MW00881149

THE BLUE GATE

A NOVEL

LL FOX

LL FOX BOOKS

NASHVILLE, TENNESSEE

LL FOX/LL Fox Books
email: llfoxbooks@gmail.com
www.llfoxbooks.com

Publisher's Note: This is a work of fiction. Names, characters, places, and incidents are a product of the author's imagination. Locales and public names are sometimes used for atmospheric purposes. Any resemblance to actual people, living or dead, or to businesses, companies, events, institutions, or locales is completely coincidental.

Book Layout ©2015 BookDesignTemplates.com

Ordering Information:
Quantity sales. Special discounts are available on quantity purchases by corporations, associations, and others. For details, contact the "Special Sales Department" at the address above.

The Blue Gate/ LL Fox. -- 1st ed.
ISBN 978-1981289226

Contents

For Senta

Alpha

The boy stood by the river throwing stones, trying with each throw to reach a point a little further than the previous attempt. The river flowed quietly and slowly to the south and the early summer sun reflected off its surface, flashing sporadically like the crystal of a chandelier in early morning light. The boy was barefoot and as he would run to the water's edge to hurl a stone, his toes would sink into the mud. His ankles and feet were caked with the wet earth, and when he stood at the river's edge, the boy could not tell what was mud and what were his feet. The boy was handsome with dark brown hair almost the color of the earth on his feet. His blue eyes flashed as he ran and threw stones and took in the whole panorama of the blue sky, crystal river, and the trees that grew along its banks.

The boy's father walked up just as the boy had worn himself out from playing. The boy threw himself down on the grass under one of the big trees by the river and his father stood looking at his son and then the river. The boy, lying on his back and breathing hard, smiled at his father, and the father returned the smile.

"You've been working hard," said the father.

"Yes, I've been trying to throw stones across the river, but I can't throw them very far," explained the boy.

"Son," said the father, "Look at the river. What do you see?"

"A river of course," he replied. "Water."

"Is it alive?" asked the father.

"Alive?" asked the boy. "It flows. Watch!" He picked up a piece of a branch almost as big as his arm, and threw it in an arc spinning over the water. When it landed, the current took it and it moved downstream. "See!" said the boy, pointing to the branch.

"Yes, it flows," said the father. "But why? Why does it flow?"

Puzzled, the boy looked at his father and then at the branch as it moved further and further downstream.

"You are looking at the branch," said the father. "Why does the river flow?"

Slowly, the boy turned his head away from the branch, his eyes moving against the current and looked upstream. And his father smiled, watching his son's blue eyes gaze at the river.

For the river now it was fall, but seven falls later. Most of the trees had changed color with some of them completely naked of leaves except for the trees along the river that in some years never turned but stayed always green. The boy was now tall and strong, carried a gun and his eyes, eternally blue watched the brush as he walked, waiting for a rabbit or anything he could kill. The autumn air was cold, but the energy of youth and the exertion of walking made him oblivious to the cold and in fact, hot. He unbuttoned his shirt as he walked through the leaves, trying the impossible task of moving quietly in leaves that were a foot deep in places. He was as big as a man, but his face still reflected the innocence of the boy throwing stones in the river. He walked further and further, more to the east and north of where he usually hunted, into land where he had been before, though not often, and not in many years. Not lost, but not exactly sure either, he half walked, half ran up and down wooded hills looking for any landmark that might tell him where he was. Then as he pushed through a thicket that tore at his clothes and topped the crest of a hill, he saw the river. His mind quickly calculated where he was, and he knew then that by following the river south, he would be able to find his way home. He sat down on the roots of a big tree by the river. His breathing slowed, and he became calm as he watched the river.

This is north, he thought, *not far upstream from where I used to play when I was a boy.* Then smiling and remembering his father, he turned once again and looked upstream. Slowly, the smile turned to reflection as he asked himself, *what is the river? If I could find its source.* Just then a rabbit shot from the brush to his left. He sprang to his feet as his right index finger switched off the safety. In one motion, the shotgun rose to his shoulder as his finger squeezed the trigger. The report echoed across the water, and the rabbit tumbled across the ground. Pleased with the shot, he ran and picked up the rabbit, and forgetting about the river, headed south to home.

What would be spring now on the river as it always would be, drew the man there again a time later. He was even stronger now, more determined and more experienced. Unlike in years past, he carried no weapon as he was the life along the river. The birds and animals there, he no longer held a desire to kill but felt rather a joy in them living. He walked with a strong, measured step that had a rhythm that would give someone watching the impression that he could walk all day and all night and never stop. Walking felt good and he enjoyed feeling his muscles work. His only discomfort was an occasional tingling in his right leg from an injury from a war in a place far away. When his leg felt that way, he remembered.

The river still flows after all these years, he thought. *It flowed seventeen years ago and seven years ago. It will flow for others when I am gone. Regardless of where I am or where I have been, when I return to the river it will always be.* He continued walking north, following the river.

The way became more difficult. The terrain became steeper. The rocks larger and the river bank in places, sheer rock walls coming down to the river's edge, making the way narrow and at times treacherous. The river would flow around small islands and somewhere in the forest, the man, following what he thought was the river, began following a tributary. It soon diminished to nothing between two hills and the man realizing that he had found only a small watershed that could not be the real source, sat down in disgust, tired and angry. Knowing time had passed and that he had wasted valuable years, the man felt a loneliness he had never fully known before, although it felt as if it had always been in him.

The day is half over, he thought. *If I return now, I will be back by dark. That would be the safest and the easiest thing to do. I am tired.* And the man sat alone in the forest.

Then, he heard it, instantly remembering the sound of sudden human pain from another forest more tropical. Rising to his feet, he slowly, then quickly, moved up the hill in the direction of the scream, not knowing if it was male or female as the sound of pain is universal. And again, cresting a hill he saw it instantly, the golden color of her hair against the dark greens and browns of the forest.

"Hello!" he shouted down the hill and across the draw. She flinched and looked up from where she sat on the roots of a big oak. Walking quickly in long strides, he came down the hill through the trees to her. "Are you alright?" he asked as he approached her.

"It's my ankle," she said. She spoke softly and slowly with no trace of the pain she felt. "I was walking and I caught my foot on this root."

"Let me see it," he said.

Then looking at him with complete trust, she extended her leg. Her white sock was torn and red with her blood. He knelt and carefully rested her leg on his knee. Slowly removing her shoe, he was taken with how delicate her foot was. As his hands took the top of her sock to remove it, her hands took the cuff of her pant leg and pulled it up. His hands seemed twice the size of hers as he carefully pulled off the sock.

She has the most perfect little feet, he thought, as he took her foot in his hand to move it to test for injury.

"Are you a doctor?" she asked as he moved her foot and ankle.

"No," he smiled.

"You seem to know what you're doing," she said.

"No, I'm not a doctor, but I have seen a lot of sprained ankles and blisters. And I think you're alright. You've just scraped your ankle. In a few minutes, we'll put your sock back on and I think you'll be OK. Let's let this scrape stop bleeding first. I would put something on it, but I don't have anything with me. But it's not bad. You'll be fine," he said.

"Thank you so much," she said as a shiver came over her when her foot was exposed to the cool air.

"You're cold," he said. "Here, this will help." He unbuttoned two buttons of his shirt and placed her bare foot against his bare stomach. With one hand under her heel and the other pressing the top of her foot, he asked, "Is that better?"

"Yes, thank you," she said, "You are very kind."

"No, not really," he smiled.

"No," she said slowly. "You are very kind." And she looked at him and saw that his eyes were dark blue like the water of the river. Neither spoke for a time. When the scrape had stopped bleeding, the man carefully put the sock back on her foot. He stood and held out his hands to her. She took his hands and stood.

Still holding her hands, he asked, "How does it feel?"

"Much better, thank you. It feels much better," she said.

He knew it was time to release her hands, but he did not want to. "Did you hurt your hands when you fell?" he asked, turning his own hands palms up while holding her hands in his to examine them.

"No, I think they are alright," she said glad that he was still holding her hands. "Your hands are warm. They feel good," she said and smiled at him. "So where do we go now? Which way is the river?" she asked.

Pausing and watching her he asked, "What do you know about the river?"

And squeezing his hands she said, "You are following the river."

He replied slowly with concern, "How did you know that?"

"Why else would anyone be here in this forest?" she asked.

"Are you here for the same reason?" he asked quietly. "Do you know where the river comes from? Do you know why it flows?"

"Yes," she said.

"If you know where it comes from, do you know how to get there?" he asked.

"I know where it is, but not how to get there," she replied. "You must find it yourself. Some are meant to find it, but most are not. Most never even know it's there."

"Are you looking for the river's source also?" he asked.

"You know where the river is," she said, looking straight into his eyes. "Follow it and I will follow you."

He smiled at her with joy and puzzlement in his eyes, not comprehending how she could understand so completely. Without saying a word, he turned and started down the hill through the forest and back toward the river. She followed. From time to time, he would look back and glance down at her foot to see if she was having any trouble. She limped slightly at times, and he wished he could do something to help the pain. She saw him looking and felt the compassion, thinking, *he will find it.*

Finally, the path intersected with the river. He saw the water and knew he would find it if he only persisted. The sun came out brightly then and warmed everything, and the water rushed past the bank. He smiled at her and stopped. Then placing his hands on the sides of her arms almost to her shoulders he said, "You know, I never asked your name. What is your name?"

She answered with a smile. Then he saw her face juxtaposed against the water and felt that her eyes were exactly like the water, and her hair the color of the sun.

"We should rest for a time," he said after they had walked quite a ways. Not tired himself, but saying *we* so that she would have to rest. "How is your ankle?" he asked as she sat down on the bank by the river. He knelt and lifted her leg to be sure the bleeding hadn't started again.

"It is much better," she answered. "It hardly hurts at all, and as we walk by the river it will continue to improve." He found it strange that she thought walking on it would help, but said nothing. He sat down by her. As he sat there, he felt warm in the sunlight and happy, and thought she was very pretty. As he looked at her, he recalled her small feet and hands. He guessed that he probably weighed almost double what she did. Still looking at her, he felt a strong desire to care for her. Then she stood and slowly knelt in front of him. Taking his right ankle in her hands she asked, "And how is your leg?"

"How did you know my leg hurts?" he asked.

"You have hurt for a long time," she said quietly. Smiling she continued, "You think no one knows. You are very kind and very brave. Will you take care of me and protect me?"

"I am not brave," he protested. She didn't say a word, but looked at him with a knowing smile and nodded. He said nothing for a while, staring at her trying to understand her crystal, perfect perception. Finally, not fully understanding, but accepting with a happiness that formed out of all the loneliness he had felt a short time earlier, he answered her question, "Yes, I will care for you and protect you."

They walked on now, refreshed by the break. Strengthened by the river and by having her beside him, he set a good pace. Walking on, they gained altitude. The way became even more rocky and often he would turn and see if she was having trouble keeping up. "I'm sorry. I'm going too fast," he said.

"No, no, you're fine. My legs aren't as long as yours," she said. But he did slow his pace and made sure that he didn't get ahead of her again. The river moved even faster and in places churned white over and around the rocks. The path became very narrow where a rock wall came down almost to the water, leaving a path only about a foot wide.

"Here, take my hand," he said. "I will go first. Let's take it slowly and carefully. It is muddy here, and it may be slick." She nodded her head and took his hand. He had just made it to where the path widened when she slipped. She pulled him down as she fell. With luck and reflex, his hand caught hold of a rock. While on his knees, he held on to her with his right hand and the rock with his left. As she dangled over the water rushing thirty feet below, she grabbed hold of his wrist with her free hand. Neither one said a word but looked intently at each other. She wondered, *how long can he hold me before I fall?* Then she felt his grip tighten until she thought her hand would be crushed and felt herself slowly being pulled up the rock face. When he had pulled her to the point that her waist was even with the path, she swung a leg up and soon was up on the path again. Releasing her hand and taking her by the shoulders he asked, "Are you alright?" He drew her close to him.

"Yes," she said, breathing hard and opening and closing her hand where he had almost crushed it. "I'm OK. I'm sorry. I'm so clumsy. I could have killed both of us."

"No, we wouldn't have died, but we would have gotten wet," he said with a smile that turned to concern when he noticed the blood on his left hand. "I've gotten blood all over you. I didn't even notice," he said.

"You're hurt," she said, taking his hand and opening his fingers. "You cut your hand on the rock when I fell." The blood ran from his hand and dripped onto the damp earth at their feet.

She reached to her shoulder where his blood had stained her shirt. Tugging and pulling, she ripped her sleeve and tore it lose. As the blood still dripped on the ground, she carefully wrapped the cloth around his hand. While he watched her every movement, she kissed his hand so lightly that he wasn't sure if he felt it or if it was just the throbbing in his hand. Again, he saw her eyes. And again, there by the river, they seemed to him exactly like the water. As the sun reflected in her eyes, it brought to him memories of water sparkling like the crystal of a chandelier in early morning light. She bent down then to where his blood had run onto the earth and took some of the earth and blood together in her fingers. And standing up, and holding the earth she asked him, "Do you understand?"

Faintly smiling, he replied, "I think so."

"You and the earth are the same creation," she replied.
"And the river flows in you."

The sun moved across the sky, and they walked on. Her ankle had stopped hurting, and the wound in his hand had sealed and no longer bled. He realized that soon the sun would set; they had gone too far to even consider turning back. As the sun made its descent, they found a bank covered in thick green moss. The moss-covered area lay in a hollow that was protected from any wind and looked down on the water rushing below. He tore two large pieces of moss loose and made pillows for them to rest their heads. He lay on his back and was surprised at how comfortable a bed it made. Then she lay down, not using the moss pillow but rather putting her head on his shoulder. With her arms around him, she held him tightly. As the sun slowly set, the only sound was the water below rushing to its omega. Listening to the water and holding her, the man felt the desire to protect her and then felt a peacefulness free of worry and free of pain.

"Why do I not worry here?" he asked out loud.

"What did your father ask you?" she replied.

"My father?" he asked.

"What is the river?" she asked again. Still holding on to him tightly as she would all night, she closed her eyes.

Thinking back and remembering, he answered, "The river is peace."

The sun was up completely when the man felt its warmth on his face. He awoke to find her still lying in his arms. Not speaking, he kissed her forehead and she awoke. Without a word, they got up and set forth again walking upstream. The water became faster still, and he knew they were close. He helped her over rocks and with each glance, with each look, he became more enchanted by her. The sun rose higher, and the water sparkled like crystal, and they were very happy. He watched her walk and saw that she did not walk on the land but rather with it and that she moved or rather flowed like the water that was her eyes. Slowly at first, then suddenly, he felt a strength come into his body that he had never known before. It was as if he had the strength of a thousand men and would maintain that strength forever.

Then just as suddenly as the strength came to him, the river slowed its rushing and widened into a body of water that seemed not really water but rather some kind of deep blue polished stone that reflected the sun with a brilliance he had never seen before. Taking her hand, his eyes were full of the excitement of what he was experiencing. They walked by the water, past the most beautiful trees that he had ever seen, lush and green. She smiled watching him, feeling his excitement, knowing that she had known he would find it. In the man, came the feeling that even though he had never been here before; he was home. He was happy and content. And looking at the girl he said, "Even more than I love you, you are love."

As the sunlight reflected off the crystal water she said, "Yes, because you love me."

The man looked at the sun on the water and then the sunlight in her eyes and smiled; it was then that she knew he understood. They walked on, only a short distance more, as their journey was almost done. Looking ahead the man finally saw the crystal rock rising from the water. As he saw it, images of his life flashed in his mind: of his father, of years ago, of the river, of times when he had been far away, of times when he had forgotten about the river, of wondering if he would ever know. There before them the river ended, or rather began. It flowed from a crystal rock that was higher than a mountain. Its surface was perfectly flat and rose straight up from the water and disappeared into the clouds.

Looking at her and holding her hands, he spoke almost shouting, "We have found it. I knew we would find it. I knew if we just kept on long enough. I knew it was there. I knew we could find it." And then calmer, "I don't think I would have found it without you. I think I would have given up."

"You did find it," she said looking at him with crystal blue eyes and golden hair and smiling. He again seeing her eyes and remembering the reflection comprehending the river and her.

"We are home now," he said. Putting his arms around her, holding her tightly, and remembering his promise to protect her, he felt even more than loving her, she was love. And then again looking into her eyes he said, "You are light and water."

And she smiled at him as *Love* replied, "And we will be this way forever."

CHAPTER ONE

Senta

Senta Miller won the annual blackberry cobbler competition two weeks before her seventeenth birthday. The contest was part of the summer celebration that occurred every year to signal the end of the planting season. Senta had never entered the competition before, but her friend Ruth and her mother had convinced her to try. Senta could hardly believe she had won! Everyone was complimenting her and making over her cobbler. When the judge called her name, she was so surprised that for a moment she froze. Her father put his arm around her and told her to go up and claim her ribbon. Standing before the crowd made her happy but nervous as she wondered if her hair was in place. Brushing a strand of hair that had fallen to the side, she accepted the blue ribbon from the judge and held it up. Everyone cheered. Senta Miller would remember that day for many years as the best day of her life.

The summer celebration was in the Amish community of Cheatham County, Tennessee. Nestled in the hills of the Cumberland River valley, the Amish community might not have been obvious to a passerby, except for the occasional horse-drawn buggy. The white clapboard farmhouses with the white fences didn't look that much different from the non-Amish houses. The Amish farms were all very well kept and orderly. The pastures that held the horses were neat with perfectly maintained fence rows. The barns were freshly painted and every door and shutter were in working order. In the spring before the celebration, a tourist driving through might notice a man with a black hat, white shirt, and black trousers walking behind a horse-drawn plow. An observant wanderer might notice a woman in a long blue dress with white apron and white cap carrying a basket with lunch to her husband in the field.

Senta was Amish, an only child who lived with her parents, Elijah and Sarah, on the family's dairy farm. She enjoyed a happy childhood of life in rural middle Tennessee, of her mother and father, the farm, the cows, school, and church on Sundays. Approaching her seventeenth birthday, she was nearing the end of adolescence and was thinking more and more about her future. She liked to daydream who her future husband might be. She observed how her mother ran the household and wondered if she would be as good a wife and mother.

Senta's education had stopped at 8th grade, as was typical for Amish children. She was an inquisitive girl and had been sorry when her schooling had ended. Although she never said it, she envied the English children who she knew had the opportunity to continue their education through high school and beyond. Senta also missed seeing her classmates every day. She looked forward to Sundays when she could talk about the future with her friends. Senta accepted her life willingly and looked forward to what lay ahead.

She had asked her parents' permission to start attending the singings. A singing was a gathering where young men and young women could meet, sing songs together, get to know each other, and would likely find a future husband or wife. Senta's parents had reluctantly agreed. Reluctantly, not because they didn't want her to participate, but because they knew it would eventually result in marriage and losing her. Not that she would be very far away, but because she was Elijah and Sarah's only child. They loved her and enjoyed every day with her. Senta was happy and kind and her being in the house and around the farm, made life complete for them. They wondered with quiet sadness what their days would be like when she would one day leave.

Permission to attend the singings also required the blessing of the bishop. That permission was granted just before the summer celebration. The week after winning the cobbler contest, Senta went to her first singing with her best friend Ruth. The girls had a great time singing and talking to the other teenagers, particularly the boys. Life was exciting and the future bright. As she returned home that evening, Senta never imagined that it had been the only singing she would ever attend.

Being an only child also meant that Senta didn't have brothers and sisters to play with, so from the time she was little, she was great friends with the family's horse, Sugar. Sugar was a black mare whose purpose was to pull the family's buggy. One day Elijah looked out in the pasture in horror to see his little daughter swinging from the horse's tail! Fortunately, Sugar was a very calm and gentle horse and it didn't appear to bother her. Elijah ran out into the pastures and calmly talked to the horse while telling Senta to come to him. Later that day Elijah told Sarah, "I was so afraid Sugar was going to kick Senta. It would have killed her. But Sugar didn't seem to mind that someone was swinging from her tail! Sugar is a wonderful horse, and we will never sell her." Sugar and Senta were the best of friends. Senta loved to brush her and of course living up to her name, the horse loved it when Senta brought her sugar cubes.

Every morning and every evening Elijah gathered the cows in the barn and milked them. It took around an hour and a half each time. As Senta had gotten older, she'd begun to help her father with the afternoon milking. Though Senta had her own day filled with chores, she didn't mind. In fact, she looked forward to spending time alone with her father.

One morning, shortly after attending the singing, Senta was coming down the stairs to the kitchen to go to the barn to help Elijah, when she heard her mother scream. She ran to the kitchen to see her mother running out the door and toward the barn. Senta ran after her and together they found her father on the ground, unable to stand. He was trying to talk but was unable to speak. The next few hours were a blur with Senta trying to understand the doctor as he explained what a stroke was.

All she knew was that her father was alive. She comforted her mother and prayed to God to spare his life. Elijah Miller did live, but was permanently stricken with a left leg and left arm that no longer functioned as before, and the inability to speak. The shock of his condition had a debilitating effect on Senta's mother, Sarah. Somewhat frail before, Mrs. Miller was even weaker now. Elijah's condition also meant he could no longer work as he had for decades, and this cast a cloud of uncertainty over the family's future.

It was at their next monthly meeting that the bishop along with the elders of the community addressed the situation of the Miller family due to Elijah's stroke. For these men, the decision was obvious. It was easy to see Senta as the solution. And so, the men with white beards decided Senta's future, changing her life forever in an instant. Permission to attend singings was revoked.

When Bishop Yost drove up to the Miller's house in his black buggy, Senta knew something was wrong. As the bishop sat in the family parlor explaining the decision, Senta's mother said nothing and nodded her head. Senta's father was unable to speak due to the stroke. Senta heard nothing beyond the part about her future, not as a wife and mother, but as a caretaker for her parents. Bishop Yost continued talking, but Senta only thought about the gate never being painted blue, never going to a singing again, and the day she had won the cobbler competition.

Senta felt as if she were shrinking. She heard the voices, but the voices sounded far away. Senta was only five feet, two inches tall, but sitting there in the parlor she felt even smaller. She felt like she was there, but not, with everything moving away from her. Senta felt alone and detached as the bishop and her mother talked.

The next day when she woke she thought it had all been a bad dream, but quickly realized it was true. And life went on. The first time Senta had experienced such feelings was when her grandmother had died. Senta had felt like everything should stop, but it didn't. There was still work to do and Senta had watched in shock as life went on. Senta buried her head in her pillow and cried, quietly but hard. It was a wrenching sobbing that signaled the end of her youth, and the beginning of an adulthood unlike anything she had imagined. Afterwards she got up out of bed, put on her work dress and brushed her long brown hair streaked with blonde from working outside. Senta braided her hair and wound it into a bun. Then she walked down the stairs and out of the house into the early morning to milk the cows.

The Millers had twelve dairy cows and selling milk to the local dairy was how the family made their living. Senta's father had always milked the cows, with Senta and her mother helping at times. But now it was Senta's job, taking care of the cows and everything associated with them. Milking them, filling the aluminum cans and getting them to the road for pickup; the cans held ten gallons each, which was about eighty pounds, and Senta couldn't pick them up to load them. She devised a system with the farm's two milk carts. She would fill the milk cans on the carts so she didn't have to lift them. Then, she'd pull the cart loaded with full milk cans to the road and leave them for the milk hauler truck. She would pull the cart with the emptied milk cans back to the barn the next day.

Tending to the cows, the house, and cooking left her completely exhausted, and she was always ready for bed as soon as the sun set. Senta would wave at friends passing by her farm if she was outside. Excluding her parents and church, she rarely saw another human being. Life went on. At least the lives of everyone else in the community went on, while Senta's life froze in time at age seventeen. Senta sensed that life was moving for the rest of the world, and not for her. Like when she would see a car drive past. She wondered sometimes who the people were. She wondered where they were going, and what their lives were like. But this was her life, the routine became her life, and she learned to live it that way.

The one bright spot in her week was Ruth. Ruth had been Senta's friend for as long as she could remember. The two girls had been best friends through school and continued thereafter. They saw each other every other Sunday at church services. Senta had always looked up to Ruth both literally and figuratively. Ruth was taller and very pretty with a classically beautiful face. Had the Amish community held beauty pageants, Ruth would have been the Amish queen of Cheatham County. Ruth was always the center of attention at the singings, and at the one singing Senta had attended, it was obvious who was the most popular girl there. Senta cherished her friendship with Ruth and never felt jealous of her friend's popularity.

Just as Senta's life stopped, Ruth's life took off at high speed, and Senta eagerly listened to every detail on Sundays when the girls had time to visit. Senta couldn't keep track of all of Ruth's suitors. It seemed that every time they spoke there was a new one, as the single men of the community vied for Ruth's favor. Ruth was giddy with all the male attention and could not wait to share the details with Senta on Sundays. Senta listened intently and was truly happy for her friend. Senta knew that soon Ruth would make her choice, then her parents would decide, and lastly the bishop would give his blessing. Then Ruth would be married. Senta watched Ruth as she talked about each suitor. It seemed that Jacob Troyer was her favorite. Senta remembered him from the singing and knew he lived about ten miles to the east. He was somewhat older, and Senta remembered him as rude, arrogant, but quite handsome.

Every day, except Sunday, was the same. Senta got up before dawn, brushed her hair, braided it, and then wound it into a bun. She wore her work dress and work shoes out to the barn to milk the cows. Her dress had been patched so many times that there was almost more patch than the original blue fabric. The walk to the barn was her favorite time of the day. The sun would just be coming up, the birds would have just begun to sing, and the mist would be hanging in the valley. It was in those moments that Senta began to fantasize. The rest of her day was too busy to even think, but for that time walking to the barn, she started to imagine herself as someone else. When she would go to the grocery store in Ashland City every other week, she would notice the magazines at the checkout counter. There were always pictures of beautiful women in beautiful dresses. She started imagining herself as one of the them; one day a famous singer, another as a princess from some unheard-of country in Europe. Senta liked to imagine herself wearing an elegant evening gown. Reality always managed to return as she entered the barn and began the next hour and a half of milking the cows. Senta talked to the cows and sang to the cows as she milked them. Pouring the buckets of milk into the milk cans on the cart, she then pulled the cart to the road in front of the farm where the dairy would pick up a short time later. By the time she was walking back to the house, she was hungry for breakfast which she prepared for herself and her parents. The smell of bacon would awaken her parents who would arrive in the kitchen just about as breakfast was ready. Senta and her mother would talk, and her father would just eat, not able to speak. Sometimes Senta would feel her father looking at her, and she'd look back at him and ask, "Is everything alright, Father? Do you need anything?" He would smile a crooked smile at her, crooked from the stroke, and she could feel his love and concern for her in his smile.

The summer passed and then held in that limbo between seasons. Fall would begin with that sensation in the morning, one day in September, when it would feel different. Senta would sense it every year. That feeling of a little cooler and a stillness that was the silent announcement that soon the days would shorten, the nights would be cooler, and the leaves would begin to change color.

CHAPTER TWO

The Lapps

The change of seasons brought another change when one day in September John Lapp drove his buggy up the drive and stopped in front of the Miller house. John and Abigail Lapp lived down the road and also operated a dairy farm. A little older than Senta, they had been married four years and had no children.

"Hello, Senta!" called John as she opened the front door. "Could I come in and talk with you and your parents for a few minutes?"

"Of course, John," Senta replied holding the door open for him to enter. "Sit down please, while I go get my parents."

When Mr. and Mrs. Miller came into the parlor, they greeted John and then everyone sat down together. Senta didn't know John very well, only from church. On occasion, he would stop to ask her father's guidance on dairy cattle issues.

"I will get straight to the point," John said. "I have a proposition for you. Abigail and I are very concerned about Senta. We see her pulling the milk wagon to the road every day, and it takes every bit of strength she has. Soon it will be winter, and I don't know if she'll be able continue. It was hard work for you, Elijah, but you were able to do it because you were stronger. We're afraid Senta will hurt herself. So, here's my idea. It has two parts." The three listened intently to John's words. "First, I would buy your dairy herd. You would no longer be in the dairy business. I know you probably don't like the sound of that, but if Senta hurts herself you'll be out of business anyway. So, I would buy your dairy cows. You would receive the money for the cows, but your revenue would end. Now, for part two. You know Aaron Campbell, the CPA in Ashland City, who does taxes for a lot of the Amish around here? He does our taxes, and I like him. Just recently he got the work of doing the bookkeeping and taxes for the Amish business that manufactures storage buildings and such over in the next county. Their financial records are a mess, and Aaron has told them they need a bookkeeper. They asked Aaron to find one for them. He was asking me, and I thought of Senta." Turning to Senta, John said, "You could work from home, Senta. You wouldn't have to actually go to the office. Aaron would deliver all the invoices and receipts every week."

"But I don't know how to do work like that," said Senta.

"I know," said John. "Aaron knows that, but he would teach you. He has two bookkeepers working for him right now in his office. He would have them teach you their system. Also, the Amish company would like it if they had an Amish bookkeeper. You're smart so you can learn how to do it. You would replace the income from the dairy operation and so you could take care of your parents."

Senta looked at her parents, first her father, then her mother, trying to read their thoughts on this unexpected proposal. She wasn't as sure as John was that she could do it. As she looked down at her hands and saw the toll from milking twice a day, she started to hope that her father would say yes. Looking up at her father, he nodded his head *yes*, and then her mother did the same.

"Senta, will you give bookkeeping a try?" asked John.

"Yes," Senta replied. "I'll do my best."

"Wonderful!" said John. "I'll check on the current prices for Guernsey cows and let you know, Elijah. And, Senta, I'll tell Aaron, and he can see about getting you trained. I think you can start next week. He needs someone now."

"Thank you, John," said Mrs. Miller shaking his hand.

Then she and Senta walked him outside to his buggy, while behind them the cows grazed quietly in the pasture as they had for years. Elijah Miller stood in the doorway watching them with an accepting sadness. He was sad to know his farm would cease to be a dairy farm but knew that John's plan was a good one and the only one that would work for his family.

The next week John came to get the cows, but first he stopped to talk to Senta. "Senta, I spoke to Aaron Campbell, the CPA, and he wants to give you a try. He'd like to come pick you up tomorrow around 8:00 a.m., take you to the office in Ashland City, let you meet Sally, and start on your training," John said.

"This is very fast," said Senta. "I've never had a real job before, in an office. But I'll be working here at home, right?" asked Senta.

"That's right," John said. "But you've got to get trained on their system, and Aaron will need to get you a computer."

"I am so nervous, John," said Senta. "I've never touched a computer. I don't have the slightest idea of what to do."

"Senta, it will be alright. Don't worry. Sally is very nice, and she will teach you everything. I really think you're going to like this new job," said John. And with that he smiled and waved to her as he went to the barn to gather up the cows. With twelve more cows to milk twice a day, John had invested in an electric milking machine. He'd also met with the dairy and informed them about the milk production moving from the Miller farm to his farm. The Millers stood in front of their house and watched as their cows were led away. The only livestock left on their farm was Sugar, their mare.

That evening as Senta and her parents ate dinner her mother said, "Senta, we don't tell you enough, but thank you. You work so hard. We hope that this new job will be easier on you. The cows and the milking were so difficult for you, but you never complained. Since your father can't work anymore, I don't know what we'd do without you. We love you very much."

"Thank you, Mother," said Senta. "I think the job will be physically easier, but I don't know anything about accounting and computers. I'm afraid. What if I make bad mistakes, mistakes that cost money? Mr. Campbell would be right to fire me. And everyone there will be so much smarter than I am. I've only been to 8th grade. I'm sure they all graduated high school, and I'm sure Mr. Campbell went to college to be a Certified Public Accountant."

Elijah shook his head and said, "Hmmm Hmmm Hmmmm."

"Your father means for you not to worry," said Senta's mother. "We know you will be fine. God will take care of us, and He will take care of you in your new job."

Senta went to sleep that night still concerned about the next day but more at peace remembering her mother's words. She woke up the next morning in a panic thinking she had overslept and that Mr. Campbell had arrived and left without her because she was still asleep. She was relieved to see that it was 4:00 a.m. She got up and got her clothes ready, her nicest Sunday dress. She made breakfast for herself and her parents but ate very little herself.

"I don't know when I will be coming back today," she said. "John didn't say. Should I pack a lunch?"

"No, no," said her mother. "Here take some money. You will probably eat at a restaurant, or maybe they will have something delivered to the office."

Senta was ready and standing by the front door a half an hour early just in case Mr. Campbell arrived before 8:00. He was right on time when he pulled up the Miller's driveway in a silver Cadillac. Pushing the button to roll down the passenger window, he called out, "Is this the Miller farm? Am I in the right place? Are you Senta?"

"He's here! I'm leaving," Senta called to her parents as she closed the front door and walked quickly to the car. "Yes, sir. I am Senta Miller."

"Pleased to meet you. Hop in, and let's get this show on the road," Aaron Campbell said, shaking her hand as she got in the car.

"This is a very nice car, Mr. Campbell," Senta said as she admired the leather interior and thought about how comfortable the seats were.

"Glad you like it. So, let's talk about today. We've got a lot to do. First the office, then you meet with Sally, don't let her forget to call Jason to get you set up with the computer tomorrow morning. I've got two meetings this morning, then you and me and Sally are going to drive to Joseph Stoll's Woodworking. There's a bar-b-que place on the way. Do you like bar-b-que? I do. That's where we'll eat lunch. Did John explain this? You're my employee, but you're Stoll's bookkeeper. Don't try to understand it. It'll work fine. Joe isn't a bad guy. Mrs. Stoll, she's kind of their office manager. I'm probably doing a great disservice to office managers everywhere by calling her one. You'll be talking with her a lot. Are you patient, Senta? John said he thought you were a patient woman. Slow to anger is good, too! Sally will explain. Mrs. Stoll can be difficult." Mr. Campbell kept talking, and it all blurred together for Senta who had never heard anyone talk so much and so fast. Aaron Campbell was older than her father with a bald head on top and white hair around the edges. He drove the Cadillac as fast as he talked. Senta was certain she had never traveled that fast! The miles to Ashland City passed quickly, and soon they were in the parking lot of the Aaron Campbell CPA accounting firm.

As they walked in the door, a pleasant looking lady in her mid-40's stood up from her desk and said, "Mr. Campbell, Mr. Walker line two, about his IRS audit."

"Got it," he said. "This is the new girl for Stoll. You know what to do."

"You must be Senta Miller," said the lady. "I'm Sally. It's been crazy this morning. Come back here to the conference room. Do you drink coffee?" she asked as she guided her to the meeting room. "OK, let's have some coffee and get you started. But first, did he scare you to death? That man can't drive slow. He gets speeding tickets all the time. Don't tell him I said that, but it's true. I was telling Suzanne, he'd better not scare our new Amish bookkeeper so bad she quits on the first day. Bless his heart, he's not a bad guy. He just talks a mile a minute and drives even faster. I'm so glad we found you. Mrs. Stoll is driving me crazy. They've got a pretty good business going there, but their books are a mess! Mrs. Stoll can be hard headed, but I bet you can handle her because you're Amish, too, and maybe she'll be more reasonable with you."

"Sally," said Senta as the two women sat at the conference table just starting to drink their coffee. "First, yes, Mr. Campbell drives very fast. Second, thank you so much for training me. I promise to do my best, but I must warn you I don't know anything about computers and accounting. And third, don't forget to call Jason to have my computer installed tomorrow morning."

"I love it!" laughed Sally. "We're going to get along just fine. We'll be great friends. I've never had an Amish friend! This is going to be a hoot!"

That morning Sally explained that they had gotten the Stoll account because Mr. Stoll had made a mess of his taxes and had hired Aaron Campbell to straighten it out with the IRS. Stoll Woodworking manufactured portable storage buildings and wooden furniture. They had grown to 45 employees. Mr. Stoll was difficult because he insisted on keeping his books in old fashioned ledgers. Mr. Campbell refused to do it that way insisting that using a computer system was much more efficient. They finally compromised by doing both. Mr. Campbell knew the company needed a staff accountant but also knew it just wouldn't work with Mrs. Stoll who would not allow a computer on the premises. It ended up with Aaron Campbell hiring Senta for the Stoll account to keep the ledgers to satisfy Mr. Stoll and maintain the computer program for Mr. Campbell. The difficult part had been that the Stolls wanted an Amish bookkeeper. Aaron was trying to figure out where to find one when John Lapp told him about the Miller's situation and Senta.

Senta and Sally got along well. Sally explained that if Senta had questions she was to call her or Suzanne. Senta was completely shocked when Sally told her she would be issued a company cell phone along with the computer. She was equally shocked when Sally took her into an office and showed her four bushel baskets of invoices and receipts from Stoll's Woodworking.

"Now don't panic, and don't you dare quit!" said Sally. "I know this is a mess, but we will get it under control!"

Sally taught her how to turn on the computer and boot up the program. She explained passwords and how Jason would help her set up her computer the next day. She showed her the two ledgers and how to tell the difference between the receipts and the invoices. She showed her the various categories of expenditure and how to code them in the system. She explained bank account reconciliation and how that had to be done every month. Finally, she showed her the payroll system and how she would enter the time cards for the payroll. Senta took notes as quickly as she could, but her head was spinning with all the information.

At noon Mr. Campbell, Sally, and Senta drove west in the Cadillac to first stop at Mr. Campbell's favorite bar-b-que restaurant and afterwards to visit the Stoll's. As they drove he said, "Now Senta, I don't want to lie to Mr. Stoll. And I'm not lying. You are a trained staff accountant. Sally has spent all morning training you. And you're Amish. So, you don't have to go into detail about your lack of experience. But it could be said you've been the staff accountant of a dairy farm. If he asks, tell him that."

Mr. and Mrs. Stoll were a bit unusual, but Senta felt kind of at home there. At the office and in the restaurant, she was the only Amish person, and she felt different and somewhat out of place. But at Stoll's, everyone was Amish. Joseph Stoll barked orders to workers, and it was quite noisy. But the Stolls were so pleased that their new bookkeeper was Amish that they asked few questions. Mrs. Stoll took Senta around and introduced her to several of the other employees. "Isaac, you'd better be nice to her," warned Mrs. Stoll as she introduced her to one of the foremen. "She processes the payroll and if she doesn't like you, you won't get a paycheck." Senta wasn't sure if she was kidding.

Finally, after returning to the office and processing more invoices with Sally, Mr. Campbell called Senta into his office and explained her salary, her vacation time, and her 401(k). She had no idea what a 401(k) was so her new boss explained that it was a retirement plan and how it worked. Senta's head was spinning from all the information as she and Sally loaded files and bushel baskets of paper into the trunk of Mr. Campbell's car. He talked nonstop all the way as he drove her back to the Miller farm. Although overwhelmed, Senta was happy and proud to be a part of it all.

"Now, you call Sally when you have questions. Either she or I will drive out and bring you the new receipts, invoices, and timecards each week," said Aaron Campbell as he pulled up in front of the house.

"I will," she replied. "Thank you, Mr. Campbell, for this opportunity. I won't disappoint you!"

"Thank you, Senta," he said. "We really need you."

It was 5:30 p.m. when Senta walked in the house. She went straight to the kitchen where she found her mother preparing dinner with her father who was seated at the kitchen table. "She's home, Elijah!" said her mother. "Come and sit down! You must be exhausted! Tell us all about it!"

Senta started telling about her first day, not chronologically but jumping around from event to event. When she explained about how fast Mr. Campbell drove and talked, her mother said, "You must be careful of the English. They're very different from us." And her father nodded in accord.

Senta told about Sally and Suzanne. "Sally is very nice and talks fast like Mr. Campbell. Her husband is the manager of something I didn't understand in Ashland City, and they have two daughters. Suzanne is very pretty, and her husband is an engineer at A.O. Smith on the Cumberland River where they make hot water heaters. I think they have two little boys." She explained about Stoll Woodworking and Mr. and Mrs. Stoll and that a man named Jason would come to their house tomorrow with a new computer for her. Finally, she explained her salary and how she would be on probation for six weeks and if she did a good job she would be a permanent employee and get a raise.

"Senta, that is wonderful! I think Mr. Campbell is being very generous with your salary. We've been so worried about how to replace the income from the dairy, but if you can do this work it will be enough for us to make it. God works in mysterious ways. John Lapp buying the cows and telling his friend Mr. Campbell about you and Mr. Campbell needing an Amish bookkeeper for Mr. Stoll. This is just amazing!" said Mrs. Miller as she hugged Senta.

The next morning at exactly 9:00 a.m. Jason Schneider from JS Computer Services arrived at Senta's front door. "Senta?" he asked as she answered the door. "Hey, good to meet you!

Did Sally tell you I was coming?"

Senta was expecting someone a little older as she greeted the young man with unkept hair and thick glasses. He didn't look old enough to be out of high school. "Jason, yes, come in," she said cautiously.

"I know. I get that look all the time," he said. "I know I don't look old enough to have my own business. I'm just a computer nerd. But here I am. You'll appreciate me when your computer locks up!"

Jason carried in the computer, and Senta showed him where to set it up in the extra bedroom no one used. That room would become her office. He helped her set up her password, *accountant16*, and explained how she would need to change it every six weeks. He gave her a brand-new iPhone and showed her how to save phone numbers in *contacts*. Senta took notes in her notebook adding to all the information she had from Mr. Campbell. He watched her as she entered the office number, Sally's direct number, and Mrs. Stoll's number. Then he had her call Sally.

"Hello, Sally," she said. "This is Senta." It was the first phone call she had ever made. "Yes, Jason has me all set up. I'll start working in just a few minutes. I know I am going to be calling you a lot."

Jason gathered up the boxes and extra cables and carried them out to his van. "Call me if there are any problems. Don't forget to back it up every day like I showed you."

As he drove down the drive and onto the county highway, Senta began her first day of work. She did call Sally a lot the first few weeks. The end of the first month was a mess just like Mr. Campbell had predicted. The bank account would not reconcile. Finally, after eight phone calls to Mrs. Stoll, Senta determined that Mr. Stoll had taken out $1,500 in cash to buy a new horse, which of course was not part of the company and which of course he wasn't supposed to do. Sally told her over the phone how to enter the $1,500 as the owner's draw.

Mr. Campbell was pleased with Senta's work. Sally dropped off the week's invoices, receipts, and time cards every Monday morning. The Millers always had coffee ready for her, and they would sit at the kitchen table long enough to drink a cup while Sally brought Senta up to date on what was happening at the office. The Stoll's business finally got on a firm financial footing. Mr. Stoll was happy. Mr. Campbell was happy although he continued to drive too fast and continued to get speeding tickets.

Senta found out about her progress at her work one evening while she was eating dinner with her parents. Mr. Campbell called and told her she had passed her probation and would be seeing a raise on her next paycheck. Senta told her parents, "More than the money, that I know we need, but more than the money, I feel very proud that I've done this. I'm doing important work. It's important to Mr. and Mrs. Stoll that their business does well. And it's important to all the men who work there and their families. They all depend on me. Mr. Campbell can help Mr. Stoll make more money and expand his business because I am keeping the books in a correct fashion. I am very proud of that."

"Pride is a dangerous thing, Senta," warned her mother. "The English are all full of pride driving around in their fancy cars and wearing their fancy clothes. Look at the English women and how they dress. Full of pride. This is why we dress the way we do, to not be caught up in pride. Be careful as you work among the English, Senta."

Thinking about what her mother said, she replied, "I think it's more complicated than that, Mother. Why shouldn't someone who does good work be proud of that work? Father, weren't you proud of your dairy cows and the milk they produced? I don't think it's wrong to take pride in your work. And I don't understand why it's wrong for a woman to be proud of herself if she's pretty. God created her that way. How is that wrong?"

Senta, her mother, and father finished the meal in silence as her mother looked at her with raised eyebrows indicating displeasure at her daughter's ideas. Had the family not been so dependent on Senta's salary, she might have demanded Senta quit the job the very next day. But Senta's father didn't look at her with displeasure. Instead, he smiled his silent smile, and Senta could hear him thinking, *you're right daughter, you should*

*be proud of what you're doing. And you are pretty and you should
be proud.*

Senta became better and faster at her work. She became
more confident as she became more skillful at solving problems
with the books. One day she made a discovery that for her was
earthshaking. One of the invoices she had received had the bottom
part torn off, removing the address for the supplier. Needing
to enter that in the system she called Mrs. Stoll to see if she
knew the address. She didn't. Next, she called Sally who said,
"I don't know, Senta. Google it. If Mrs. Stoll doesn't know, just
Google it." Sally told her how to find Google on her browser
and how to enter the company's name. Sure enough, there it was,
complete with the address and phone number. "You can find
anything with Google," explained Sally. "Just pick a subject, any
subject. Y'all had dairy cows. Type in *Dairy Cows* and you'll find
hundreds of articles about cows. Click on *images* and you'll find
hundreds of pictures of cows. It works that way for anything."

After she hung up with Sally, Senta sat at her desk almost
in disbelief. Slowly, she typed in *Dairy Cows* and just as Sally
had said, instantly there were more articles about dairy cows
than she could read in a lifetime. Clicking images, there were
pages of pictures of cows. Next, she typed in *Tennessee*. Next,
she tried *Ashland City TN*. And finally, she typed in *Hairstyles*.

Senta had been right in her intuition of Jacob Troyer; he
and Ruth were married in June. The wedding was on a Saturday,
a beautiful sunny Saturday in June. Everyone came, and there
was a long line of square black buggies with orange triangles on
the back, lined up outside of Ruth's home. Ruth was a strikingly
beautiful bride, and Jacob was a handsome groom, making for
a picture-perfect couple. The wedding turned into a three-day
holiday for Senta. First, was the wedding on Saturday. Senta
hitched up their black mare to the carriage, and she and her
parents drove to the bride's home. The ceremony was lovely,
and the reception outside under the trees was perfect. Senta was
very happy for her friend. They returned Sunday for church
services, and then Senta saw her friend and her new husband

again on Monday as it was traditional for the new bride and groom to spend their first week of marriage calling on their friends and relatives in the community. Everyone anxiously awaited the sound of the horse's hooves and wheels on gravel as they knew the newlyweds had come to visit. It wasn't until Sunday two weeks later that Senta sensed something was wrong.

The look on Ruth's face as Senta walked toward her the next week at church, immediately concerned her. Gone was the happy, carefree girl, the smiling bride brimming with joy. Whispering, Ruth said to Senta, "It's terrible. He's so mean to me. Don't ever get married, Senta."

"Here comes your husband," whispered Senta forcing a smile. "Hello, Jacob."

"Good morning, Senta," said Jacob. "Time to go inside, Ruth." He quickly ushered her into the house where services were being held that Sunday. There was never time for Ruth to talk in detail, although she probably wouldn't have told Senta details. Every other week, Senta saw her friend a little paler, more drawn, and never smiling. Senta wondered at what her friend's words meant but didn't understand. She remained confused and scared for her friend. She wondered at times if her friend was right about marriage being terrible, or if it was just Jacob.

The leaves turned, and the days got shorter. The men worked constantly in the fields to bring in the harvest before the fall rains began and made it too muddy to get into the fields. The rains held off until November, and the harvest was a success. Senta and her parents attended the harvest celebration, and Senta marveled at how quickly another year had passed, and all that had happened that year. Several friends reminded her of the day she had won the cobbler competition. Senta laughed and thanked them. She wondered if she would ever enter the cobbler competition again. Christmas came and went, the skies were gray and cold.

On a sunny day in January which was a bit warmer than normal, Senta's father decided to wash the buggy. He got out a bucket and rolled out the garden hose. He washed off the road dust and the mud on the wheels. After he put everything away, Elijah Miller sat down on the back porch to rest until lunchtime.

Peacefully, he sat looking out on the pasture as he had thousands of times before over the years. When Senta came out on the porch to tell him lunch was ready, he was gone.

CHAPTER THREE

Elijah

Senta never thought about why her parents had only one child until her father died. She never found the answer to that question, but only the question itself. Her father, Elijah Miller, hadn't married until he was thirty years old. He was a quiet man who worked hard on his small dairy farm. His life was his wife Sarah and their daughter. Elijah Miller was a man of few words; it was often difficult to tell if he was happy or sad. When he smiled, it was a slight smile, not a big smile, but one with just the corners of his mouth slightly elevated. There were few things that would bring about that response, but the main one was Senta. Elijah Miller adored his daughter even if it wasn't apparent to most. Though he loved his wife, it was his daughter who brought him the greatest joy. Her presence transformed the hard work on the farm into something approaching fun. Just watching her milk a cow or scramble an egg made him feel that all was right with the world.

The years had passed, and Senta had grown from a child into a young woman. Elijah had thought with some sadness about the day when she would start attending the singings and would eventually marry. Around her sixteenth birthday when Elijah had been at the hardware store, he'd bought a can of blue paint.

Driving through the countryside of Cheatham County dotted with white farm houses surrounded by white fences and white gates, a house with a blue gate could occasionally be seen. A blue gate indicated the home of a young woman of marriageable age. It was a sign of her coming of age. When Elijah had returned home, he sat the can of paint on the kitchen counter instead of in the barn, purposely that day for Senta to see. When she did, she broke into a big smile and then bit her lower lip as she saw her father watching her. They looked at each other, knowing what the other had been thinking, their silent communication of smiles. That same communication of smiles that would become so important after Elijah's stroke when he could no longer speak.

The day of Elijah Miller's funeral was cold and gray, even colder still because of the wind that bit at the somber faces of the community as they stood in the cemetery. Lines of black suits with black hats and black dresses with black caps, all silently listening to the pastor read the passage from the Bible. Senta heard little. Immediately after having found her father, she had frozen and everything had become an unreal dream. She would cry and then comfort her mother, then cry more. A blur of three days of people and funeral and cemetery all contained in three days of grief. She would cry frequently in the coming weeks, but as before, life would continue and there would be work to do. Now it was just her mother and her. If Senta's world had been small before, it became even smaller yet with the loss of her father.

Senta and her mother drove home from the cemetery in the buggy followed by three more identical black buggies. At the Miller house, the neighbors unhitched the mare and put the carriage away in the shed. Senta and her mother went in the house with the women while the men stood outside and talked. Senta tended to her mother until she herself started to cry, and then her mother would tend to Senta, holding her close while stroking her head. The neighbors left around 9:00 p.m. and Senta got to bed shortly before midnight, the latest she had been up in years. Morning would come early and there would be work to do, but she couldn't sleep. Her mind kept jumping from images of her father, to the cemetery, to finding him on the porch, to her mother, to imagining tomorrow she would see her father at breakfast.

Outside the wind blew, mixed with light snow causing a branch on the tree outside Senta's window to lightly hit the glass. Finally, needing to escape the images in her mind, Senta pictured herself as a beautiful girl in a white silk dress walking along the river in Paris. Then, overcome with guilt for indulging in such frivolous thoughts on the day of her father's funeral, she asked God to forgive her, and cried herself to sleep.

Morning came early and for a fleeting moment, Senta thought it had all been a dream. But reality came rushing back along with the responsibilities of daily life. She got out of bed and dressed. As she stood in front of the mirror brushing and braiding her hair, tears began to fall. As she stood in front of the mirror she thought how her own hair reminded her of her father's. *How many years will it be until my hair will start to show gray?* Shaking off the thought, Senta chided herself for feeling such vanity.

Downstairs, Senta began to go through the motions of what would now be a *normal* day. She made breakfast for her mother, but Sarah Miller wouldn't get up. Her mother said she was still tired. So Senta ate alone. She did the laundry alone. At noon, when her mother still didn't want to get out of bed, Senta went out to the barn to feed and water Sugar. Afterward, Senta dusted, took care of some sewing, and worked at the computer on the invoices.   Seeing the time on the computer screen read 5:00 p.m., she realized she had been alone all day.

John and Abigail Lapp stopped the next day at the Miller house as they were taking their buggy into Ashland City to visit the supermarket. "There's no need for you to make the trip by yourself," John said. "There's plenty of room. You and your mother can come with us; or if she's not up to it, she can stay here and you can do the shopping. We'd like the company." So Senta started going to town every other Thursday with the Lapps to buy groceries at the Food Lion. Senta's mother, Sarah, who was becoming more and more reclusive, left the house less and less. "If your mother doesn't feel up to going to church Sunday, just come out to the road and we'll give you a ride," said Abigail. "There's no need for you to hitch up your rig for just you."

Over the next few months, Senta and Abigail became better friends. Even though they only lived a quarter of a mile apart, they hadn't known each other very well until then. John and Abigail were a little older than Senta and had been married six years. Senta loved riding to church and to town with them and she liked being with them for a reason she never spoke aloud. Senta saw something in them that was very different than what she saw in her friend Ruth. They were happy.

Senta sometimes thought about what a perfect husband might be like. She had liked a few boys at school, but none of them met her idea of who her husband should be. Sometimes she wondered at herself because she couldn't really describe what he should be like. Watching Ruth and Abigail in their marriages was a way to imagine what it might be for her. Ruth's unhappiness shook the foundation Senta's idea of marriage was built on. She wondered if Ruth was right and that marriage was torturous. She wondered if her parents had been miserable. Perhaps she just hadn't noticed. She pondered it, remembering moments from the past, concluded that they seemed happy. She considered other couples and wondered. She thought about the terrible things Jacob did to Ruth and wondered what they were. And then was afraid to imagine what she could be talking about.

"Were you and Papa happy?" Senta asked her mother one day at breakfast. To Sarah the question came out of the blue.

"What kind of a question is that, Senta?" asked her mother. "Of course we were happy. Why do you ask this?"

"It's Ruth, Mother. I'm not sure she's very happy," said Senta. "I think Jacob is mean to her."

"Some men are mean, Senta, but your father wasn't one of them," said her mother. "He was a good man and was always very kind to me."

Her mother's words gave her hope. John and Abigail gave her hope. She observed them as they rode together to Ashland City on Thursdays. She watched them laugh as they talked, and seeing how they looked at each other made Senta believe they were in love. And noticing how Abigail sat close to her husband and held his hand convinced Senta that she didn't fear him and felt safe with him.

The days and the weeks blurred into her routine of invoices, the farm, and her mother. The months brought four Sundays and two trips to Ashland City with the Lapps. Another year and another harvest; the time ran together. One day Senta was standing in the driveway by the road, waiting for the Lapps when she began to focus on how long she'd been riding to town with them. Her knees felt weak as she did the math in her head and realized it had been fifteen years. As she stood in the cool autumn air, waiting on the buggy ride to town, tears came to her eyes. *Are the best years of my life already behind me?* She started to panic as she felt a tremendous loneliness come over her. A confusing loneliness because she still had her home and her mother. Senta closed her eyes.

Senta prayed. Not the mechanical prayer spoken before a meal. Not a polished prayer prepared for public recitation in church. But a pleading, desperate prayer of, *is this my life, and is there not something else for me?* And finally acquiescence, *I don't even know what I want. I don't even know what to pray for, but You have given me this life.*

Senta stood in the gravel by their mailbox looking down at her tears falling on her shoes. "Senta!" shouted Abigail. "Get in!" Senta looked up and saw the Lapp's buggy in front of her. "What's wrong, Senta?" asked Abigail. "Get in. I've got to talk to you. We have news!" Senta opened the buggy door and climbed in. "Are you OK? Have you been crying?" asked Abigail.

"Yes, I'm not sure why. I'm OK," answered Senta, wiping her eyes.

"Senta, I can't wait any longer. We're so excited!" said Abigail. "John, you tell her. Tell her the good news!"

Smiling, John turned to look at Senta as the horse pulled the buggy onto the pavement. "We didn't think it would happen. We thought there was probably something wrong," he said. "But there isn't. Everything is fine. Abigail is pregnant!"

"Can you believe it!" she exclaimed. "After all these years and now God is blessing us with a child!" Senta hugged her friend and they all cried with happiness. As they rode toward Ashland City, Senta sensed that God was telling her something. Something about trusting Him and patience.

When shopping was complete and they were loading the groceries in the buggy, Abigail said, "I almost forgot to tell you about my idea. It will be harder now with the baby coming, but we can do it."

"What are you talking about, Abigail?" Senta asked.

"John thinks I'm a little crazy," said Abigail. She gave her husband a grin. John smiled back amused. "It's an idea for us, and you, to make some money." Senta looked at her friend and exhibited a questioning smile. "You know Mrs. Belier and Mrs. King started selling baked goods at the Farmers' Market in Nashville last year. They have been doing very well selling their breads and pastries. Most of the time they sell out completely! That gave me the idea that we should sell something. What if we sat up a booth at the Nashville Farmers' Market on Saturdays, too?"

"But I'm not the best at baking bread, Abigail, and truthfully you aren't either," remarked Senta. John couldn't help but chuckle and Abigail gave him a stern look.

"No, no, not baking, something different!" exclaimed Abigail.

"Just tell her, Abigail," said John. Senta looked back and forth at John and Abigail. With a smile and a look of anticipation on her face, Senta listened eagerly.

"Cheese!" exclaimed Abigail. "We have the cows and, therefore, the milk. We can make cheese, that is, after we visit Mrs. Stolzfus and she schools us. Then you and I can sell it at the Farmers' Market!" Abigail watched for Senta's reaction to what she was certain was an excellent idea.

"But Nashville is so far away. How could we do it?" asked Senta not wanting to discount her friend's idea, but not understanding how it could work.

"No, no, I have it figured out," said Abigail. "Mrs. Belier and Mrs. King are picked up by the van service some Amish use to transport them places that are far away. Nashville isn't that far if you're in a van. And the best part is they drive right past us. They could pick us up on Saturday mornings early and then drop us off on the way home. It's really perfect!" Abigail held her hands clasped together in front of her mouth, then looked intently at Senta, awaiting her response to the idea. A few moments passed before Senta answered.

"I think we could do it," Senta replied. "I think it's a good idea!" Abigail squealed with joy and hugged her friend while John smiled as he drove the buggy down the country road to Ashland City.

Something changed that day. Life changed. Senta's life took on a new aspect. She thought about it sometimes while she was working. She wondered why everything felt so different. She concluded that for the first time in many years she had a dream. A future that held promise and excitement. And she realized as she went about her daily chores, which weren't different from before, life had somehow gotten better. Better because now she saw a future. Senta had heard it said that people should learn to live in the present, enjoying each day. And now having found a future to look forward to, the present was no longer empty.

When they arrived at Senta's house that day, John Lapp drove the buggy up the drive to the house so Senta could get the groceries in easier. "You have to come in!" said Senta. "Just for a minute to tell my mother!" Senta, John, and Abigail each carrying bags of groceries came in through the kitchen door as Senta called out, "Mother, where are you?"

"I'm here," said her mother. "Is something wrong?"

"Wonderful news, Mother!" said Senta. "Here's Abigail and John! They can tell you themselves!"

"Mrs. Miller," said Abigail. "We do have some wonderful news. God has blessed us with a baby. I'm pregnant!" Everyone turned to Mrs. Miller to see her response.

"This is, indeed, wonderful news!" she said, crossing the kitchen to embrace Abigail.

"And there's more!" said Abigail. "We're going to go into business with Senta. We've decided to make cheese to sell at the Farmers' Market in Nashville."

"Cheese?" questioned Mrs. Miller. "You're dreaming, Senta. What do you know about making cheese?"

"Nothing, Mother," answered Senta. "But we're going to learn!"

CHAPTER FOUR

Jerrick

Jerrick Douglas woke at 4:25 a.m., the only thing visible in the stateroom being the red numbers on the clock. He knew he could sleep longer but thought of the morning and getting underway made him want to begin sooner rather than later. He stretched out his legs and his arms feeling the cool of the sheets against his naked body, cool where his legs hadn't been just a moment before. Then he moved his legs back to the warm spot where he had been when he woke up. As he stretched his arms above his head, he felt the coolness of the mahogany bulkhead that would have been a headboard had the bed been in a regular bedroom on land. His head almost against the bulkhead, his feet would have extended a few inches over the foot of the queen-sized berth had he not been lying a bit diagonally. The cool of the air-conditioning felt good on his arms and shoulders, and he lay there listening for the sounds he had listened for instinctively now for years. The most important being bilge pumps kicking in. But he heard nothing other than the hum of the air-conditioning pushing cold air through the boat, and then a different hum of the refrigerator cycling in the galley. All good sounds. He lay still feeling for motion and listening for the sound of water lapping against the hull but heard nothing and felt no motion. As the weather had forecast, it would be a still, windless morning.

43

Getting out of bed, he walked naked through the boat in the darkness, out of his cabin, down the passageway, then up three steps with a single red light on each step. Red to see the steps at night, but also red because that color of light doesn't affect one's night vision, something needed when operating at night. Then immediately to starboard at the top of the last step, he was in the galley and pushed the button on the coffeemaker. The coffee was already prepared, Casi Cielo from Guatemala, which he had ground the night before. He looked out the galley window through the Diamond Seaglaze glass at the Clarksville Marina. No one was up yet. The only movement being the fountain of water at the entrance to the harbor. Going back down below, he went into the master head, shaved, brushed his teeth, and took a shower while looking out the portside porthole at the harbor. He smiled to himself thinking about how much he enjoyed taking a shower when underway. Since the boat was moving, he could see the water pass by through the porthole. But that rarely happened because he always had to be at the helm. Unlike the other three boats in the group, he was alone.

Operating 64,000 pounds of yacht by himself was difficult at times, especially docking and going through locks. But he had gotten used to it and had developed strategies to make it work, although having another person on board would have made the journey easier. He had been alone for many years now. It had become normal to travel alone on the boat and as well as in life. Drying off after his shower, he quickly ran a brush through his damp hair and noticed the gray that was starting to show up against the dark brown. Stepping back into the stateroom, he got an old pair of khaki cargo shorts out of the drawer. They were so old and worn that the edges had frayed and were unraveling. He knew he should throw them away, but he liked them because they were comfortable and because it seemed he had had them forever. He put on an old, slate blue T-shirt that read *BVI Tortola* in faded letters. Then, he added a dark blue sweatshirt that had *Grand Harbor* embroidered on it. He knew that even though it would be a hot day, this early in the morning the temperature would still be cool. He thought about the two Grand Harbors, Grand Harbor where the Tennessee met the TennTom at the juncture of Tennessee, Alabama, and Mississippi. And Grand Harbor on Malta at Valetta. He knew both Grand Harbors. The coffee maker beeped completion but before going to the galley, he meticulously made the bed taking pains to ensure the sheets and blanket and then bedspread were perfectly straight and tight. He made the bed for no one other than himself. Though an unmade bed would never be seen, he would see it and he liked order.

Pouring his coffee, he walked through the salon then out onto the aft deck, and up the starboard side deck while scanning the dock lines to be sure nothing had moved in the night. He smiled to himself, taking a sip of the hot coffee while admiring the coiled lines on the dock. He had a dislike for janky dock lines and would joke that he was beautifying America's docks, one dock at a time, with his neatly coiled dock lines. He walked forward on the dock until he could see around the bow of the boat. Standing in the darkness, he looked across the water at Clarksville, Tennessee. Only a few cars were moving at this hour. The sign on the Mexican restaurant flickered, juxtaposed against other old dark buildings behind, some from before the Civil War.

> *Reverse morning darkness, Profits come to a halt*
> *Gently the darkness holds you in his arms*
> *'Til morning will start you may never feel*
> *The quake of artillery in the early morning hours*
> *In fear awaken. Peace in our time.*

Remembering something he had written a long time ago, and again thinking juxtaposition of words of *reverse darkness*, as light being the reverse of darkness, or maybe he should have said reverse light. It didn't matter, of course, because he had never told anyone he wrote poetry and never would.

Seeing the light come on in the salon of Sam's boat, he looked at his watch and decided he'd better perform the engine room check. Stepping from the dock through the side gate to the starboard side, he entered through the pilothouse door, stopping long enough to hit Spotify. Perhaps he'd listen to some Selena while checking the engines. Down the stairs to the salon and then down again to the passageway that connected the two staterooms to the rest of the boat, he entered the sound deadening door to the engine room as Selena was singing "Como La Flor." First checking the engine oil, and singing along. Then checking the coolant level in the heat exchanger, checking the transmission fluid level, strainers, and finally belt tension. Then, with Selena singing "I Could Fall in Love," he laughed, thinking that he did love the big, continuous-duty John Deere diesel. He loved that it could run for weeks on end, and while he would never take this boat around the world, knowing that it could do so, pleased him.

Back up in the pilothouse, he turned the key and pressed the start button. The diesel sprang to life, and he held his finger on the oil pressure gauge to watch the pressure come up before doing the same with the genset. Then, refilling his coffee, he went out on the dock again. Standing behind the boat, he watched the exhaust ports to be sure both engines were pumping water. There were two sets of fenders on the starboard side, the regular ones that were cushioning the hull from the dock and three big round ones that were riding just above the level of the dock. The big round ones were for locking through Cheatham Lock, about ten miles ahead, the only obstacle between Clarksville and Nashville.

Looking down the dock, he saw activity on the other three boats. They were all doing the same thing he was doing, preparing to get under way, get through Cheatham Lock and get tucked in at Rock Harbor for the weekend. Back in the pilothouse, he brought the radar online and the array on the radar arch began turning. One by one he switched off the AC circuits before switching from Shore Power to Ship's Power. He flipped the AC circuits back on, then brought the DC circuits online, and finally hit Nav Lights as the red, green, and white lights came on outside of the yacht. With no wind and plenty of room, he reeled in the power cord and brought in the forward, aft, and spring lines, throwing them in a pile on the aft deck to be coiled later. Then in the pilothouse, checking all the gauges, looking at the radar screen and adjusting the alarm to 3 miles, and seeing the icon of his boat on the chartplotter screen, he pushed the transmission forward for two seconds, then to neutral, then to reverse for two seconds, repeating as he side-stepped the boat away from dock. Once in the turning basin, he slowly turned the boat, and at dead idle, 700 rpm, he coasted through the marina as the other three boats in the group did the same. It was not quite dawn. The line of boats was hardly noticeable to the few people driving by the marina, appearing only as a line of white and green lights ghosting through the harbor.

Cheese

"I don't know, Abigail," said Senta voicing a bit of concern. "Do you think we can do this? I had no idea how complicated cheesemaking was. No wonder it's so expensive."   John and Abigail Lapp and Senta drove down the country road in the Lapp's buggy on their way back from visiting Mrs. Stolzfus. Abigail had wasted no time in setting up the meeting with her to get her guidance on making cheese.

"Senta is right," said John. "It is complicated and very labor intensive. I thought you just made the cheese, let it age a week or two, and then you could sell it. It sounds like it takes at least three months to age, and you must brine it every week during the aging process. Not to mention that it has to be kept at 50 degrees."

"You two are so negative," scolded Abigail as she adjusted herself in the seat, trying to find a more comfortable position. She realized that as the pregnancy progressed it would only get more uncomfortable, but she was happy to bear it and thought lovingly about the baby growing inside her. "You two see only negatives, but they're really positives! Yes, cheese is expensive because it's hard to make. If it was easy, everyone would do it. That means we can charge a good price and make more money. We can start off making a small batch to see how it turns out and then increase the quantity when we get it down right."

"But where are we going to store all these batches at 50 degrees?" asked John. "That's not being negative, that's being realistic."

"We have two cellars on our farm," answered Senta. "Mother and I only need one so we could use the other cellar for our cheese. Also, I can make a schedule and do the brining weekly. We have plenty of milk. We'll make cheese once a week. I can take the cheese to my house and age it in our extra cellar. After three months, we can take the first batch to market for sale."

"There you go, John!" chided Abigail. "Oh, ye of little faith. No problem at all. We just happen to have an extra cellar!"

So, it began two weeks later after they had bought the equipment and the supplies. They started with eight gallons of milk and ended up with 4 pounds of cheese. Senta read Abigail's notes from Mrs. Stolzfus aloud as they worked. The kitchen was a mess, and they weren't exactly sure they had done it right. John took Senta home in the buggy carrying the cheese in the back. Senta carried the cheese down into the unused cellar. The next day she marked the date on the batch and made an Excel spreadsheet with columns for batches and 14 weeks of brining and ageing. The skills she'd learned from her work for Mr. Campbell were surprisingly helpful with making cheese.

The time passed quickly as every week Abigail and Senta made more cheese. Mondays were the days Sally brought invoices and receipts, Tuesdays were for cheese making, every other Thursday was for going to Ashland City for groceries, every other Sunday was for church, and soon Saturdays would be for the Farmers' Market in Nashville. Senta's life had quickly become much busier. *I don't think I have ever been so busy*, Senta thought. *But I like it and it's fun. And I can't wait to start selling our cheese at the Farmers' Market!*

The first batch of cheese surprised them all as they cautiously took bites of their creation. "Mrs. Stolzfus said it would be a success if we followed her recipe," said Abigail.

"She was right," said John. "This is really tasty."

"This is delicious," said Senta. "I guess we should wait

until next week though to make sure we don't get sick before taking it to the market."

"You two are so negative!" exclaimed Abigail. And they all laughed as they enjoyed sampling the cheese. Senta took some home to her mother who also thought it was very good. She also shared some with Sally the following Monday when she came with the paperwork from Stolz Woodworking. Sally gave her approval as well.

I think we can do this, Senta thought, as she sat at the kitchen table that Monday with her mother and Sally. *I'm a staff accountant for a CPA firm and now I'm making cheese. I'm supporting myself and my mother and we're doing fine.* She thought about her future and was happy but still felt an absence of something. Something that somehow left her incomplete. She knew of course what it was. Senta felt alone. Even though she had her mother, her work friends, and the Lapps, she knew it wasn't the same as sharing her life with a man, her man. *Why has no man ever paid me any attention? Why have I never met anyone who interests me?* Such thoughts came to her from time to time, but she usually pushed them aside. She was busy with her work, and she liked not having time to think about it; it was easier.

One day, in her bedroom office, after her eyes were tired of looking at invoices, she stood and stretched. As she did, she saw herself in the mirror and stood there looking at herself. *Am I pretty?* she asked herself. Then taking off her cap and pulling the barrette from her hair, she shook her hair lose. Looking at herself she began wondering if men thought she was pretty. Thinking that perhaps her face was at fault she turned her head left and right scrutinizing her features. Then wondering if her figure was the problem she turned sideways, stood very straight, and took a deep breath, as she critiqued what she saw. Finally, she concluded that she probably wasn't pretty.

Preoccupied with her appearance, she went to her computer and typed *Hairstyles* in Google, and spent the next twenty minutes looking at pictures of various styles and their descriptions. *Why am I wasting my time looking at hairstyles*, she thought. *I'm Amish and I couldn't try any of these styles if I wanted to.* But then she went back to Google and typed in

Shoes. She spent another fifteen minutes looking at everything from flip flops to Manolo Blanik. Then she clicked on a fashion link and ended up in a site called *Net-a-Porter* where she read the fashion blog and looked at the latest designs off the runway in Milan.

That night after dinner was done and the kitchen cleaned up, Senta told her mother good night and went through the house turning off lights and locking the doors. Back in her room she put on her night gown, and said her prayers. Just as she started to turn out the light, Senta went to the closet for a pillow to take to bed with her. It wasn't the pillow she rested her head on but an extra pillow. Then lying down on her side, she wrapped her arms around the pillow pretending it to be a man. When Senta did this she felt at peace and her worries disappeared. Even though she couldn't picture what he looked like or who he was, she held him and imagined him holding her as she drifted off to sleep.

The next morning brought a new day of making breakfast and eating with her mother, followed by going to the bedroom office to tackle the invoices from Stoll Woodworking. About ten o'clock she took a break, walked downstairs to talk to her mother a bit, then walked outside enjoying the sunshine before going to the cheese cellar behind the barn to brine the cheese.

It took her about ten minutes to pour the salty mixture over the cheese and she thought about how she'd arrange the various batches which would eventually have 12 different dates in 12 different points of production in the cellar. Then, she considered what would happen if they doubled their production making each batch twice as big. Looking at the wooden shelves, she envisioned it would take up all the space and realized the amount of cheese they could make would be determined not by milk but by cellar space. Walking up the steps from the cool cellar into the warmth of the day, Senta saw the horse and buggy tied up in front of the house as her eyes adjusted to the bright sunlight. She wondered who it could be as she walked back to the house.

"Just stopping by to see how you and your daughter are

doing," Senta heard Eric Yost, the bishop, telling her mother as she came into the house from the kitchen door. Senta stood quietly in the kitchen listening to Bishop Yost and her mother talk, a sense of dread running through her. Her mind went back to the day when Yost had stood in that same room with her mother and father after her father's stroke. She remembered Yost delivering the news of the decision that changed her life forever. She only saw him at church services and knew she shouldn't be angry with him. Senta struggled with these feelings at times. She loved her parents and wanted to take care of them, but she couldn't help but feeling that Bishop Yost had robbed her of her own life. She knew she should forgive him, but couldn't, not so much because of how he had decided her life for her, but because she didn't like him, didn't trust him. She couldn't say why exactly, but she felt uneasy around him.

"I have to say, Mrs. Miller, I don't approve of Senta working outside the home for the accountant in Ashland City," said Bishop Yost. "It's not good for women to be out in the world among the English like that."

"I know, Bishop Yost," Mrs. Miller replied, "but Senta actually works for the Stoll's, the Amish woodworking company. And she works right here at home. I don't understand the technology, but I'm so grateful for computers and the internet because it means Senta can work from home."

"A computer? You have internet in this house?" demanded Yost. "This is not acceptable!"

"Bishop Yost, Senta and I depend on this job. We don't have the cows anymore so we need the income from her work," said Mrs. Miller.

"Good morning, Bishop Yost," said Senta walking into the parlor.

"Your mother has been telling me you have a computer in this house," said Yost. "Is this true?"

"It is," said Senta, thinking ahead to her response and also thinking it not a good idea to mention the cell phone, much less the cheese making enterprise with the Lapps. She didn't trust him and feared he might order Abigail and her to cease their cheese business.

"This is unacceptable," he said, raising his voice. "The internet is full of evil, sinful things that you should not be looking at."

"Bishop Yost, I was only trained on the bookkeeping program for Stoll Woodworking. That's the only thing I know how to use the computer for. There may be bad things on the internet, but I don't know what they are or how to see them, and I don't want to see them. Bishop Yost, how do you know about these sinful things on the internet?" asked Senta.

"That is enough!" said Yost, bringing his fist down hard on the arm of the chair. "I will not tolerate your insolence. Does Mr. Stoll know you have a computer?"

"He does," Senta replied. "He bought it for me to use. You should visit Mr. and Mrs. Stoll sometime, Bishop Yost. They have a wonderful business, and I help them by keeping all their invoices, receipts, and payroll straight. Mr. Campbell, the CPA in Ashland City, isn't Amish like we are, but he is very nice. I feel blessed to have him as my boss. And I am blessed to be able to provide for my mother and myself."

Bishop Yost stood up, said his goodbyes, and stormed out the door to his waiting horse and buggy. He wasn't sure what had just happened, but he had the feeling he'd been outmaneuvered by the Miller girl! While he knew there was nothing wrong with what she was doing and the church would do nothing if he should bring it up, he still felt Senta needed to be taught a lesson. He didn't like it that she was independent and self-sufficient. Yost recognized that he had caused this when he decided she was to stay home and care for her parents, and it galled him. If he had not done that, she might well have been married by now and her husband would be providing for her and her mother. She was an annoyance, and he was not about to let her get the best of him!

"I don't like that man," said Senta, as she watched the black horse and buggy turn onto the road.

"Senta, you should be more respectful of your elders," warned her mother.

"How about respect for me?" replied Senta. "He was implying that I'm using the computer for sinful purposes, and

I'm not. I wouldn't even know how to do that if I wanted to. Besides I'm just doing my job to take care of you and me, just like he said I should after Father had his stroke. I'm not strong enough to be a dairy farmer, but I'm smart enough to be the bookkeeper for Stoll Woodworking. I'm a different kind of strong that Bishop Yost doesn't like at all!"

That night as Senta prayed, she asked God's forgiveness for lying about only knowing how to use the accounting program. She did know how to use Google. She had looked up all sort of things that had nothing to do with work, but none of them were sinful. She reasoned with God that looking at fashion, shoes, and hairstyles wasn't sinful. It was just interesting to her. She wasn't going to buy a Chanel dress or a Prada bag. But then she admitted to God that she wanted to be more attractive, and asked for forgiveness. Turning off the light and getting into bed, she hugged her pillow and drifted off to sleep.

Three months passed quickly. Abigail's pregnancy progressed as did the cheese making business. Abigail had spoken with Mrs. King and made the necessary arrangements for Senta and herself to be picked up on Saturday mornings for the trip to Nashville. Abigail found an old cash box in the attic to use for making change. Senta made a sign that simply said "Cheese $7." They would be bringing twenty-five one pound cheeses to market. If they could sell them all, it would be $175. The van service and rent for the space at the market was $60 which left $115. That would be $57.50 each for she and Abigail.

The night before their debut at the Farmers' Market, Senta was so excited she could hardly sleep. She would need to get up at 5:00 a.m. to get the cheese out of the cellar, prepare breakfast, and meet the van in front of the house at 6:30 a.m. She lay in bed thinking about all the new people she might meet. She knew that many Amish were very skeptical and cautious with the non-Amish or English as they called them. But her experiences with co-workers at Mr. Campbell's office had all been positive. She liked everyone at the office and had been surprised at how much they had in common. But the Farmers'

Market was going to be completely different. She wondered if she might even meet people from other countries, certainly from other parts of the United States.

Her alarm went off at 5:00 a.m. and she jumped out of bed. Her mother told her to be calm at breakfast and cautioned her about not going anywhere by herself at the Farmers' Market but to stay close to Abigail, Mrs. King, and Mrs. Belier so she wouldn't be kidnapped. Senta had never heard of anyone being abducted from the Farmers' Market and thought her mother was probably worrying needlessly.

The black van rolled up the driveway right on time. Senta was waiting in front of the house with two baskets holding the twenty-five pounds of cheese, their first batch to take to market. Mrs. King and Mrs. Belier were already in the big black van with their cargo of various breads. They were in their mid 50's and had a serious and reserved air about them that bordered on judgmental. Senta sensed immediately that the two women were very suspect about her job keeping the books for the woodworking company. Only a short distance down the road, they pulled in and picked up Abigail. As they rode on to Nashville, the two older ladies regaled the two younger women with words of advice of how to conduct themselves at the Farmers' Market, what to watch out for, and what not to do.

Senta and Abigail were both excited to see how their cheese would sell, but Senta was excited for another reason. Although no one knew it, she had made a discovery about herself, and it was all due to Google. Ever since she had learned how to use the search engine, she realized that she could find out about anything, but more importantly she had discovered a world that she never knew existed. The thought of spending one day a week in that world filled her with expectation!

Soon they were entering the Nashville traffic, and even though it was Saturday, the van slowed down. Senta was amazed at how many cars were on the multi-lane interstate and wondered where everyone was going. Off in the distance, she saw the city skyline and thought it incredible that so many people lived so close together. When they pulled into the Farmers' Market parking lot, the driver took them directly to their building to unload.

The market was a series of big metal roofs supported on brick columns open on all sides. Mrs. King explained that it was a nice set up compared to other farmers' markets she'd seen because the roof kept the sun and the rain off. The concrete floors of the buildings had yellow lines forming boxes with numbers in each. They were in Shed B, numbers 14 and 15. On rectangular folding tables, the four went to work arranging, stacking bread and cheese, and taping up the signs. Abigail looked at Senta as they put up their sign that said *Cheese $7*, a look of, *I hope this price is alright and not too high*. Then they took one block of cheese, cut it up in little pieces on a plate, and set it on the table next to a sign that said *Free Samples*. Even though it would cut into their profit a bit, they felt it was a good idea.

Soon cars started filling the parking lot and people started pouring into the market. They quickly found out that any worry about the customers liking the cheese had been needless. They sold out by 9:30. Abigail and Senta looked at each other and laughed. "I'm sorry, ma'am, but we've just run out of cheese," said Abigail, as Senta took down the sign. "But we'll be back next week with more."

Senta gave Mrs. King the money for their part of the van service and the space. With nothing left to sell, they decided to walk around the Farmers' Market and explore. There were hundreds of people. They walked from space to space and building to building looking at all the things that were for sale: vegetables, fruit, preserves, ceramics, and wooden items. "I need to tell Mr. Stoll about this," said Senta. "I imagine he could sell lots of his wooden chairs here."

"No wonder we sold out, Senta," said Abigail. "I've not seen anyone else selling cheese, and there are hundreds of people here!"

"We must increase our production," said Senta. "But even if we make the most we can make, we'll still be out by noon... if it's always like this."

The last building was different from the others. It was enclosed and as they walked through the glass doors, they found themselves in a building with a variety of vendors and a food court in the middle. They spent an hour looking at everything from an international grocery store to candles. Then they decided on bar-b-que and purchased their lunch from one of the stands in the food court. They sat down in the center of the building and ate. Senta watched the customers, seeing people of all ages and all colors. She listened carefully and heard several languages she couldn't identify. "Did you hear all the different kinds of music, Abigail?" asked Senta as they ate.

"Yes, everyone has a music system and plays their music," said Abigail.

"I've never heard so many different kinds of music," said Senta. "And can you believe how some of the people dress?"

"Well, Senta, you know some people may say that about us!" laughed Abigail.

Senta smiled and nodded, "You're probably right. But at least we're decent. Did you see that large woman with the tight white pants you could see through? I tried not to stare, but I couldn't help but look. How in the world did she get those pants on? I'd be afraid they would rip out the seams!"

"And what about the man with all the metal piercings on his face? The English are different," Abigail said.

"But all our customers today were very nice, and I enjoyed talking to them," said Senta. Abigail nodded and the two ate their sandwiches and French fries.

When the van dropped Senta off that evening, she was bursting to tell her mother all about the day's adventure. As the two women prepared dinner, Senta chattered away about how well their cheese had sold, and all the people she had seen. Senta suggested that maybe one Saturday her mother could go with them as there was room in the van. But Mrs. Miller declined the invitation saying she would rather stay home.

Senta walked up the stairs to her room and soon was in bed. As she lay in bed thinking about the day, she marveled at how many people there had been at the Farmers' Market. *I don't know for sure how many, but there could have been over a thousand people there today. Nashville is so big. There must be a million people living there.*

Her mind returned for a moment to the thought that she had never met a man who found her interesting, and that there were millions of men she had never met. But quickly she fell asleep.

CHAPTER SIX

The River

Jerrick Douglas didn't grow up with boats. Many people assumed he did. It started one day when he was in his early twenties. He was at a marina and while walking the docks and looking at the boats it hit him that he should have a boat. Not because he wanted one, even though he did, but rather he wouldn't be complete without one. It was as if having a boat had always been a part of him even though he had never been around boats. He bought a 22-foot sailboat and that began his love affair with boats and water. While spending a weekend on the boat was always fun, what he loved most was traveling by water. Sometimes that would be a four-day trip to Nashville on the Cumberland River, sometimes a two-week trip to Chattanooga and back on the Tennessee River, or sometimes three or four months down the TennTom to the Gulf and on to the islands. There was something adventurous, fascinating and nostalgic about arriving at a port by water, something just not possible from arriving in a car. Nostalgic as in connected to the past.

He thought about this off and on for years and finally concluded that he must have had ancestors who had spent a lot of time on boats and that somehow that was in his DNA. Boats made him feel more whole. The work involved in operating the boat, didn't seem like work at all, and he got satisfaction from everything running correctly. He liked operating the systems, monitoring the engine gauges, managing the electricity from the genset through all the various batteries, inverters, and buss bars. He liked watching the electronics, observing an approaching vessel miles away on the radar, and changing the autopilot one degree left rudder to adjust course to the chartplotter. The final satisfaction came with arriving, whether in an uninhabited cove or a city, hailing the harbormaster to get a dock assignment on the transient dock, or watching the bottom contour on the chartplotter to determine the best place to drop anchor and to multiply that number by seven to put out that amount of chain.

His personal life had been as bad as his professional life had been good. His marriage had only lasted four years. She had been pretty but increasingly demanding as time passed, never happy with anything and always wanting more. Increasingly materialist and infected with a serious case of keeping up with the Jones' she had constantly demanded more things, always in an attempt to keep up with her competitive friends. She liked boats though, not for the experience of voyaging, but for the cache it gave her with her friends. Completely focused on working, he didn't discern how she was at first, but little by little he started to see it and did not like what he saw. She had a harshness with anyone she felt to be below her and that was just about everyone. He started to grasp how incredibly selfish she was, always putting herself ahead of others.

More and more the situation bothered him as he came to understand her true nature. It was on a Saturday that he decided to observe her and study her actions. He was hoping to see some example of kindness from his wife, but there was not even one during the entire day. He continued to watch closely in the days and weeks to follow. Sadly, he began to see patterns of manipulation and deceit.

Toward the end of the marriage, she demanded a swimming pool. He explained that a swimming pool would have to wait because the cost didn't fit in the budget for that year. She threw a fit and informed him there would be no more sex until she had her pool. Reluctantly, he gave in and she got what she wanted. Realizing he was being manipulated ate at him.

Ironically, it was while sitting by the pool, and watching his wife that Jerrick had an epiphany. He no longer wanted her. It didn't matter how attractive she was, he just didn't love her any more. In fact, he didn't even like her. About a year later the divorce was final. Fortunately, there were no children.

Now, years later, that part of his life didn't seem real. It was as if he had never been married. Most of the details had long faded. In a way, it was like a movie he had once watched but only vaguely remembered–a movie Jerrick had no interest in watching again. He had never looked back or second guessed his decision to end the marriage. As time passed, he had no idea where life had taken her of if she was even alive.

His business, however, was another matter. The divorce gave him new energy. No longer fighting with his wife, no longer constantly trying to make her happy, and no longer spending immense amounts of money on her, he focused on business. He predicted the coffee house phenomenon by noticing how Europeans and Latin Americans loved to gather at coffee shops, drink cappuccinos and lattes, and converse. The trend was just starting in the United States, and he expected it would continue. Instead of trying to develop a chain of stores, he focused on supplying independent coffee shops across the country with premium coffee from Guatemala. He learned from his Guatemalan contacts that most of the premium coffee in the world went to Europe. The Europeans knew good coffee, appreciated good coffee, and were willing to pay more for good coffee. Believing that Americans would start to do the same, he made his contacts with some fincaros, coffee plantation owners, in Guatemala and hit the road in the US driving from city to city selling their premium coffee under his own label. Explaining the concept that the independent coffee shop could differentiate itself from the competition with better coffee, one by one he signed up new customers. After ten years of working seven days a week, the coffee shops were calling him. With 55 employees and distribution in 48 states, he had become a big deal in the coffee business even though the average coffee drinker had never heard his name. It was in the eleventh year that a major food conglomerate contacted him and offered him eight figures for his company.

It was years before that Jerrick Douglas had read a book by an American author named Stribling. The main character in the book was a man named Colonel Vaiden. Colonel Vaiden was on track as a young man to become very wealthy in the cotton business, but the Civil War changed the economics of that track to wealth. After the war, the previously prosperous Vaiden, now poor, sat on the park bench in Florence, Alabama, watching the people walk by, trying to understand what had happened. After sitting there for one year, it dawned on him that everything was constantly changing. Cotton had been a great path to success but then after the war, it wasn't. Watching the people walk by as they shopped, he saw a country on the verge of a consumer economy and decided to open a general store. He was successful but after ten years returned to sit on the bench on the square once again to try to determine what would be the next evolution in the economy. He saw the growth of wealth and opened a bank, riding that train to yet another level of wealth. Jerrick had always remembered that book, that character, and had thought of it when he started the coffee company. Knowing that nothing in economies lasts forever, he accepted the buyout offer, sold his company, and retired.

His first purchase in retirement was a new boat, a Krogen 48 NorthSea. A full displacement hull meant it was slow and very fuel efficient. A Nordhavn 40 had circumnavigated the world a few years back and he knew the Krogen 48 could do it with no problem. Jerrick had no plans to sail around the world, but had been around the Carribean a couple of times already. He thought going through the Panama Canal and then working his way up the west coast all the way to Alaska sounded interesting. The Krogen was built like a tank with everything constructed heavier than was necessary. He had been through several severe storms with her, and it barely fazed the 32-ton vessel. But the boat was just about the maximum one person could handle. That was made possible with the autopilot that steered the yacht while Jerrick did other things, although he always had to maintain a lookout. The alarm on the radar also alerted him to anything up ahead.

He had guests from time to time, and the big trawler could sleep five comfortably. Most of the time guests would be a couple, but when he made long crossings having to stay awake for 24 to 48 hours or longer, he would call on a couple of friends who liked to cruise. They would stand watch letting each other sleep. When they did this Jerrick would sleep on the settee in the pilothouse so he would be right there if the man standing watch needed him for anything. The key to an easy, event free crossing was patience. It was well worth it to sit tight in Apalachicola for a few extra days waiting for the weather window. While it was tempting to get impatient and take a chance with less than perfect weather, it was always better to wait. It wasn't that the boat couldn't take the pounding that bad weather would give; it was whether the crew could. Jerrick learned this the hard way when he had crewed ocean races in sailboats.

Once, crewing the Rolex Middle Sea Race in the Mediterranean, a confluence of three weather fronts hit at the same time. The next two days had been terrible with everyone seasick and increasingly tired from not being able to sleep or eat. Going below to rest when off watch was like trying to sleep in a dryer. An Australian boat, *Loki*, tore out its rudder when it fell off a wave. Steering a confused sea is very difficult if not impossible at times. With no rudder and water pouring in faster than the bilge pumps could pump it out, the *Loki* sank quickly with 18 men on board. Miraculously, the Italian Coast Guard rescued all 18 men with helicopters in horrendous winds and no one died. The captain of Jerrick's boat called it quits and they limped into Siracusa, Sicily. Exhausted the men, waited out the storm for the next three days in that safe harbor. Jerrick had no desire to repeat that voyage although the three days in Siracusa were very enjoyable. He learned to watch the weather carefully and never left safe harbor without a good weather window. He would sometimes remember that race and remembering always caused him to smile. They had sailed back to Malta from Marzememi at night, the wind perfect and the sea flat. The captain loved 70's disco and Motown. The sailboat's sound system blared Donna Summers and BeeGees all night long while they drank Jack Daniels and sang along.

It was always interesting if he was at a party and someone who knew him would say, "Jerrick, tell about when you were shipwrecked on Sicily." He would tell the story and as he did, watching their faces, knew sometimes they thought he was making it up. "Honest to God, it's true," his friends would say. "You can't make that up. It happened and he's actually leaving some of it out. Go Google *Loki* and read about it." Sometimes he would think about all the things his friends didn't know about him. All the things that had happened to him in his life and how it was amazing he had survived them. But he'd generally stop with the Sicily story because they might have thought he was fabricating had he told more.

After his first wife, he'd spent most of his energy on building the business. He had dated occasionally, mostly when well-meaning friends fixed him up with a blind date. Maybe it was because his first wife had been so self-centered and materialistic that he saw those tendencies in other women. Or maybe it was because so many women were self-centered and materialistic. He reasoned that culture dictates behavior, and the culture of his time told women to be strong which often came across as harsh and selfish. He had no problem with women working or achieving success outside the home but noticed that so many of them somewhere along the way had forgotten how to be women and tried hard to be very much like men. He thought they could be both successful and feminine. He believed that the pressures and strains of life were hurting women, making so many of them unhappy.

Sailing into a new marina and tying up the big trawler at the dock in front of the bar almost always got him attention from local women who would hang out at the marina bar. But they didn't interest him. He was put off by their forward and aggressive manner.

When he was home he didn't go out much, his world shrinking a lot since he'd sold the business. He lived in the woods and spent most of his time alone working around the house, cutting and splitting firewood. If asked what his perfect morning was, he would have answered, "There are two of them. The first is to wake up on my boat at anchor in a wilderness anchorage, no people, no houses, no boats, just the forest and the water. Then sit on the aft deck, drink coffee and watch the sun come up. Once when I came up on deck in an anchorage like that, the boat was in a cloud of white butterflies. It was magical. The other is to wake up at home in winter and to open the curtains and see snow. Then sit by the fire, drink coffee and watch it snow." Jerrick liked simplicity and peace. He wondered at times if there were any women who liked simplicity and peace. If anyone like that existed.

CHAPTER SEVEN

The Market

Senta had taken over paying the farm bills when her father had died. She stayed very busy working on Stoll Woodworking's bookkeeping, making cheese on Tuesdays, and selling cheese on Saturdays. But she felt her most important purpose was taking care of her mother. Her mother continued to gradually do less and less, both around the house and outside the home. She never went grocery shopping anymore when Senta went with the Lapps on Thursdays. Mrs. Miller made it to church less than half the time. Mrs. Miller did help in the kitchen and still did quite a bit of the cooking. More and more she lived her life vicariously through Senta. Mrs. Miller enjoyed Mondays when Sally brought the Stoll paperwork for Senta and then brought Senta up to speed on what was going on in the office in Ashland City. She also looked forward to hearing about the Farmers' Market when Senta returned.

One Saturday evening after talking to her mother about the market, Senta said, "Mother, John Lapp thinks we may be needing a new roof in the next year or so. Do you remember how old our roof is?"

"It must be over twenty years old now, if I remember correctly," answered Mrs. Miller. "You were still in school."

"We're doing well on money, Mother," said Senta. "We've never had to spend any of the money from the cows. I'm making enough to pay our bills. And now with our cheese business, I'm saving that money. So, it shouldn't be a problem to get a new roof. I'll ask John who he recommends and see about doing that next year."

"Senta," her mother said. "You're in charge now. This is your house. You make all the money and you're taking care of all the business. I trust your judgement."

Tearing up, Senta hugged her mother. "I love you, Mother. You and Father were the best parents anyone could want. I'm glad I can help."

"I just worry about you, child," said Mrs. Miller. "Someday when I'm gone, you will be alone."

"God has taken care of us all along, and He won't stop now," said Senta. "Remember how I got the job with Mr. Campbell? Now I'm selling cheese in Nashville!" Her mother smiled and nodded her head. Considering her daughter's words, Mrs. Miller decided she needed to have more faith.

The next day, Sunday, Mrs. Miller didn't feel up to going to services, so Senta walked down to the road and stood by the mailbox where John and Abigail picked her up. Abigail's pregnancy was now starting to show although most wouldn't have noticed. The Amish women made their own dresses from patterns of old dresses, generally making them several sizes too large. The excess fabric would hide a pregnancy for quite some time. Senta decided she needed to make herself a new dress or two. Senta didn't know what size her dresses were. She decided that she was going to cut the pattern down a bit for two new ones. She didn't want to cut it down too much or people might notice and talk if she made her new dresses too tight. Particularly for the market, she wanted dresses that fit a little better. She enjoyed watching all the people and how they dressed though what she saw made her more self-conscious.

One Saturday at the market, a particularly beautiful and well-dressed woman came through and stopped at their table. She bought cheese and bread. As she walked away and was out of ear shot, Senta said to the other three ladies, "Wasn't she beautiful!

Did you see her shoes? They were Christian Louboutin."

"What are you talking about, Senta?" scolded Mrs. King. "Do you expect me to believe that you can tell what brand of shoes that woman was wearing just by looking? Next, you'll tell me you know how much they cost."

"I can tell, Mrs. King, because they had red soles; those shoes cost about $600," replied Senta with a trace of defiance in her tone. Abigail looked at her with raised eyebrows as if to say, *Senta be careful, you're going to get yourself in trouble.*

"Well, Miss Miller, I'm starting to wonder as to your sanity," laughed Mrs. King. "There are no shoes on earth that cost that much!"

Giving Senta a look again that said, *don't say another word*, Abigail intervened, "She's just joking, Mrs. King. She does that all the time. You should hear the stories she comes up with when we're making cheese!"

Later, when Senta and Abigail had sold out of cheese and had walked to the food court to have lunch as they always did at the Farmers' Market, Abigail said, "Senta, I know you're probably right, but you can't say that, you know, the comments about the lady's shoes. They're going to start questioning how you know things like that. You must protect your job with Mr. Campbell. Bishop Yost doesn't like you working outside the home. If he gets word that you're becoming prideful, he may make you quit your job. Then you and your mother would be in such trouble."

"But I am right, Abigail, and I'm not prideful. I just like to observe. I like to hear the different accents our customers have when they have lived in other places. Did you see the young man earlier today with the US Army cap that read *Afghanistan*? Did you see how he limped? He was probably wounded there. I see people from all these different places, every one of them special and unique and I wonder what their lives are like. Some are happy, but some seem really down. I wonder why they're unhappy, and I feel sad for them," Senta said. "I know you're right, and I'll try, but I don't like being accused of something that's not true. And Eric Yost will never make me quit my job. He may try, but he can't. I like my job, and it's my life not his."

"I know," said Abigail, reaching across the table and

squeezing her hand. "You have a point, Senta. You're very brave." Looking at her, Abigail studied her friend's face. "You're very different, my friend. You see things others don't see. You think about things others don't even consider. You hear music everywhere. Something tells me your life is just starting. I don't know why, but I think there's going to be more for you than the farm, Mr. Campbell, and cheese."

"Oh, I hope you're right," said Senta. "Have I told you about Spotify? It's a way to have any kind of music you like on a phone. Mike, who sells ceramics down the aisle in our Shed, showed me how to put it on my phone. I have the free version so I must listen to commercials sometimes, but when I hear a song I like, I ask the name, then I find it in Spotify and I have it forever. I can listen to it over and over. Don't tell Bishop Yost, or he'll have me shunned!" laughed Senta.

"You are such a rebel, Senta!" said Abigail laughing. "What am I going to do with you? Just do my best to keep you quiet around Mrs. King and Mrs. Belier. I need to buy some duct tape!"

"You are such a good friend, Abigail!" said Senta. "Thank you. I will try to do better. I just get very excited when I discover something new. Speaking of which, when we finish lunch I want to show you something out back where the trucks are, where the produce is unloaded. Everyone there speaks Spanish. I think they're from Mexico. They have their own music. And, Abigail, they dance. There's a young couple and they dance something called bachata. It's beautiful. I don't understand what the words mean, but it's beautiful and romantic. I'm sure it's about love."

"Senta, you've been wandering around out back?" asked Abigail. "I can't leave you alone for a minute. You don't know these people. They may be dangerous."

"They're not dangerous," said Senta. "I've made a new friend. Her name is Luisa Fernanda. Let's go see if she's there today. If her boyfriend is around, maybe they will dance some bachata for you."

"Senta, the English are not like us," warned Abigail.

"Abigail, they're Spanish not English!" said Senta, laughing. Then they both laughed and walked out of the food court to go in search of Luisa Fernanda. Senta almost had to drag Abigail to get her to leave the actual Farmers' Market and go behind it to where the produce trucks were parked. "Luisa Fernanda!" called Senta when she saw her friend along with several others sitting in the shade eating lunch.

"Qué tal, Senta?" said Luisa Fernanda, getting up from the milk case she was sitting on to greet her friend.

"Luisa Fernanda, this is my friend Abigail, the friend I make cheese with," said Senta. "I've brought you a gift," said Senta, retrieving a block of cheese from the pocket in her white apron. "Carlos!" Senta exclaimed as a man walked up to them. Abigail stood quietly, wondering what her friend had gotten her into and wondering if she should tell John and if he would be angry.

"Qué tal, Senta?" said Carlos, greeting Senta and then looking at Abigail.

"Bien gracias!" said Senta, laughing. "You see, Abigail, I'm bilingual, or with the Pennsylvania Dutch and English, tri-lingual!" They all laughed except for Abigail who was still being very serious. "I'm kidding, Abigail. Luisa Fernanda has taught me maybe three or four words of Spanish, so I'm trying to be funny. It's a joke." Abigail smiled, then laughed a little and relaxed a bit.

"Here's some of our cheese. I hope you like it," said Senta, handing the block of cheese to her friend. "But it comes with a condition. Could you and Carlos show my friend Abigail bachata? I've tried to explain it to her, but I can't." Carlos looked at Luisa Fernanda with a look of *why not*.

"You know, '*Déjà vu*,' the one by Shakira and Prince Royce. You put it on my Spotify, and I really like it," said Senta. Abigail gave Senta a puzzled look having never heard of Shakira, Prince Royce, or Spotify. Luisa Fernanda picked up her iPhone, which was synced to the mini sound system sitting by the truck, and searched through her playlist for the song.

"Abigail, you're not going to believe how beautiful this is!" exclaimed Senta. "It just flows. It's so graceful." Carlos walked over to Luisa Fernanda, extending his left hand and taking her right, then led her onto the concrete where the trucks unloaded. The music started with guitars, slow, while the two dancers came together, then shifted gears into the bachata rhythm. The two moved together in perfect unison, spinning and turning effortlessly as Senta had tried to explain. "Abigail, see how they flow," Senta said. Abigail nodded as she listened to the music with words she didn't understand. She agreed they did indeed flow as sometimes the turns and spins were so rapid that she wondered, *How do they do that?*

"I think it's because they're in love. I think that's why they can dance like that," said Senta as she and Abigail walked back to their space in Shed B after saying their goodbyes to their friends when the song ended. Senta and Abigail didn't say a word to the other two ladies about where they'd been upon returning to their tables in Shed B. Then the two younger women sold bread while the two older women took their turn for lunch. Abigail watched her friend as they worked and saw in her eyes that she was still hearing the music and was thinking about dancing.

CHAPTER EIGHT

Dutchman

June 2nd, was just another Saturday, but it would become the best day of Senta's life, replacing that day so long ago when she had won the cobbler contest. Senta went out to the cheese cellar to load the cheese into the baskets. She wanted them to be ready for when the van arrived with Mrs. Belier and Mrs. King to go to Nashville. There was a slight fog hanging on the pasture, white against the grass and the forest behind. Senta walked back from the cellar with the two big baskets full of cheese. Her thoughts turned to her father and when there had been dairy cows grazing in the pasture. The green of everything was the fresh green of spring and early summer. The red and white impatiens in the pots by the kitchen door were bright against the terra cotta of the pots; everything was quiet and peaceful as Senta brought the cheese in the house and started breakfast.

Once again, Senta's mother cautioned her at breakfast about the English and about the dangers of the Farmers' Market. She listened respectfully, and nodded in understanding of her mother's words, and promised to be careful. She heard this every Saturday morning and smiled as she drank her coffee, grateful to have been blessed with such a caring mother. After washing the breakfast dishes, Senta went upstairs, showered, and put on one of her new re-sized dresses and after brushing her hair, one of her new caps. She had also modified the new cap just a little. The old ones were so big that barely any of her hair was visible. The new one exposed more of her hair. She wasn't sure why she was doing this, but it felt right. She looked at herself in the mirror and smiled.

Senta told her mother goodbye and took the baskets out the front door. As she waited on the van, her mind turned to the cheese business. She thought about how the cheese sold out every time they went to market. She thought about Abigail and her progressing pregnancy and wondered if they would be able to continue when she had the baby. Senta thought about why she wanted to continue by herself if Abigail couldn't, and decided it was because she enjoyed the Farmers' Market. More than the extra money they made, she liked traveling to Nashville and experiencing the people and the excitement of the market. Soon the black van pulled into the drive, and Senta loaded her cheese baskets in the back and climbed in the side door.

Senta was greeted by Mrs. King and Mrs. Belier, "Good morning, Senta. How are you this morning?"

"I'm fine, thank you," responded Senta. "I think we have a beautiful day for the Farmers' Market. I'm sure we will have lots of customers."

"I think so. Spring always brings people out," agreed Mrs. King. "You look different today, Senta. Have you lost weight?"

"I don't think so," said Senta. "I think I'm the same. We don't have scales, so I don't know how much I weigh. Maybe I should buy scales with some of my cheese money. On second thought, that's not a good idea. Then I'd know how much I weighed and if I gained a pound, I'd start worrying about it."

Everyone laughed. Mrs. King said, "Well, I don't think you need to worry about that, Senta. You could afford to gain some weight. I think you could gain a few pounds and look just fine. I don't think you eat enough."

They picked up Abigail, who was starting to show. "What a beautiful morning!" she said as she climbed in the van a little slower than she normally would. "Are we all ready to sell lots of bread and cheese today!"

"You are always so happy and positive," said Mrs. Belier. "There will come a time when you will not be able to continue this."

"Oh, I don't know. The pioneer women worked the fields and stopped long enough to give birth and then went right back to work," commented Abigail. "My life is pretty easy compared to that. Selling cheese at the Farmers' Market isn't that hard. It's possible I may miss a few weeks, but I'm not planning on giving up our cheese making. How about you, Senta?" Senta returned a smile. It was a smile of agreement and harmony expressed in the secret language she'd shared with her father when he was alive.

Through the countryside, through the traffic, and then up Rosa Parks Boulevard to the Farmers' Market, the van was soon parked by Shed B. The sun was up high and the temperature was starting to rise. Senta made Abigail rest and not work too hard by insisting she sit while Senta unloaded, set up tables and arranged the cheeses. Due to the heat and her dress, Senta started to get overly warm as she worked. She watched some of the ladies at an adjacent space wearing shorts and tank tops and thought it had to be more comfortable to dress in less clothes when it was hot. But it occurred to Senta that she would feel almost naked wearing so little clothing. Finishing setting up, she sat down with Abigail and shared a drink of water while they waited for the market to open. As she waited contentedly with her friend, Senta had no idea that her world was about to change. It had never entered her mind that life had been preparing her to bring her to that place and to that moment in time.

The morning went quickly with the sunny Saturday bringing out lots of customers. At times, there were so many people in the aisle between the rows of vendors that it was hard for people to get through, but then the crowd would thin out. Senta kept a close eye on Abigail, making her sit down and take a drink of water during the quieter moments.

All the cheese from the first basket had been sold and half from the second basket when Abigail saw a new group of customers walking up. There were six of them, three men and three women, apparently couples out for the day. They approached the Amish tables, smiled at the four ladies, and started asking about the cheese and bread. Senta explained a bit about the cheese making process. Taking pieces from the free samples dish, they all agreed it was delicious. Three pounds were quickly purchased, with Abigail getting each of the ladies their cheese and Senta taking the money and making change. Then the group moved on a few feet and started talking to Mrs. King and Mrs. Belier about their bread.

Senta was making change for the last man when she glanced up and saw another man, a fourth man, walking up the concrete aisle. He was scanning the crowd, looking for someone, and when his eyes found the man in front of Senta, he smiled. She stopped as she gave her customer his change and watched the man. Mesmerized, Senta couldn't take her eyes off this man. He was tall, strong, and tanned. His dark brown hair was windblown like he'd just stepped onto land after a long voyage. Effortlessly, and in long strides, he seemed to flow instead of walk. She noticed how graceful, yet determined, his movements were. He wore old khaki cargo shorts and a worn polo shirt with faded embroidered writing on the chest. Flip flops were on his feet, a watch on his left wrist. As he came closer, Senta felt a shiver move across her body when she realized he was walking straight toward her.

"Hey, what's happenin', Captain!" hailed their customer, smiling at the taller man as he came to a stop directly in front of the cheese table.

Smiling and looking around for the others and spotting them one table down buying bread, he said, "Lost y'all for a minute. So, what have you found here, Joe?"

"Amish cheese, buddy. Here try a sample. It's great. These two ladies here make it themselves. Milk the cows and everything. You've got to buy some," said Joe, but he'd lost his friend at "Amish cheese, buddy". The friend had taken a sample of cheese and turned to look at Senta, his dark blue eyes met hers; she froze, unable to move and unable to talk.

He put the little square of cheese in his mouth, savoring the flavor, then looked at Senta and said, "It's very good. So, you actually make this from scratch?"

While all the activity of the Farmers' Market carried on-while hundreds of people were buying things-while thousands of words were being spoken, only ten words had been spoken to Senta at that moment. She heard them but was transfixed. Her brain could comprehend, but she was unable to respond. Something was happening inside of Senta that she had never felt before. She couldn't understand it or that it was all beyond her control. With eyes locked on him, she saw, as if with a microscope- every movement, every nuance, and every detail. She was captivated by the way he walked and the confidence in his movements. She saw the scar on his left cheek and how his nose was just a little crooked as if he might have broken it in the past. She noticed the little bit of gray in his hair. She watched his hand, tan and strong, as he reached out for the cheese sample. She saw the tendons and sinews in his arms move as he brought the cheese to his lips. And she watched those lips as he ate her cheese. But she was frozen.

"Senta," prompted Abigail looking at her friend with a puzzled look. When Senta didn't respond, Abigail turned to the man. "Yes, sir. We make the cheese from scratch. My husband and I own the cows. Actually, Senta's family used to own some of the cows, but now she's an accountant for a CPA in Ashland City. Senta and I make the cheese by hand and age it for three months before it's ready to bring to market."

"It's delicious. I'll take a pound, please," he said, watching Senta. He retrieved his billfold from his back left pocket and took out seven dollars as indicated on the sign. Returning his wallet to his back pocket, he handed the money to Senta. But Senta was still not able to move and take the money. The man looked at her a little questioningly and a little amused. Abigail looked at him and then back at Senta. Abigail began to think that she would have to take the money for her friend who for some reason seemed to be paralyzed. But the man leaned forward across the table and took Senta's right hand in his left and placed the folded bills in her hand. Then with his other hand, he took her left hand and placed it over her right hand with the seven dollars inside, her hands between his.

The hundreds of people present at the market noticed

nothing. But to her, it was like magic or an out-of-body experience as he held her hands. She thought he must be at least a foot taller than she because her face would have been even with his chest had the table not been between them. Senta couldn't look at him any longer as she found his presence unnerving. She looked down at her hands and saw them enveloped in his. She had never felt electricity before but felt something like it move up her arms and into her chest and then down lower into her legs. She steadied herself certain she was on the verge of collapse.

"So is your name really Senta?" he asked, still holding her hands.

Abigail was the only witness to all this as everyone else was preoccupied with their own business. Just when it appeared Abigail might have to answer even that question for her friend, Senta finally spoke, "Yes." It was all she could utter.

"I've never known anyone named Senta before," he said. "I recognize the name but never actually knew anyone named Senta. I'll have to come back sometime and buy more cheese. Are you here every Saturday, Senta?"

"Yes, ... every Saturday," managed Senta. Then slowly regaining the ability to talk she added, "We may miss a few times in the future when Abigail has her baby, but we're almost always here."

"That's great," he said releasing her hands and smiling kindly at Senta. "Hold on to that money now. Don't lose it." He picked up his cheese and started to walk away but turned and said, "I'll be back some Saturday, Senta. And I won't wait seven years."

Then he walked away quickly, hurrying to catch up with his friends. Senta backed up a few steps to Abigail's folding chair and sat down, unable to stand any longer. "Senta, are you alright?" asked Abigail putting her hand on her friend's shoulder. Abigail was very concerned about her friend's odd behavior.

"I don't know, Abigail. I haven't a clue as to what just happened to me. It was like I was in a dream. I could hear him talking and I could hear you, but I couldn't speak," Senta said and put her face in her hands. "Oh my, Abigail, what did I do?

He must think there's something wrong with me."

"What's going on?" asked Mrs. King as she walked over to the two younger women. Abigail was kneeling by Senta, rubbing her back while Senta sat with her face in her hands.

"It's OK, Mrs. King," said Abigail. "It's just the heat. Senta felt a little faint. She'll be alright. We're almost sold out of cheese, so I'll take her to the food court and get her a cold drink in just a minute." Abigail got up and helped another group of customers who had just arrived and were sampling the cheese. They bought everything that remained. Abigail returned to Senta and said, "We've sold out of cheese. Let's walk to the food court building and get you something to eat and drink."

The two women chose Chinese food. Abigail got water to drink but got Senta a lemonade thinking maybe some sugar would help her. Sitting down, they both prayed silently before beginning to eat. Still being affected by the encounter with the man, Senta barely touched her food. "I think it was because he was so handsome. Didn't you think he was handsome, Abigail?" asked Senta.

"Well, yes, he was a nice-looking man, but I think you were more taken with him than I was," answered Abigail. "You two were just standing there looking at each other. I don't know if I've ever seen anything like it. You were spellbound by him." Abigail and Senta ate for a while in silence. "You did notice he's not Amish, Senta. And he is probably married." Senta didn't respond but only looked down at her uneaten food. Then Abigail continued, "You don't even know his name."

"I don't," Senta said. "But I do know he's a captain because his friend Joe called him *captain*. I don't think he's married because he was by himself, and his friends all had their wives with them. And he wasn't wearing a wedding ring. I know you're going to say that lots of men don't wear wedding rings. We Amish don't wear wedding rings, but look at you," said Senta looking at her friend's protruding stomach, "You're obviously married, and you're not wearing a ring. So, you can't tell for sure."

Abigail laughed and said, "That's true, but you shouldn't be thinking about him like that."

"He liked my name, Abigail," said Senta. "He liked my

name, and he said he would come back and buy more cheese. So maybe I will see him again. They're not from here. I think they're from the United States but not from Nashville. They were traveling, and they were traveling by boat."

"Senta, for heaven's sake, traveling by boat! Do you see any water here? I'm starting to worry about you, my friend," said Abigail looking at Senta with heartfelt concern.

"Abigail, all of them were wearing boat shoes. All people with boats wear them to not put marks on the deck like regular shoes would. The one lady wore a necklace with an anchor pendant, and another one wore a bracelet with signal flags. They were on a boat or maybe several boats. I'm sure of it. And Abigail, just a short distance from here is the Cumberland River. That's a big river; it runs right by Ashland City. One can go anywhere in the world from here on that river," said Senta.

"Senta, I swear you should have been a detective!" chuckled Abigail. "And what are signal flags? And traveling by boat, how would a person eat and sleep? And what do you know about boats anyway, Senta?"

"I don't know that much really," confessed Senta. "But there is a program on my computer called *Google*. I use it in my work. Abigail, you can ask it about anything, and it will tell you. His polo shirt said MiddleSea Race 2001 and RMYC. I don't know what that is, but I am going to find out. His watch, Abigail, it was a marine watch, I'm pretty sure. I will google it and find out. But I'm almost certain they were on a boat."

"I thought you had slipped into a coma, and you saw *all* that?" her friend said, laughing and shaking her head. "But really, you mustn't get so worked up about him. You should just let this go."

"Abigail, I don't know what happened," said Senta. "All I know is that I am 36 years old, and I have never felt like that before. In a way, he scared me, but I wasn't afraid of him. He was kind. When he put the money in my hand and put his hands around mine ...... I can't explain it. It was kind. But he unnerves me. When he looked at me, it was as if he could see right through me and read my thoughts! He seemed dangerous at first in the way he was always looking around and scanning everything, but he was gentle. I didn't want him to let go of my hands." Abigail didn't know what to say. Senta sat in silence with her friend and then said, "I'm afraid I'll never see him again. I don't know who he is or where he lives. I want to get up and run through the Farmers' Market and find him before he leaves, but I know I can't do that."

The two women walked back to their stall, stopping along the way for Abigail to go to the restroom, something she found herself doing with more frequency as her pregnancy progressed. Senta waited outside, watching the people walk by hoping he might just happen to come that way. Abigail came out of the restroom, and the two walked back towards their stall. "What did he mean when he said he'd come back, but he wouldn't wait for seven years?" asked Abigail looking to her friend. Senta shrugged her shoulders, raised her eyebrows, and shook her head. But she wouldn't forget he had said it, and Senta would try to figure out what it meant.

Abigail and Senta didn't talk any more that day, about what had happened. Senta wanted to talk to her friend about it but didn't dare because Mrs. King and Mrs. Belier would question it. She had to find out what Abigail had seen and what Abigail's impressions were. Her mind replayed the encounter over and over on the drive from Nashville later that afternoon. Remembering every word, remembering every nuance of him, and placing her right hand over her left hand she recalled the feeling of the moment when he had put the money in her hand. She had not put the seven dollars, a five and two ones, in with the rest of the money. She'd told Abigail that she was going to keep those bills and that they would reduce her part. As the van drove through the Tennessee countryside, she sat holding her hands, eyes closed, thinking she didn't want to wash her hands because she didn't want to lose a single molecule of him that might still be on her skin. The encounter had absolutely enraptured her.

When she got home, Senta found her mother in the kitchen, and kissed her, and gave her a long hug. "Did you sell out again today, dear?" asked her mother. "How was everything in Nashville? Tell me all about it."

Senta wanted so badly to tell her mother about the

interesting man she had met and how he had made her feel, but she knew she couldn't. She knew her mother would be angry and would likely be afraid that he was dangerous. She also knew that her mother might even pressure her to give up the Farmers' Market. After today, she knew she would never give up going to the Market.

"It went well, Mother," she said. "We sold out by noon. Abigail and I had lunch in the food court. It's air-conditioned there and that felt so good since it was hot today. We saw lots of interesting people. There was one curious group who bought cheese. They were traveling in boats on the river. Isn't that interesting, Mother? Wouldn't that be fun, to travel somewhere far away on a boat?" Her mother smiled at her and shook her head thinking her daughter had quite an imagination. But that was as close as Senta came to talking about him with her mother.

Senta went upstairs right after dinner. She gave the excuse that she was tired from the day at the Farmers' Market. But she didn't go to her bedroom immediately, but rather to the office bedroom where she quietly closed the door, sat down at the desk, and turned on the computer. Remembering the words embroidered on his polo shirt, she typed in MiddleSea Race RMYC in Google and pressed enter. She immediately saw Royal Malta Yacht Club and then recognized the red and white triangular flag with the crown she'd also seen on his polo shirt. Then she read about the Rolex MiddleSea Race being an ocean race of 607 miles in the Mediterranean Sea that went from the island nation of Malta up and around Sicily and back to Malta. Selecting *images*, she saw pictures of sailboats, Mount Etna, and a volcano named Stromboli. Remembering the tiny letters on the face of his watch, she typed in Rolex watch and touched *enter*. Going to *images*, she scrolled through the pictures until she found the watch, *Yachtmaster*.

Sitting back in her chair, she thought, *captain, a sailboat race, and boat watch. I know I'm right; he came on a boat.* She turned off the computer and went to her room. She got ready for bed, turned off the lights, and got under the covers. For the first time in her life, she knew who she was hugging when she held her pillow. She drifted off to sleep as she imagined his strong, tanned arms around her as her head rested on his chest.

The next day, Sunday, was church, which was at the Belier's house. Senta's mother got up and decided she would go also. The mother and daughter walked down to the mailbox where John and Abigail came by a short time later to pick them up in the buggy. "Good morning, ladies," said Abigail as they climbed in the buggy. Abigail looked at her friend as she got inside and their eyes met. Senta knew Abigail was trying to determine if she had regained control of her emotions from the previous day. Lips together, Senta smiled as if to say, *Yes, Abigail I'm alright*, and *No, Abigail I'm falling apart*. Of course, on the ride to church, on the ride back, and during the service Senta could focus on nothing but what had transpired the day before.

Back at home after church, Senta sat at the kitchen table with her mother and quietly ate lunch. "Senta, are you OK?" asked her mother. "You seem distracted. You're not talking much, and it's like you're somewhere else."

Senta hadn't realized she was that obvious. She hadn't expected anyone to notice, but yes, her mother was right. While she was sitting with her mother, her mind was miles away in Nashville replaying the day before. "I'm just tired I guess, Mother. After I clean up the kitchen, maybe I'll take a nap," she said, standing up and carrying her dishes to the sink. Her mother got up and started helping her but looked at her questioningly. It wasn't that she didn't believe her daughter, but she still felt something wasn't right.

Senta washed the dishes and her mother dried. After everything was put away in the cupboards, Senta went upstairs but didn't go to her bedroom. Once again she went to the office bedroom and sat down at the computer. Returning to Google, she typed in boats but got millions of pictures of every kind of boat imaginable. Senta didn't know what she was looking for and knew she didn't. She clicked on several articles and read some of them. One article was about a couple who were cruising to the Bahamas from Florida. Looking at the pictures of their boat made her wonder if the captain's boat was like that one. She started seeing the word *yacht* frequently and figured out that a yacht was a larger pleasure boat. The word *cruising* was used a lot and she understood that to travel by water was to cruise. Senta found an article on fuel polishing from a magazine called *Passagemaker* but didn't read it because it was too technical. Finally, after reading and looking at photos for over an hour she stood up, stretched, and walked to the window. Gazing out over the pasture beyond the barn, she turned to view the road and saw the heat waves rippling off the pavement as the afternoon sun heated up the asphalt.

Senta started to turn off the computer, but just before she did, one more search came to mind, *Senta Seven Years*. A second later there it was – 273,000 results. And her name was everywhere! An opera by Richard Wagner, *Senta's fidelity and love*, the *Captain can only return to land every seven years, Der Fleigende Höllander*, a *portrait of the Captain*. Senta clicked on the first link, Wikipedia, after scanning the first page of hyperlinks all containing her name and references to a sea captain. As the Wikipedia story came up, Senta sat down and read with her hands over her mouth, leaning forward, hardly believing what she was seeing. In the story of the *Flying Dutchman*, the two main characters were a ship's captain and Senta. She sat there almost shaking. *What is this? Who am I? He knows. He knows my name and he said seven years. Who is he?* She clicked the print icon and the printer immediately started zipping out the words and sentences of the story about the opera.

Grabbing the pages, Senta ran downstairs looking for her mother and found her sitting on the front porch. "Mother, my name, *Senta*. Why am I named *Senta*?" she quickly asked sitting down on the swing next to her mother.

"Is something wrong, Senta?" asked her mother. "What is this all about? Why do you suddenly want to know about your name?"

"It's an unusual name, Mother," she said, trying to calm herself. "I've just never known anyone else with that name."

"Well, it was your father's idea," she said. "I'm not really sure where he found it. We talked about lots of different names, both for boys and girls when I was pregnant. We didn't know if you were a boy or a girl until you were born. When your father suggested Senta, I liked it. We agreed Senta Miller sounded nice."

"Did Father like opera?" asked Senta. "Did he ever mention anything about opera or Richard Wagner?"

"Not that I recall," said her mother. "But his father, your grandfather, liked opera. I believe. I only knew him a short time after we were first married, before he died. But it seems like I remember that. Why are you asking all these questions, Senta?"

"It's nothing, Mother. I just didn't know about my name. I've got to run down to Abigail's to ask her about cheese making on Tuesday. I'll be back shortly." Senta clutched the papers and ran across the yard toward the road, leaving her mother sitting on the porch watching her daughter run down the road in the heat of a late Sunday afternoon in June, wondering why she was acting so strangely.

Fortunately, the Lapp farm was only a short distance down the road. Senta ran up to the kitchen door of the Lapp farmhouse, her hair having fallen from under her cap. She banged on the door and called out, "Abigail!"

Abigail was in the kitchen kneading dough. "Come in, Senta. Is everything alright?"

Breathlessly, Senta opened the screen door and rushed into the kitchen. "Yes, everyone is alright. Where is John? Is he in the house?"

"He's out in the barn getting ready to milk," said Abigail. She grasped Senta by the shoulders and steered her to the kitchen table and sat her down. "Senta, calm down. What is going on?"

"Abigail, you're not going to believe this. I don't even believe this. Remember when we talked about using Google? That's how I know all these things that I wouldn't know otherwise. Well, I am right. My captain is a captain. His shirt is from a sailboat race in Malta, in the Mediterranean, you know where Paul and Luke were shipwrecked in Acts in the Bible. His watch is a marine watch, the kind of watch people with boats tend to use. But, Abigail, my name and the seven years. I looked it up on Google. There's an opera written by a composer named Richard Wagner, and it's about a sea captain who is cursed, who can only come to land once every seven years. He can only break the curse by finding the love of a woman. He finds that woman, and her name is Senta." Senta handed the pages of the explanation to her friend. "I printed it because I had to show you. I know you would want to believe me, but it's too much, and it's even hard for me to believe."

Seated at the table with her friend, Abigail held the printout in her flour-covered fingers while studying the content. Everywhere she looked she saw her friend's name. *Senta*. "This is something, Senta. Does the captain have a name?"

"I don't think so," said Senta. "I didn't see any name, just the Captain."

"This explains why he was so interested in your name," said Abigail. "And why he said he wouldn't wait seven years to come back."

"He has to come back," said Senta tears welling up in her eyes. "I know you probably think I'm crazy. Even I think I'm crazy. But I've never felt like this before. He must come back. If he doesn't come back, I think I may die."

Abigail put her arms around her dear friend. Senta cried on her shoulder until Abigail's dress was wet with her tears. After she was cried out and there were no more tears, Abigail walked her out to the road. "Are you OK to walk back? I can have John take you back in the buggy." Senta shook her head no and wiped her eyes again. "Alright then, you go home and get some rest. I'll see you Tuesday when we make some more cheese. I don't understand all this, Senta, but it will be alright. Everything will work out." Senta walked down the gravel shoulder along the county road. Not one car passed as she walked the quarter mile to her house. She needed to hide her red eyes when she got home so her mother didn't see that she had been crying. She needed to act normal but nothing about her life was normal anymore. She was in such uncharted territory that she had no idea how to behave.

When John came in the kitchen door from milking that evening, Abigail had dinner ready for him. After John had given thanks for the meal, Abigail spoke. "John, I'm going to tell you something that you need to know. I don't completely understand it, and I can't image where this is all headed, but I want you to know it. You must not tell anyone. I'm sure you won't, but this must remain with us. It's about Senta." She explained what had happened the day before at the Farmers' Market. She showed him the Wikipedia printout about the opera and told him about the Captain and the seven years. John listened closely and nodded in agreement.

Senta went to bed as soon as she got home. She prayed to God to help her. She pleaded that she didn't understand what to ask for exactly because she was so confused. She asked God's protection on the captain and begged God, if it was His will, to bring him back to her. Lying in the darkness and holding her pillow, she thought, *he said he would come back*. Then remembering him, his face, his hands, and the sound of his voice, she imagined he must be on his boat now, maybe hundreds of miles away, at anchor somewhere, in his bed asleep. And she wished she was with him as she drifted off to sleep.

Monday started a new work week, and Sally came by early with Suzanne. "Good morning, Senta," she said. "I've got Suzanne with me today. I'm going on vacation the next two weeks, so she's going to be taking over some of my duties, including coming to see you on Monday mornings." The three women greeted one another as they carried in the boxes of paperwork. Senta had the previous week's work all neatly packed in one box ready to transport back to Ashland City.

"This week Senta will reconcile the Stoll's bank account," said Sally to Suzanne. "So you'll pick up the ledgers for Mr. Stoll to check over, and then return them to Senta the following week. Now that the business part is done, let's go to the kitchen and have a cup of coffee!"

"Come in, ladies," welcomed Mrs. Miller. The four women, Sally, Suzanne, Senta and her mother, sat at the table, sipped some coffee and caught up on the news from the office in Ashland City.

"How about you, Senta? Anything exciting happening with you? Is everything good with Abigail and the cheese business?

How is she doing? Is it much longer until the baby comes?" asked Sally. Senta so badly wanted to tell Sally and Suzanne about the man she had met Saturday, but she couldn't because of her mother's presence. She simply smiled and said that everything was fine. Sally and Suzanne looked at Senta questioningly, sensing Senta was holding something back. The women chatted away, an interesting mixture of two worlds coming together because of coffee and sharing life.

"Our cheese business is doing well. We sold out again Saturday," said Senta. "Abigail is coming along well with her pregnancy." Soon it was time for Sally and Suzanne to return to Ashland City and the office.

Senta walked them to the door and out to Sally's car. Looking back over her shoulder to make sure her mother hadn't followed them, she said, "Sally, Suzanne, I have something I must tell you. I couldn't say anything because of my mother." The two women looked at her with a look of alarm. "Saturday at the Farmers' Market in Nashville I met a man. We talked, well he talked mostly. He bought some cheese. I've never in my life met anyone like him. He said he would come back to buy more cheese." Sally and Suzanne looked at Senta not quite understanding what the big deal was.

"Senta, that's interesting. What's his name?" asked Sally. Seeing Senta's excitement about this man, she asked a basic question.

"I don't know his name. I know that's strange. He was on a boat." Senta said.

Puzzled, Suzanne asked, "He came to the Farmers' Market on a boat, and you don't know his name?"

"I know, I know it doesn't make sense. He must have left the boat on the Cumberland River and have come with his friends to the market, probably in a taxi."

"Senta? Is he Amish?" asked Sally carefully.

"No, he's not," answered Senta. "That's why I can't tell anyone. Except Abigail knows because she was with me. And I can tell you because you're not Amish either. I just have to tell someone. I know I'm not explaining it very well. You see, when I met him I couldn't speak. I've never met a man that made me feel like that before. You have to keep this between us."

"He must have really been something," said Sally. "He obviously had quite an effect on you. I must ask one more question, and maybe you don't know this either. Is he married? Do you know?"

"I don't believe so because he wasn't wearing a ring, but I'm not certain," said Senta pursing her lips and shrugging her shoulders. "You probably think I've gone crazy, but I've never felt this way before. I told you when I met him, I was tongue-tied!" She didn't tell them about the *captain* part or the significance of her name. She didn't want them to think she had lost her mind. That story would have to wait for another time.

"You know, Senta, he could have travelled by boat," said Suzanne. "There's a restaurant we like by the bridge to Ashland City. It's the Riverview. They serve great catfish. There's a big dock, and I've seen large boats come in there. Boaters will tie up and go to the restaurant for lunch. Sometimes they stay docked there all night. These are big boats with radar, electronics, and big diesel engines. People don't realize there are boats like that here, but there are. My husband's boss has a big boat at Cedar Creek up on Old Hickory Lake. He takes it down the rivers to Mobile Bay and then on to Florida every fall, returning in the spring. The man you met may do that as well."

The two friends hugged Senta, and she promised to tell them when he returned. She watched Sally's car turn out of her drive onto the county road as it headed back to Ashland City. Having been able to tell someone, to share her excitement and her story, made her feel better. She thought about the captain and imagined by now the anchor was up and the boat was moving. A wave of sorrow came over her when she considered the boat was probably moving further away from her. She waved goodbye to her friends even though they were now almost out of sight. Then she turned around and went upstairs to her office to start the week's work.

Time blurred for Senta. She functioned, but on a kind of autopilot. Her mind was somewhere else. She did her work for Stolz Woodworking. She did her housework with her mother. She made cheese with Abigail on Tuesday. Her mother asked several times if she was alright. Her mother would ask a question and Senta, not paying attention, wouldn't answer. She was in another world thinking about the man from the Farmers' Market, trying to understand her feelings. One Tuesday while making cheese she asked Abigail, "How did you know John was the one? How did you know you loved him?"

"Well, I noticed him long before he noticed me," Abigail replied. "He's a few years older than I am. I think he always thought of me as a child. Our families were friends so I'd known John my whole life. I always liked him. No, it was more than liking. I always wanted him to notice me, to talk to me like I was his equal not like I was a child. He was always nice to me but never took me seriously until one day when I was about sixteen he did. My family was at his house for a picnic. He would have been nineteen. I noticed him watching me. When he realized he'd been caught, he smiled. He sat with me while we ate, and then we spent the whole afternoon together just talking. That's when I knew," Abigail said as she stirred the milk as it heated on the stove. "I must ask John when he knew."

Senta asked her mother the same question and got a response very similar to Abigail's. Her mother's family had known her father's family. Her father was older than her mother, and she noticed him first. And just like with Abigail, he hadn't considered her anything more than a child. Then when her mother grew into a woman, he did notice. *So, it's all about noticing*, thought Senta. *The women seem to notice first. With my parents and Abigail and John, they lived close and they saw each other a lot. It took years for them to grow up. I'm already grown. Did he notice me? There won't be a picnic or a church social for him to attend. Did he notice me? Have I crossed his mind, or is his life so busy that my memory has blurred into all the other memories only to be forgotten?*

There was one other person she wanted to ask this question of and that was Ruth. She was very concerned with Ruth's answer because unlike her parents and the Lapps, Ruth was not happily married. Senta saw her standing alone by the buggies the next Sunday. Not seeing Ruth's husband around, Senta ran to her. "Ruth, I've been wanting to ask you a personal question for a while. It's about you and Jacob." Ruth gave her a sad smile and nodded as if to say, *go ahead.* "How did you know Jacob was the one? When you met him, did you feel something? Did you love him immediately? What was it like?"

"That's a hard question, Senta," she said. "Thinking back, I doubt that I ever loved him. I believed I did, but I think I was in love with the idea of getting married. I also was in love with all the attention I was getting. I had so many men courting me. It made me feel happy because so many men wanted me. I wonder how Jacob would answer that question? I think he probably just wanted me because so many others did, too. It probably had nothing to do with me really."

Then everyone started walking to the house where services were that week. "Thank you, Ruth," said Senta.

"Why are you asking this?" asked Ruth. But Senta was saved from having to make up an answer as another family joined them on their walk to the house and started another conversation. During the service, Senta didn't hear any of the sermon. As she had done ever since meeting him, she was present in body only. Finally, ignoring everything around her, she closed her eyes and prayed. She prayed sincerely and fervently asking God to guide her. She thanked Him for letting her be part of the cheese business that had taken her to the Farmers' Market and ultimately to him. She prayed for his protection wherever he might be. She gave her fears to God, trusting Him to help her. Finally, she promised to stop worrying and obsessing over it all.

That day back at the farm before eating lunch, Senta's mother said, "Senta, I'm very concerned about you. I don't know what's happening, but something is wrong. You're not as happy as you used to be. You look worried all the time. You've also stopped eating, and you're losing weight."

Senta looked at her mother, wanting to tell her what was going on in her life but knew she couldn't. Her Mother would not understand and would not like it at all that she had feelings for a man who wasn't Amish. But already she was feeling better. Her prayer had helped, she felt more relaxed, and she was hungry. "I'm sorry mother. I know I've been different lately. But I'm OK. Really, I am. And I'm going to start eating more. I promise."

For the first time since that Saturday she cleaned her plate and didn't just pick at her food. After the dishes were washed and the kitchen cleaned up, Senta said, "I'm going to take a walk, Mother. I'm going to walk down by the barn and around the pasture down to the creek. Would you like to come?"

"No, Daughter, I'm tired from church. But you go ahead," said Mrs. Miller. Senta went to her bedroom and changed from her church clothes into her old work dress, the old one she had worn so many years ago when they had dairy cows. Still mostly patches of various shades of blue, she looked at herself in the mirror and smiled, thinking about how she loved the old dress because it reminded her of her father. Heading out of her bedroom she picked up her iPhone and went downstairs, stopping to tell her mother that she was leaving.

Walking toward the barn, down the gravel drive from the house, she found the Spotify icon on her phone. She was amazed at all the different kinds of music she heard at the Farmers' Market. Mike, the man who made and sold ceramics at the Farmers' Market, had put Spotify on her phone and showed her how to add songs. When she heard a song she liked, she would listen to the words and search for the title, adding it to her playlist named *Senta*. Luisa Fernanda had helped her save some bachata and salsa songs in Spanish and two Selena songs. Senta had saved some songs she had heard in the food court also. The problem was that she could rarely listen to them. Her mother would not have approved of her listening to any music that wasn't church music. Luisa Fernanda had shown her the place in the bottom of her phone where she could plug in ear phones, but she didn't have earphones and didn't have any opportunity to buy them. So, that Sunday afternoon she walked and listened to her songs. She walked behind the barn, stopping to pet Sugar, and continued down the fence row to the path that led to the creek. When she got there, she sat on a log by the side of the creek and watched the water slowly moving past her, flowing. For a moment, she wondered where it might go and concluded that it probably flowed to the Harpeth River and then to the Cumberland. She thought about the captain and wondered where he was at that moment. Then she started to worry again but stopped herself, resolving not to think about it. Looking at her playlist, she found a song she'd only heard the end of the previous Saturday at the food court at the Farmers' Market. She had liked the way it sounded even though the noise in the food court made it difficult to hear. She wasn't sure she had found the right song. The Three Degrees, "When Will I See You Again" As she touched *play*, the violins started and the smooth voices of the 70's trio sang.

Sitting on the log as the creek flowed by, the music flowed and Senta was overcome with emotion as she listened to the song. She listened to it three more times before she left the spot and walked back home. When she got to the house and turned off the music, she decided to ask Sally or Suzanne if they knew where she could get some earphones for her iPhone. Unsure if the song helped her or hurt her, she wanted to hear it over and over because it made her feel like she had when she first met him that Saturday at the Farmers' Market.

Monday came again and Suzanne delivered the week's work and picked up the ledgers for Mr. Stoll to inspect. They had coffee with Senta's mother and talked about Sally and her family being gone on vacation to Florida. Senta walked Suzanne out to the car and just before getting in Suzanne asked, "Have you heard anything, Senta?"

"No, nothing," Senta replied. "He didn't come to the Farmers' Market last Saturday. But I'm OK. He will return when he can." Suzanne gave her a warm hug and hoped that she was right.

"Senta, watch the weather this afternoon. Last night the weather man said something about possible bad weather today. I should pay more attention, but I can hardly stay up long enough to hear the weather." The two women laughed because they both had trouble staying awake when it got dark. Senta waved goodbye to her friend as Suzanne pulled out of the drive and headed west to Ashland City.

CHAPTER NINE

Storm Warning

Senta went upstairs to her office and started on the invoices. Whenever there was work to do, she always tackled it immediately. She would work hard on Mondays and Tuesdays so she could get ahead and was often finished by Thursday. It just made her feel better to stay ahead of the work. Senta and her mother had leftovers from Sunday for lunch. Mrs. Miller even commented that Sally and Suzanne were very nice women considering they weren't Amish and that she enjoyed having them for coffee on Monday mornings. As Senta washed the dishes, she looked out the kitchen window and noticed how dark the sky was to the west. "That sky looks angry, Mother," she said. "Suzanne said the weather man is predicting bad weather today. We'll need to keep an eye on the sky."

Senta's mother went to her bedroom to work on some sewing. Senta went upstairs again and dove into recording invoices into the accounting program. She was so engrossed in her work that she forgot to check the weather occasionally. What finally got her attention was the room had gotten darker; then it dawned on her that it was much too early for the sun to set. She ran down the stairs and out the front door. Standing in the front yard, she watched the sky. Senta had only been in one tornado, years ago when she was a child. What she recalled was how quiet it was before it hit and how a strange feeling hung in the air. Then looking up, she remembered the strange, almost green color in the sky. As she watched the sky, her cell phone rang. She retrieved it from the pocket in her apron and pushing the green button on the screen said, "Hello."

"Senta, this is Suzanne. There's a tornado. It's very close, almost to Ashland City. We're all going down in the basement now. Get your mother and head to the cellar now! Do you hear me, Senta? Go now!"

"Yes, we're going. Thank you!" said Senta. They hung up, Suzanne going down the stairs into the basement of the Campbell accounting firm building and Senta running back into the house. "Mother, it's a tornado! We've got to get to the cellar now!" she yelled as she ran to her mother's bedroom. "We have to get Sugar in the barn."

"Yes, Daughter, I'm coming," said Mrs. Miller. "I'm slow. You go ahead, and I'll catch up. There's no time to chase the horse."

"No, Mother, we'll go together. We'll make it in time. Thank God that Suzanne called!" Senta cried. The two women made it to the kitchen door, and with Senta's help, Mrs. Miller got down the three steps to ground level. The wind was starting to pick up as branches started to break off high in the trees. Lightning struck close by as they ran across the yard to the cellar door. It had started pouring rain, and the wind and rain stung their eyes as Senta opened the latch on the door. With all the strength she had, Senta managed to open the heavy door. Squeezing in and pulling the string to turn on the light, Senta pulled the door shut. They were enveloped in silence. Taking a deep breath, they looked at each other for a moment, realizing they were soaking wet. "I hope Sugar had enough sense to get in the barn," Senta said.

"Get the candle and matches ready," said Senta's mother, pointing to a candle and box of matches on the shelf next to Mason jars filled with tomatoes. Senta nodded, got the candle down, and set it on the little table in the middle. "Chances are, the power will go out soon." The two sat down to wait out the storm.

"I hope John and Abigail are alright," said Senta. "And the cows." She remembered hearing about how tornadoes would pick up cows, suck them up in the vortex, and throw them miles away. "I think everyone at the office got down to their basement in time. Thank God for Suzanne calling and thank God for this cell phone." The light went out a short time later; Senta struck the match and lit the candle. They waited, listening to the sounds outside. Senta's mother thought it was a good sign that she didn't hear anything that sounded like a railroad locomotive. After about ten minutes Senta asked, "Do you think it's safe to look outside now, Mother?"

"Slowly, carefully .... it might not be over," said her mother. Senta got up from the bench and moved to the door and cautiously moved the iron bolt to the open position. Both knew they might open the door to see their house gone, or possibly with very little damage. Tornadoes were like that, very selective in how they caused destruction. When she opened the cellar door, she was blinded for a second, seeing nothing but white. But the wind had ceased and it was quiet. Stepping outside into the whiteness, she realized that it was hail. "Mother, the house is OK, I think, but everything is covered in hail. Her mother stepped out, looked at the house and then the barn.

"Let's go check on Sugar," said Mrs. Miller. Walking on ice that was about the size of golf balls, the two women went to the barn and found their black mare, scared but unhurt. Stepping out of the barn and looking back at the house Mrs. Miller said, "Well, there's no doubt we'll need a new roof after the pounding this hail has given it." Mother and daughter walked back to the house. Senta, with her arm around her mother, knocking ice off the steps, helped her up the three steps to the kitchen door. "I'll check the windows to make sure none of them are broken," said her mother as she went inside.

Senta stood on the kitchen steps looking at the surreal landscape of ice in June and broken limbs strewn about. It was then that her phone rang. Retrieving it from the pocket of her apron, Senta answered it.

"Senta, this is Suzanne. Are y'all ok? Good, Good! We're fine. Looks like some damage in town here, but we're ok. Senta, listen to me. Can you talk? Are you alone? You're not going to believe this. He called. The man from the Farmers' Market. He called here looking for you. I gave him your phone number, Senta. He's going to call you."

"He called you, looking for me?" Senta asked in shock. "How?"

"He knew you worked for a CPA in Ashland City. So apparently, he started calling CPA's in Ashland City. We're Campbell, the first one on the list alphabetically. We had just come back upstairs when the phone rang. I answered it. It's him, Senta. He told me that he knew it was probably against company policy to give out employee phone numbers but that he saw that a tornado was headed for Ashland City, and he wanted to know that you were alright. I tried to be cool, but Good Lord in Heaven, first a tornado, now your man calls looking for you, and Sally isn't here. She's going to be so mad!"

"He called for me?" said Senta again, not believing what she had heard.

"That's right," said Suzanne, "so I'm going to hang up and get off this line because he's going to call you any minute. Good luck, Senta!"

Senta stood in the yard in shock, thrilled that he had tried to find her but almost afraid to answer the phone. Then deciding that she had to be alone when he called, she ran back in the kitchen. "I'm running down to Abigail and John's to see if they're alright. I'll be right back."

"The windows look alright," said her mother. "Hurry back, and be careful of downed power lines."

Senta headed down her drive, walking around a big branch that she would need to ask John to help her with. When she was almost to the mailbox, her cell phone rang. The phone was in her hand because she had not put it back in her apron pocket. For weeks, she had thought about him, prayed about him, dreamed about him, and wondered who he was. Now he had found her and was on the other end of her cell phone, just a touch away from talking to her. But just like at the Farmers' Market, she found herself frozen, unable to act. *Answer the phone before he hangs up*, Senta told herself, and pushed the green button on the touch screen. "Hello."

"Senta?" he asked, the sound of his voice immediately bringing back the memory of that Saturday at the Farmers' Market.

"Yes," she answered, forcing herself to answer even that one word.

"Are you alright?" he asked.

"Yes, I'm OK," she answered.

"Did the tornado hit anywhere close to you?" he asked.

"Yes, I think. I don't know for sure. There are branches down, and we had lots of hail. Are you OK?" she asked.

"I'm fine. It passed south of me. But on the radar it looks like it hit somewhere around Ashland City. Did your friend Suzanne call you?" he asked.

"Yes, she told me you called. I would have recognized your voice though, even if she hadn't told me to expect your call. I know it's you, but I don't know who you are. I don't know your name," she said, second guessing her choice of words and wondering if she'd even made sense.

"That isn't fair, is it?" he said with a laugh. "I know your name, but you don't know mine!"

There was silence for a few seconds as she waited to hear the name she had wondered about for the past three weeks. "Are you going to tell me your name?" she asked feeling a bit awkward.

"Yes," he said. "I'm just playing with you. My name is Jerrick. Jerrick Douglas. And you are Senta Miller. Your friend told me your last name. I'm pleased to meet you, Senta Miller, now that we're formally introduced."

"I am pleased to meet you," Senta said as her mind raced, processing the flood of feelings of finally knowing his name and discovering that he had been worried about her. He had gone to so much trouble to track her down. Once again, Senta froze, being concerned to say something wrong and cause him to think badly of her.

"Your friend Abigail. Is she alright? Does she live near you?" he asked remembering that Abigail had said they lived close by.

"I don't know yet, Mr. Douglas," she said. "Abigail and

John live just down the road. I was walking there to check on them when you called. And now I'm standing here under a tree in front of my house by the road, talking to you." *Did I just say that*, she thought? *Why did I say that? He must think I'm an idiot.*

"You can go ahead and walk to their house while you talk to me. Just watch out for cars and downed power lines," he said. "And do I have to call you Miss Miller since you're addressing me as Mr. Douglas? Or can you call me Jerrick so I can call you Senta?"

"You sound like my mother warning about the downed power lines," she said. "Yes, you may call me Senta." She could hear the smile in his voice.

"You just seem a little distracted, probably the shock from the tornado," he said, knowing that it was he who was causing the distraction but wanting to give her an excuse. "And was that correct, *Miss* Miller not *Mrs.* Miller?"

For many years now, she had felt a sadness when she was introduced as Miss Miller. It was fine, expected, to be Miss when she was 18, but with each passing year, as the other girls her age married and now had children, it didn't feel like something positive. But now, for the first time since her father had bought the can of blue paint that still sat on the shelf in the barn, she answered with pride and hope, the four words, "Yes, it's Miss Miller. I'm not married. I live with my mother on our farm. My father passed away fifteen years ago."

"Abigail's husband is John? Has she had her baby yet?" inquired Jerrick.

"Yes, that's right. Their last name is Lapp. Their farm is a quarter of a mile from ours on the other side of the road. I'm still walking. There are no cars out. Some branches are down but nothing too bad. I know the Lapps are probably checking on their dairy cows. There wasn't time to get them in the barn, not that that would help much if the tornado directly hit the barn. Dairy cows are very expensive, and it hurts to lose even one. No, she hasn't had her baby yet. It's about another month and a half before it's her time. They are very excited. This is their first baby. I can see their house now and the barn. Everything seems alright."

"That's good. I'm looking at the weather radar, and I think the tornado hit west of Ashland City. Are you east of Ashland City?" he asked.

"Yes, we're east," she answered, "Mr... Jerrick," she said, for the first time saying his first name instead of his last. She enjoyed feeling the sound of the letters on her lips. For some reason, it was difficult to call him by his first name even though he requested she do so. "Where are you? And, maybe I shouldn't ask this, but are you on a boat?"

"Wow, you're good!" he said, laughing. "I'm in Haven Harbor, Kentucky. That's about 120 river miles from you. And yes, I'm on a boat. I'm impressed! How did you know that?"

"When you were at the Farmers' Market, you and all your friends were wearing boat shoes, Sperry's. You were wearing a shirt from a sailboat race, and your watch was a marine watch. Your friend called you *Captain*." She wondered if she'd said too much, giving it away that she had payed a lot of attention.

"Wow, again!" he said. "I thought you worked for a CPA, not a private investigator. You're correct. Yes, we were on boats, four of them. Sometimes a group of us will cruise up to Nashville for the weekend. We dock at Rock Harbor which is very close to the Farmers' Market. The women love to go to the Farmers' Market. The men do too, but not as much as the women. So, we take Uber from Rock Harbor to the Farmers' Market. We'll go out to eat and catch a concert on Saturday night. Sometimes we keep going on up to Old Hickory Lake and stay at Cedar Creek Yacht Club. It just depends on how much time we have."

"I thought the ladies looked nautical, too," said Senta. "I noticed an anchor necklace and a bracelet with nautical flags. Does your wife like traveling in the boat?" Senta held her breath, not believing she had dared to ask the question that could destroy all her hopes. It seemed as if her heart might stop as she waited for the answer.

"I'm not married, Senta," he answered. "The other three guys are. They let me tag along solo."

"Do you live on your boat all the time?" Senta asked quickly, trying to get away from her last question. She felt elation, learning that he was single. Standing in the Lapps' drive with

104 | LL FOX

her eyes closed and her right hand over her heart, Senta did her best to sound calm on the phone.

"No, I have a house, too, but I do spend a lot of time on the boat," he answered. "Now changing subjects, I'm planning on being in Nashville the weekend after this coming one. I thought I'd stop by the Farmers' Market because I'm completely out of cheese. Will you and Abigail be there?"

"Yes, yes, we'll be there." She answered trying to be calm and not betray her excitement at the possibility of seeing him again.

"Great, maybe I'll see you then," he said.

"Yes, you will," she said. "Jerrick, thank you for being concerned about me and the tornado."

"I'm very glad it missed you," he said. "I'll see you soon, and Senta, if it looks as if you'll sell out of cheese before I get there, hold back a pound for me."

"I will. I promise," she said. And with that he was gone. Senta stood in Abigail's drive, once again feeling like she wasn't in her own body. A whirlwind of feelings, thoughts and ideas racing through her mind. But overall, she felt absolute elation as she ran toward the barn where Abigail and John were checking on their cows.

"John, Abigail, are you all OK?" said Senta as she ran into the barn where the Lapp's were moving cows into their stalls and checking them for injuries.

"Yes, it missed us," said John. "All the cattle are here and uninjured. We got lucky on this one. How about you and your mother?"

"We're fine," Senta answered. "The roof may be damaged from the hail so I may be asking you for the name and number of your roof man."

"Are you finished with me, John?" asked Abigail leaning against the barn door and holding her back. "I'd like to go back to the house and rest."

"Yes, we're fine here. You go ahead. Go back to the house. You can rest and visit with Senta," said John.

The two women walked back to the house, Senta wanting to get her friend inside and seated before she shared the incredible news. They entered the kitchen door, with Senta holding it open for her pregnant friend. They got some iced tea and sat down on the front porch.

"I'm really ready to have this baby," said Abigail. "I get tired so easily, and I'm so awkward and clumsy. You said your mother was OK?"

"She's fine," said Senta. "Abigail, I have news. Unbelievable news! Wonderful news!" Abigail looked at her friend with raised eye brows indicating, *tell me, I'm listening.* "He called me, Abigail. I was just talking to him, standing right here in front of your house. His name is Jerrick Douglas."

"You mean the man we met at the Farmers' Market?" asked Abigail. Senta nodded. "Oh, my, really," said Abigail. "How in the world did he find you?"

"It was thanks to you, Abigail," said Senta. "When you were explaining how we make cheese, you said I worked for a CPA in Ashland City. When he saw the tornado on the radar, he could tell it was headed for Ashland City. He was afraid it might hit me, us, he asked after you also. So, he started calling CPA's in Ashland City. Campbell is the first one alphabetically on the list. He talked to Suzanne, and she gave him my number." She stopped for a second to let Abigail absorb it all. "He's coming to the Farmers' Market in two weeks to buy cheese. He's coming to see me."

"Senta, honey," said Abigail speaking quietly and reaching out to hold Senta's hand. "You have to get hold of yourself. I know you're happy he called. It was very nice of him to call you. It's fine that he's coming back to buy more cheese. But Senta, he's not Amish. Also, he is probably married."

"He's not married. He told me," said Senta.

"OK, but he could be lying. Still, he's not Amish. You have to stop thinking about him like this," said Abigail.

"Abigail, I don't know if I can explain this. I probably can't because I don't understand it myself. But I can't stop myself. From the first second I cast eyes on him, I was different. You know because you were there. I couldn't even talk! When he looked at me, it was like he could see inside of me, like he understood everything about me. I know this seems crazy. I realize he's not

Amish, but I don't care. It doesn't matter. Even today, just now, just on the phone when he isn't here, his voice does something to me. I see all the problems, Abigail, but I can't stop feeling the way I feel," Senta said taking her hand from Abigail and burying her face in her hands.

"I know," said Abigail. "I just don't want you to be hurt. You have built him up in your mind, but you don't know anything about him. He's a stranger."

"I know he was on a boat," Senta said. "I was right when I observed all the nautical clues. His friends were in boats, too. They enjoy traveling to Nashville, and the wives like to make a stop at the Farmers' Market. The harbor is close to the Farmers' Market. But he was by himself. He isn't married. And he's kind, Abigail. He cared enough to find me and call, just to see if I was hurt in the tornado."

The two women talked for another thirty minutes before Senta walked back home. Abigail gently tried to convince Senta to forget about her captain, and Senta tried to explain how she couldn't help herself.

About half way home, Senta stopped and got out her cell phone. Going to *recent*, she made a new contact for Jerrick Douglas. It made her smile, imagining how wonderful it would be if her phone rang and his name appeared on her iPhone screen. Then her mind returned to his voice, how it sounded strong and confident just like she remembered from the encounter at the Farmers' Market. She delighted in recalling how nice it was when he spoke her name. She thought about how easy it was talking to him even though they had never really spoken before. And even though she hardly knew him, she trusted him.

The next week and a half was both elation and torture for Senta. At first elation because she was actually going to see him again. She knew, in her heart, that he was coming to see her and that buying cheese was just an excuse. The torture came as she tried to imagine how it might unfold. Would he just come by, purchase some cheese and leave? Or would he talk to her? But talking to her at the cheese table with Mrs. King and Mrs. Belier present wasn't a good idea! Did he realize that? Maybe if he got there at the right time, he could eat lunch with her and

Abigail. That would be a perfect opportunity to talk. Then she would agonize over what they would talk about. *I must speak intelligently and be interesting,* she told herself. *I can't freeze up. He is very smart. I can tell by the words he uses. I don't want him to think I'm stupid or backward.* Then finally she agonized over how she looked. She wanted to look nice for him. She wanted him to notice her and find her attractive. The frustration built as she came to grips with the fact that she couldn't change her clothing, her hair, and lack of makeup. *My shoes are so clunky,* she thought, looking at her big black leather shoes. One of her favorite pastimes at the Farmers' Market was looking at women's shoes. She wanted to look feminine. She wanted to look pretty.

What is this I'm feeling? she asked herself every night as she lay in bed thinking about Jerrick Douglas. *I've never felt anything like this before. I have been around men before, but none have affected me like he has.* She was afraid to even think it, but deep down she knew.... She loved him even though she didn't dare let herself think it because it was too soon. Every night she held her extra pillow that she pretended was him. Contented, she drifted off to sleep after giving the pillow his good night kiss.

CHAPTER TEN

Winds of Change

On the morning Jerrick was to return to the Farmers' Market, Senta got up earlier and shampooed her hair. Standing in the shower letting the water rinse the shampoo out of her hair, she felt the warm water run over her naked body and wondered how it would be if he were in the shower with her. Snapping out of her dream, she felt guilty for having such ideas. Finally, she admitted to herself how she'd been feeling. She had never wanted anyone to kiss her before, but she did think about Jerrick Douglas kissing her.

In the years since her father's stroke, there were times that Senta experienced struggle as her faith collided with her feelings and the circumstances of her life. There were moments of anguish when it was easy to be angry with God, feeling like she had been forgotten. Senta would remind herself that faith was just that, faith. She recognized that being angry with God was not the answer. And in her heart, she knew she didn't really believe she'd been forgotten. Yet, from time to time, Senta had to remind herself of that.

And now, things looked and felt so differently. Today, she would see Jerrick. Somewhere far away, he was up and getting ready to drive to Nashville, perhaps even taking a shower just as she was. As Senta finished showering, she offered a prayer of thanks to God for bringing her to that day and time when her path in life had crossed Jerrick's. For any number of reasons, Senta might have missed him that day, but God had made it happen. He had not forgotten her.

Telling her mother goodbye, Senta ran out the door to see the van coming up the drive. Her mother was pleased to see her happier and also eating more. Mrs. King and Mrs. Belier gave Senta their typical formal good mornings. Then a few minutes later when Abigail got into the van, Senta caught her friend's eye and they shared the excitement of the moment. Senta remembered how she had done that with her father, communicating with just a look.

The trip to Nashville was quick, and soon they were unloading and setting up for business. The Farmers' Market opened for customers at 8:00 a.m. and soon Shed B was full of people. Senta kept an eye out looking through the groups of people, looking for her captain, but she didn't see him. Abigail noticed this, and again the two women exchanged a look in which Abigail said, *Be patient, he didn't say when. He's coming.*

But noon came, and Jerrick Douglas hadn't arrived. As usual, they ran out of cheese shortly before lunch time. Senta had kept back one block of cheese. "Let's go eat lunch, Senta," said Abigail. "I'm hungry, but what's new? I'm always hungry." Abigail tried to be lighthearted to cheer up her friend. As the two walked out of Shed B and across to the Food Court building, Abigail said, "It's a long drive, Senta. There could be construction that slowed him down." Senta looked at her friend with concern and nodded her head. "How does Mexican food sound today, Senta? I'm thinking a burrito." The two walked through the food court and got in line at the Mexican restaurant. When it was their turn to order, Senta heard his voice.

"These three are all on one ticket," came the voice from behind them. Senta's heart leaped as she recognized it and turned around to find him standing behind her. "I meant to get here sooner, but there was construction on Interstate 24," he said. "Have you sold out of cheese, and did you save me some?" Jerrick asked looking at Senta, smiling, then looking at Abigail.

"Yes, I saved you a pound of cheese," said Senta smiling from ear to ear. "Abigail, you have met Mr. Douglas before, but let me introduce you. Jerrick, this is Abigail Lapp."

"It's nice to meet you, Abigail," said Jerrick. "You know, I need to apologize. I'm crashing your party. I hope you don't mind if I join the two of you for lunch?" he asked as they walked with their food to the tables in the center of the food court.

"No, that's fine," said Senta trying hard to appear calm. "After all, you did buy our lunch." The three found a table for four. Jerrick sat his lunch down and then pulled out chairs for Abigail and Senta. Not being used to such treatment, Abigail gave Senta a quick look as she sat down. Senta knew she was impressed even though Senta knew her friend was looking for flaws in his character. Abigail folded her hands, Senta followed suit, and Abigail said grace. When they looked up from their prayer, they saw that Jerrick had prayed, too. Senta watched him as he unwrapped his two tacos. She noticed his clothes. Unlike the first time, he had on khakis and a neatly pressed blue shirt that matched his eyes. He wore the same watch that he glanced at and then at her, smiling.

They dove into their tacos and burritos and Jerrick asked, "Abigail, how is the pregnancy coming? You're pretty close to due date, aren't you?"

"Yes, I am," said Abigail. "Thank you for asking, Mr. Douglas. I'm ready any time the baby is ready."

"Are your farms alright after the tornado?" Jerrick asked, looking back and forth at Senta and Abigail.

"They're fine, just minor damage, Mr. Douglas," said Abigail. "But what we'd like to know is more about you. Where are you from? What do you do? Are you married?"

"Abigail, please," said Senta, looking at her friend pleading for her to be polite.

"No, it's OK," he said. "I know it looks strange. I buy some cheese, then a few weeks later I track you down," his eyes moved to Senta, "and call you after the tornado. And now here I am buying you lunch. The truth is that I wanted to see you again. Even though we barely spoke, I found myself thinking about you, wondering who you were. When I saw the tornado on the radar heading for Ashland City, I had to know you were alright. I'm back here today not for the Farmers' Market, but for you, to talk to you, to know you better." Senta's heart soared as this man she barely knew told her he felt something for her. She couldn't take her eyes off him and as before couldn't say a word.

"What do I do? Well, I guess I'm retired. I sold my company a few years ago. It was a coffee company. I bought coffee in Guatemala and sold it to independent coffee shops in the US. I sold out to Proctor and Gamble. I still own part of two coffee plantations in Guatemala so I go there several times a year. I own a boat, which Senta figured out," he continued, as Senta smiled at him, "and I like to cruise. I like to travel by boat. Maybe that's a short trip up the Cumberland River to Nashville or maybe a longer trip down to the Gulf and the islands in the Caribbean. I just like the water. Lastly, I'm not married. I was years ago. I'm divorced." There was silence at the table although all around them was the noise and activity of the food court.

Wanting badly to make conversation with him, Senta said, "I think I told you, but I'm not married. I live with my mother on our farm. I work for Aaron Campbell the CPA in Ashland City. I'm the staff accountant for Stoll Woodworking, west of Ashland City. Abigail is married, obviously," she continued as Abigail gave her an *of course I am* look. Senta looked back with an, *it doesn't hurt to say so*, look. Jerrick smiled. "This is Abigail and John's first baby, and we're all very excited for them. John and Abigail bought our dairy cows when my father had a stroke. They have a nice herd of Guernsey dairy cows, and they sell their milk to the dairy except for what is held back for our cheese. And we're Amish."

Jerrick laughed, "I hadn't noticed!" Senta didn't know whether to be mad at herself for saying something so obvious or to be mad at him for teasing her. But she couldn't be mad at him, so they all laughed. "Look, I'm sorry about the Amish thing. You're probably not supposed to even be talking to me. I don't want to cause you any problems. I considered returning to the Farmers' Market sooner but then decided I shouldn't since you're Amish and I'm not. If I'm bothering you, please tell me. If you want me to leave, tell me and I won't come back." He'd said it. He'd thought about it a lot. *An Amish woman! What am*

I thinking? There are billions of women on the planet, and I find an Amish one. This will be way too complicated. But he had kept thinking about her and had to call when he saw the tornado at Ashland City.

"I believe that would be very much for the best," interjected Abigail, standing up and gathering her empty paper cup and plate for the trash. "Senta, it's time for us to be getting back. Mrs. King and Mrs. Belier will be needing our help."

Senta's heart fell as she looked in shock at her friend who had answered the question he had asked her. *No, no, no, I don't want him to leave. I want to see him every Saturday, every day.* The possibility that this moment could end everything and she would never see him again scared her more than anything. At that realization, Senta gathered up every bit of courage she could muster and said, "Thank you, Abigail, but I'm going to stay and talk a little longer with Mr. Douglas. I'll be back soon." Somehow Senta felt she should call him *Mr. Douglas* around Abigail, as if *Jerrick* was too personal.

Abigail looked at her friend very seriously before responding. "Don't be too long. Thank you for lunch, Mr. Douglas. It was very nice to meet you." And with that Abigail walked away, throwing away her trash as she left the food court.

"I'm sorry for my friend's behavior. She is really a very fine person and my best friend. She is just concerned for me," Senta explained, her hands clasped together almost appearing as if she was praying. "But I don't want you to stop coming here to buy cheese or to see me. I didn't mind at all when you called me. I don't know what to say about me being Amish."

Reaching out his hand to hers and taking both hers in his, he said, "Then I will. Let's not worry about our differences right now. I just want to spend time with you. Can we just talk? You're doing much better talking today than the first time I met you," he said with a twinkle in his eye.

But she wasn't so sure about that because once again when he touched her hands she felt the feeling all over her body that moved from her chest then lower. She watched his jaw, his eyes, and lips. Senta found herself wanting to touch his face, clean shaven, so unlike the Amish men she knew. "Yes, I would like that.... for us to get to know each other," she finally answered.

"I just want to learn more about you," he said. "But not like I'm reading your CV. More about you, how you feel and how you think."

"My CV?" Senta asked, not understanding.

"Your curriculum vitae, your resumé, like for a job," he said. "I know you live on a farm, and you work for a CPA. But I want to know what you love. I want to know how you feel."

Senta's mind raced. *He is handsome and smart,* she thought. *Sometimes he says things I don't understand. Sometimes I think he changes what he's going to say, to say it so I understand.* "How I feel? I don't believe anyone has ever asked me that before. Why do you want to know?" she said, finally responding to his question.

"I want to know because it's who you are. Look at all these people here in this food court. They're all in the same place doing the same thing. To just look at them, you might think they're alike. But they're not because they all feel differently. Tell me about yourself. What do you love? What makes you happy? What are you afraid of?" he asked and then waited patiently for her to think.

"I love my parents," Senta answered quietly. "My father has been gone for many years now. I don't have any brothers or sisters. I don't even have any cousins. My mother is the best mother anyone could want. I know she worries about me. I'm concerned about her because she's getting older and her health.... She won't go to the doctor."

"You're a good daughter," Jerrick said. "I can tell."

"I love to walk down to the creek and listen to music," she continued. "There is a creek on the back side of our farm. I like to walk down to the creek and sit on a log at a place where the creek bends. It's very beautiful and peaceful. It's relaxing to sit there and watch the water flow. I have songs in my iPhone, and I like to listen to them. Music makes me feel things, things I already feel, but even more. It's like the songs are about me." He smiled, watching her as she considered his questions, taking them very seriously.

Contemplating her fears, she thought, *I'm afraid he could never be interested in me.* Then taking a deep breath and summoning her courage she said, "And what am I afraid of? I'm afraid that I will never see you again." Senta looked down, unable to look at him after having shared something so personal. She wondered how he felt about what she had just said, hoping her honesty didn't scare him away. Then wanting to lighten the seriousness, she said, "Can we walk now? I want to show you something."

"Of course," he said and stood to gather their trash and dispose of it. He considered everything she'd said and felt her goodness and kindness. He had asked questions like that before and had never received such heartfelt answers. "What do you want to show me?" he asked.

"This way," she said. Fearing that her answers hadn't made sense, Senta looked for a sign of how Jerrick felt. *Maybe most people don't feel things like I do. Or maybe they used to and life crushed those feelings.* Her mind flashed for a moment to Ruth and wondered if she saw life differently than before she was married. Then Senta returned to the present and wondered how Jerrick would have answered his own questions. She wanted to ask him but didn't dare. "I said I like music. We Amish only have church music and don't listen to any other kind. One of the things I like about the Farmers' Market is all the different music. You hear it here in the food court. Some of the vendors also play songs. A friend put Spotify on my phone and when I hear something I like, I find it, and save it so I can hear it later. I can't listen to it at home because I know my mother wouldn't approve. But I can listen at the creek. My friend told me I should get some ear buds. That way I could listen, and my mother wouldn't hear. So, I'm going to find out where to get them and buy some." She looked up at him as they walked, watching his eyes to see if he found her conversation interesting. Knowingly, he smiled when he saw her look up at him as he opened the door for them to walk out of the food court building. It had been cool and refreshing in the air-conditioned building, but outside was getting warmer and more humid.

As they left the Farmers' Market and ventured behind where the produce trucks were, Senta thought for a fleeting moment about her mother's warnings of kidnapping. But immediately she dismissed the thought because the truth was she felt comfortable and safe with him. "So I want to show you a new kind of music I discovered. Back here behind the Farmers' Market, I've met some people from Mexico. They play this music and dance to it. I don't understand the songs because the words are in Spanish, but I love to watch them dance," she said, leading him back to the trucks.

"Do you know what it's called?" Jerrick asked.

"Yes, it's called bachata," she said. Walking around the trucks, Senta spotted her friend. "Luisa Fernanda, hello!" greeted Senta as she approached with Jerrick.

"Qué tal, Senta!" said the Hispanic woman, wearing jeans and a white blouse, her hair up, trying to stay cool in the heat. "And who do you have here, Chica? Tu novio?"

"Luisa Fernanda, this is my friend, Jerrick Douglas. Jerrick, Luisa Fernanda," said Senta.

"Mucho gusto," said Jerrick gently shaking her hand. "Es un placer conocerla." It was then that Senta realized that Jerrick could probably speak Spanish because of his coffee business.

"I was telling Mr. Douglas about bachata," said Senta. "I was hoping you might be playing some bachata music and dancing today so he could watch."

"Everyone has gone to eat lunch," said Luisa Fernanda. "I can play some bachata but there's no one to dance with unless you want to dance with me, Señor Douglas?"

Senta looked at Jerrick as it dawned on her that perhaps he already knew about bachata, too. She asked, "Do you know about bachata? Do you know how to dance bachata?"

"Yeah, I do," he said, not wanting to diminish her excitement but not wanting to lie to her.

"Que ganga, Chica!" said the Latina swiping her finger on her phone to send the music to the little portable speaker on the tailgate of the truck. "Te gusta Prince Royce y Shakira?" she asked Jerrick.

"*Déjà vu*?" asked Jerrick as Luisa Fernanda smiled and nodded yes, "Por supuesto." Looking back at Senta, Jerrick shrugged his shoulders as Luisa Fernanda took his hand and pulled him out on the concrete pad that was their dance floor. The music started. He spun her and turned her. They moved together like they had danced together before. Senta stood with her hands over her mouth, caught up in the music and the motion, as it all flowed together.

When the song ended, the two walked back towards Senta, "OK, you can have him back now," said Luisa Fernanda. "But if you don't want him, I may want to replace Carlos." They all laughed.

"Oh my, I didn't know you could dance like that," said Senta. "That was really good. Where did you learn how to do that?" she said complimenting him.

"I learned how to do that years ago by a river in Guatemala," he said. "And do you see it yet?" he asked.

"Do I see it?" she asked puzzled.

"What does a river do? What does bachata do?" he asked watching her to see if she understood the connection.

Pondering it, she answered, "They both flow?"

Smiling, he said, "That's right. They both flow. Think about why."

"I wish I could do that. Dance like that. But there's no way. I'm way too clumsy and uncoordinated," she responded at the same time thinking about what he'd said.

"But you can," he said. "May I show you?" He extended his left hand, palm up to her. Hesitating, she then surrendered, placing her right hand in his. As he asked Luisa Fernanda to play the song again, Senta realized that she couldn't tell him no. There was no way she would ever try this with anyone else. She smiled as he led her out on the concrete, thinking, *I can't tell him no. Anything he wants, I will say yes to. And I think he knows it.*

The music played, and he took her hands in his. "Basic bachata is pretty simple; it's one, two, three, tap. I move to my left, and you move to your right. Then we come back; one, two, three, tap." They repeated it for several measures as she watched her feet and his. "Now, I don't want you to watch your feet. I want you to feel it." He placed her left hand on his shoulder and then placed his right hand on the small of her back. "You can tell what you're supposed to do by feeling it. If I move left, you feel it and move with me. If I turn, you turn because you feel it. That's called following. I lead; you follow." Senta was trying to pay attention, but being so close to him left her overwhelmed. She could feel his hand on her, and it felt as if it belonged there. She wanted to press against him and wrap her arms around him. "Senta, are you paying attention?" he asked, fully aware of the effect he was having on her. "Now, I'm going to show you how to turn. If I raise my left arm and push you here on your waist, you will naturally turn under and come back around. That's the lead for that turn," he said, gently pushing her waist to bring her under his arm. She did the turn and smiled up at him, proud of not stumbling. "Very nice," he said. "Now if I bring my left hand up across your face at an angle, you're naturally going to turn the other way," he said as he turned her the other direction. "You're doing great," he said as she completed that turn. "The last one is trickier. I bring my left hand back around you, but I take your other hand in my right. Then as I turn you, I don't let go," he said as he turned her. "Don't let go. See you end up like this with your arm behind you. Getting out of this one will be two turns because we have to unwind you," he said as he spun her back around twice to get her back to the basic position. It was a little too much, too fast, and she lost her balance as she came back and fell against him. She only stayed against him for a moment, but oh, she thought about that moment every night for weeks. Her face against his hard chest, his arms around her catching her as she fell into them. She remembered his scent, clean with just a hint of cologne.

He laughed and told her it was alright. He told her it was impossible for her to do it wrong and that she was a great dancer. She knew she wasn't, even so she didn't want the song to end. He stopped spinning her and just danced bachata with her, close, pulling her against him. He dropped her right hand and brought his left arm around her, holding her close. She wrapped her right arm around him. She could feel him move and sensed his strength. She tried to remember every note of the music, every movement. *I love his arms around me*, she thought. *I don't know what could be more perfect. My God in Heaven, what if we made love? I can't even imagine how that would feel.*

When the song ended, they stood holding each other for a moment. "You did great!" he said.

"I made a lot of mistakes," she said. "I've never danced before."

"Listen to me," he said, gently. "You can't make mistakes. With dancing or other things. It's not possible." She thought about his words, wondering what he meant.

"We should probably get you back to Abigail. You've been gone quite a while," he said, "But before you go, I want to ask you something." She looked at him, smiling but still completely undone by the dancing. "I have to be back here in Nashville on Thursday. I won't be done with my meeting until around 5:00, but when I'm done, I'd like to take you out to dinner. Will you join me?"

Hearing his words, Senta felt like she was in a dream. "Yes," she said. "I would love to." She heard her voice saying yes and thought about all the years, about holding the pillow at night. "Jerrick, I have never been on a date before."

"You're worrying again. Don't worry. You can't do anything wrong. I'm going to take you to a restaurant in Nashville. May I pick you up at 6:00?"

"My mother," she said. "I can't tell her. I want to tell her so badly. I want her to meet you." She had considered it all before and was certain that her mother wouldn't like him because he wasn't Amish. But Senta knew she didn't care. In fact, Senta liked it that he wasn't Amish because he was so different. "I will tell my mother I have a dinner meeting with the staff at Mr. Campbell's. I'll be waiting for you at 6:00. My mother won't come to the door. She won't know." They walked back and said goodbye in front of Shed B. Jerrick walked on to the parking lot then turned around to see if she was still there or if she had gone back to her friends. She was still there and gave him a last wave goodbye.

Senta walked down the aisle of Shed B in a dream state. *He danced with me*, she thought. *I must find that song on Spotify, "Déjà vu," Shakira and Prince Royce. I can't believe he likes me. He really likes me. He's taking me out to dinner. I can't believe he wants to take me on a date. He is so different. He doesn't talk like other men. I don't always understand him. He moves so nicely, graceful but strong. When we danced, I thought I'd collapse! He wants to know how I feel. I love him. I love him like I've never loved anyone or anything. I'm going to see him Thursday night.*

"Senta," called Abigail. "Over here." Senta had walked right past the cheese and bread table, oblivious to everything. Mrs. King and Mrs. Belier both looked at her, suspiciously.

"Oh, there you are," Senta said turning and walking toward the space between the yellow lines to get behind the tables.

"We're in the same place we always are," said Mrs. King. "Where have you been all this time, and what have you been doing?"

"I left her in the food court," said Abigail. "She said she wanted to look at some of the vendors selling candles."

"When I saw her, she was with a man," said Mrs. Belier, accusingly. "She was talking to him and laughing."

"Well, yes, I did talk to one of our customers," Senta replied. "We were looking at candles, and he began asking about our cheese." The two older ladies looked at her with doubt. *Why do I have to lie like this?* she thought. *I've done nothing wrong. I don't like lying.*

The rest of the day passed in almost total silence, the four women talking to each other only when necessary. When the van came to transport them back home, they loaded their baskets and rode home through Nashville and into the countryside in silence. Abigail was the first to get off and Senta said, "I'll see you tomorrow for church." When Senta got off a short time later, the two older women said nothing. Senta walked up the sidewalk carrying the empty cheese baskets while feeling a cascade of emotions. *He's taking me to dinner,* she thought. *Mrs. King and Mrs. Belier saw me with* Jerrick. *I want to tell my mother so badly.*

Senta went in the house, gave her mother a hug and told her about the day at the market. Of course, no reference to Jerrick Douglas was made. It caused Senta pain to keep that detail a secret. After dinner, she asked her mother if she would like to take a walk, knowing she would decline. Walking down the gravel drive toward the barn, Senta retrieved the iPhone from her apron pocket and went to Spotify and searched the song they had danced to, "*Déjà vu.*" Once out of her mother's sight, she touched *play*. With eyes closed, Senta moved with the music, remembering the magic of dancing with him. Three times she played the song and danced, lingering in the memory. All too soon it was time to return to the house. But Senta wanted to listen to one last song as she walked back.... "When Will I See You Again."

Senta's mother heard her enter through the kitchen door. "Senta, did I tell you Bishop Yost came by today?" asked her mother from the front parlor.

"No, you didn't," replied Senta. "What did he want?"

"Just checking on us. He cares about us you know," said Mrs. Miller. "He's such a good man. He was asking about you, too."

"That is very nice, Mother," replied Senta. "But I don't trust him. I don't think he likes me at all." Mrs. Miller closed her eyes and shook her head not being able to fathom why her daughter felt the way she did.

"Bishop Yost was also telling me about Mrs. Yost. She's not doing very well," said Mrs. Miller. "You know she has been in poor health for some time and is continuing to decline. He is very concerned."

"I will pray for her," said Senta in total sincerity, but also thinking that perhaps dying would be better than being married to Bishop Yost. Senta said goodnight to her mother and went upstairs.

Senta brushed her teeth, put on her nightgown, and got her extra pillow out of the closet. She knelt and said her prayers as always, but tonight Senta did something she'd never done before. She asked God to forgive her ahead of time. Listening at her door to make sure her mother was still downstairs, Senta stood in front of the full-length mirror and slowly removed her nightgown and then her panties until she was naked. Looking at her reflection, she wondered what Jerrick would think if he saw her. Since no one had ever told her she was pretty, she didn't know if she was or not. She looked at her breasts and found fault, and then her hips and legs, almost concluding that there was no way he would be attracted to her. Shaking off those thoughts, Senta shifted her focus to the positive. *But he came back*, she told herself, *and we're going on a date Thursday.* Then turning off the light, she did another thing she'd never done before. She got in bed naked. The sheets felt good against her bare skin, the cool of the fabric arousing her. Wrapping her arms around her pillow, she drifted off to sleep thinking about Jerrick, dancing with him, and lying with him, her head resting on his chest, and pretending to hear the beat of his heart.

CHAPTER ELEVEN

Waypoints

Sally came by as usual on Monday. Senta was so excited to tell Sally about Saturday that she could hardly wait to conclude business and coffee with her mother to tell Sally that Jerrick did return to the Farmers' Market. Senta revealed that Jerrick had asked her out on a date for Thursday night, and she had accepted. Sally was thrilled for her friend and equally thrilled to get back to Ashland City and give Suzanne the latest news. Sally hugged Senta and wished her well.

Tuesday evening came and Senta walked down to Abigail's for cheese making. Senta almost didn't want to go because she was afraid Abigail was mad at her. As they worked making the cheese Abigail said, "Senta, I'm sorry I was so harsh with Mr. Douglas. He doesn't seem like a bad person. But we don't know anything about him, other than what he's told us. I'm just trying to protect you. I'm afraid he will hurt you."

Senta said, "I don't want you to be upset with me. I know I was gone too long. I just lost all track of time. Abigail, I'm helpless with him. I think he's wonderful. I just don't know what to do now." She had decided not to tell Abigail about their upcoming date Thursday night and was grateful that their regular shopping trip to Ashland City wouldn't conflict with seeing Jerrick.

"Of course, you don't know what to do next," said Abigail. "But I have no doubt that Mr. Douglas knows exactly what to do with you next." Senta looked slightly puzzled at her friend but very quickly understood the implication. "And Mrs. Belier saw you. I'm afraid she may tell her husband, and then the bishop may find out. I don't know what might happen."

Senta walked home that night feeling alone but more convinced than ever that Jerrick Douglas was the love of her life. *I don't care what everyone thinks*, she told herself. *I love him.* But then realizing the futility of the whole situation, she started to tear up. Taking out her iPhone, she found a song she'd added to her Spotify, "Unlove You" by Jennifer Nettles. And walking home down the country road in the dark, she cried as the song talked about a situation that Senta felt was exactly hers although most would believe it was about something entirely different.

Wednesday brought a surprise when Sally stopped by again, something she never did except on Mondays. Senta opened the door when she heard the knock. "Senta, I forgot to bring you something Monday," Sally said, winking. "I don't have time to come in because I've got to get home. You might need this." With a whisper, she added, "I had this little bottle of Dolce Gabbana Light Blue. It might be nice for tomorrow night." Sally handed Senta some papers with her right hand and with her left a small thin perfume bottle with a light silver top. "Not too much now, *just a little.*"

"Thank you, Sally," said Senta. "You don't know how much this means to me. Yes, I will use it, just a little." The two women hugged and then Sally ran back to her car. As Sally drove away she gave Senta a thumbs-up. Senta carried the papers and the perfume upstairs, putting the papers in the office and the perfume in her bedroom.

She had been thinking about details like this ever since Saturday-what to wear, her hair, her nails, and her shoes. So much of it, she couldn't change. She didn't have any other shoes besides the big, black clunky ones. Her dresses were all the same, with the exception of size. The older ones were just too big, with the one she'd made most recently fitting only a little better. She decided to make a new dress cut down slightly smaller still. A new dress that would, hopefully, fit her better.

She had it finished by Tuesday evening. Putting it on and standing in front of the mirror, she was pleased. Then checking her profile, she saw that she had a figure. She decided to not wear the white apron or the white cap. She considered wearing her hair down, but her hair was almost to her waist and after trying several possibilities she decided it was better up, just without a cap. She wished she had some more feminine shoes, something with a little more heel to make her taller, but she didn't own any.

By Thursday, she was so nervous she could hardly work. "I forgot to tell you, Mother, that we have a staff meeting for everyone this evening at Mr. Campbell's in Ashland City. Sally is going to stop by and pick me up. I don't know how long it will take, but I'll be quiet when I come in and try not to wake you," she explained to her mother that morning. Her mother nodded and smiled and suspected nothing. Senta tried to concentrate on her work but found herself repeatedly going to her bedroom, checking to make sure she had ironed her dress perfectly. She sat down for lunch with her mother but ate very little due to sheer nervousness. She sincerely wanted to tell her mother about her dinner plans but knew her mother would forbid it. Senta knew there were dangerous people in the world, but she felt safe with Jerrick Douglas, protected actually. Abigail had implied that he would take advantage of her, but Senta didn't think so. Her mind raced from thing to thing. *Where is he taking me? I hope it's not too fancy with so many forks that I don't know which one to use. What if someone sees us? I must remember to talk. What if we could dance again? Should I ask him if I don't understand something or just act like I do? What if this doesn't go well? What if he doesn't want to see me again?*

At four o'clock, she showered and shampooed her hair. Wearing her robe downstairs to make dinner for her mother, Senta reminded her that she wasn't eating at home due to the evening meeting. Still unsure how she was going to leave the house without her cap and apron, she would just have to cross that bridge later. She decided to not put on the perfume until she was outside for fear her mother would notice it and ask questions. After dinner, she went to see what her mother was doing, and found her in the chair in her bedroom asleep. Senta quickly went to her room and dressed, fixed her hair, put her perfume in her purse and checked to be sure she had her house key. She tiptoed down the stairs and out the front door, carefully closing it as quietly as possible. Finally, she took out the bottle of Light Blue and put just a drop behind each ear. A short time later she saw the white SUV pull up the drive and stop. She stood there watching as if her whole life had been lived to get her to that day, to that moment. Her eyes never left him as he got out of the vehicle, walked around in front, through the gate, and then up the sidewalk. Jerrick Douglas was wearing jeans and a white shirt that contrasted handsomely against his tanned skin. His hair just slightly messed up. Senta thought, *I love him in that white shirt.* He smiled as he came to a stop in front of her.

"You look great," he said. "Different. No apron, no cap? You are beautiful." Senta's heart skipped a beat from the compliment. *He does think I'm pretty*, she thought. Coming beside her and putting his hand gently on her back, he guided her to the SUV and said, "We should probably get going before your mother sees me and gets the shotgun!"

"We're Amish; we don't believe in guns," she said, seriously. But then seeing him smile, Senta knew he had been kidding. *I'm messing up already*, she thought. Jerrick opened the passenger door, took her hand and helped her into the vehicle. She found the seatbelt and put it on while he walked around to his side. The interior was all two-toned leather, beige and coffee. *Oh, my*, she thought, *this is even nicer than Mr. Campbell's Cadillac.*

Getting in and fastening his seatbelt, he started the SUV, pushing a variety of buttons. Suddenly, but very subtly, Senta felt the whole vehicle rise. "Did your truck just get higher?" she asked.

"Yes, it did," he said. "When you push this button here, it makes it move up or down. I lowered it to make it easier for you to get in. Some people have shorter legs than others, and this SUV sits high, so it adjusts, for people who are vertically challenged." He smiled as he said it, poking fun at her. *Is he saying I'm short?* she wondered. But then she saw him grinning at her and thought, *he's always kidding around with me. I'm not used to that. I'm used to everyone being serious with me.* "You know they say good things come in small packages," he said, and reaching in the center console he produced a small box wrapped in silver paper with a tiny silver bow. "This is for you," he said.

"Thank you," she said, more impressed with him for giving her a gift than even caring what the gift was. "But it's not my birthday or anything," she said.

"When is your birthday?" he asked.

"May 15th," she answered.

"So I missed your birthday," he said. "It's just a really late birthday present. Go ahead and open it."

Carefully, she removed the silver paper and bow and inside found a pair of ear buds for her iPhone. "Oh, thank you," she said with delight. "I will use these every day." *And I will think of you every time I use them*, she thought. *It's amazing how he listens to everything I say and remembers it.*

"Are you comfortable?" he asked as he pulled out on the road and accelerated. "You can adjust your seat on the side by your right hand."

"Yes, thank you. It's very comfortable," she answered quietly. Wanting to make conversation, Senta added, "Your car is very nice. What kind is it?"

"It's a Range Rover," he said. "It's diesel, but you can't tell, can you? It's so quiet. I don't know how they do it, but it's as quiet as a gasoline engine." He glanced over and saw her looking down and holding her hands together. "Are you nervous?" he asked, knowing she was.

"Yes," she answered.

"It's OK to be nervous," he said. "Remember, you can't do anything wrong."

"You've only seen me at the Farmers' Market. You have no idea how badly I can mess up," she said.

"Are you one of those girls that spills stuff, knocks over her drink," he asked laughing. "Like really clumsy?"

"No, not normally," she said, now smiling.

"So there you go. How bad could it be?" he asked. "You don't get drunk on a date, do you? That's really bad, to get drunk on a date, especially a first date. Embarrassing." He had continued kidding her to make her laugh and feel more relaxed.

"No, of course not," she said. "I don't drink alcohol!"

"Never?" he asked.

"No, I never have," she said. "I'm afraid I'd get drunk."

"If you'd like a glass of wine with your dinner, you may have one small glass. No more," he said. "I don't want to have to carry you out of the restaurant." She smiled and wanted to playfully slap his hand because she knew he was teasing. But she wasn't sure if that would be appropriate.

"So, have you been listening to any more music?" he asked.

"Yes, every day I take a walk and listen," she said. "And now with the ear buds you gave me, I can listen more at home."

"Have you found any more bachata you like?" he asked.

"No. I think "Déjà vu" is my favorite. What do the words mean?" she asked.

"The song is pretty sad, really," he said. "Her boyfriend has left her and she's heartbroken. So, she gets mad at love. She swears off love because it hurts too bad. She challenges anyone to defend love, to say it's good. She wants to see a show of hands to see if anyone can explain why love is good. So, she swears not to love again." He glanced at Senta to see how she was taking the explanation. "Have you heard 'Qué Bonito'?"

"No, is it bachata, too?"

"Yeah, Vicky Corbacha. I think she's from Spain. Qué bonito means how beautiful. You'll hear qué bonito a lot in the song. She's talking about her boyfriend, and she's saying that everything about him is beautiful," he said, tapping the touch screen three times and bringing up the song. "This vehicle has 23 speakers, great sound. You'll like it."

Senta smiled as the song began to play. Jerrick translated occasionally, explaining all the ways the singer found her lover beautiful. They listened to it together as they drove. When it finished, he asked, "Did you like it?"

"Yes, very much," she said.

"You want to hear it again?" he asked.

"How did you know?" she asked. "When there's a song I like, I'll listen to it over and over."

"I'm not surprised," he said. "I do the same thing." He touched the screen again and replayed the song. "Sit back and close your eyes," he said as he reached over and took her hand.

She looked up at him. Feeling his hand on hers, she remembered the first time he had touched her hand. *This is just so perfect*, she thought. She placed her right hand over his hand, then sat back, closed her eyes and listened as the song played again. If only she could spend time with him every day. She wanted the moment to last forever.

When the song ended, he continued to hold her hand and she his. "Have you been to downtown Nashville before?" he asked.

"No, I've only been to the Farmers' Market," she said. "You're going to find that I've not been anywhere, really. Not like you. You've probably been everywhere."

"Oh no, there's lots of places I haven't been," he said. "And lots of places I'd like to see. But I wanted to warn you, downtown Nashville is crazy. I don't think it ever stops. There are always people, tourists mostly, walking around down on Broadway, hitting the bars and restaurants. But you need to see it just to say you've been there. I'm taking you to a restaurant called The Southern. It's next to the Nashville Symphony and only about a block from the Cumberland River."

"Thank you so much for tonight," she said. "Do you think I'm dressed appropriately?"

"Now you're worrying again," he said, glancing over at her and she looking back with a look that confirmed his guess. "You look fine, really. You see, this is Nashville and everything and anything goes. At the symphony, some men dress in blue jeans and others in tuxedoes. Both are OK. I was at the open house for a company, Horace Milan, last year. They'd just moved into a beautiful new building on Blair Avenue. A friend of mine, Ellie McMillan, from Ellie Media, shares the building with Horace Milan. Anyway, I'd been invited to their party, and like you, I was wondering what to wear. Ellie told me to wear whatever I pleased. So, I wore a Tennessee tuxedo, that's jeans and a sport coat. I'm not kidding. There were men in real tuxedoes, women in couture gowns, and guys there who had just come in from the farm. One guy still had mud, I hope that was mud, on his boots. So, I was dressed just fine; you are, too. Does that make you feel any better?"

"Yes, a little," she said. "I can't help thinking that I may look odd… because I'm Amish."

They had turned off the interstate highway and were crossing the Cumberland River. The lights of the city were in front of them. "Senta," he said quietly, still holding her hand, "I didn't think you'd go out with me because I'm not Amish. But you agreed, and here we are. Have you wondered why I came back to see you at the Farmers' Market and then asked you on this date tonight?"

"Yes," she answered.

"So why do you think I asked you out on this date?" he asked.

"I have no idea," she said. "I can't imagine why."

"But you said yes," he said. "Why did you agree to our date?"

"You already know," she said. "Do I have to say it?"

"Yes, why?" he insisted.

Taking a deep breath and looking at his hand between hers she said, "Because I've never met anyone like you. I've never met anyone who makes me feel like you do." She sat in silence, wondering how he would take her declaration.

"I feel the same way about you," he said. Her head spun, hearing the words and feeling them impact her. She couldn't imagine that he felt the same way she did.

They turned onto Broadway, and, just as Jerrick had said, there were people everywhere. The sidewalks were full on both sides. Doors and windows of buildings were open and music poured from inside. There were horse-drawn carriages and strange things called pedal bars. These odd-looking contraptions on wheels plied Broadway. They were moving bars that twenty people pedaled like bicycles while they drank. Senta had never seen anything like it. Jerrick took his hand back to drive in the traffic. Turning off Broadway, they were one block from The Southern. They pulled up in front, Jerrik lowered the Range Rover, and the valet took it to parking. Jerrick guided her into the busy restaurant. Senta had never seen so many people. She didn't think they would be able to find a table, but the maître d' took them immediately to a booth. "This place is really hopping tonight," Jerrick said, and Senta nodded in agreement.

"This is going to be fun," he said, smiling at her as their water glasses were filled. The waitress started rattling off dinner specials, drink specials and dessert specials. It was somewhat overwhelming for Senta.

"Would you like to try some wine? Do you know what you like?" he asked.

"No, you chose something for me," she said.

"I'll have an Old Fashioned and the lady will have a glass of Reisling," he said. The restaurant was full of people and alive with activity. Jerrick thought about oysters on the half shell for appetizers but changed to shrimp because he thought Senta might not care for oysters. When it came time to order the entrée, the waitress escorted them to the kitchen where they each chose a steak.

"This is a very expensive restaurant," she said to Jerrick after the waitress left.

"Please don't worry about that," he said. "I know it's expensive compared to Ashland City, but for Nashville it's not that bad. It's OK, really." When the waitress brought the drinks, Jerrick said, "Drink just a little of your wine now. Wait until your food gets here to drink most of it. If you drink with food, it doesn't affect you as much. Men metabolize alcohol faster than women, and men tend to be bigger than women. So, men generally can handle more alcohol. That means women get drunk faster than men. So, you're only getting one tonight."

Senta took a sip from her glass of Reisling and made a face. Jerrick laughed. "It's not too bad," she said. "You'd better not tell my mother!" she said laughing.

"Reisling is rather sweet so I thought you might like it for your first wine experience," he said. Senta smiled and nodded her approval. They enjoyed their food as well as watching all the people around them. Jerrick asked her about her job with Aaron Campbell, and she explained how it worked and what she did. He was impressed with how seriously she took her work and how she felt a real obligation to the people at Stoll Woodworking.

Senta asked him about his boat. "What kind is it? I know there are different types," she said thinking about how she'd wanted to know about his boat ever since that first day at the Farmers' Market when she suspected he was on one.

"My boat is a displacement hull cruiser," he said. "Also known as a trawler. That type of boat is slow but very fuel efficient. It's a Krogen 48 NorthSea."

"I'm not familiar with that type of boat," she said. "Is it big? Does it have rooms inside?" She had Googled enough boats to know that *boat* could mean anything from a kayak to a ship.

Looking around the restaurant and estimating distances, he said. "Do you see the end of the bar over there?" Senta nodded. "It's about as long as from where we're sitting to there." Senta looked at him trying to determine if she had misunderstood or if he was exaggerating. "So it's 53 feet overall. It displaces 64,000 pounds or 32 tons. Yes, it has rooms inside." He got out his iPhone and touched photos and brought up a picture. Turning the phone to her, she studied it.

"It has another boat on top," she noticed.

"That's called a tender. If there isn't a dock and you have to anchor out, you put the smaller boat in the water and take it to shore. The mast here," he said, pointing to the white mast on the upper deck, "serves several purposes. One is to hold the radar and antennas but also to lift and launch the tender."

Senta listened intently and asked, "What are the little windows?"

"The little windows, as you called them, are portholes. But you're right, they're windows, but watertight windows to keep water out. There are two bedrooms and two bathrooms," he said, pointing to the forward section of the boat, "Back here is where the salon and galley are. Salon means living room, and galley means kitchen."

"Jerrick, this is a big boat," Senta said seriously. "Do you drive it all by yourself? Or do you have help? Does Ellie help you drive it?"

Jerrick looked at Senta and smiled, "Ellie is married to John Luke. They're friends of mine. I told you, I don't have a girlfriend. Yes, I operate it by myself. Driving it is easy most of the time because it's on autopilot. It drives itself. Docking and going through locks are times having help would be nice. But often there are people on the dock who will help catch lines for me."

She continued to look at the picture on the iPhone, annoyed at herself for asking about Ellie but relieved to find out Ellie wasn't a girlfriend. Then Senta began to wonder what it would be like to cruise on the boat with Jerrick. *I could learn how to do lines, tie knots, drive the boat*, she thought. *I could help him.*

"What is the name of your boat?" she asked.

"*Arcadia*," he answered just as the waitress walked up to ask about dessert. "We'll take two cookies, Amoretti, to go and the check," Jerrick said. Then turning to Senta, "We're only a block from the water. We'll walk out on the pedestrian bridge and eat our dessert there." Senta looked at him with surprise but delighted. "Doesn't eating an Italian cookie on the bridge sound better than here in the restaurant?" he asked. Senta nodded *yes* and thought, *I don't know what dates are supposed to be like, but this just can't be any better. I can't wait to tell Sally and Suzanne. What am I going to do? I wish I could tell Mother and Abigail. What if he wants to take me on another date? If he doesn't, I'll be crushed. But what if he does?"*

Jerrick paid the bill, and the waitress brought the cookies. Jerrick guided her out of the restaurant and out onto the sidewalk. "You can't eat it yet. You have to wait until we're on the bridge," he told her. She laughed and thought about how she loved it when he told her she couldn't do something like eat the cookie or have more than one glass of wine.

"Jerrick, I have to tell you something about the wine," she confessed. "I can feel it. I feel funny. And I want to talk a lot. I'm having to stop myself from talking so much. I'm sorry about asking about your friend Ellie like I did."

"It's OK," he said putting his arm around her as they walked down the street. "It's not too noticeable. I'm glad I cut you off at one though." She looked up at him knowing this time that he was teasing her again. She thought about how much she liked that. And she thought of how wonderful it felt to walk by him and feel him next to her with his arm around her. "I like your perfume," he said and Senta was pleased that he did.

They walked down 3rd Avenue and turned right onto the bridge approach and then followed it to the blue pedestrian bridge. It was all lit up and had a surprising number of people walking back and forth, looking at the river and the skyline. Halfway across the river, they stopped at one of the balcony overlooks. "OK, now we can eat the cookies," he said as they looked out over the river and up at the lights of the tall buildings of downtown Nashville. "Down there," he said pointing below, "is the municipal pier. I've tied up there before, but I don't like to even though it's convenient to downtown. Sometimes, late at night, drunks will throw beer bottles at the boats. It's important to dock either right under the bridge or far enough away that they can't hit your boat."

Senta looked down to the municipal pier and then downstream, thinking about the river and how it continued to Ashland City, and then on to Kentucky and finally to the sea. "Thank you for tonight," she said, "for asking me on a date, for dinner, and for dessert on the bridge."

"You're very welcome," he said finishing his cookie. "Thank you for saying *yes*." Standing by the rail next to each other, overlooking the water, he once again placed his right hand over her left. Then turning he took both her hands in his and said, "Senta, you're very concerned about whether I have a girlfriend. I don't want you worrying about that, so from now on if anyone asks me that question, including you, I'm going to say that I do." Senta looked at him, puzzled, as he continued. "I'm going to say that *you* are my girlfriend." The moment, the wine, the lights of the city, standing above the water, and most of all his words shook her from her head to her toes rendering her speechless once again. Then because of the awkward silence Jerrick added, "Unless you don't want to be my girlfriend."

Still unable to speak, Senta threw her arms around him and pressing her head into his chest hugged him as if she would never let go. Finally, she did and said, "Yes, that would be wonderful." Then he lifted her chin upward and taking her in his arms kissed her. A soft gentle kiss, his lips brushing hers and then with lips pressing harder against hers, her world exploded into a million pieces. Senta was trembling from excitement, struggling to regain control. Jerrick gently touched her cheek. He looked into her eyes for a moment then turned and they walked back the way they had come. Back down from the bridge, up 3rd Street, stopping in front of the Southern while the valet brought the car up. Jerrick opened the door and helped her in.

Soon they were driving down Broadway and retracing their route out of the city and back to the country to Senta's house. Jerrick didn't speak until they were on the interstate. "Senta, I don't know how we're going to do this. I know you being Amish, or rather, me not being Amish, is a problem," he said. "We're going to work that out. But let's not talk about that now. Right now, I need to tell you something, and I don't want you to be upset. I'm leaving the country Saturday on business to help a friend. Remember I told you about the coffee plantations in Guatemala? I have a friend, Mario, who has just inherited a coffee finca from his uncle. Mario doesn't know very much about coffee so he's asked me to come look at his operation and give my opinion and recommendations. His finca is way up in the mountains. There aren't even paved roads there. No telephone, no cell phone signal, no radio, no TV. So, for the next several weeks, I'll be out of contact. I can't call you, and you can't call me. I don't know how long I'll be gone. Three or four weeks, probably." He said nothing for a minute or two letting it sink in. "But I will be back. I'll call you as soon as I'm back in the United States. Then we can figure this all out together."

Senta was simultaneously thrilled and devastated. Thrilled at the real possibility of a future. Thrilled beyond description that he wanted her to be his girlfriend. Thrilled with him, how he thought, how he was, how he treated her. *I've never known anyone like him*, she thought. Thrilled beyond explanation as to how she felt when he touched her and especially when he'd kissed her. But the thought of his leaving, going to another country, especially another place that was so remote, scared her. *I have lived my life to find him. I can't lose him*, she thought. She reached over and took his hand in hers and kissed it.

"I promise I'll be back soon," he said, reassuringly. Because he didn't want to worry her, he kept the potential danger of the trip to himself.

"One of the songs I like is called 'Get Here,'" said Senta with a sniffle and wiped her eyes with her hand. "It's by a lady named Oleta Adams. She's telling her boyfriend to hurry up and come home. She says she doesn't care if it's in a boat or a plane, a car or a camel, she just wants him to get back as soon as he can. So, I'm going to listen to that song every day until you come back."

"I'll be quick. I promise," he said, stroking her hair. She tried to burn every second into her memory so she could think about it again and again over the next few weeks. "Besides, I want to take you to the Commodore's Ball. It's coming up in about six weeks. That's at the Dominion Yacht Club at Haven Harbor. I think it's only appropriate for my girlfriend to be my date."

"Yes, I'll go with you. I don't know how I'll work it out. I don't have the right things to wear. But I don't care. *Where you go, I will go and where you stay I will stay.*" She stopped talking for fear she would start crying again. They exited the interstate and drove through the darkness. Realizing the evening was almost over and he would be gone, Senta tried to cherish each moment. When they pulled up in front of the house, he pushed the button that lowered the SUV. He walked around and opened the door for her.

They walked to the front door as she found her house key. As she unlocked the door, he turned her to him one last time and kissed her. Overcome with emotion, she felt her knees go weak as she felt a warmth in her heart that moved down lower through her body. He turned and quickly walked back to the vehicle. She stood in the doorway as he drove down the drive and turned onto the road. She watched intently as the red tail lights got smaller and finally disappeared.

Senta went inside and made it to bed without her mother awakening. Unable to go to sleep from all the excitement, she lay in bed reliving the evening. Hours passed before she finally slept. The next morning, she was unable to get up on time. She drifted through the day unable to keep her mind on her work.

When she caught herself making accounting mistakes she had never made before, Senta thought it best to stop working and to try again the next day. Hopefully, she would be more herself.

She walked down to the creek in the afternoon and thought about the previous night, trying to understand it. She hadn't known who she was, almost as if she was lost. But then Jerrick Douglas found her and she saw things she'd never seen before; had feelings she'd never known before. She pondered it all afternoon trying to understand it, and ended up with, *Jerrick, you make it feel like love. Love is everything you are. And I have been transformed by that love.*

The next day Senta told her mother she was walking down to see Abigail. Only one car went by as she walked down the country road in the hot summer sun. It occurred to her that she never used to notice cars, didn't even know the different makes, until recently. From now on, she would keep her eyes open for a white Range Rover. She just had to share her magical evening with someone, and while she was partly afraid to tell Abigail, she was the only person Senta could confide in. She walked up the driveway finally reaching the shade of some trees which gave a little relief from the heat. She walked around back to the kitchen door gathered her courage and knocked.

"Senta, is that you?" called Abigail. "Come in," she said wiping her hands on a dish towel.

"Hi, Abigail," said Senta entering and closing the screen door behind her gently so as not to make a noise. "How are you feeling today? Any contractions yet?"

"No, not yet, but soon I suspect," said Abigail. "You're hot from the walk in the sun. You should have waited until evening. Let's get something to drink and relax a bit." Abigail made two lemonades with ice, and the two women went out to sit on the front porch.

"Mr. and Mrs. King stopped by this morning on their way to Ashland City," said Abigail. "There's bad news from the Yost's. Mrs. Yost passed away last night. She'd been ill for some time. I understand Eric Yost isn't your favorite person, but Mrs. Yost was a good woman." The two sat in silence, drinking lemonade and watching the occasional car drive past.

"So, what's wrong, Senta?" asked Abigail. "I can tell something isn't right. You're too quiet."

"Abigail, you're my best friend," said Senta. "Don't be alarmed, and don't be upset with me. I must talk to someone and that someone is you. Now please don't be distressed."

"OK, I'll do my best," answered Abigail.

"It's about Jerrick Douglas," Senta said as Abigail looked at her with a serious and concerned look. "l went out on a date last night. With Jerrick." Senta watched and waited for Abigail's reaction. There was no response, not a clue, so Senta continued. "We went to a restaurant in Nashville. It was wonderful, Abigail! And downtown Nashville is so exciting. The food at the restaurant was delicious. Jerrick is so nice, such a gentleman. The restaurant was expensive, but he didn't seem to mind at all. We had cookies for dessert. We walked to a bridge over the Cumberland River and that's where we ate our cookies." Senta paused and took a sip of lemonade, trying to discern her friend's reaction. Abigail still said nothing. "He kissed me, Abigail. It was incredible. I've never felt anything like this. I love him, Abigail."

Neither spoke, each one waiting for the other to say something. Senta felt it had been best to leave out the part about the glass of wine and that Jerrick had asked her to be his girlfriend. *Have I made a mistake in confiding in Abigail?* Senta thought. *Is this too much for her to handle? I can't lose my best friend.*

Finally, Abigail said, "Senta, I want you to be happy. Part of me is happy for you, but part of me thinks this just won't work. I'm also concerned that he may hurt you. All you know about him is what he has said. Boats, coffee plantations in Central America, sailboat races in Malta? That's very unusual. Most people don't have lives like that. Maybe he's lying to you to impress you. I'm worried he's trying to take advantage of you."

"He is different," agreed Senta. "That's one of the reasons I find him so attractive. He's unlike any other man I've ever known. But I haven't seen anything from him that seems like he's trying to take advantage of me."

"And perhaps you're right," said Abigail. "Maybe it's all true, and maybe he has no ulterior motives. But it doesn't change the fact that he isn't Amish. What are you going to do about that, Senta? I can tell you he isn't going to become Amish."

"No, probably not," said Senta. "And I wouldn't expect him to. But I could stop being Amish. I could leave the order. If he asked me to, I would. It's not like he's a different religion, Abigail. He's Christian just like us, just a different denomination. I know we Amish think we're right and that we've got it all figured out, but so does everyone else. Look how we're changing. Today, Amish women can work outside the home just like English women. We ride to the Farmers' Market in a van. We can't own a car, but we can hire someone else to drive for us. Does that make sense? There are Amish in Illinois and Wisconsin that own cars and trucks and tractors. I'm not so sure we have all the answers, Abigail." The two sat in silence. Finally, Abigail spoke.

"We love you, Senta," she said. "John and I really want you to be happy. I have no doubt that you're in love with him. If he loves you and he wants a life with you, then you will have our blessing even if it means you leave us. That won't make us very popular with neighbors like Mrs. Belier and Mrs. King, but our friendship is more important. If God has sent this man to you, then it is certain to be a good thing. I agree with you on some of the Amish rules and ways. It's hard, Senta, trying to figure out how to live in this modern world while keeping our traditions. Remember, the reason we're opposed to materialism is because material possessions can make a person prideful and take focus away from God and Jesus."

The two talked for a while, Senta feeling much better being able to talk openly and honestly to her friend. "But remember," said Abigail, "if you go with him, it won't be easy. The community will feel you are rejecting them. They will shun you. The bishop will remove you from the order." The two hugged and Senta walked down the road toward her home remembering all that Abigail had said. Senta considered how fortunate she was to have a friend who understood her and she could confide in.

"Mr. and Mrs. King stopped by while you were at Abigail's,"

said Mrs. Miller as Senta walked into the kitchen. "Mrs. Yost passed away last night. There won't be any Farmers' Market tomorrow, Senta. It will be Mrs. Yost's funeral. It will take most of the day. I want to drive our own buggy tomorrow. Sugar hasn't been working very hard of late. We ride with the Lapps so often that she doesn't get much exercise other than being out in the pasture." Senta agreed.

Saturday came, and it was the day Jerrick would be boarding an airplane and flying thousands of miles away. Senta checked the calendar, looking three to four weeks out to determine when he might be back. Jerrick was on her mind as she dressed for the funeral. Senta had a sense of foreboding, and she didn't know why. Everything was perfect except for the Amish issue. At last, she decided it was for fear the airliner might crash. Saying a quick prayer of protection for Jerrick on his trip, she walked back to the house.

After the mail arrived, Senta walked to the mailbox expecting bills. Senta never received personal mail. She didn't buy anything online; she wasn't on any mailing lists. As she walked back to the house thumbing through the various envelopes-electric bill, water bill, real estate taxes-Senta stopped in her tracks. One hand-written letter was addressed to her. Curiously there was no return address. Senta's heart soared, immediately thinking it was from Jerrick. Opening the envelope carefully so as not to tear it, she read:

> Dear Senta,
> I'm flying out tomorrow. I miss you already.
> I had a great time last night. I'll call you as soon
> as I get back. Be sure to save me some cheese!
>
> Your boyfriend,
> Jerrick

PS For your Spotify playlist. "I Don't Want To Miss A Thing" / Aerosmith

Fighting back tears of joy, Senta ran to the house and

then up the stairs to her room to find her cell phone. She put in the ear buds and typed in the title. In a few seconds, the song was playing. Holding the letter and reading it over and over, she pressed it to her cheek. When the song ended, she took out the earbuds only to find her mother calling for her. Quickly, she pulled herself together and joined her mother to leave for the funeral.

The mother and daughter, both dressed in black, came out the kitchen door and climbed into the black buggy. The summer heat was oppressive as the steam rose from the asphalt. As they made the three-mile journey to the Yost house, they were joined by other black buggies that soon became a convoy. Senta recognized John and Abigail ahead of them. At the Yost's house, the black buggies lined up in perfect order and the occupants filed into the house in silence.

Inside, there was a long line of people waiting to pay their respects to Mr. Yost. When it was their turn, Senta's mother spoke, "Bishop Yost, we are so sorry for your loss. Mrs. Yost was a fine woman and will be sorely missed by everyone." Senta stood by her mother and nodded her head in accordance to her mother's words. Eric Yost also nodded his appreciation of the condolences, and smiled a forlorn smile at Mrs. Miller. Then he turned to Senta and gave a stern look which turned into a devious smile. The look made a shiver run up Senta's spine, as she felt fear and apprehension. She tried to shake off the feeling.

The funeral service at the Yost home was long and hot. The burial was in the cemetery down the road. Senta felt an overwhelming sadness. Perhaps it was because her father was buried there, or perhaps it was Eric Yost. All she knew was that she wanted the service to end, and she wanted to go home. When it finally did end and she and her mother were walking back to the buggy, Abigail came running up. "Abigail, you shouldn't be running," said Senta. "In fact, you should be at home resting."

"Hello, Mrs. Miller," said Abigail almost out of breath. "I need to talk to you, Senta," she said looking at Senta and glancing at her mother. "It won't take but just a moment. It's a cheese question. I need to ask you something about the cheese for next week." Senta nodded, put her mother in the buggy, and then walked around the back of the buggy to where Abigail was waiting.

"What's wrong?" asked Senta.

"Yesterday evening, Eric Yost came to the house," said Abigail, still catching her breath. "He knows about Jerrick. Mrs. King told him. He asked John and me what we knew about him. Of course, John doesn't know anything. I said he was a customer who buys cheese from us. I told Bishop Yost his name. That's all I said. I didn't say anything else. He's furious, Senta. I don't know what he's going to do, but he's irate."

"His wife just died, wasn't even buried yet, and he's doing this," said Senta. "I could feel it when we paid our condolences. He is very angry with me. What if he orders us to stop selling cheese at the Farmers' Market?"

"Bishop Yost doesn't like it that you have an English *friend*. You should have seen him when I said his name. It was pure hatred," said Abigail.

"I'm afraid," said Senta. "Thank you for telling me, Abigail. I'm going to take my mother home now." With a parting hug, the two women returned to their buggies.

"Is everything alright?" asked Senta's mother as they drove home.

"Yes, everything is fine," Senta lied. A short while later Senta asked, "Mother, did you see how Mr. Yost looked at me today?"

"Yes, he was sad. He's very distraught. Losing your spouse is one of the hardest things you can ever go through, Senta," said Mrs. Miller. Senta nodded but knew her mother had not noticed. Senta wondered with dread as to what might happen next. *What would he do and how would he do it?* She began feeling apprehensive the next day, Sunday, when she would be in the same building with him again. Would he say something to her mother? Sunday came and went with nothing happening out of the ordinary. Monday morning, however, would be different.

Sally arrived with the invoices on Monday morning. After talking business over coffee, Senta walked Sally out to her car. Sally always looked forward to that time to hear about what had happened with Jerrick. She then would update Suzanne back at the office. Senta excitedly told her about the date and the letter and how Jerrick called her his girlfriend. Then she told her about how Mrs. King had seen them together at the Farmers' Market and told the Bishop. Sally hugged her and told her it would all work out.

Back inside, Senta went upstairs and started to work. Time passed quickly as she processed invoices. Mid-morning, Senta looked up from her desk and saw something that filled her with fear. It was as if an alarm was sounding the warning of an impending attack. A line of black buggies was approaching the Miller home. Senta was filled with dread as she ran downstairs and informed her mother that company was coming.

"Who would be coming to see us on a Monday morning?" asked Sarah Miller as they walked through the parlor to open the front door. From the doorway, Senta and her mother watched as buggies were being tied up. Senta found a certain amount of comfort that her friends, John and Abigail, had gotten out of the last buggy. Bishop Yost and eleven senior men of the Amish community began making their way to the front door. Also, accompanying Yost was a stranger, a distinguished looking older gentleman wearing a black suit. "What is going on?" Mrs. Miller asked her daughter as the group passed through the gate and up the sidewalk.

"Mrs. Miller," said Eric Yost in a serious and stern tone. "May we come in? We have some pressing business to discuss with you and your daughter."

"Yes, of course," said Mrs. Miller. "There aren't enough chairs for everyone. I wasn't expecting so many people. I actually wasn't expecting anyone."

"We don't need chairs for everyone, Mrs. Miller," answered Eric Yost. "Some of us can stand. Let's just make sure Abigail Lapp has a chair due to her condition. Mrs. Miller, you and Senta can sit there," said Eric Yost indicating two chairs that were positioned side by side.

When everyone was inside, either seated or standing, Eric Yost began. "We are here today, Mrs. Miller and Miss Miller, to investigate the whereabouts and activities of one *Jerrick Douglas*."

"Jerrick Douglas? Who is Jerrick Douglas?" asked Mrs.

Miller.

"I think your daughter may know more about him than anyone here," said Eric Yost turning to Senta. "Perhaps you should ask her."

Thoroughly confused Senta's mother turned to her daughter. "Senta, do you know him? Are you acquainted with someone named Jerrick Douglas?"

Senta looked at her mother and then turned her head to look at Eric Yost, "Yes, I know Jerrick Douglas."

"And can you tell everyone here how you know him?" demanded Yost.

Taking a deep breath and sitting very straight, she answered, "Abigail Lapp and I make cheese and sell it at the Farmers' Market in Nashville. We go with Mrs. King and Mrs. Belier every Saturday. Jerrick Douglas is one of our customers." Mrs. Miller looked back and forth between her daughter and Yost, baffled as to where the conversation was headed.

"Is your relationship with Jerrick Douglas solely a business one, or is it more? Let me remind you, Miss Miller, that we already know it is more. We know you have been eating lunch with him and gallivanting around the Farmers' Market with him, laughing and behaving in a manner very inappropriate for an unmarried woman. Give me your cell phone!" Yost ordered. Senta reached into her apron pocket and handed over her phone. He tapped the iPhone bringing up Contacts, and there was the name he was looking for. Holding up the phone for all to see, the name *Jerrick Douglas* was displayed on the screen. "Proof! Proof that our sources are correct! Have you ever spoken to Jerrick Douglas on the phone?" he demanded.

"Yes," Senta said. "One time. He called after the tornado to see if I was alright." Abigail sat in the corner holding John's hand so tightly that it was sure to leave marks. Senta's mother sat in disbelief at the information being presented.

"Who is Jerrick Douglas?" asked Mrs. Miller.

"That is an excellent question, Mrs. Miller," said Yost. "A question we would all like to know the answer to. Especially you, Miss Miller. Do you really know who your *friend* is?" Senta said nothing and sat as still as if she were dead, almost wishing that she was. "Well, we have the answer to these questions," said Yost as he extended his hand toward the English visitor in the suit. "We have been investigating this and have enlisted the help of Mr. Ethan Ward. Ethan Ward, the Attorney General of the State of Tennessee." The room was silent as Mr. Ward stepped forward.

Mrs. Miller, was shocked. With her eyes closed, Sarah Miller shook her head and spoke. "Senta, what have you done?"

"I am Ethan Ward, Attorney General of the State of Tennessee," stated the distinguished looking visitor. "I was contacted by Mr. Yost on this matter, the matter of Jerrick Douglas." Mr. Ward paced a few steps, then turned to the group. "Jerrick Douglas is a convicted felon. He's done time in the Kentucky prison system for bank fraud, as well as mail fraud. Basically, he is a con man. We're not sure how many times he's been married, but it's several. He preys on women, widows mostly. He romances them, marries them, takes their money, and then leaves them. Now, it appears he's operating in Tennessee," said the Attorney General, looking directly at Senta. Mrs. Miller stared at her daughter in disbelief, wondering how all this could have been going on without her knowledge. Eric Yost stood back with his arms folded, glaring at a heartbroken Senta Miller. The others looked on sternly while Abigail sat in the back, tears running down her cheeks.

"Miss Miller," continued Mr. Ward. "I have some delicate and personal questions to ask you. This is difficult and I'm sorry, but I must ask. Have you given Mr. Douglas any money?"

"No, of course not," said Senta. "He's never asked for anything."

"Alright, that's good. Apparently, the con hadn't reached that point yet," said the Attorney General. "My next question is a more difficult one. Has your relationship with Mr. Douglas become romantic?"

Senta thought quickly, hoping they were only aware of the Farmers' Market and what Mrs. King had told them. "He is my friend," she said, not lying, but not telling the whole truth.

"Very well then," said Mr. Ward. "And the final question is this. Have you had sexual relations with Mr. Douglas?" Senta's mother gasped.

"I have not!" said Senta, indignantly. "I resent such a question!"

"Very well," said Mr. Ward. "I had to ask. Mr. Douglas generally romances women, has sex with them, marries them .... sometimes.... before he steals their money."

Senta's mind was in turmoil. *This can't be true!* she thought. *Please, please, God, don't let this be true! Was Abigail right when she was skeptical of him?* Then something came to her, and with as much courage as she could muster, she asked the Attorney General, "If Mr. Douglas is a con man, why would he bother with me? Wouldn't he have asked me questions, trying to find out if I was wealthy? I'm not a wealthy widow. I don't have anything."

"We don't understand the twisted mind of a criminal, Miss Miller," offered the Attorney General. "We just try to protect and serve the decent law-abiding citizens of our great state." Yost and the other men all solemnly nodded their approval to his answer. Senta thought, *he's the Attorney General, he must be right, but he can't be.* She turned to her mother. With a deep look of disappointment and humiliation, her mother turned away and shook her head.

"Miss Miller, as Attorney General I am ordering you to have no further contact with Jerrick Douglas. He is a dangerous man and will very soon be back in prison. If not here, in some other state. Don't talk to him, don't write letters to him, do not call him. This is for your protection," warned Ethan Ward.

"Thank you, Mr. Ward, for taking time out of your busy Monday to deal with this urgent and most serious situation," said Eric Yost handing the cell phone back to Senta. "She won't be calling him as I have blocked his number. I've also removed his name and number from Contacts." The elders nodded in approval while John and Abigail looked on in silence. "Miss Miller, it is very fortunate we were able to get this stopped before it ended badly," said Yost. "Jerrick Douglas has left a long line of destroyed women in his wake. We are all glad you won't be one of them. Don't be angry with Mrs. King or the Lapps for telling us about this. We only have your welfare at heart. Thank you all for coming and doing this today. The meeting is adjourned."

One by one they filed out along with Yost and the Attorney General. The last man to walk outside was John Lapp. Abigail gave him a look of *I'll be out shortly*. Senta who had held her composure throughout the interrogation turned to her mother and reached out for her hand. Sarah Miller jerked her hand away from her daughter, refusing to even look at her. Then she stood and left the room. Senta turned to Abigail and then broke into tears.

"It's OK, Senta," said Abigail, comforting her friend in an embrace. "We will get through this. Your mother will come around. Just give her time."

"What have I done, Abigail?" cried Senta. "Is this possible? I can't believe these things about Jerrick. When he gets back from Guatemala, he will straighten this all out."

"Senta, sweetheart, he's not coming back," said Abigail, trying her best to console her friend. "He's not in Guatemala. And saying he can't be reached for weeks at a time.... that's not true. He's in Kentucky or Arkansas, working on another con." Senta sobbed on her friend's shoulder until it was wet. "There was no coffee company. There's no boat. Those are all lies. Senta, you're right. He figured out you didn't have any money to steal, so he moved on."

A short time later, the last buggy had left the Miller farm. Senta went to her mother trying to talk to her again, but she had locked the door to her bedroom. Neither Senta nor her mother ate dinner that night. Senta lay in her bed, reading the letter over and over searching for a clue somewhere in the words that would explain it all. Finally, after the sun set, she cried again and fell asleep, emotionally exhausted.

The next day Senta made breakfast and tried to get her mother to come out from the bedroom to eat, but she wouldn't. Though in a daze, Senta worked on her invoices, trying to forget what had happened the day before. Her mind kept moving between accepting what she'd heard from the Attorney General and believing there was some explanation. Sarah Miller finally came out of her room and ate some lunch but would not speak to her daughter. Senta tried to hug her but was pushed away. It wasn't until the next day that her mother spoke, "This is why you have been acting so strangely and asking all those questions. I knew something was different. You lied to me. You may still be lying to me."

"I did lie to you, Mother," Senta said. "I'm sorry. I hated lying to you, but I knew you wouldn't approve of him. I knew you would forbid me to talk to him. I love him, Mother."

"Foolish, foolish girl," snapped her mother. "Did you not hear the Attorney General? He is a criminal! I am so ashamed of you, that you have been so stupid!"

"I'm sorry, Mother. Please forgive me," said Senta.

Still refusing to look at her daughter, Mrs. Miller said, "I guess I should be grateful that this isn't worse than what it is. I'm glad that Mrs. King saw you and your *friend* carrying on together and told her husband." Finally, she let her daughter hug her, and the two reached some reconciliation. It was clear to Senta that her mother would never understand. She stopped trying to explain her feelings and was grateful her mother would speak to her again.

The week passed in a quiet truce. Sarah Miller gradually became kinder with her daughter. Remembering the questions Senta had asked her in the previous weeks, Sarah came to realize that her daughter had truly been in love with the man at the Farmers' Market, or at least Senta believed she had been. The stress and strain of the week made Sarah feel her age. She worried about what could happen to Senta when she was gone.

When Saturday came, Senta and Abigail stayed home and didn't go to Nashville for the Farmers' Market. Abigail needed rest. Mrs. Miller had forbidden Senta to go. Senta hoped that time might change things.

That afternoon Senta and her mother worked on a quilt that Mrs. Miller had started back in the winter. It was a double nine patch pattern. They were using some of Elijah's clothing to make the solid black squares of the pattern. The quilt was very close to completion, and Senta was helping her mother with the finishing touches. Working on the quilt together had been therapeutic for both of them. The pieces from Mr. Miller's clothing had made this quilt special, almost as if he was with them.

Senta and her mother discussed the newly finished quilt over supper. They were very pleased with how it had turned out. Senta couldn't wait to show it to Abigail.

It was after dinner, that Mrs. Miller complained of feeling ill, describing what seemed to be an upset stomach. Later in the evening, she started having trouble breathing. Senta recognized the situation had become serious and called 911. While waiting for the ambulance to arrive, Senta held her mother's hand and said, "I'm so sorry I've caused so much grief, Mother. I didn't...."

"Shhhh, Senta," interrupted her mother between labored breaths. "I'm sorry, too."

"I love you, Mother," said Senta. "Please forgive me."

"Yes," her mother said. "And I love you."

Senta finally felt that everything was right between them. Senta prayed silently as her mother drifted in and out of consciousness.

When the EMTs arrived, they quickly determined Mrs. Miller needed to be transported to the hospital. Senta was allowed to ride in the ambulance with her mother since she didn't have a car to follow behind. Senta heard one of the paramedics direct the driver to Vanderbilt Medical in Nashville. It was a heart attack. Senta knelt by her mother, holding her hand and stroking her hair while the paramedics worked. Sirens, flashing lights and taking corners at high speed blurred time for Senta as her mother fought for her life. Despite the oxygen and IV's, she was unconscious as they turned off Hillsboro Avenue to the emergency room entrance. The staff at Vanderbilt Medical did all they could, but Mrs. Miller was pronounced dead twenty minutes later.

Once again Senta found herself alone, this time more alone than she had ever been. Her father was gone, Jerrick was gone, and now her mother. She cried in the waiting room at the hospital feeling responsible for her mother's death due to the stress from the Jerrick Douglas ordeal. A nurse at the Emergency Room who was from Ashland City took Senta home when her shift ended. The nurse asked if she'd be alright alone. Senta nodded yes. She walked in the quiet, empty house and then ran outside into the darkness. Stopping at the pasture fence, she was reminded that even the cows were gone. Running on into the barn she found Sugar and cried on the mare's neck until she had no energy left. Not wanting to go back in the house, she walked down the road to the Lapp's house where she knocked on their door at 3:30 in the morning. John and Abigail welcomed her and cared for her.

The funeral was the next Tuesday. Just like before, time ran together for Senta. John and Abigail stood by her until Abigail had to sit down due to contractions. Sally, Suzanne, Mr. Campbell, and everyone else from the Ashland City office came. Senta heard none of the bishop's words as he preached her mother's funeral. After the service at the Miller home the long line of black buggies made its way to the cemetery, then back again to the house. Senta was in a daze; she was functioning but not actually aware as she talked to friends and neighbors. It was a Godsend when Abigail went into hard labor. Senta came out of her malaise, focusing on helping her friend. Senta thanked everyone and sent them home. She and John got Abigail in the buggy and back to their house where they waited for the midwife.

Abigail labored through the afternoon and into the evening. Although exhausted from the events of the past week, Senta refused any rest. She stayed by the midwife's side, assisting with the birth. Then, at 7:02 p.m., the Lapps were blessed with a perfect baby girl who was given the name Rachel. Senta had never seen John so overjoyed! As Senta held the newborn, tears streamed down her face as the dam of emotion inside her broke. It was more than the sense of relief that Abigail and the baby were fine. The birth of baby Rachel was the culminating point at which Senta exchanged the feelings of sadness and loss for joy and hope.

"Would you stay here with us tonight?" asked John. He made the request partly because Senta was such good help and partly because he was concerned about her being alone in her house."

"Yes, I will," said Senta. "There is much to do for Abigail, the baby, and for you, John. You've not had anything to eat. I will ask Abigail if she feels like eating anything, and then I'll go prepare some supper."

The next day Senta walked back to her house. She loaded some clothes, her computer and files for work into her buggy that she'd hitched to Sugar. She called Sally and told her she'd moved temporarily to Abigail's house to help with the baby and asked that her work be delivered there for the next few weeks. Sally was happy to comply.

The summer dragged on, and the hot days melted together until they were almost indiscernible. Farmers watched the weather closely, praying for rain as the oppressive heat threatened to destroy their crops. Senta poured all her energy into her work and the infant. Baby Rachel was an easy baby. John and Abigail didn't mind that Senta had stayed on as she was always ready to rock the baby, change the baby, bathe the baby and help in the kitchen. In between all those duties she worked on her bookkeeping. Sally and Suzanne loved coming to the Lapps to see Senta, Abigail, and the new baby. Both made the trip to deliver the paperwork even though one would have been sufficient. The tradition of drinking coffee after making that delivery was continued now in the Lapp's kitchen. John Lapp was very content with the arrangement and appreciated the help Senta afforded his wife.

The cheese making had ceased due to the new circumstances in their lives. Since quite a bit of inventory remained in Senta's cellar, Abigail and Senta had given it to Mrs. King and Mrs. Belier to sell at the Farmers' Market. When the last of it was sold, Abigail and Senta received their money in an envelope, thus ending that chapter.

As Senta divided the bills in half, fives and ones. She remembered a five-dollar bill and two one-dollar bills she still had in a box in her bedroom a quarter of a mile down the road. Stopping in the middle of her counting, she wondered where Jerrick Douglas was, what he was doing and if he was well. Had he even given her another thought? She pushed all that away; it was best to think of other things. She didn't want to start crying again. Senta finished counting out the money then went to check on baby Rachel who was always a sweet and welcome distraction.

After working all morning, Senta said, "Abigail, do you think John would mind if I brought Sugar here to your farm? It would be easier because I have to walk down everyday to give her water and some oats. I will pay you for her keep."

"I'm sure John won't mind. And we won't let you pay us for Sugar's keep after everything you do for us," said Abigail.

"Thank you, Abigail," said Senta. "I'll go and bring her back before lunch."

Senta walked down the road toward her home, the sun not quite as hot as it had been in August and the light wind just a little cooler. When she got to the house, she went upstairs and took the box from her closet. She removed the letter and the seven dollars and put them in the pocket of her apron. She walked through the house making sure everything looked alright and then thought she should call the post office to see if she could get her mail delivered at the Lapps. She went out the kitchen door as she had thousands of times noticing how quiet the house was and how she almost expected to see her mother walk around the corner at any moment. She went to the barn looking for Sugar who was out in the pasture. Sugar came running as she always did, and Senta put a halter on her to lead her back to the Lapps. As Senta walked out of the barn leading her mare, she froze in her tracks. There, standing directly in front of her in the gravel drive, arms folded, was Eric Yost.

"Well, if it isn't Miss Senta Miller," said the bishop. "What are you doing here? And what are you doing with my horse?"

Not being sure if she had heard him correctly, Senta answered, "I am living with the Lapps and helping them with the baby. I walk home every day to feed and water Sugar. I thought it would be easier to take her to the Lapps."

"That would be fine if that was your horse, Senta," said Yost. "But that's not your horse, it's mine. So technically, you're stealing my horse, and technically, you're trespassing on my property."

Not believing what she was hearing, Senta said, "What are you talking about? Your property and your horse? This was my parents' farm. Now that they are gone, it is mine."

"Come along," said Yost, turning and walking toward the front of the house where his horse and buggy were tied up. "Let me enlighten you." Senta, not trusting him, followed at a distance, leading her mare.

When Yost got to his buggy, he reached inside and retrieved a large manila envelope. "Tie the horse to the wheel here," he said pointing to the wheel of his buggy. "And come sit with me on the front porch. I'll explain this all to you."

Senta followed him to the front porch where she sat as far from Yost as she could on the swing. Yost opened the envelope and removed a document that he handed to Senta. "Your mother was very concerned about you and distressed about what would happen to you when she was gone," said Yost. Senta read the document, not fully comprehending its meaning. But seeing *Quit Claim Deed* and the name *Eric Yost* clarified everything. "Your mother was afraid that without a man to take care of you there would be no telling what kind of trouble you'd get in. Your actions of late with the Jerrick Douglas incident only confirmed your mother's concern. So, she put the farm in joint name with me just in case she might pass. Now that she is gone, ownership reverts to me, not you. I own the farm, the house, and your horse.

Senta sat in the swing almost physically shaking while inside her emotions and thoughts ran wild. *Can he do this?* she thought. *Is there anything else that I can lose?* "Can you do this?" she asked, her voice shaking.

"I didn't do this," he said. "Your mother did. She did it for your own protection. I know how badly you must feel, alone, deceived by that Douglas fellow, losing your parents, and your farm. It must be painful, but I want to help you."

Doubting Yost's every word, Senta responded, "You have never wanted to help me. You were the one who decided I couldn't go to the singings after my father had his stroke. You have always despised me. I don't know why. I've never done anything to you. You don't like it that I work for Mr. Campbell. And you didn't like it when you thought I might have a boyfriend."

"Now, Senta, I'm going to just let all that pass because

I know how upset you are over the loss your mother and the humiliation of being used by Douglas. I'm here to help you. There is a way to make this all work out for you, and for you to continue to live on your farm. I am a widower now and in need of a wife. I want you to be my wife," said Yost. He reached over and put his hand on Senta's knee, moving it up slightly as he watched her reaction. Slapping his hand and jumping up, she ran down the stairs of the porch to the buggy where she untied her mare.

"I should call the police and report you as a horse thief," yelled Yost as Senta took off running down the drive with Sugar in tow. "But I won't. The horse is old, Senta, like you! You'd better reconsider! You're not 18 any more, you know! No one will ever want you!"

Senta ran all the way back to the Lapps' farm, looking behind her from time to time to see if Yost was following. A feeling of complete abandonment overwhelmed her as tears streamed down her face. The thought of Yost wanting to marry her was revolting, and remembering his hand on her knee almost made her ill. *I've lost both my parents*, she thought. *Jerrick has abandoned me, if he ever really wanted me. What will become of me? The bishop is right. I'm no longer 18.*

When she got to the house she ran to the kitchen where John, Abigail and the baby were eating lunch. Senta cried, pouring out her heart about what had happened. They listened and Abigail comforted her as she sobbed on her shoulder. John reassured her that she had a home with them.

Abigail was appalled by the ordeal Senta had endured. *Yost is so evil,* she thought. *He has even stolen her home. I am afraid he will have us shunned for letting Senta live with us. But if she can't live here, she will be homeless.* "There is nothing we can do except pray for God's help," Abigail said. "Pray that He will intervene. Pray that He will show us a way out of this."

CHAPTER TWELVE

A.G. Ward

Three days later at 9:32 a.m. Jerrick Douglas pulled into the Lapps' driveway. Upon his return, he had phoned Senta, but there was no answer. Fearing that something was wrong, he'd called Sally at Aaron Campbell's office, but she had hung up on him. He had driven for three hours to Senta's house only to find it deserted. He walked back to the barn and saw that even the horse was gone! Not knowing where else to turn, he drove to the Lapp farm, parked in front of the house, walked up to the front door and knocked.

"I hear wheels on the gravel out front," said Abigail. "Do we have visitors, Senta?" Senta went to the parlor and looked out the window. She saw the white SUV and immediately recognized it. Jerrick stood outside the door knocking while Senta stood just a few feet away on the inside wanting desperately to answer it but knowing she shouldn't. From the kitchen, Abigail said, "Get the door, Senta. Someone's at the front door."

Senta hurried back to the kitchen. "It's Jerrick. He's here," she whispered, not knowing what to do.

"Oh, no! Don't answer it," said Abigail. "I can't believe he's come back. I thought we'd seen the last of him. Stay away from the window, Senta. He'll think there's no one home and leave." Jerrick stood at the front door and knocked even louder, but when no one came, he walked around the house and back toward the barn.

Upon entering the barn, he saw John Lapp who was cleaning the milking equipment. "Are you John .... John Lapp?" asked Jerrick.

"Yes, I am," answered John. "What can I do for you?"

"My name is Jerrick Douglas. I'm a friend of Senta Miller. I also know your wife, Abigail," he said. "I'm looking for Senta, and I can't find her. There's no one at her house."

"You're not welcome here. Leave now," John said with a stern look as he continued to clean the milking equipment.

"John .... may I call you John? I am sorry to interrupt your work, but I thought perhaps your wife might know where Senta is," Jerrick said.

"And I said you're not welcome here; get off my property!" ordered John. "We do not want criminals here!"

"Criminals?" Jerrick said. "What are you talking about? What do you mean by that?"

"I mean that you're a felon, Mr. Douglas. I mean that you've been in prison in Kentucky. I mean that you take advantage of women and steal their money. Now get out!" said John.

"John, I realize we've never met," said Jerrick. "But I have no idea what you're talking about. I really don't. Do you have me confused with someone else?"

"*Mr.* Douglas," said John *sarcastically*. "You can stop with the act. The Attorney General came here and told us all about you. We know. Senta knows. It's over!"

"The Attorney General?" asked Jerrick, still trying to understand what was going on. "The Attorney General of Tennessee?"

"That's right," said John. "He came with the bishop to the Miller house and spoke with Mrs. Miller and Senta. The bishop requested Abigail and me to be there also. We heard it with our own ears. Now, I won't tell you again. Get off my land!"

"John," said Jerrick. "I will leave, but please, just a few more questions. Was the Attorney General named Ethan Ward?"

"That's right," said John.

"And he was here? When?" asked Jerrick.

"He was at Senta's house, a month ago," answered John.

"What did the Attorney General look like?" asked Jerrick.

"Oh, mid-60's, gray hair, beard," said John.

Jerrick got out his iPhone and quickly started tapping the screen. "What are you doing?" demanded John.

"John, look at this man in this picture. Is this the Attorney General?" asked Jerrick, holding up his phone for John to see.

John looked closely at the picture and responded, "No, that's not the Attorney General. That's a young man."

"John," said Jerrick calmly typing more words into his phone. "I understand that I'm a stranger to you. It sounds like you have been told all sorts of things about me. It may be hard to believe and perhaps you don't want to believe me, but look at this photo from the newspaper. This is the Attorney General. He's in his thirties, no beard." He waited briefly for John to read the newspaper caption. "John, I have no idea as to what's going on, but you have been deceived. The man who you're talking about was not the Attorney General."

John looked at the photograph again. Then half angry and half confused asked, "But why would someone pretend to be the Attorney General?"

"I have no clue," said Jerrick. "But I'm going to find out. We need to get to the bottom of this. Your bishop needs to know. We all need to know. John, will you help me?"

"Maybe. What do you have in mind?" asked John cautiously.

"Can you give me a couple of hours?" asked Jerrick. "I must go to Nashville right now and see the Attorney General. And I need you to go with me!"

John looked at Jerrick, wanting to trust him, but then remembered the Attorney General's warning that Douglas was a con man. But .... what if the Attorney General wasn't the Attorney General. What if it was a lie?

Understanding John's turmoil, Jerrick chose his words carefully and continued, "John, please. Senta needs your help. Will you, please, do this for her?"

John considered Senta and the tragedies she'd been

through before finally responding, "Let's go. I'm not going to tell Abigail and Senta. Let's go, now!"

"They're here, in the house?" asked Jerrick. "I didn't think anyone was home. Is Senta alright?"

"They're fine. They probably didn't answer the door because they're afraid of you," said John.

In the kitchen, Abigail was looking out the window above the sink while Senta sat at the kitchen table holding baby Rachel. "What is John doing talking to him?" asked Abigail. "Why doesn't he tell him to leave? Now they're walking around the front."

Abigail ran through the house to the window in the parlor. "What is John doing? Senta, he's getting in Douglas' SUV." With the baby in her arms, Senta scurried to the parlor window, just in time to see the two men drive away and turn on the road heading east. "Senta, I'm afraid," whispered Abigail.

"Abigail," said Senta softly. "Try to be calm. Didn't John leave willingly? I don't believe Jerrick would force him to go. I know terrible things have been said about him, but I just can't believe Jerrick would hurt John."

The white Range Rover headed toward Nashville while the two men sat in silence. Finally, Jerrick asked, "How is Senta? When I stopped by her house and she wasn't there, I didn't know what to think. I'm glad to hear that she was with you and Abigail."

"She's doing alright, considering," said John. "She is living with us now; it's for the best."

"Living with you?" Jerrick asked with surprise. "Why has she moved in with you? How about Mrs. Miller?"

"Mrs. Miller passed away several weeks ago," said John.

"Oh my God, I had no idea!" said Jerrick. "Poor Senta. How did it happen?"

"She went very quickly. The doctors said it was a heart attack," answered John. "Then the very day of the funeral, Abigail went into labor and our daughter was born that night."

"Abigail has had the baby! A girl?" exclaimed Jerrick. "I can't believe all this has happened. What is her name? Are she and Abigail OK?"

"We named her Rachel. And, yes, they're both doing

fine. Senta has been so much help for Abigail."

"That's good news," said Jerrick. "So Senta is living with you to help care for Abigail and the baby?"

"Originally, yes," said John. "Senta didn't want to be in the house alone after her mother passed. And we have appreciated the help, but now there's another reason." John paused and sat in silence considering whether to tell Jerrick about Bishop Yost. Perhaps he'd already said too much.

Jerrick waited for the response that didn't come so he finally asked, "John, what is the other reason Senta is living with you and Abigail?"

Taking a deep breath, John said, "She's lost her farm. Apparently, Mrs. Miller put Eric Yost's name on the farm a few months ago. The bishop convinced Mrs. Miller that Senta wasn't capable of handling the farm. Senta had no idea her mother had done this. When she passed, the farm became Bishop Yost's property."

"But why? This isn't true. Senta is perfectly capable of handling her own financial affairs," said Jerrick. "And then there's this crazy story about the Attorney General and his story about me. Why?"

"Senta and the Bishop got in quite a fight," continued John. "The bishop is recently widowed. His wife had been ill for some time. Yost proposed marriage to Senta. I think he may have tried to use the farm to get her to agree to the marriage .... so she could get her farm back."

"Unbelievable!" exclaimed Jerrick processing all the news. "John, you said earlier that Bishop Yost .... that's Eric Yost, right? He came to Senta's house with the Attorney General who said I was a con man and convicted felon, right?"

"Yes, that's correct," answered John.

"That son of a bitch," said Jerrick. "Eric Yost wants to marry Senta?"

"Yes, he proposed to her," said John. "But she said no."

"That's it. There's your motive," said Jerrick. "I'm competition. He had to get me out of the way, hoping then that Senta would marry him out of desperation to reclaim the family farm. That Attorney General was an actor, someone Yost got to pretend to be the Attorney General for the performance you saw."

John shook his head, trying to get it all straight. "But where are we going now?"

"We're going to Nashville to see the Attorney General, the real Attorney General."

"But you can't just walk into the Attorney General's office," John said.

Jerrick glanced over at John and said with a smile, "You can if you know him. Watch me." Jerrick touched the phone icon on the steering wheel and said, "Call Contact. Call Ethan Ward." After two rings, Ethan Ward answered.

"Jerrick, how are you?" asked the friendly voice that came through the sound system of the vehicle enabling John to hear the conversation as well.

"I'm good," said Jerrick. "But, there's a problem. I need to see you. A friend of mine has a problem that involves you."

"Really," said Ethan. "How so?"

"It's more than complicated," said Jerrick. "You're not going to believe it. You can't make this stuff up. I need to tell you in person, and I have someone with me I'd like you to meet. Could we stop by your office?"

"Now you've got me curious, Jerrick," said Ethan. "Sure! Where are you? Kentucky? Guatemala? When can you come by?"

"We're only about twenty minutes out," said Jerrick.

"Well, then come on," said Ethan. "They've got me in the John Sevier Building. It's kind of a mess right now because all the offices for the legislature are being moved. It'll be nice when it's done, but for now it's a mess. Just come in the front door, and someone will direct you. See you shortly."

"We'll be right there," said Jerrick. "Bye."

John sat in the copilot seat trying to process everything he had just heard. "*That* was the Attorney General," he said.

"Yep, the youngest Attorney General in Tennessee history. He's only thirty-two," said Jerrick.

"And you know him?" said John.

"Yep, I've known him for years," said Jerrick. "I was at

the ceremony when he graduated Belmont Law. He's been to my house, and he's been on my boat so many times I can't count them."

"Guatemala," said John. "So that's true....... the coffee company? And the boat....... that's true?"

"Yes, John, that's all true," said Jerrick. Shortly thereafter, they took the I-65 exit and were soon parking at the John Sevier Building. The receptionist directed them to the Attorney General's office where Ethan Ward's secretary showed the two men into the office of the Attorney General of the state of Tennessee. John Lapp had gone from being angry to completely confused about everything that had transpired.

"Ethan, I said you're not going to believe this, so let me get right to it," Jerrick said after introductions had been made and the three men sat down together. "I met a woman named Senta Miller at the Farmers' Market here in Nashville back in the spring. Miss Miller and John's wife, Abigail, make cheese on their farms over in Cheatham County. The women sell the cheese at the Farmers' Market. Miss Miller and I became friends and now we are dating." Ethan smiled a curious smile, and John looked at Jerrick with surprise as they heard the word *dating*. "I know, I know, she's Amish and I'm not," he continued. "I've been gone to Guatemala and when I get back all hell's broken lose. Sorry, John," as he looked over at his Amish friend. "Now, Ethan, here's where it gets interesting."

At that point, Ethan Ward couldn't help himself. With a laugh, he said, "Oh, I'd say it's already interesting."

"A man named Eric Yost, another Amish farmer in Cheatham County," Jerrick continued, "who is also the bishop of the Amish community there, arrived at the Miller house with a man who claimed to be the Attorney General of Tennessee." Ethan Ward sat up straight and leaned forward in his chair, raising one eyebrow. "The Attorney General, a man in his mid-60's, with a beard no less. John Lapp was there and saw this. He proceeded to tell everyone present, including Senta and her mother, that I'm a felon. That I've been in prison in Kentucky. That I'm a con man who preys on women and steals their money. He said they were tracking me and were going to arrest me. Soon after, Mrs.

Miller passed away, possibly from the stress of discovering her daughter was seeing me. Senta hadn't told her about me since I'm not Amish. After the funeral, Senta was told by Yost that her mother signed the farm over to him and that the only way she could get it back was to marry him."

Ethan sat back in his seat and exhaled, "Wow, I've never had anyone impersonate me before. That's a first. Mr. Lapp, you witnessed all this?" asked the Attorney General.

"Yes, sir!" said John. "And there's something else. Maybe it's nothing, but it might be important. About five years ago, Eric Yost bought the Yoder farm next to his when Mr. Yoder died. The story was that Yost told the widow she would have to pay a lot of taxes if she sold the farm because it had gone up so much in value from the time of purchase thirty years before. He offered to *solve her problem* by buying it from her for the original price thus eliminating the tax problem."

"This Bishop Yost sounds like a real prize," laughed Ethan. "Classic projection, don't you think, Jerrick? He accuses you of what he does." Ethan sat and considered everything he'd heard. "So, we have the Miller Farm problem, potentially the Yoder Farm problem, your defamation of character problem, and the impersonation of me problem."

"I need you to get Miss Miller's farm back for her," said Jerrick. "And to bring Yost to justice."

"Yep, we can do that," said Ethan turning to John Lapp. "John, I need statements from you, your wife, and Senta Miller. Will you be home this afternoon? Let's say two o'clock this afternoon?" asked the Attorney General, looking at his watch.

"Yes, we will," said John.

"Miss Thompson," said Ethan pushing the intercom on his phone.

A few seconds later, Miss Thompson entered AG Ward's office. "Yes, sir," she said.

"Miss Thompson, rearrange my schedule for this afternoon. We're going to Cheatham County. John, would you go with Miss Thompson and give her your address," he directed. "We'll be taking statements from three people. Hmmm......, this is Tuesday. John, where is your church located?"

"We don't have church buildings," explained John. "We worship in private houses. We have services every other Sunday, and we rotate houses. This coming Sunday will be at Bishop Yost's house."

"Perfect! That's just perfect," said Ethan. "OK, John, I must stress this to you, and I'll say it again to you, your wife, and Miss Miller this afternoon. This is an *ongoing investigation* so you must not talk about this to anyone. No one. Do you understand?"

"I understand," John answered. "We will say nothing." John went out to Miss Thompson's desk and gave her the address.

After walking his visitors to the door, Ethan shook Jerrick's hand. "We'll take care of this," Ethan promised. "We'll get her farm back for her."

"Thanks, Ethan," said Jerrick. "I appreciate it. Call me if you need anything else from me."

Soon Jerrick and John were on the road heading back to Cheatham County, leaving the traffic of Nashville behind. "This is just unbelievable," said John. "Abigail and Senta, what will they say when I tell them?"

"I don't know, John. You have your hands full. All this and a new baby," said Jerrick. "Has Senta said anything about me? I can only imagine what she must have felt when she heard all the lies about me."

"She was devastated," answered John. "She's not the same person she was. We have been very concerned about her."

"Thank you for looking after her," said Jerrick. "For taking care of Senta. You don't know how much I appreciate that."

The two drove on in silence, each man lost in his own thoughts about the incredible developments of the day. Soon they were heading down the country road to the Lapp farm.

"They're back," said a very relieved Abigail who had been sitting in the parlor rocking the baby while watching for her husband. Senta ran in from the kitchen and the two women peeked out the window as John Lapp got out of the white SUV and walked up the sidewalk to the house. By the time he was to the front door, the Range Rover had pulled onto the road and was disappearing from sight.

Senta stood in the middle of the parlor, frozen again. It was that familiar feeling that something was about to happen. Senta had the foreboding sense of more bad news. She stood petrified as Abigail opened the door and John walked in. "John, what happened? Where did you go? Why did you go with him? We were worried to death!"

John looked at his wife and then at Senta. He had been rehearsing this conversation all the way from Nashville. He wasn't the most eloquent man, and this situation was particularly tangled and complicated. "Abigail, Senta, sit down, please," he said. "I don't know where to begin, so I'll just start explaining. What I'm about to tell you will be hard to believe, but I assure you this is the truth, finally, the truth." Abigail and Senta looked at each other and then back at John with dread as to what he might say.

"Yes, I went with Jerrick Douglas. We went to the Attorney General's office in Nashville." Abigail looked at her husband with surprise; Senta looked at him with dread. "Senta, I know how upset you have been over the situation concerning Jerrick. Senta, Jerrick didn't deceive you. We were lied to. We have all been mislead." Senta at first thought she had misunderstood and didn't dare believe that she had heard correctly.

"What do you mean we were lied to? The Attorney General himself told us," said Abigail, bewildered.

Shaking his head, John said, "Except the man who came here wasn't the Attorney General. I just met the Attorney General, the real Attorney General. None of the things the imposter said are true." Then, turning to Senta he said, "Senta, none of those things are true. He's not a felon. He doesn't steal money from widows. He's not been in prison."

Senta, holding her hands in front of her mouth, could hardly breathe. Almost unable to think, she slowly processed John's words. *I knew it wasn't true*, she thought. *I knew my Jerrick couldn't have done those things.* Then looking at Senta, John said, "And Senta, Jerrick really was in Guatemala. He really did have a coffee company. He really does have a boat. It's all true. He wasn't making that up." Feelings of total shock were followed by total relief. Tears of joy started streaming from Senta's eyes as she gasped for breath, still unable to talk.

Perplexed, Abigail managed to ask, "But, John, how do you know all this?"

"When Jerrick came to the barn I told him to leave," said John. "But he wouldn't, and he was obviously dumbfounded. I repeated all the things that the Attorney General had said. I even told him, 'You're a criminal. You steal from widows.' He got mad, poor man. Now I realize how wrong I was. But more than mad, he was genuinely confused. He kept asking me how I got the idea that he was a criminal. So, I told him that the Attorney General said so." John paused for a moment to collect his thoughts. "Abigail, Jerrick Douglas knows the Tennessee Attorney General. They're friends. He knew it couldn't be true especially coming from his friend. He asked me if I would go to Nashville to the Attorney General's office to get to the bottom of it. And I did."

"Oh, my God in Heaven!" exclaimed Abigail who sat on the couch with her arm around a sobbing Senta. "What have we done? How could this happen? But who was that man, the imposter Attorney General?"

"Abigail, Senta, we are going to find answers very soon. At two o'clock, to be exact. The Attorney General is coming here to our house to take our statements. He is investigating all of this. Senta, Jerrick told him to get your farm back and the Attorney General said he would. But we can't talk about any of this to anyone. Mr. Ward will explain when he gets here." At that point, the baby started crying so Abigail jumped up to get her. John patted Senta on the shoulder and then followed his wife.

As Senta sat alone in the parlor drying her eyes, she went over the turn of events in her mind. Jerrick was who he said he was, and everything else was a lie. Then came anger at Yost for what he had done to Jerrick. *Eric Yost was planning this all along*, she thought. *He hates me; yet, he wants to marry me. Just to torture me? He is so evil! When Mrs. King told Yost I might have a boyfriend, he did this to make me turn against Jerrick. Thank God, John listened to Jerrick. Thank God, Jerrick knows the Attorney General.* Senta's emotions turned to Jerrick. She wanted to see Jerrick and hold him and feel his arms around her. She wanted to kiss him a thousand times and say she was sorry for ever doubting. *Why didn't we answer the door when he came back with John?* she asked herself. And then, *why didn't he come in once they returned? Why didn't he come in and tell* us? *Is he angry with me for doubting him? Has he given up on me? I couldn't blame him if he did. Thank you, God, for bringing him back safely and for revealing this deception. Please, let him forgive me for doubting.*

After eating a quick lunch, Senta and Abigail straightened the house while awaiting the visit from the Attorney General. Right on schedule, a shiny, black Suburban with blacked out windows drove up in front of the house. "He's here," said Senta who had been watching eagerly from the front window. Abigail had just fed the baby and put her down for a nap. She and John met Senta by the front door as she opened it to the four people coming up the front walk. Two men were plain-clothed Tennessee state troopers dressed in suits and aviator sunglasses. The third man, Attorney General, Ethan Ward, was also wearing a suit. He was followed by Miss Thompson, his secretary, attractively dressed in a white blouse and black pencil skirt. One state trooper was carrying a case containing a printer. Miss Thompson was carrying her laptop computer in a computer satchel.

"Hello, John!" said the Attorney General, extending his hand as they reached the door. "It's good to see you again. Hopefully, the next time will be under better circumstances."

"Come in, Mr. Ward," said John as the group entered the house one by one.

"Let me introduce everyone. I'm Ethan Ward, the Attorney General. The real one," he said, giving Abigail and Senta a warm smile. It was an effort to lighten the mood a little from what was obviously a very tense situation for the women. "This is my assistant, Miss Thompson. And these two gentlemen are Sergeants Stevens and Jones. They are Tennessee state troopers who go with me on assignments like this one, for protection."

"This is my wife, Abigail, and this is Senta Miller," said John.

"It's very nice to meet you," said Ethan, shaking Abigail's

hand first and then Senta's. "So you're Senta. I've heard a lot about you." Senta's eyes got wider, not knowing how to take his statement. "It was all good," he said smiling. "Jerrick told me about you, and it was all quite positive." Senta relaxed a bit and wondered just what Jerrick had said.

"What we're going to do now is take your statements. May we use the dining room or kitchen for Miss Thompson to set up her computer and printer? I will talk to each of you, one at a time, while Miss Thompson records your statement. Then she will print it. You will read it for accuracy and then be asked to sign it," Ethan explained.

"The kitchen would probably be best," said Abigail directing Miss Thompson. "And, Senta, let's get everyone some lemonade."

The state troopers smiled and obviously liked the idea of lemonade. This would be a very pleasant afternoon's work for them. Miss Thompson set up her equipment on the kitchen table while Senta poured lemonade. The Attorney General, Miss Thompson, and John went to the kitchen first while Abigail, Senta, and the two state troopers waited in the parlor. When John was finished, Abigail was next. Finally, it was Senta's turn.

Sitting down at the kitchen table, she said, "Mr. Ward, I am so sorry we didn't know who you were. I'm sorry we didn't realize the other man was an imposter."

"That's OK," he said. "Most people can't even come up with the governor's name much less what the AG looks like. In fact, I've had people doubt I was the AG because I'm rather young to be an Attorney General."

"Thank you for helping us," Senta said. "Somehow I've found myself in circumstances that were more than overwhelming. I've always believed God doesn't give us more than we can stand. Things have been so hard recently, but this resolves everything. You don't know how much I appreciate you clearing Jerrick's good name."

"That's my job, to help the people of our state," he said. "I'm glad to do it. So, let's get started. I have strict instructions from our mutual friend to get your farm back for you." Ethan asked questions, Senta answered, and Miss Thompson typed.

Senta told her story while Ethan jotted down notes from time to time. When they were finished, Ethan took Senta back to the parlor while Miss Thompson gathered all her papers and equipment and packed them in the case.

Back in the parlor the Attorney General addressed everyone, "We're all done. I have what I need. Tomorrow I will call the State's Attorney of Cheatham County, and we'll coordinate our investigation." He paused for a moment, then continued. "Mr. Yost probably doesn't realize it, but he is in serious trouble. It is likely he has been doing things like this for years, and because he wasn't caught, he was emboldened to continue. But now he's been found out. Both the Yoder farm situation and your farm situation, Senta, are under the 15-year statute of limitations. Mr. Yost has perpetrated theft of property under false pretenses. These are either Class A or B felonies, depending on the value of the farms. Impersonating me to injure Mr. Douglas is a Class B misdemeanor. That's up to six months in jail and a fine. But together with the two felonies, it could be up to 25 years in prison. We also will be tracking down the individual who was posing as me, and arresting him." John, Abigail and Senta heard these words with shock as the gravity of such a sentence registered with them.

"I'm pretty sure Mr. Yost will be happy to cooperate in signing your farm back over to you for a reduced sentence. But for now, I want to remind you that this is an ongoing investigation. Do not say a word to anyone about this. Stay away from Yost. Don't talk to him. I have one last question before I leave. Are you all planning on being at Mr. Yost's house on Sunday for services?" The three all nodded their heads in the affirmative. "That's good. I really want you all to be there. Especially you, Senta. This is going to be a service they'll be talking about in Cheatham County for years."

The four said their goodbyes and walked down the sidewalk with their equipment to the black Suburban. John, Abigail and Senta stood in front of the house, watching. Before getting in the big SUV Ethan turned, waved, and called, "See you Sunday!"

When they went back inside, Rachel was crying and Abigail

went to get her. They all sat in the kitchen while Abigail fed the baby and rehashed the Attorney General's visit. "Yost is in serious trouble," said John. "He's going to prison."

"I agree. I can't believe it," said Abigail. "Mr. Ward said it probably wouldn't go to trial because there's just no denying any of this. The bishop did these terrible things." And then turning to Senta took her friend's hand and added, "I hope he can get your farm back, Senta."

"Yes, I want the farm back," said Senta. "And even more than that, I'm just so happy that those things weren't true about Jerrick. It seems that Mr. Ward really likes him, really respects him."

"What does he mean about Sunday?" asked John. "Why would he see us Sunday unless he plans on being at Yost's house for the service? And why would he come to an Amish service?"

"I have no idea why the Attorney General would want to come to our church service," said Senta. "I guess we'll just have to wait and see."

Senta went to her room and closed the door. Her cell phone was on the small table in her bedroom that also served now as her office since she had moved in with the Lapps. Picking up the phone and sitting down on the bed, she went to *contacts* and looked for a way to retrieve Jerrick's number, but she found none. Moving over to the computer, she brought up Google and entered *Jerrick Douglas* and then *Jerrick Douglas Haven Harbor Kentucky*. She was searching for a phone number but had no success. *I must talk to him*, she thought. *I must apologize. Why doesn't he call me?* Then remembering that Yost had blocked his number, she thought that maybe Jerrick had tried to call and the call wouldn't go through. She gave up and got his letter out of her drawer and read it again. Finally, she prayed. Senta thanked God for Jerrick. Then, she thanked God for sending Ethan Ward to help them. *Heavenly Father*, she prayed, *I put all my trust in You. I am helpless to solve these difficulties and am completely dependent on You. But, please, help Jerrick to not be angry with me. I want the farm back, but above that, I need Jerrick. I believe You have given him to me. Please don't take him away.*

Senta lay in her bed, exhausted, praying, and thinking

about Jerrick as she slipped into sleep.

CHAPTER THIRTEEN

Uncovered

Sunday was dreamlike for Senta as she got herself ready for church then helped Abigail with Rachel. It wasn't different from any other Sunday, but to Senta it seemed as if everything was moving very slowly and like she was someone else watching everyone get ready for church. The drive to the Yost house was like that, too, surreal. Senta wondered what the morning held in store as they made the journey to the Yost farm.

The black buggies converged and parked in front of the bishop's house. Inside, everyone was very attentive to the recently widowed Eric Yost. He was in the spotlight as the service was at his home, and as he would be delivering the message. Only John, Abigail, and Senta had any idea that the service might be anything out of the norm as they waited to see if the Attorney General showed up. Not a word had been said to anyone about their meeting. Yost preached on the sin of covetousness, proclaiming that pride could cause one to covet. Only Senta, who had seated herself by a window saw the black suburban, two Cheatham County squad cars, two more cars, and two television vans advancing up the drive. The service continued inside, while outside the antenna dishes on top of the vans moved up to position and locked on their satellites. The Cheatham County Sheriff conferred with the Attorney General while reviewing various papers. TV cameras were set up on tripods, and cables attached to microphones were fed back to the vans. When the service ended and the front door was opened for the congregation to file out, they were met with a most unexpected sight of reporters, cameras, and law enforcement officers.

"Is this the home of Eric Yost?" asked the sheriff. "We are looking for Eric Yost."

"Yes, it is," answered Mr. King as he was the first out the door with Mrs. King at his side. "What is going on?" Congregants close behind who had heard the sheriff went back into the house to summon Yost.

"I am Eric Yost," said the bishop arriving at the front door of his house. People filed past the sheriff and then gathered in front of the house. "What is this all about?" he asked, confronted with the mass of vehicles, law enforcement, and media in his front yard. A camera man from a Nashville TV station got closer, zooming in on the sheriff and the bishop. Two deputies stood behind the sheriff. Off to the side and next to the Suburban stood the Attorney General with his state police escort.

"Eric Yost, you are under arrest for two counts of theft by deception, and one count of conspiracy to impersonate a government official with the intent to defame and defraud. 'You have the right to remain silent. Anything you say can and will be used against you in a court of law. You have the right to speak to an attorney and to have an attorney present during questioning.' You are entitled to one phone call. You will get that call when we return to the jail in Ashland City. The judge will determine your bail, but that won't be until tomorrow since this is Sunday. Cuff him." One of the deputies moved behind Yost and taking the handcuffs from his belt, pulled Yost's hands behind his back and secured the handcuffs around his wrists. The onlookers stood in the front yard in complete shock. Everyone except John, Abigail, and Senta. Senta watched with tears of righteous indignation as she saw her tormentor brought to justice. Cameras rolled and two reporters gave account of what had just happened.

"Sheriff, may we have a statement from you?" asked a reporter.

"In a minute," said the sheriff. Then turning to Yost he said, "Eric Yost, there's someone who would like to talk to you. He's a friend of yours, I understand." Then turning to the assembled congregation he continued, "Several of you had the opportunity to make the acquaintance of our state's Attorney General recently. Mr. Yost, here, is a close friend of the Attorney General, I understand. Well, Mr. Yost, guess who's with us today? That's right, the Attorney General, just to see you. Mr. Ward," announced the sheriff, waving to Ethan Ward.

As Ethan Ward made his way up to where the sheriff and Yost were standing, the cameras were recording. The men who had been present at the Miller home a few weeks before looked on in utter bewilderment. Ethan Ward glared at Yost with contempt then turned to the crowd and said, "Hello, I am Ethan Ward, Attorney General of the State of Tennessee. Some of you are probably confused right now because I am not the same man you met at the Miller farm a few weeks ago when Bishop Yost brought a paid actor to that meeting." The Attorney General then turned to Yost. "Eric Yost, impersonating the Attorney General is a crime!" Yost crumbled and hung his head in defeat, saying nothing. Then Ward addressed the crowd again, "And everything said at that charade about Jerrick Douglas was a lie. None of those things were true." The people in the crowd looked at each other aghast and then turned to Senta. "And why would you go to so much trouble to do all this, *Bishop* Yost? I'll tell you why," said the Attorney General turning to where Senta stood and pointing to her, "To steal Senta Miller's farm!" The crowd was stunned. "I don't know how the church hierarchy works in the Amish community, but I'm thinking y'all are going to be needing a new bishop." With that, Ethan Ward walked to Senta. One of the cameras followed him and the other stayed on the sheriff and Yost. Ethan Ward approached Senta and hugged her. Then he turned so the camera could get a good shot as he said to the camera, "Today justice is being done in Cheatham County as a grievous wrong is being righted." The camera made Senta nervous while the Attorney General seemed to enjoy it. The deputy escorted Yost to the squad car where he was placed in the back seat. One by one, the congregation passed by the car as they went back to their buggies. Yost sat hunched over in utter shame, totally exposed. The sheriff made a prepared statement concerning the case to the reporter.

Miraculously, baby Rachel had somehow managed to sleep through the whole ordeal but now had woken up and was getting fussy. "I think she's hungry," said Senta as she and Abigail headed for their buggy. John stayed behind to talk to a group of men and discuss the happenings of the day.

"Senta," called out the Attorney General, following her and Abigail. Senta stopped while Abigail went on. "Senta, thank you for your cooperation. This is all going to work out. We have so much on Yost that he will gladly sign the farm back over to you for a reduced sentence. He's going to do time in prison, as will the man who impersonated me."

"Thank you, Mr. Ward," she said. "This means so much to me. Thank you for all this."

"You should thank Jerrick," said Ethan. "If it hadn't been for him, Yost would probably have gotten by with this."

"I want to thank him," she said. "I want to tell him I'm sorry for doubting him. But I don't have his phone number any more. Yost deleted it from my phone. Do you have Jerrick's number?"

"Well, I do, but I don't see a reason to give it to you." Ethan grinned at the bewildered look on Senta's face. "There's no reason for you to use the phone when you could tell him in person." Ethan's eyes looked off to the left toward where the Suburban was parked. Senta followed his gaze and there saw Jerrick leaning up against the Suburban, arms crossed, watching her.

"Oh, my God. He's here," she whispered.

"Of course, he's here," said Ethan, reassuringly. "He wanted to see justice done, too, both for you and for him. He didn't want everyone in Cheatham County believing all those lies about him. And he has been very insistent that you get your farm back. If I don't get your farm back, I don't think I'll ever be invited to his boat again," said Ethan, laughing. "Now get over there and talk to him."

Senta walked slowly across the grass toward the Suburban.

She had to pass the squad car holding Yost to reach the vehicle. As she walked by, Yost glanced up at her through the window and then immediately looked down again when he realized it was her. She saw how much smaller he looked now, weak and conquered. She no longer feared him. He wasn't going to hurt her any more. Walking on toward Jerrick she prayed, *please, God, don't let him be too angry with me.* Dressed in denim jeans and a blue oxford-cloth shirt, Jerrick was still watching ... waiting. *My goodness*, she thought, *he's handsome even when he's angry.* She stopped in front of him, although a bit farther away than she normally would have, hesitant to get much closer.

"I'm sorry about your mother," Jerrick said. Senta nodded and once again was at a loss for words when she was near him. "I should have been there. I'm sorry."

"No, I'm the one who's sorry. I'm heartbroken that I ever doubted you," she said. "I knew it couldn't be true, the lies about you. But when the Attorney General says something, you think it's true except that ... he was a fraud. Thank you for getting my farm back. And I'm sorry, so sorry. Please, forgive me." She took a step forward but then stopped to look into his eyes for any sign that he would forgive her. Jerrick continued to lean against the SUV with his arms folded, still watching her. Then, he broke a slight smile, moved away from the Suburban, and unfolded his arms. Senta, reading his thoughts, knew that Jerrick wasn't angry with her, and ran into his arms.

"I don't blame you," he said as she held onto him as tightly as she could and cried into his chest. "I'm not mad at you. I didn't want to leave, but I'd promised Mario. Everything is going to be alright," he said holding her and stroking her head.

"I blame myself for my mother," she said sobbing. "Like I caused her to die."

"It's not your fault, Senta," he said. "The man sitting in that squad car .... he's responsible. There is no telling how many people he's wronged besides you and your mother and me. Now, he will pay."

"After John got back, when the two of you went to Nashville, after the truth came out," she said, wiping her eyes. "I worried as to why you didn't come in and tell us yourself.

We didn't answer the door when you first came. I'm so sorry. I wanted to answer the door, but I was afraid. Then later when you didn't come in with John, I thought you had given up on me. That you didn't want to see me anymore."

"I considered coming in but decided it best to let John explain it all and then to let Ethan take care of it. It's alright now. It's going to be OK," he said brushing some hair that had fallen, moving it out of her eyes.

About half the congregation had gone, the other half still lingered to discuss the shocking scene that had just been witnessed. The camera crews were packing up their equipment while back at the TV station the lead story was being written for the evening news. The headlines would read, "Amish Bishop in Cheatham County Arrested." One by one the congregants noticed Jerrick and Senta. Abigail came back with Rachel to the group where her husband was standing to find everyone gazing across the lawn at Jerrick and Senta. As she walked up, Mrs. Belier said, "There he is! There's that Jerrick Douglas! I know him from the Farmers' Market. Look at how she is behaving. She's all over him."

"Mrs. Belier," said Abigail. "Shut up. Leave her alone. After all she's gone through, how dare you say one bad word about her! That man you see over there is her boyfriend. He is courting her. So, leave her alone."

"Courting her?" asked Mrs. Yoder. "But he's not Amish. They can't do that."

"Yes, they can, and they are. And just to make it official, tomorrow John and I are going down to the Miller farm and we will be painting the gate blue. Isn't that right, John?" said Abigail, to which John nodded wholeheartedly.

Jerrick and Senta, oblivious to what the others were discussing, continued in their own world. "Senta, I have an idea," Jerrick said.

"An idea?" Senta asked, looking up at him and brushing the hair from her eyes.

"When we went to dinner in Nashville, do you remember that I mentioned the Commodore's Ball?" he asked.

"Yes, I remember," she said. "And I remember wanting

to go with you while at the same time being scared to death."

"Well, the Commodore's Ball is next Saturday night," he said. "And I want you to be my date because you are my girlfriend after all." Senta's heart skipped a beat every time he called her his girlfriend. "Now, here's my idea. The ball is in Haven Harbor, Kentucky. Right now, my boat is at Rock Harbor in Nashville. Why don't we cruise to the ball together?"

Senta's mind raced. Such a short time before, everything seemed lost. Now he was wanting to take her with him. Then fear began to creep in. What if something went wrong and he changed his mind about her? "Jerrick, I want to. I really do, but my job, and I don't have anything to wear to something like that," she said. At the same time, she wondered where she would sleep but was afraid to ask.

"Can you call Mr. Campbell and ask for a week's vacation?" he asked. "We will take care of the dress situation. We'll go to Green Hills Mall and find the perfect dress for you. And you would have your own bedroom and bathroom aboard *Arcadia*." She looked at Jerrick in disbelief, feeling as if he had just read her mind.

"Yes," she said, biting her lower lip. "I will go with you." She hugged him again, savoring every second he held her. "You must be very patient with me. Your world is completely different from mine. There are so many things I don't understand."

"I will," he said. "Every time we've been together, we've had to worry about other people. There was Mrs. King at the Farmers' Market. You had to sneak out of your house so I could take you to dinner. On the boat, it would be just the two of us, separated from the world. I really want us to do this."

"That would be quite a second date," said Senta smiling.

"That it would," he said. "If at any point you want it to end, you tell me. We will stop at the next town, I'll rent a car, and take you back. I never want you to feel pressured into something you don't want to do. If you absolutely don't want to go to the Commodore's Ball, I won't insist."

Reaching for his hands and looking up at him, she thought, *He really cares how I feel. He wants to know how I feel. Of course, I want to go to the ball. I'm just afraid I will make a mistake and embarrass him. I can't believe he wants to take me with him.* "Yes, I like your idea. Yes, I'll go," she said. "When do we leave, Captain?"

"Right now, if you can," Jerrick said. "I rode with Ethan in the Suburban. You can go with us, and they'll drop us off at Rock Harbor."

Senta had dreamed about something like this ever since she'd met Jerrick in the spring. And now she was just minutes away from it becoming reality. *I'm not dreaming. This is real*, she thought. "Let me go talk to Abigail. I'll be right back. Don't leave," she said. Senta walked quickly back to where the people were gathered, this time not even noticing the squad car with Yost in the back.

"Is everything OK with Jerrick?" asked Abigail as Senta walked up.

"Everything is better than OK, Abigail," said Senta. "He wasn't upset with me." Senta paused for a moment, looking around at the scene of people and police cars. Then she glanced back to be sure Jerrick was still there. "Jerrick has invited me to a ball at his yacht club in Kentucky. It's next Saturday. He's cruising there from Rock Harbor where his boat is docked. He wants me to go with him now, Abigail."

Nodding her head and smiling, Abigail said, "Go with him, Senta. Do you remember how I told you once that I thought life had more in store for you? Well, this is that moment. Go with him. Of course, you realize you're leaving the order by doing this, but go with him. We'll take care of Sugar and your house. You'll need to call Mr. Campbell. You must call Sally tonight so she doesn't drive out with your work tomorrow. You can explain the situation to her so she can talk to Mr. Campbell on your behalf. We'll work everything out." Abigail embraced her friend as the others looked on.

"Thank you," said Senta. "I love you, Abigail. I cherish our friendship. I want to always be friends, even if I'm not Amish anymore. I don't know how not to be Amish, but I will do anything for him."

"I understand," said Abigail. "And, Senta, we will always be friends. Nothing will ever change that. Wait here for a minute. I want to talk to Mr. Douglas. I need to apologize." Abigail retraced the path Senta had just taken across the yard and by the squad cars, looking on at Yost with disgust as she passed.

"Abigail," said Jerrick, as she approached him.

"I must apologize, Mr. Douglas," she said. "I was thinking very badly of you. I was deceived by the bishop and his actor. I am sorry I didn't see through it. Senta is going with you. She is very much in love with you, and I want her to be happy. Be kind to her. She is fragile. She has had such a difficult life, yet she's still so positive and happy most of the time. I don't know how she does it. You are the best thing that has ever happened to her. So, please, be good to her."

Jerrick closed the distance between Abigail and himself and hugged her. Then they turned towards the others, and together they walked back to where Senta was talking to John. "I love her too, Abigail," he said as they walked. "I will be careful with her. She's always afraid that she will do something wrong that would make me mad at her. I don't think she's capable of doing anything that would anger me. This week is important for us because I want us to get to know each other more. I will take good care of her. I promise." Abigail looked up at him with tears welling up in her eyes and nodded her approval. With that Jerrick rejoined the group of officials with whom he'd arrived.

One by one, the buggies left. A deputy locked Yost's house. The camera crews and the TV vans drove away. The sheriff, deputies and Yost left in the squad car, heading to the jail in Ashland City. The state troopers, the Attorney General, and Jerrick were waiting in the Suburban. Senta said her goodbyes to the Lapps, John, Abigail, and baby Rachel and then ran to the Suburban, getting in the back next to Jerrick. Where so many people had been just a short time before, now it was just the Lapps waving goodbye as the Suburban pulled out onto the county road.

"Thanks for the lift, Ethan," said Jerrick, as the big SUV rolled east. Senta felt the change of mood from the seriousness of the official state business. The Attorney General and his two stone-faced state trooper bodyguards were suddenly smiling. It was a welcome change from the intensity of the day.

The two troopers were in the front and the other three were in the back. "Well, I couldn't have you walking all the way back to Rock Harbor. After all, you vote," said Ethan. "Hold it. Stop the car, and let him walk. He's not a resident of Tennessee. He doesn't vote here. Now, Senta's vote is important so she gets to ride." Senta saw the trooper in the front seat crack a smile and then caught Jerrick and Ethan smiling at the joke.

"Hey, Ethan!" Jerrick asked. "Where is Miss Thompson today?" Senta looked at Jerrick, surprised he would ask that.

"I didn't want to make her work on Sunday, and there's the overtime," Ethan laughed. "We have to keep the payroll under control."

"I can tell you like her. And I can tell she likes you. So, have you asked her out yet?" Jerrick asked.

"No can do," said the Attorney General. "Attorney General office protocol. No interoffice dating."

"So she's not Presbyterian?" asked Jerrick. Senta who was seated between the two men looked back and forth between them trying to understand the conversation.

"No, she's actually Presbyterian," said Ethan.

"The right kind of Presbyterian, the conservative kind?" asked Jerrick.

"Yes, she's even my kind of Presbyterian," responded Ethan.

"I'm not believing this. And she's pretty. Senta, didn't you think Miss Thompson was pretty? You know, Ethan's assistant who came to the house for the statements," prompted Jerrick.

"Yes, I thought she was very pretty," replied Senta quietly, still not catching on and quite puzzled by the conversation.

"How about you guys up front. What do you think? Is Miss Thompson nice looking?" Jerrick asked.

"Yes, sir!" both troopers responded in unison.

"I know, but the rules," said Ethan.

"I realize there's been some confusion about who the Attorney General is lately," teased Jerrick. "But I'm pretty sure it's you. So, change the rules, and ask her out on a date! All in favor of the Attorney General changing the no-dating rule and taking Miss Thompson out on a date say 'Aye!'"

Everyone in unison shouted "Aye" and then laughed for the next two miles. Taking it all in, Senta watched Jerrick as he laughed and thought, *Jerrick likes to kid people. He likes to kid me. I suspect he only kids people he likes.* Then Jerrick said, "Or you could fire her. Then you could date her!"

Again, everyone laughed, and then Sergeant Jones who was driving added, "But then she'd hate you for firing her and wouldn't go out with you!"

"Bad idea," said Jerrick. "Just change the rules. That way she gets to keep her job." And they all joined in the laughter.

The miles passed. Listening to the conversation and banter among the group, Senta found herself beginning to relax. Senta thought, *I assumed these people were serious all the time, but they're regular people.* It seemed like no time before the Suburban reached the cityscape of Nashville. Enjoying the ever-changing urban scenery as the vehicle made its way across and through town, Senta was surprised to be passing through an older residential neighborhood. *This doesn't seem like a harbor*, she thought. But she was even more surprised when they pulled into a parking lot, and the Suburban stopped.

"Ok, we're here," said Ethan. "Senta, I have your number. I'll call you if I need any more information, but I think I have everything. By the time you return, the farm should be in your name. Don't worry. We'll take care of it." Everyone got out of the Suburban, said their goodbyes, and the SUV drove around the parking lot and back onto the street that would take them to the interstate.

CHAPTER FOURTEEN

Aboard

Jerrick and Senta stood alone in the parking lot, Jerrick in jeans and a button-down shirt and Senta in her Amish dress with white apron and white cap. "Are you ready?" he asked, taking her hands. She nodded. "Let's think of this as the beginning of a week-long date. Senta Miller, will you have dinner with me tonight?" he asked. "I don't know about you, but I'm hungry. With all that happened back in Cheatham County, we didn't have time to eat lunch."

"Yes, I'd love to go to dinner with you. But where? We don't have a car. And where is the harbor, and where is your boat?" she asked, looking around the parking lot.

"I'm taking you to the Blue Moon," he said, taking her hand. She smiled, having decided to always trust him even if it didn't make sense at first. They walked to the far end of the asphalt, then by some big buildings where boats were being repaired, and down a gangway. He watched her to see her reaction as the water and the floating, Blue Moon restaurant came into view.

"This is the restaurant! I didn't see it before. And here's the harbor. It's kind of down in a hole," she said looking down at the floating restaurant and the docks.

"Rock Harbor used to be a stone quarry. When the wall of rock between it and the river was dynamited, the water rushed in, and the quarry became a harbor. It's unusual, isn't it?" said Jerrick as they walked down the gangway to the Blue Moon. "It's not the prettiest harbor. Kind of industrial."

I'm going to have to get used to this, Senta thought. *Everything about this life is so different. Everything is so much fun. More than I ever dreamed!* Senta walked carefully on the steel grid of the gangway that sloped steeply towards the Blue Moon. She could see through the grid to the water below.

"Let's eat outside. The evenings are getting cooler, and it's nice sitting outside," Jerrick suggested as he guided her around the deck on the outside of the restaurant to the seating by the water. There were only a few other diners there since it was a Sunday evening, so they had their pick of seats. Jerrick chose a table by the water overlooking the marina. Directing her to her seat, he pulled it out for her.

He pulled my chair out for me, she thought. *Just like he did at the food court.* "Thank you," she said as he gave her a smile and walked to the other side of the table and sat down. "Is your boat here?" she asked.

"Yes," he said, pointing directly across the water from where they were sitting to a white trawler with the name *Arcadia* on the transom. "That's your home for the next week."

Senta looked at it, studying all the details, remembering some of the terminology. "*Arcadia* is beautiful," she said. "And big. I couldn't really picture how big."

The waitress walked up and took their order. Senta ordered the catfish plate and Jerrick the seafood plate, and they both ordered lemonade to drink. Jerrick considered wine but thought better of it due to all that had happened that day. "I hope you'll like it, being on the boat," Jerrick said. "It's different traveling by boat. It takes some getting used to. After we eat, I'll give you the tour. Getting you moved in will be easy since you don't have anything to move in. Tomorrow we'll go shopping and take care of that situation. I hope you'll be comfortable in your cabin and head, bedroom and bathroom," he said, translating the boat-speak to English.

"I will. I'm certain I will," she responded. "How do you do that? How do you know what I'm thinking? Do you always know my thoughts or just sometimes?"

Jerrick smiled and answered, "Not all the time. Just sometimes. I can see it in your eyes."

"I can't tell what you're thinking," she answered. "But today I could tell you weren't upset with me. I could see it in your eyes."

"So, you *can* tell what I thinking," he responded, smiling and looking at her with affection. *I am helpless*, she thought. *He is wonderful. Can this be happening to me?*

They ate dinner as a boat came into the harbor. They watched it glide smoothly into its berth on the dock. "He did that very nicely," commented Jerrick as they watched the captain and a woman tie up the boat to the dock. "Most of the time that's how it goes, but occasionally you get someone who can't operate their boat. That's when it can get very exciting, and not in a good way. If that ever happens, get away. If a boat rams the dock, it can throw you into the water." Senta nodded in understanding. When they were finished, Jerrick paid the bill and Senta noticed that he left the waitress a generous tip. *He is kind*, she thought.

They left the outside restaurant deck. As they stepped onto the dock that would lead around to *Arcadia*, Jerrick took her hand. Slowly, they walked together. Senta took in the whole scene of water, boats, and docks all contained within the rock walls of the harbor. "Jerrick, do you remember when we first met, that first Saturday, when you said you'd come back, and you wouldn't wait seven years?" she asked.

"Yes," he answered. "I remember. Did you understand? I didn't think you did, but do you understand now?"

"No, I didn't understand. Abigail heard it, too, and she didn't understand what you meant," she said. "I was confused and intrigued by it. I thought about it all day. I went home and googled it, *Senta* and *Seven Years*. I didn't know what my name meant and hadn't given it any thought. And then I was sure you were a captain because your friend called you, 'Captain'. Then I read about the *Flying Dutchman*. I didn't know what to think."

"I wondered if you heard me when I said it," he answered. "When I first met you, that first time at the Market, I was taken by you. Although unlike you, I could talk," he said, smiling and giving her hand a gentle squeeze. She smiled back and thought, *Of course he noticed that I'm at a loss for words around him. And he can tell what I'm thinking most of* the time.

"When Abigail called you 'Senta', it made me think of the opera. That's why I said I'd come back and not wait seven years. You're Senta and yes, I'm a captain, and I do kind of wander around in my boat. But I'm not cursed like the captain in the story. He had to sail almost endlessly and only could come into port once every seven years. Only finding true love would break the curse. Then there was Eric, the woodcutter, like in the opera who Senta was engaged to marry. When I found out about Eric Yost wanting to marry you, I thought, '*This is just like in the opera.*' But in the opera, the captain thinks Senta wants to marry Eric so he boards his ship and sails away. Senta sees the ship leaving and in desperation jumps from a cliff. Her love redeems him and breaks the curse. Then the captain and Senta ascend together to heaven." They continued walking slowly around the dock to *Arcadia* as Senta listened to Jerrick explain the story she had read. Upon arrival at the yacht, Jerrick said, "That's where the opera ends. Some crazy similarities aren't there?"

Senta looked at Jerrick and agreed. "When I read about the opera, I asked my mother about my name," Senta explained. "She said it was my father's idea to name me Senta. Perhaps my grandfather liked the name. In the story, Senta saved the captain. But I feel like you saved me. I feel like I was lost and didn't know it."

"We found each other, and perhaps we've saved each other," Jerrick said. "Of course, it's just a story. And look, my boat is the *Arcadia*, not the *Flying Dutchman*." Jerrick pointed to the transom of the yacht and the name *Arcadia*. "Let's get you on board and settled in and to bed because tomorrow I'm taking you shopping."

Stepping from the dock through the starboard gate and onto the boat, Jerrick kept hold of Senta's hand to guide her. *I feel like my heart is going to explode with love for him,* she thought. *From the first time I met him, I loved him. I never knew anyone like him existed.* They stood on the aft deck as Jerrick said, "First, I'm going to ask you to take off your shoes. Tomorrow, we'll get you some boat shoes, so the decks don't get marked up by the black soles of your shoes."

"I'm sorry," she said, quickly taking off her shoes. "I knew better. I read that on the internet. That's why people on boats wear those shoes for traction and to not mark the deck. I won't do it again." Then saying something she would have never said before, "Are you going to punish me?" *Oh, my God, why did I say that*? she thought. *He knows what I think. I shouldn't have said that.*

"I might have to," he said with a grin. "I am the captain, and you have to obey." Senta smiled and blushed, looking away.

"So first, I'm going to give you a tour, so you know where everything is. We use different words on boats," he said, as he opened the aft door into the salon and they stepped inside the boat. "This, for example, is like a living room, or as you call it, a parlor. On a boat, it's the salon."

Senta was struck with how grand the inside of the boat was. While the outside was all white except for the teak hand rail that went all the way around the perimeter, the inside was all wood. The floor was made of teak and holly laid down in alternating strips of dark and light wood. The walls were all mahogany. The overhead was white with strips of teak. There were two white upholstered chairs and a white sofa. A flat screen TV was built into the mahogany bulkhead forward. A highly polished wood table with a compass rose inlayed in the top sat in front of the sofa. "It's amazing," she said, touching the table top. "I didn't know how marvelous boats were inside."

"Thank you," he said. "I'm very proud of her. All the woodwork inside is perfect. Notice how all the grain matches up." Jerrick pointed to the walls. It was hardly noticeable where one piece ended and the next began. "And moving forward, here is the galley, or the kitchen as it's called in a house."

Senta looked at the granite countertops and mahogany cabinetry and thought that it was almost too elegant to use. Looking out the window at the harbor, Senta imagined herself making breakfast for Jerrick. "The sink is here, closer to the center line of the boat instead of outboard under the window," he explained. That's because the motion is less in the center when the boat is moving. See how deep the sink is? That's to keep water from splashing out when the boat is moving." He opened what appeared to be a cabinet, and then she realized it was the refrigerator. "There are two sets of stairs here," he said indicating the stairs forward of the galley. "One set goes up to the pilothouse, and the other set goes below to the staterooms or bedrooms. Let's go up to the bridge first."

They walked up three steps to the pilothouse. In the center was a big, elevated leather chair in front of a stainless-steel steering wheel. Three big windows faced forward, overlooking the bow. From that vantage point, Senta had the feeling she was high above the water. In front of her was a confusing array of screens, gauges, and switches labeled with words like radar, chartplotter, AIS, start, stop, parallel. Behind the big chair was a step up to a built-in settee with another handsome table on a stainless-steel pedestal. "This is where I operate the vessel from," Jerrick explained. "It's called the pilothouse or the bridge. It has lots of technology. Back here is a place you're going to like," he said pointing to the settee. "It's a great place to sit and watch the world go by while cruising. There's another bridge above us. It's called the flybridge. It's outside which is a great place to be when the weather is good. But the inside bridge is much better if the weather is bad, too hot or too cold. It's heated and air-conditioned like the rest of the boat, so it's more comfortable."

"How fascinating," she said, looking at the woodwork and then the instruments. "And complicated. It's very comfortable. I'm not used to air-conditioning. We had electricity on the farm, but we only used it for lights and the refrigerator. We didn't have things like TV or air-conditioning." She looked outside through the windows at the marina.

"There are doors on each side to go outside to get to the foredeck or up to the flybridge. Do you see the machine all the way forward that controls the anchor?" he said, pointing out the window. She nodded. "It's called the anchor windlass. Don't touch it. You could hurt yourself. Only I operate the windlass. Do you understand?"

"Aye, aye, Captain," she said, and then thought she might touch it sometime when he was looking. *Stop that, Senta*, she thought. *He can read my mind. What's wrong with me? He's trying to keep me from hurting myself, and I'm having thoughts like this. Why does the idea of him punishing me excite me like that?*

"Come back down to the galley and I'll show you your cabin," he said leading the way down the stairs. Senta followed.

As she followed, Senta couldn't help but notice a big glass panel with what looked like a hundred different switches by the stairs. "What are all these?" she asked.

"Electricity," he answered. "There are AC circuits and DC circuits. We can get AC from shore power like we are right now, but we can also get it from our battery bank by running it through the inverter, or we can make our own AC by turning on the generator. All these switches are for controlling how we get electricity, store it, and manage it." She looked at all the breakers, switches, and meters and wondered, *How does he know how to do all this? I knew he was smart, but I had no idea. Sometimes I feel so inadequate. Maybe he thinks I'm smarter than I am. Does he know that sometimes I don't have a clue as to what he's talking about?*

"Come on down," Jerrick said, standing at the base of the stairs looking up at Senta as she studied the electrical controls. She followed him down the three stairs from the pilothouse and then turning at the galley down four more to the lower deck. "So here are the washer and dryer," he said, opening a beautifully crafted paneled mahogany door in the passageway. "And down here on the left is your bedroom." She followed him down the hallway to the next door. "But on a boat, we'd call it your cabin or your stateroom," he explained. She followed him into the room and instantly liked the way it felt. It wasn't big, but it wasn't small. Just like the rest of the boat, it was all wood. There were the port holes she'd seen from the outside. Her bed was built into the mahogany furniture, perfectly made up with crisp sheets and matching pillow. There was a built-in desk and a chair and a closet he called a hanging locker. "There's lots of storage," he said. "It's empty now, but we'll take care of that tomorrow. So how do you like *Arcadia*?" Jerrick asked with a proud grin.

A jumble of emotion welled up inside as she thought about everything that had happened. Images began to flash through her mind-losing her mother, losing the farm, then that scoundrel Eric Yost. Then came images of Jerrick and his kindness and how gentle he was with her. She started to cry. Jerrick took her in his arms and held her. When she was able to speak she said, "Your boat is wonderful. I love it. Yes, I'll be very comfortable here. I don't know why I'm crying again." His strong arms around her felt safe.

"It's OK," he said. "You've had a hard day, a hard year. It's OK to cry."

"It's been the worst year of my life, and the best year of my life," she said, wiping her eyes. "The best because of you." He waited for her to pull herself together. "I'm sorry I'm such a mess," she said.

"It's going to be alright," he said. "You just need some rest. Let me show you your bathroom. That's what we call the head." Directly across the hall from Senta's cabin was another door that opened to her bathroom. Senta was struck with how simply elegant it was, all white except for the dark granite counter top of the vanity. They walked to the end of the hallway. "This is my cabin," he said, opening the door.

Senta was surprised at how large the master cabin was. It was much bigger than hers. All mahogany with an elevated queen bed in the center with lots of built in drawers and lockers. There was a flat screen TV on the bulkhead, positioned for lying in bed and watching a movie. A door from the master cabin led into the master head that was also much bigger than Senta's bathroom. "It's so elegant," she said. "I had no idea there was so much room inside. *Arcadia* looks big when standing outside on the dock, but there is so much more room inside than I expected. It's bigger than some houses."

"You haven't seen it all yet. There's the lazarette and the engine room, but I'll show you that tomorrow. The engine room isn't as pretty as all this, but it's pretty in its own way," he said. Then turning to a hanging locker, he opened it and took out a hanger with a perfectly starched and ironed white dress shirt. Holding the shirt up to her, he said, "I know you don't have anything to sleep in. Do you think my shirt would work? It's a bit large. It almost comes to your knees, but the sleeves can be rolled up. Tomorrow we have to remember to get you some pajamas."

"It will work just fine, but I don't want to mess it up," she said. "It's so perfect." Senta recalled the first time she'd met him. He was wearing the old shorts and frayed T shirt, a total contrast to the perfect white shirt. Senta found the idea of sleeping in his shirt quite romantic.

"You won't hurt it," he responded. "It's just a white shirt. You're just going to sleep in it."

"Thank you," she said. "You think of everything."

The sun was setting; it was getting dark outside and also in the boat so Jerrick switched the lights on in the cabin. "There are light switches everywhere just like in a house." Jerrick looked at her and saw exhaustion on her face. "Are you getting sleepy? Would you like to shower?" he asked.

"I'm tired," she said. "It's been a long day. And yes, a shower would be nice."

"The water is just like in a house, hot and cold, adjust it as you like. Remember, we're below the waterline so you'll need to turn on the pump when you shower," Jerrick explained. "You see, we are standing lower than the level of the water outside the boat. So, gravity won't drain the shower like it does in a house. You'll need to turn this switch on when you shower to do that. There's soap, shampoo, and conditioner in the shower. I'm going to give you my robe. We'll get you one tomorrow."

"Jerrick, about tomorrow," she said. "I don't have any money. I don't have anything but the clothes I'm wearing."

"Yes," he said. "Don't worry about that. I will take care of the money. I don't want you to do anything other than rest and enjoy this week. Don't forget to call your friend Sally and let her know what's going on. Then tomorrow you can call your boss and ask for vacation."

"But Jerrick, you're spending a lot of money on me," she said with genuine concern.

"I know you think I am," he said. "Just let me. It's my

pleasure to spend money on you. Now go take your shower and get ready for bed. Let me know if you need anything. I'm going to the engine room to check everything there, so that when we leave on Tuesday everything is ready." Senta walked down the hallway with his white shirt and his white robe. She turned right into her cabin and smiled at him as he walked past. Then looking around the corner at him, she saw him lift the stairs that went up to the galley revealing another room. He turned on the lights, and she could see a big engine and more machinery.

Closing the door, she hung the white shirt in the locker, laid the robe on her bed, and sat down next to it. Looking around the cabin at the everything, Senta was still not sure whether this was a dream. Then she thought, *This is only the third bed I've slept in my entire life, and it's on a boat. Until Abigail and John's house, I'd never slept a single night anywhere but in my house. I've never even slept in a hotel,* she thought. *And now I'm here, on this yacht, with this handsome man who's doing something in the engine room, and I'm going to go take a shower.* Then she thought, *I always imagined that I would feel a boat rock, but I don't. There's no motion at all.*

Senta slowly stood up and looking at herself in the mirror, took off her cap, then her apron. She unwound her hair and let it fall all the way down her back. Then she took off her dress and hung it in the locker. Standing naked in front of the mirror, she looked at herself wondering if he would be pleased with what he saw, then quickly put on the robe. She wrapped the belt tightly around her waist feeling the cotton against her body. Pressing the lapel against her nose, she inhaled an aroma of soap and him. The smell made her knees weak as she closed her eyes and savored it. She opened the door and stepped across to her bathroom, looking down the hallway towards the engine room door. "Senta, there's a new toothbrush and toothpaste in the locker above your sink," he called from the engine room.

"Thank you," she answered. She thought of her friend Ruth as she closed the door behind her and found the toothbrush and toothpaste. *Jerrick is so kind to me. He thinks of everything. Every time I think he can't be any more wonderful, he surprises me.* She turned on the water in the shower and adjusted the temperature and stepped in. She noticed that it was just like a shower on land. Then on her tip toes, she looked out the porthole and saw the restaurant across the water where she had just had dinner. Standing under the showerhead, she let the warm water run over her. Then perusing the various bottles of shampoo and conditioners she read *L'Occitane, en Provence, Shampooing pure fraîcheur.* Recognizing the word *shampoo,* she put some on her hand and immediately the shower was filled with the most wonderful aroma. She shampooed her hair and was enjoying every second of it when she realized the water was rising to her ankles. *Oh, no! I forgot,* she thought. She quickly reached outside the glass shower door and turned on two switches, not knowing which one was the shower pump. Immediately, the water started to pump out of the shower and an exhaust fan came on, pulling the steam out of the shower. She relaxed once again and enjoyed her shower. Afterward, Senta dried off, put on the robe, and towel dried her hair, wrapping the towel around her head. She turned off the fan and the pump and stepped out into the hallway. She felt both very exposed as she was naked under his robe, and covered as his robe came all the way to her feet. She started to go to her cabin, but then saw the engine room door was now closed, so she turned and went up the stairs to the galley and salon.

Jerrick was sitting in one of the white chairs in the salon when he saw her at the stairs. "How was your shower?" he asked.

"It was glorious," she answered. "The shampoo smells wonderful. Everything is perfect."

"If you need more towels, they're in the linen locker. I'll show you. And there's a hair dryer in your bathroom, if you prefer," he said, standing up and walking toward her. "Your hair is so long," he said, touching the towel gently. "That may take a while to dry." Senta felt very vulnerable and was very aware she was naked under his robe. "You look so different, not wearing your Amish clothes. You really are beautiful," he said. Once again she was at a loss for words and couldn't even manage "thank you". A shiver came over her. "Here, come back down. I'll get you some more towels. Maybe a flannel shirt would be warmer than the white one. Then come up to the salon when you're ready, and we'll talk a little before we go to bed." He got her two more towels and a flannel shirt and left her in her bathroom. When she came up to the salon, she was drier and warmer although she knew her shivering wasn't from being cold. He had a blanket ready and wrapped it around Senta as they sat down on the white sofa together.

"Thank you for everything," she said, feeling more comfortable being more covered.

"You're welcome," he said. "Did you figure out the buttons and switches in the head?"

"Yes, but I did forget the shower pump at first," she admitted.

"Everyone does," he smiled. "It doesn't hurt anything, unless you let it overflow into the rest of the boat." Senta thought for a moment of who else had taken a shower in that bathroom and if there had been other women who had been there before her. "I want to talk to you about tomorrow," he said. "We're going to go to a mall called Green Hills and do a little shopping. I'm just not sure how to do it .... because you're Amish. I don't want you to feel forced to dress like we do."

Senta sat holding the blanket around her with her hair still wrapped in a towel. She thought, *I look terrible and he's seeing me like this.* "Jerrick, I'm Amish and I don't know if I'll ever not be Amish. I don't think I can change just by changing what I wear. I don't know what to do. Here I am on your boat, wearing your shirt and robe. I do want to go with you. I'm so honored that you want to take me to the Commodore's Ball even though I'm scared to death I'll do something wrong. I want to be pretty for you, but I don't know how to shop. I have no idea what is right or wrong for me to wear. I've never had to make decisions like that. All my dresses are the same. I'm not even sure what size I am," she said, biting her lower lip.

"I'm not trying to change you," he said. "I don't want you to be anything other than what you are. What if we go shopping tomorrow and we have the sales associates in the women's department help you? We can get you some outfits for everyday and a dress for Saturday night. You should decide what you like. It's not just what others say is fashionable. It's what you like and what works for you. How does that sound? Would you like to try that?" he asked.

"Yes, I'd like that," she answered. "Thank you for being so considerate and understanding."

"Ok then, it's a plan. If there's anything you don't like or are concerned about, you must tell me, OK?" he told her and she nodded her head in agreement. "I'm sleepy, how about you?" he asked.

"Yes, I am," she answered. They both stood and walked to the stairs leading to the bedrooms. Senta was nervous as he followed her.

"I'll come check on you in a few minutes," he said as she turned into her cabin. She turned down her bed, then went to the bathroom and came back. Taking off his robe, she decided to sleep in the flannel shirt he had given her because it was warmer and also because she didn't want to wrinkle the white one. She got in bed and got under the covers bringing them up to her chin, her hair still damp. Although tired, she felt very sensual wearing just his shirt and feeling the cool sheets on her legs. A few minutes later he was standing in her doorway, wearing only pajama bottoms and no shirt. "Are you ready for lights out?" he asked, walking over to stand by her. Once again, she couldn't answer. She couldn't take her eyes off him towering over her. His tanned chest and tight muscles, blue eyes and messed up hair had her entranced. "Are you warm enough?" he asked. Hearing no response, he went to the salon and brought back the blanket from the sofa and put it on her, carefully covering her. Sitting on the bed so close to her, he leaned over and kissed her on the forehead and said, "I love you, Senta." He stood and turned off the light. Then stopping at the door he said, "If you need anything in the night, I'm just down the hall."

Senta lay in her bed, almost ready to explode with happiness. *He loves me! He told me he loves me! And I couldn't say anything, but maybe he's getting used to that. I can't believe that out of all the women in this world he loves me.* Then as she did every night, she prayed. She thanked God for Jerrick and asked for God's help with their relationship, wanting to please both Jerrick and Him. She thought of all the nights of going to sleep in her room holding the pillow, and thought of how at this moment it was almost real. She thought about how his sweet kiss felt on her forehead and how special it was to be with him every minute. She thought about Jerrick's muscular arms and his chest and how she wanted to touch him. When he turned off the light in his cabin, the light shining down the hall disappeared leaving Senta's cabin completely dark. She thought, *He's just down the hallway.* She listened closely to see if she could hear him breathing and then drifted off to sleep.

CHAPTER FIFTEEN

First Mate

Jerrick was up, showered and dressed before Senta even stirred. It had been quite a dream-filled night for Senta. In one emotionally exhausting dream, Senta and baby Rachel were riding Sugar, trying to escape Yost. Around two o'clock in the morning, Senta had awoken a bit disoriented; she didn't know where she was. In that dream, she was on a boat with Mrs. King and Mrs. Belier who were baking bread in the galley. When Senta realized she really was on a boat, her heart stopped for a moment, thinking the Amish ladies were on board also. Relieved that it was a dream, she finally went back to sleep.

Having gotten out of bed, Senta peered around the corner of her doorway. Down the hallway, she saw Jerrick's bed was made. Then she heard a woman's voice. *Who's that?* she wondered. After listening more closely, it turned out to be a meteorologist giving the weather report on television. Suddenly, Senta remembered the need to call Sally. It was still early enough to catch her before she left for work. Sally was thrilled to hear what had happened and told Senta that she would gladly talk to Mr. Campbell. With that taken care of, Senta got ready for the day. She put on her blue dress but not her cap or apron. She twisted her hair and wore it up for the day.

"Good morning, Captain," she said as she walked into

the galley and saw Jerrick sitting in the salon drinking coffee and watching the news. "I'm afraid I overslept."

"No, you didn't," Jerrick responded. "We have no appointments to keep today. I think you needed a good night's sleep. Did you sleep well?"

"Yes, I did, thank you," Senta said. "I dreamed a lot. I dreamed I was sleeping on a boat and then woke up and found I was sleeping on a boat!" She looked out through the windows seeing the marina again in sunlight, seeing the boats, the water, and people eating breakfast at the Blue Moon across the way. "It's so different, this world of boats and water."

"What do you like for breakfast?" Jerrick asked. "I've prepared some fruit if that sounds good to you. Some pineapple, nectarines, and bananas. It's in the refrigerator. Why don't you get it out, and we'll eat out on the aft deck."

"Fruit sounds wonderful," exclaimed Senta opening the refrigerator to find a fruit plate with everything he'd just named plus grapes and blueberries. *But I'm supposed to make breakfast for him*, she thought.

"Get out the orange juice, too," Jerrick said from the aft deck through the open doors from the salon.

Senta got two glasses along with the orange juice and took them to the aft deck where Jerrick was positioning a small teak table between two teak deck chairs. "I should have been up earlier and made breakfast for you. I will do that tomorrow. I want everything to be perfect," she said as she placed the glasses and orange juice on the table and hurried back to the galley for the fruit, plates, and forks.

They sat and watched boats go by as they ate. "Cool mornings are so nice to have breakfast on the aft deck," Jerrick said. When they were finished, Senta took the dishes to the galley and brought back the coffee carafe. She poured Jerrick some more coffee and then poured herself some. "Senta," Jerrick said. "Sit down. I want to tell you something." Senta sat down holding her coffee between her hands enjoying its warmth and looking at Jerrick as he continued, "I want this week for us. I want it to be perfect, too. But, Senta, we're not perfect. I'm not. I have my flaws. You're incredible, but you have some faults.

Not that you have to be perfect to be wonderful. I don't want you to stress over doing everything correctly. If you think I feel the way I do because you're perfect, you're mistaken. I feel the way I do because you're you."

Senta heard his words and considered them carefully. She looked out toward the Cumberland River and watched a towboat push five barges past the opening to Rock Harbor. "But you are perfect. I love you so much. I just don't want to disappoint you," she said.

Jerrick stood up and moved the teak table to the side. Then he moved his deck chair next to hers to where they touched. Picking up his coffee mug, he sat down next to her so that her arm touched his. "I'm not perfect, Senta. I never have been, but I know being with you makes me a better man. So maybe two imperfect people can make a perfect couple?" They sat in silence, watching the boats and the water. "Let's just sit here and enjoy this perfect moment," he said and Senta leaned to rest her head against his shoulder.

They sat quietly, watching the water. Then Senta spoke, "There's something about water, isn't there? Something peaceful." Jerrick looked at her and smiled. "Jerrick, can I ask you something, something that I'm worried about?"

"Of course," he answered. "You can ask me anything."

Taking a deep breath, Senta started, "Today we're supposed to go shopping. I don't have anything, and I know I need some things. But I'm afraid I can't do it. A complete wardrobe, shoes, purses, makeup, the dress for the ball. It's so much. It's like last night. This is only the third place I've ever slept. I didn't realize how much of a change this would be." She watched his face for any reaction but saw none. "There's no place I'd rather be than here with you. And everything is wonderful. It's just so different. I hope this doesn't sound silly. But I've never worn pants before, and I'm not sure if I can. Even I don't understand it. I remember seeing women at the Farmers' Market wearing shorts and thinking they were lucky, wishing I could wear shorts. But now that I can ...." She paused for a moment, collecting her thoughts. "Would it be alright if today we just shopped a little? Maybe just a simple dress or two. I like dresses I suppose because that's what I've always worn. Maybe, and I'm not certain, but one pair of jeans. Perhaps it's because jeans are tighter. I've seen some of the women at the Farmers' Market, and you can see everything. Everything of their figure. Do you know what I mean?"

"Senta, of course we can do that," he said. "We'll go to Green Hills and just shop a little. You don't have to do anything or wear anything you don't want to. Sometimes I go overboard. No pun intended," he smiled at his own joke. "Fashion is very tricky. It's especially hard for women. How to be attractive but classy. It also differs from woman to woman. What might look good on one woman could look terrible on another. And some women do wear their jeans too tight. There are ladies in the women's department at Nordstrom who can help. They can guide you on sizes and style. If you just want a few things, that's fine. The only thing I insist on is a pair of Sperry's."

Senta was relieved. Reaching across to Jerrick's arm, she pulled herself to him and rested her head on his shoulder again. *He never gets upset with me*, she thought. *He doesn't even know he's perfect.*

"About the Commodore's Ball," he continued. "We don't have to go. I thought you'd enjoy it, but if it makes you uncomfortable we don't have to attend."

"Oh, Jerrick, I'm being so difficult," she said. "I don't know. I want to. The thought of going to the ball with you, makes me feel like a princess. I've dreamed about things like that. Before, when we had the dairy cows and I would help my father milk them, I'd fantasize about going to a ball and wearing a beautiful gown. And now, here you are actually wanting to take me to a ball, and I'm afraid."

"Can I make a suggestion?" Jerrick asked. Senta nodded. "If you decide to go, and you don't have to .... But if on Saturday you want to attend the ball, jeans are not an option and neither is this dress," he said gently, touching her blue, Amish dress. "Also, there is no place between here and Haven Harbor to buy an appropriate dress. But there is here in Nashville. So, what if we found the right dress and bought it, then should you decide to go you'll be ready. But if not, it's no problem, we'd just return the dress. What do you think?"

"I like that," Senta said smiling. "Dresses like that are expensive, aren't they? I'm worried that I might spill something on it."

"And what if you did?" Jerrick asked. "It would just mean you're normal. Don't think you're the only person who's done that. And it always seems to happen when wearing something nice or new. Last year I did it. I couldn't believe it. A light blue Zegna suit and what did I do? Spilled marinara sauce right here," he said, pointing to his crotch." Senta almost laughed but stopped herself. "I did it. A combination of embarrassing and no one to be mad at but myself. But, did it matter? It didn't. It's just a suit and some spaghetti."

"I can't believe you did that," Senta said trying not to laugh.

"Ah, so you see I'm not perfect," he said. "And that's only one of many things I've done. You have no idea!"

"Was the suit ruined?" she asked.

"No, it was fine. The dry cleaners got it out. It's as good as new. You see, it really wasn't a problem at all. It seemed like it at the time, but it really wasn't anything."

They finished their coffee, talked some more, and Senta felt a little less apprehensive about shopping. They called an Uber driver to take them to Green Hills, and Jerrick had him drop them off in front of Nordstrom. They found two associates in the ladies' department who were very helpful with Senta. Jerrick had originally planned on buying her a lot more than he did, but he didn't push it, letting her get used to a world so different than what she had known, and at her own pace. He'd thought about a makeover session at the cosmetic counter and then a trip to the beauty salon for her hair, but decided against both. Senta ended up with two knee-length casual dresses, a pair of Sperry deck shoes, a pair of jeans, three tops, pajamas, three bras, seven panties, a full length black Adrienne Papel evening gown with a black clutch and black pumps with a modest heel. He'd wanted to get her the Carolina Herrera gown but knew if she'd seen the price she would have refused. When it came time to check out, Jerrick said, "Why don't you wear one of these dresses now, Senta?"

"Can I do that?" she asked, surprised.

"Of course, and the boat shoes, too," Jerrick said as an associate took her back to the changing room while Jerrick settled the bill. Then he put the receipt in his pocket instead of in the bags where she might see it.

"There's a captains' meeting you have to attend," Jerrick said to Senta as they walked out of the department store with their bags. "And it's going to be at Martin's Bar-B-Que on Belmont Avenue. Are you prepared?" He said it partly to play with her because she wouldn't know what he was talking about but also to divert her attention from the purchases and worrying about the cost.

"What's a captains' meeting?" she asked, looking up at him. "You're playing with me again, aren't you? Was that expensive? We bought so much. I'm sorry to be so expensive."

Ignoring her last two questions and focusing on the first one, he said, "A captains' meeting is a meeting for the captains and first mates held the night before a trip. They talk about the destination, how far they plan to travel the next day, where they're going to stop for the night and when they need to leave the next morning. It's also an excuse to eat and drink."

"What is a first mate?" she asked, questioning the new term.

"That would be you," he said. "I've not had a first mate before, but now I do. Since there aren't any other boats going, it'll be just you and me. We'll talk about when we're leaving tomorrow, and about locking through. I should teach you how to do that. We'll practice on the dock."

"Aye, aye, Captain," she said as the Uber driver pulled up. *Is every day like this?* she thought. *Can it be that every day is this much fun? I have no idea how much he spent, but it was a lot. I couldn't see the price on the dress for the ball, but it had to be expensive. I feel so spoiled.*

After getting settled in the car and telling the driver where they wanted to go, Jerrick said, "I'm glad we were able to find a more reasonably priced dress for Saturday night. Did you see how much that Carolina Herrera dress was, or that Chanel?"

He's doing it again, she thought. Senta looked at him to see if she could tell if he was just trying to make her feel better about the cost. *I swear he knows what I'm thinking and then answers my questions without me saying a word.* "I'm glad it wasn't too expensive. I didn't see the price. How much was it?" she asked.

"I don't know. I can't remember," he lied but gave her a wink. "But it was a lot cheaper than those other dresses." He smiled and put his hand on her knee. "I really like this new dress," he said. "It's very pretty."

"Thank you," she said, feeling his hand on her leg. "I really like it, too. I'm still not sure about the jeans. You're sure they're not too tight?"

"They're just right," he said, moving his hand up just a little higher to where she didn't know if it was purposeful or if it was just random. Then he leaned over and kissed her. His hand on her leg and the kiss on her lips made her warm all over. A murmur escaped her lips.

At Martin's Bar-B-Que, they ate the best bar-b-que sandwich Senta had ever had. "I wonder if Mr. Campbell has ever eaten here?" Senta asked. "He really likes his bar-b-que."

"Was Mr. Campbell OK with you taking a week's vacation?" Jerrick asked.

"Yes, he was wonderful," she answered. "Sally had already talked to him, and he agreed even before I asked."

"So, Senta, we're leaving tomorrow. We're heading downriver toward Haven Harbor," Jerrick explained. "I think we should leave tomorrow morning by eight o'clock. Cheatham Lock is 23 miles downstream. We'll pass by Ashland City on the way. You can wave at your coworkers as we go by." Senta smiled, knowing he was kidding with her. "It will take us a little over two hours to get there. We cruise at 8.6 knots. That's 10 land miles per hour, but we have the current with us. So, two hours more or less. Then when we enter the lock, you have to lasso the bollard."

Senta looked at him wide-eyed as he continued, "Inside the lock chamber are big slots in the concrete walls. There are floating steel boxes with a big post on top called bollards. I'm going to show you how to put a line around them and secure

Arcadia to the lock. Then the water leaves the lock chamber, and we float down about 26 feet to the level of Lake Barkley. You don't cast off until the gates are open and the horn sounds. Then you cast off, and we'll head out of the lock to Clarksville which is only about ten miles or so from there. Don't worry, I'll help you," he said, knowing it was confusing.

They got another Uber to take them and Senta's purchases back to Rock Harbor. Once aboard *Arcadia,* they carried everything to Senta's cabin and Jerrick left her putting things away. Then he went out to the dock to prepare the lines for Senta's class on locking. Senta stood in her cabin in front of the mirror looking at herself in her new dress. *The lady at Nordstrom said this was a sun dress*, she thought. *The colors are so pretty, yellows and reds. I like it because it's full everywhere except up here*, she thought, touching her bust. *It makes me self-conscious because it's so form fitting. Jerrick will be able to see my figure, some of it.* Then she opened another bag and looked at the new lingerie. *This is so lovely*, she thought, touching the delicate lace on the bra. *I've never had anything like this before.* She put everything away and then went up on deck to find Jerrick.

Senta walked through the salon, out the aft doorway, and then up the starboard side deck. Looking down, she saw Jerrick moving a trash can across the dock. "How do you like your new dress?" he said, looking up at her as she stood holding the rail. "The style looks great on you."

"Thank you for all the clothes," she said. "I love them."

"There's just one problem with your new dress," he said, and she looked back with concern. "It's September, and it's starting to get a little cooler. You're going to be cold in that dress soon. You'll need a sweater. But we'll take care of that," he said, positioning the trash can by the midship cleat. "Are you ready for your lesson?"

"Yes, but you have more confidence in me than I have in myself," she said. Jerrick looked from the dock and smiled.

"OK, here's what you have to do," he said. "I will be in the pilothouse, operating the boat as we enter the lock. The lockmaster will open the gates for us, and we'll just drive in. You'll be standing right where you are now." Then reaching over the rail, he brought a dockline through the hawse pipe. "You'll hold the line here with your left hand and here with your right so you have a big loop. Now, pretend that this trash can is the bollard. Just swing the loop back and forth until you loop it over the bollard." Senta swung the loop and missed the trash can. Jerrick laughed. Senta made a face at him, and he laughed again. "It's OK to miss. Just don't let the line go under the boat and wrap a screw. That's a propeller. Getting a line wrapped around a propeller is bad, and I'll be upset because I'll have to dive under the boat to cut it free."

"But what do I do if I can't get it," asked Senta, trying again.

"Then I'll come out of the pilothouse and help you," he said. "There's no rush in getting it done. The lockmaster is patient."

Senta tried again and on the third try got the loop over the trash can. "Good job!" said Jerrick, walking up to the trash can. "Now, loop it around the trash can one more time. Then bring the line back through the hawse pipe and cleat it off," he said, walking back down to the gate and stepping aboard *Arcadia* to show her how to cleat the line. He took her hand and guided her. "You bring it around the base once, cross it, then turn it under and cross it again. Now, try it by yourself."

They practiced some more and Senta got better at catching the bollard. "Don't even attempt it until we're close. Remember, it's my job to get you close to the bollard. I'll get you right up next to it so it's easier," he said, putting his hands on her bare arms and moving around her on the side deck. As he did, she felt his body pressed against her back. He went in the pilothouse, and she stood on the side deck feeling warm all over even though it was getting cooler outside. "I think we've worked hard enough today, don't you?" she heard him say from inside the pilothouse where he was getting out the chartbook for the Cumberland River. Senta walked to the pilothouse door. "I think it's time for a glass of wine on the aft deck," he said. "No, let's sit up on the flybridge and have that glass of wine."

"Do you have the kind of wine I had at the Southern?" Senta asked, following him down the steps into the galley.

"We do," Jerrick said with a wink, "Isn't that coincidental! I believe that was Riesling, and I believe you liked it." Senta watched him take the bottle from the refrigerator and open it with a corkscrew. *I can't imagine how wonderful it would be to live like this every day,* she thought. He got two white wine glasses, and together they went up to the flybridge. They sat down and Jerrick poured them each a glass of wine. The view was better there because the flybridge was 16 feet above the water.

"A toast to a good first day," he said, holding up his glass and clinking it against hers.

"A great first day," she said, and they both took a drink.

"Did you have fun today, Senta?" he asked.

"I can't describe what a splendid day I had," she said. "Can you tell how overwhelmed I am almost all the time? I still can't believe you asked me to go with you like this."

"I hope you're overwhelmed in a good way," he said. Senta smiled. They sipped their wine and watched the boats go by. "You know tomorrow is when it really begins. I can't explain it, but travelling by water is so different. You'll see it tomorrow. You'll feel it. Tomorrow night we'll be in Clarksville. It's a nice harbor there. I'm going to take you to the Blackhorse Saloon for dinner."

"This is all so new to me," she said. "But for you it's normal. Isn't it?"

"I guess so," he answered. "But it's never exactly the same. The weather changes. The seasons change. You'll see."

"Jerrick, can I ask you a question?" Senta asked.

"Of course. Remember, I want you to know me and I want to know you," he said.

"Jerrick, are you rich?" she asked. "I mean, you spend a lot of money and it doesn't seem to be a concern you. You are so generous with me. When I first met you, you were wearing old clothes, and I had no idea. I'm sorry. I've been very rude."

"I'm very rich, Senta," he said. "But not because of money. I'm rich because of you. I was poor before I found you. I know you're talking about money. I have been very blessed financially, but that's not what makes a person rich."

Senta thought about his words and the concept that she

made him rich. *Truly, he is different from anyone I've ever known,* she thought. "I'm going to stop drinking wine now," she said, "before I say something stupid." Jerrick watched her and smiled. "Jerrick, could we do something?"

"What would you like to do?" he asked.

"Could we dance again, like we did at the Farmers' Market?" she asked. Jerrick smiled and led her down to the salon where he picked up his iPad and a Bose speaker. Placing it on the table on the aft deck, he touched the screen a few times and then stepped through the starboard gate onto the dock. Turning and extending his left hand to Senta, she took it and stepped onto the dock.

"Do you remember bachata?" he asked.

"Sort of," she answered.

"Don't try to remember how to do it. Just feel it. Let me lead you," he said. "Let the music flow through you." A new song she'd not heard before played, and there on the dock, he pulled her to him and started dancing. "Close your eyes," he said. She did and focused on the music while the touch of his hands guided her as she turned and spun. She felt the music lift her, and she felt him press against her as she came back to him from a turn. She relaxed and became the music.

When the song ended, he said, "You can open your eyes now." Senta was standing on the dock, holding onto him .... entranced. Slowly, she opened her eyes.

"That was incredible," she said.

"Priceless," Jerrick added. "That's why we're rich."

"Can we dance every day?" Senta asked.

"We can," Jerrick answered.

"I love you," Senta said.

"I love you, too," he answered.

CHAPTER SIXTEEN

Locks

Senta was sound asleep when she felt his hand brushing the hair away from her face. "Senta, time to get up," Jerrick said. Senta opened her eyes and saw him sitting by her on the bed, watching her. She smiled and then saw that her cabin was lighted from sunshine coming through the portholes.

Seeing that he was dressed and ready for the day, she said, "Oh my, I've overslept again. I don't know what's wrong with me. I sleep so soundly on the boat.

"I'm glad," he said. "There's no rush. We don't have an appointment with the lockmaster. Take your time. I'll be up in the pilothouse when you're ready." He laid his hand on her cheek and gently caressed her face as he stood and walked out of her cabin.

Senta lay there for a minute, savoring the touch of his hand. Then, she quickly got up, put on his robe, and crossed the hall to her head. Shortly thereafter, she was up on the bridge. "I'm ready now. What shall I do to help?" Senta offered.

Jerrick had noticed her disappointment when he had made breakfast the day before, so he had only made coffee this morning. "I'd really like some scrambled eggs and sausage for breakfast, and I'd like to eat while we're making our way to the lock. You can go down to the galley and make breakfast while I get us ready to leave. Let me know if you can't find everything you need."

Senta eagerly went to the galley and started getting eggs and sausage out of the refrigerator. As she was looking for a frying pan, she heard a low rumbling noise and felt the slight vibration as Jerrick started the engine. She saw him on the stairs by the electrical panel as he switched off rows of breakers, turned a round knob, and then switched them on again. "Don't start cooking yet. I need you on deck to cast off first. Then you can do the eggs and sausage and bring them up to the bridge," he said. She cracked the eggs and mixed them up in a bowl and had everything ready when he called her. She stood on the side deck as he untied the lines on the dock and handed them to her. He stepped onto the boat, closed the starboard gate and said, "When we're clear of the dock, bring in the fenders, then come up to the bridge. I want you to feel what it's like when we leave. Then it will be time for breakfast." He left her and went to the pilothouse.

This is much more complicated than I imagined, she thought. Then she heard a noise that was the thrusters and felt the boat move sideways away from the dock. Senta brought in the fenders as instructed, then ran up to the pilothouse door and went inside and stood by Jerrick as he operated the controls. The boat slowly moved through the marina toward the rock cut that would take them onto the Cumberland River.

"This is a no wake zone, which means slow," he said, pointing to the tachometer. "Dead idle. Over here, on the chartplotter screen, you can see us moving out of Rock Harbor. On the radar you can see the cut so if we were doing this at night or in a storm we'd know our exact position." He brought the boat out into the river and engaged the autopilot. "I'm turning on autopilot so she'll steer herself." The boat moved toward the center of the river and Senta felt the gentle motion as the vessel cut through the water. "What do you think?" he asked.

"It's powerful," she answered. "It's not like a car or a horse and buggy. It's big and powerful, but it's quiet. I almost can't tell we're moving, but I can see we are."

"How about making breakfast now? Then, we'll eat here

on the bridge," he said, walking away from the wheel and looking out the port window.

"Don't you have to drive the boat?" she asked, looking at the abandoned wheel.

"No, it's steering itself. Remember the autopilot?" he answered. "I just have to watch out for traffic and monitor the systems.

Senta went down the stairs to the galley, still intrigued with the idea that they were moving and she was going to make breakfast. She turned on the stove and scrambled the eggs and fried the sausage, turning from time to time to look out the galley window to see the distant shore pass by. Soon, she was finished and brought the breakfast and orange juice up to the bridge. Behind the wheel and helm chair was a settee with a table, and she set the plates there. Then she and Jerrick sat down to breakfast while the autopilot steered the boat. "I still don't understand how it knows where to go," she said.

"There's a device called a flux gate compass onboard that knows where north is," he said. "The chartplotter/GPS positions us on the chart. The autopilot follows the blue track line and makes little corrections to keep us on course." Amazed, Senta watched all the controls as she ate. "The autopilot can't tell if something is coming, like a big barge or a little fishing boat. So, we can't just walk away and ignore it. We must maintain a watch and make corrections if something is in our way. I'll teach you how to do it, just not today. But isn't autopilot nice! I don't have to sit at the wheel and drive. I can walk around, eat breakfast, or whatever."

They finished breakfast, and the scenery changed as they left the industrial area close to Nashville and started to see more forest and rock cliffs. "You're going to be surprised, but for most of the way, it's just wilderness. We may go for hours and see no sign of civilization," he said.

Senta watched the shore pass by and felt the gentle motion of the boat. "Shall I clean up the kitchen .... galley now?" Senta asked, correcting herself.

"Yes, and then come back and we'll rig fenders for the lock," he said. "I hope you're liking this. I know it's not what you're used to."

"Oh, I do," she said, smiling at him. "It's just so different. You said it would be. There's so much for me to learn." She took the dishes below, cleaned up the galley and then returned to the bridge. "Jerrick, this is embarrassing," she said as she found Jerrick looking out the pilothouse windows with the binoculars.

"What's wrong?" he asked, lowering the binoculars and turning to her.

"I have to use the bathroom. Can I do that while the boat is moving?" she asked, looking away.

Jerrick laughed, "Yes, everything works whether we're moving or not. You go right ahead." Senta turned around and went down the stairs.

Upon returning, she said, "I'm so embarrassed. That was a stupid question, wasn't it?

"No, it wasn't," he said, trying to be serious. "I've never had anyone ask that before, but it's better to ask if you're not sure of something. So now that you're back, I want you to sit here," he said, pointing to the helm chair. "You drive, and I'm going to rig the big round fenders for the lock."

"No, no, no," she said, shaking her head. "I don't know what to do. Don't leave."

"I'll just be outside," he said, pointing to the side deck just outside the pilothouse where they were. "I've got to rig the fenders. And remember the boat is driving itself. You don't have to do anything. You can monitor the instruments. Make sure we have oil pressure in the engines. Make sure they're running at 180 degrees. Make sure the voltage from the alternator is in the green. Watch the chartplotter to see we're on the sailing line. Watch ahead to see if anyone is coming." Senta climbed up in the pilot's chair and tried her best to remember all the things *she didn't have to do* as Jerrick stepped out on the side deck and rigged three big, white, round fenders on the side of the yacht. Senta could see him as he worked and felt much better knowing he was a few feet away. When he finished and came back in, she was sitting up very straight and looking out the windows with the binoculars. "See anything?" he asked.

"There's a fishing boat up ahead, but he's not in our way,"

she answered.

"You see, you're getting the hang of it already," he said. Senta got down from the helm chair.

"It's your turn to drive now," she said.

At that moment, a voice came over the marine radio, "Hello all stations, Hello all stations, Hello all stations, United States Coast Guard, Ohio Valley Sector, Consolidated Broadcast for the Cumberland and Tennessee Rivers, 22 Alpha. Senta looked at Jerrick with a look of *what is that?*

"It's just the Coast Guard broadcast. They're going to report on conditions and hazards on the river," Jerrick said as he switched the marine radio from Channel 16 to Channel 22. Senta listened as the voice on the radio reported on various construction sites at different places on the rivers and missing navigation buoys. She watched Jerrick as he listened to the report. When it was finished, Jerrick switched back to Channel 16 and said, "That's good. Nothing close to us." Then looking over at her said, "Come here." Senta moved over and stood by the helm chair, and he put his arm around her while she put her head on his shoulder. "There's the Ashland City bridge coming up. We're about an hour to the lock. Here, in a minute, let's go out on the foredeck. It almost feels like you're flying when you're out there. We'll need to get a couple of PFD's out for the lock. You must wear a PFD in the lock chamber. The lockmaster can write you a ticket if you don't." Senta didn't have to ask because Jerrick read her mind. "A PFD is a Personal Flotation Device, a lifejacket," he said. Senta remembered how she and her father used to communicate with looks and smiles. She thought about how much she missed her parents. *Father would be happy for me and would want to hear all about this trip on the river*, she thought. *Mother wouldn't approve at all because I'm living with Jerrick, alone, even though we're in different bedrooms.* Then she thought about Abigail and John back on the farm that wasn't very far from where they were. Then, baby Rachel and finally Sugar, her horse.

The river got wider, and there were sweeping forests and gray stone cliffs on both sides as they came around a bend. Cheatham Lock and Dam was ahead. Jerrick called the lockmaster on the marine radio. The lockmaster told them to come on and he would have the lock open for them. Senta put on her PFD and took her position on the starboard side deck by the midship cleat with her line for the bollard. As they approached the gates, she was surprised at how big the lock was. *Don't be nervous*, she told herself. *I've got to do this right.*

Arcadia entered the lock at idle speed and slowly moved forward in the chamber. They were the only boat locking through. As the boat moved forward, the lockmaster zipped by in a golf cart and waved at Senta. She waved back and looked up at the pilothouse, wondering if Jerrick had seen him, too. Slowly, Jerrick worked the big trawler up to the bollard. Senta thought, *Wait, Jerrick said he'd get me close so I can't miss.* Finally, she saw the big groove in the concrete wall and saw the floating bollard. "There it is, Senta. I'll get you closer," he said from the pilothouse. When it was right by her, she flipped the line over the bollard and looped it over again. Then she heard Jerrick call out, "Good job! First time, too!" and he came down the deck to help her cleat it off. Then, he went back to the pilothouse and she heard him say on the radio, "Cheatham Lock, *Arcadia* is secure." Shutting off the engine, Jerrick came out to stand with Senta. She jumped when a load horn sounded, and the huge steel gates slowly closed behind them. "You really did well," he said. She looked up and smiled at him, very happy that he was proud of her.

The water dropped, and Senta finally understood how a lock worked as the boat lowered into a concrete chamber. When they had entered, she had been looking out on the grounds around the lock. But as the water lowered, the boat sank deeper into the lock chamber. All she could see was the slimy concrete walls of the lock. Then the lower gates slowly opened, Jerrick restarted the engine, and Senta released the line to the bollard after the horn sounded. She heard the thrusters and felt the boat move away from the lock wall. She looked up at the huge steel gates as *Arcadia* passed through them, and soon they were on their way again.

Senta ran inside the pilothouse and stood by Jerrick as they once again pulled into the river. Jerrick took off his PFD, and Senta did the same. As Jerrick reset the autopilot, he said, "Pretty cool, huh?"

"That was just amazing," she answered. "I never quite understood how locks worked."

"That one was just a drop of 26 feet. Wilson Lock down in Alabama on the Tennessee River is 97 feet. You feel like you're down in a well on that one. It takes a lot longer," he said.

Senta was watching the scenery when her phone rang. "Who can this be?" she asked. "No one ever calls me, except you," she said, smiling. "Hello."

"Hello, Senta, this is Ethan Ward," came the voice on the phone. "Put your phone on speaker so I can talk to both of you." Senta handed the phone to Jerrick, and he touched the screen twice so that Ethan was on speaker.

"Ethan, how are you?" asked Jerrick.

"I'm good," he answered. "I'll get right to it. I have some news for you, Senta. Eric Yost spent Sunday night in jail. He made bail yesterday. We just met with the State's Attorney there in Cheatham County, along with Yost and his attorney. Yost has agreed to sign the farm back over to you, Senta. His attorney advised him to not go to trial, so he plea bargained. He could have gotten twenty-five years, but we settled on ten. He'll serve five with good behavior. I'm sure the Amish community there will be finding a new bishop. The most important thing is he won't be doing this again, and you've got your farm back, Senta."

"Thank you, Mr. Ward," said Senta. "I can't thank you enough."

"You're welcome, Senta," he said. "So, Jerrick, I got her farm back. Does that mean I'm invited to the boat next Memorial Day?"

"It does, Ethan!" Jerrick laughed. "I just think you need to bring Miss Thompson with you!"

"OK, I'll work on that," Ethan said. "Have a good trip. Bye."

"He did it!" exclaimed Senta after they'd hung up. "I can't believe how bad everything was, and now everything has turned around." Senta started to tear up. "I wish my parents could have known you. My father would have liked you. My mother was always afraid of anyone who was English. She always thought someone was going to kidnap me at the Farmers' Market."

Jerrick put his arm around her and gave her a hug. "Your mother was right," he said. "I did sort of kidnap you."

She looked up at him and said, "I don't think it's called kidnapping if I'm willing."

The autopilot steered, and the river miles ticked off. They went out on the foredeck. Standing on the foredeck with Jerrick behind her, his arms around her. *It does feel like flying. I couldn't be any happier*, she thought. An hour later, Clarksville came into sight and soon they pulled off the river and into the marina. Jerrick was familiar with the harbor and knew where the transient pier was. Soon they were tied up to the dock, the engine was shut down, and the systems were switched to shore power. Jerrick and Senta walked up to the office to find the harbormaster and pay for the night's dockage. As they walked back to *Arcadia*, Senta asked, "Why is it important that Miss Thompson be the right kind of Presbyterian for Ethan?"

"Ethan has very high standards for the future Mrs. Ward," answered Jerrick. "He's really particular. That's not a bad thing. It just takes some of us a long time to find the right woman. We all kid him about it." Jerrick watched Senta to see if she understood. She looked at him, and he knew she did. "He's just going to have to figure out a way to get around the rules. He could switch her to a different department, but then he wouldn't get to see her every day, and I think he likes seeing her every day. Time will tell," he added, shrugging his shoulders.

Back on the boat, Jerrick said, "May I take you out to lunch for some Mexican food?" as he pointed to a Mexican restaurant next to the marina. "Then we can walk through old Clarksville. They've got some interesting antique stores and some women's boutiques. There's also another captain's meeting at the Black Horse Saloon this evening."

"I'd like to walk," she answered. "That sounds like fun." *He's so good to me*, she thought. *I can't believe he loves me. Whenever I make a mistake, he just laughs. He never gets upset with me.*

"Sounds like a plan, First Mate," he said. "Give me 15 or 20 minutes. I want to go down in the lazarette and check the hydraulic system pressure for the steering. I could be imagining it, but I thought the wheel felt a little sluggish. If you need to do anything or just relax, I'll be ready in a few minutes."

Senta watched as he opened a hatch in the aft deck and disappeared down a ladder. She went to her cabin and brushed her hair, experimenting with parting it on the side or in the middle. Finally, she made a pony tail and then turned it into a French twist like she'd seen on the internet. Looking at herself in the mirror, she decided to change clothes and put on her new jeans and a red sleeveless top. Walking up the stairs and into the salon, Senta stopped in her tracks. Looking out the window, she saw Jerrick talking to a very attractive young woman on the dock. The woman was wearing blue jean shorts and a white short-sleeved blouse with the top two buttons undone, displaying serious cleavage. If that wasn't enough, she had beautiful dark brown hair that cascaded down onto her shoulders. Senta watched intently as Jerrick talked, although she couldn't hear what he was saying. But she could hear the woman laugh and see her smile at him. *Oh, my, she's striking!* Senta thought. *How am I supposed to compete with that? Her legs, her figure, her smile.* Senta watched until the woman walked away. Senta also noticed when she turned around and waved goodbye again. When she was finally gone, Senta went out on deck. "Are you ready?" she asked.

"Hey, look at you!" he said. "You're wearing jeans. You look great. I just have to get used to you looking different. But I like it!"

Jerrick and Senta walked up the dock to the office, around the parking lot to the sidewalk and then on to the Mexican restaurant. "Is something wrong?" Jerrick asked, as they were seated at the Mexican restaurant. "You seem different," he said, studying Senta.

"I'm just concerned about something," she said.

"So what are you worried about?" he asked.

"Have you had a lot of girlfriends?" she asked.

"Senta, you shouldn't ask me questions like that," Jerrick answered.

"But you said I could ask you anything," she said.

"I did," he answered. "Does this have anything to do with the woman I was talking to on the dock?"

"Well, maybe," she said. "Who was she anyway?"

"Just a girl who was looking for a friend's boat and couldn't find it," he said. "I sent her over to the next pier."

"She was very pretty," said Senta. "And she liked you. I could tell."

"She was pretty, and she was flirting with me," he agreed.

"Does that happen to you very often?" asked Senta.

"Not often, but occasionally," he said. The waitress, a pretty Mexican girl, approached their table and Jerrick ordered two tamarindos for them.

"Just occasionally?" said Senta when the waitress was out of earshot. "She likes you, too! I saw how she smiled at you. You're so charming. Jerrick, how can I compete with all the beautiful women there are?"

The waitress came back with the drinks and took their food order. Before she left, Jerrick said to her, "¿Disculpe, señorita, tienes un canal de bachata? ¿Puedes cambiar la mùsica a bachata?"

"Por supuesto, Señor," she answered.

"What did you say to her?" asked Senta. Jerrick stood and extended his left hand to Senta just as the music changed to bachata.

"I asked her if she could switch the music to bachata, so I could dance with you," he said. Senta stood and he led her to an open area of the restaurant.

"You want to dance right here?" she asked. Jerrick looked at her. "Yes, you want to dance right now," she said, answering her own question.

Not many people were in the restaurant as it was just past the lunch hour, but the few who were there watched Jerrick and Senta as they danced. The song was "La Carratera." As they danced, Jerrick whispered "You don't have to compete with anyone, Senta. There's no competition because I chose you." Senta looked into his eyes and felt the music flow in them. He twirled her twice as the song ended. And the other customers applauded.

They returned to their booth, as the waitress was bringing

their food. "That was very nice bachata, señorita," complimented the waitress. "Most Americans can't dance like that. Where did you learn?"

Senta smiled, very pleased with the compliment and answered, "At the Farmers' Market in Nashville." Then pointing to Jerrick, she added "And my teacher."

With a knowing smile, the waitress said, "I think you have a good teacher." With that, she returned to the kitchen. Jerrick could tell she was talking about them to the other waitress.

"Thank you," Senta said to Jerrick. "I just get nervous sometimes. I think about those weeks when you were gone to Guatemala and how I thought I'd lost you. I don't want to ever lose you." She took a drink of her tamarindo while Jerrick listened. "I really liked that song. I like it when we dance, and we do it perfectly together. What was that song?"

"It's another Prince Royce song, 'La Carretera.' Remember, 'Déjà vu?' That was Prince Royce and Shakira. We should dance every day. Because every time we dance, we discover each other a little more. We get better because we're part of each other," Jerrick said.

"I am getting better, aren't I?" she asked. Jerrick nodded. "I was really bad at first. I was nervous because I didn't know how. But you made me close my eyes and feel the music. I want to dance with you every day."

After lunch, they walked down the street that followed the river and Jerrick showed her the municipal pier. Turning right, they walked up the hill away from the river into Old Clarksville where they browsed through a few shops. At a store called Couture Crush, Jerrick bought her a sweater and another top that would go with the jeans. "You've got to stop spending so much money on me," she said. "But, thank you." Then she thought, *He likes to buy me things. It's just how he is. I wish I could do something for him.*

Wandering around the old downtown, they found a coffee shop called C3. They ordered cappuccinos, and Senta was amazed at the intricate coffee art leaf pattern the barista made in the espresso. "Jerrick?" she asked as they drank their coffee. "You know all about me. But tell me about you."

"Well," he started. "I'm originally from Southern Illinois. I was a business major at UT, the University of Tennessee at Knoxville. My parents still live in Southern Illinois. I have one brother. And you know I like boats."

"You told me you were married," she asked. "What was she like?"

"I met her in school," he said. "She was pretty but very self-centered, selfish. She was very materialistic, always spending money."

"But you're always spending money on me. I don't want you to think I'm like that," she said.

"You're nothing like her," he said. "You're kind and generous, always thinking of others. You don't have a selfish bone in your body." Jerrick paused and took a sip of coffee. "You're also prettier."

"I'm jealous, you know," Senta said, looking down at the table.

"I do," he said. "Try not to be. I didn't matter to her. Now, I can't even remember the marriage. And it's all good because we've met each other."

"And what do you love?" Senta asked, remembering when he had asked her that question and she had wondered how he would answer.

"I love peace," he answered. "Every day I thank God that we're not at war. That we can sleep in peace without fear." Senta looked at him and wondered why he would say that but couldn't bring herself to ask. "And next would be, what do I hate?" he said. "I hate people who abuse their power. People who use their position to get what they want and hurt others with no regard for them. It's wrong to do that. It's wrong to abuse power."

Senta hadn't expected any of that but felt he was referring to Eric Yost. *Why does he think like that?* she wondered. *He's very careful with me, and protective, but there is a part of him that scares me. With Eric Yost, he was angry .... a silent, frightening kind of angry. Yost is going to prison. Ethan saw to that, but if he hadn't, I'm afraid Jerrick would have done something. When most people are mad, it's obvious .... but Jerrick is quiet. I just have the strong feeling that Eric Yost is lucky Ethan sent him to prison.* Jerrick studied Senta and read her mind.

Leaving the coffee shop, they decided to explore the old downtown until dinner time. As they walked, Jerrick said, "So you see I'm not perfect."

"You said we should get to know each other better," Senta responded. "I love you. I think you're the most wonderful man I've ever known." They continued walking. "You're very complicated and sometimes I don't understand you. I forgive you for anything you've ever done wrong, and I forgive you for everything you may do wrong in the future."

"So, you really are Senta .... just like in the opera," he said, smiling. "I don't deserve you."

"No, I'm the one who doesn't deserve you," she said.

When they got to the Black Horse, it was packed. "It looks like quite a wait," he said. "Why don't we order a pizza and take it back to the boat." She nodded in agreement, so they ordered a pizza to go and called an Uber for a ride back so the pizza wouldn't get cold.

As they were riding, he asked, "Do the Amish watch movies?"

"I'm not sure about all Amish, but we didn't," she answered.

"So, would you like to watch a movie while we eat our pizza?" he asked. "I've got lots of DVD's on the boat; there's a classic called *Captain Ron* that you've got to see." Jerrick laughed and added, "I feel like I'm corrupting you, asking if you want to watch a movie."

"I've always wanted to watch movies," she said. "Is *Captain Ron* a good movie?"

"It's a great movie, and everyone who's ever been on a boat needs to see it," he said, laughing. "It's a comedy. You're going to love it, and you're going to enjoy it more because you understand boats now."

The Uber driver dropped them at the marina, and they entered the code to get through the gate and back to the boat. Jerrick found the DVD and put it in the player while Senta got plates and drinks. Senta enjoyed her first movie. Jerrick found the expression on her face priceless as the yacht owner and his wife got caught in the shower and then came spilling out when Captain Ron opened the shower door. They both laughed until they hurt.

When it was over, Senta said, "Our voyage is very calm compared to theirs, and your boat is in much better shape. I couldn't believe what the little boy said to the General." They laughed some more and talked about the movie.

"It's time to do the engine room check," Jerrick said when they'd finished discussing the movie. "We're leaving Clarksville tomorrow morning, unless you want me to take you back."

Senta looked at him with concern. "Of course not. Why do you think I'd want to go back?"

"I just got a little intense back at the coffee shop, and I thought I may have scared you," he smiled. "Remember, I can tell what you're thinking sometimes. But I want you to understand me."

Senta smiled and said, "Jerrick, you've told me I don't have to be perfect." Jerrick responded with a smile. "Well, you're being too hard on yourself. I think you're wonderful. I wouldn't change anything about you. I think you're perfect." Senta hugged him and pressed her face against his chest. "I don't understand everything, but I know I have lived my life to find you. Everything that's happened in my life has been to bring me to you. For a long time, it almost felt like God had forgotten me, but I see now that He was just arranging it all so I could find you."

Jerrick did the engine room check, and Senta got ready for bed. Lying in bed, she waited for him with the covers up under her chin. He came in and kissed her goodnight. Without lingering, he retired to his stateroom. *I hope everything is OK,* she thought. *He seems distant, like he's thinking about something .... like he's deciding something.* The light went out in the master cabin; soon the captain and the first mate were asleep.

CHAPTER SEVENTEEN

Charts

Senta woke up early. She guessed it was just after dawn. A front had blown in during the night, bringing a heavily overcast sky that covered Clarksville from horizon to horizon. She lay in her bed still thinking about the night before, worried that something was wrong. *He asked me if I wanted him to take me back*, she thought. *Why would he think that? Maybe he wants to take me back and was just hoping I'd say I wanted to go back. It seemed like everything was going so well. Who am I kidding? There's no way he could truly like me. He has his pick of pretty girls, so why would he pick me? But he tells me he loves me. He tells me he chose me. But he hasn't* kissed *me again like he did in Nashville. Why doesn't he? It's because he's going to take me back. He's just being nice to me.* Then she heard footsteps overhead and thought, *He's up already.* She jumped up, made her bed, and with her clothes, hurried across the hall to the head to get ready. She showered and was done in record time.

She ran up the stairs to the galley and looked in the salon. No Jerrick. In fearful expectation, she turned and ran up the stairs to the bridge. "There you are," he said. "Did you sleep well?" She stood still, once again reverting to speechlessness. "Are you OK?" he asked with a faint smile. "Is something on your mind?"

She stood before him, studying his face and his voice, looking for any clue that he was about to say he was taking her back. "Come here," he said. She crossed the few feet between them and fell into his arms; while hugging him as hard as she could, Senta broke into tears. "What's wrong?" he asked, holding her.

"I am afraid you are going to send me back," she cried. "Do you want me to stay?" She looked up at him, trying not to cry.

"Of course," he said. "Where did you get the idea I don't want you to stay?

"It's just me," she said, wiping her eyes. "Maybe it's because I still can't believe you would want me. That someone like you would want someone like me."

Jerrick held her again, stroking her hair. "Is it because of the girl on the dock, or is it because I'm mostly behaving myself around you?"

"Both, I guess," she answered. "I know I don't kiss very well, and it was probably disappointing when we kissed on the bridge."

"Senta, it takes every ounce of willpower I have to not kiss you like that again," he explained. "And I haven't because I know that if I did, here, I wouldn't be able to stop myself. Do you know how difficult it is to put you to bed in your cabin and then walk down the hall to my bed? To know you're lying there just a few feet away?"

Senta listened to the words, contemplating what they meant. *He is attracted to me*, she thought. *I was afraid he didn't want me like that.*

"Abigail told me to be careful with you, to be gentle," he said. "You've been through so much. You're fragile, and I'm trying to go slow. But honestly, I can't do that much longer. So, stop worrying that I'm sending you back or that I don't like how you kiss or that you don't turn me on. OK?" Senta nodded and wiped her eyes. "Now, I would like some cinnamon rolls for breakfast. They're in the refrigerator. Let's you and me go down and get that oven preheated to 350 degrees." They went to the galley together and went to work. Jerrick helped, all the while watching Senta to make sure she was alright.

Senta looked at him as she broke open the tube of cinnamon rolls, and he poured orange juice. *I've got to stop crying all the time*, she thought. *He does think I'm attractive. He almost said that I turn him on. I don't understand how that can be, but he said it. Stop worrying, Senta! He told you to stop worrying. Don't be so emotional.*

"Set the timer for the oven and pour us some coffee. Let's go to the bridge, and I'll show you where we're going today," he said.

Up on the bridge, Jerrick had the Cumberland River chart book out. "Maps are for land, and charts are for water," he said, as he turned the pages in search of something. "Right here. This is where we'll be spending the night." Senta looked at the book of maps that he called charts while she held her hands on her coffee cup, enjoying the warmth. "A cold front came through last night. It's still moving through. That's why it's so cloudy. It will start raining in a few hours, continuing through the night. You haven't been outside yet, but it's colder," he said, looking at her dress. "I really like your new dress, but I'm afraid you're going to get cold."

Senta looked up at him and then put her coffee down to open the starboard pilothouse door. The cold wind and light rain hit her and she quickly shut the door. "Oh, my! It *is* colder!" she said.

"Told you," Jerrick smiled. "We're expecting two deliveries this morning. I've ordered some supplies, and they'll be delivered right here to the boat. We'll leave after breakfast and after we receive those deliveries. We have about a four-hour cruise today," he said.

"Is it another harbor like this one?" Senta asked.

"No, it's not," he answered. "No town, no restaurants, no people. It's a wilderness anchorage."

"You mean there's nothing there?" she asked.

"Just us," he said. "I guess it's possible other boats could be anchored there, but I've never had that happen. It'll be just us."

Senta imagined what that would be like to not be tied

up to a dock, with nothing but forest in view from the water. *Arcadia* would feel like an island. "So we'll use the anchor and windlass?" she asked, and Jerrick nodded.

They ate the cinnamon rolls in the salon because it was too cold and wet to eat on the aft deck. When they were finished and enjoying a second cup of coffee, Jerrick spotted someone on the dock. "I think this guy is looking for us." He went out the aft door and met the delivery man. Taking three sacks, Jerrick thanked him and gave him a tip.

Senta looked perplexed as Jerrick came in. "I thought you were getting some oil or something for the engines. Those bags are from Crush Couture, the store where you bought my sweater yesterday.

"Yes, I don't want any complaining," he said, playfully. "These are more clothes for you. I had the lady who helped you yesterday pick them out because she knows your size. Socks because your feet will get cold. Another sweater. A couple more tops that will be a bit warmer. Another pair of jeans. A jacket."

Senta took the items out of the bags one by one and admired them. "They're so pretty. The lady at the store really knows how to pick things for me," she said. "These look like me, or how I think I would like to look. Does that make sense?"

"I'm glad you're pleased. And it makes perfect sense. You're learning what you like. What looks right on you and what doesn't. You're discovering your own style," he answered.

"Thank you," she said, standing and giving Jerrick a hug. "You know, I can't kiss you because you're so tall, unless you lean down a little." Jerrick smiled and leaned over, and Senta kissed him on the lips, a very quick kiss but a kiss, nonetheless. The touch of their lips sent that feeling of electricity through her again and she thought, *I kissed him. Am I getting brave or what? There's that feeling again. He's so handsome. Settle down, Senta!* "I'm going to go down and put these away. And you're right. It's colder, so I'm going to change into something warmer. Thank you."

Senta went down both sets of stairs to her cabin and put away her new clothes. Then she changed into her new jeans, a pair of warm socks, a new top and a pullover sweater. She quickly redid her hair as it had partially come down when she put on the sweater. *This is so cute*, she thought as she looked in the mirror. *The jeans fit nicely, not too tight.* Senta turned around and studied herself from the back. She went up the stairs and saw Jerrick going out the salon door again to the aft deck to another delivery man. She couldn't see what he had until he walked back in a second later with a vase full of red roses. *Oh, my goodness!* she thought. *He's brought me red roses!* With her hands over her mouth, Senta was astounded.

"These are for you so you'll believe me and stop worrying that I'm going to send you back," he said, presenting her with the roses.

"They are beautiful," she cried, taking the vase from him and setting it on the salon table. "No one has ever given me flowers before. I don't know anyone who's gotten red roses before. Abigail hasn't. Ruth hasn't. Oh, my!" She stood, admiring the flowers and then him while thinking, *He does love me. I'm not going to cry again. I'm not going to cry.*

Again, she hugged him. Then he tilted her chin up and kissed her. "I'm never going to ask you that question again. I was just kidding," he said. "I'm glad you like the roses. Now, let's put the vase in the sink and pack some towels around it so it won't tip over if we hit any rough water today. When we're safely at anchor you can set them out again on the table."

"Jerrick, I've never told you. I've wanted to tell you from the very beginning," Senta said. "I love you. I think I loved you even before I knew you, if that's possible." Jerrick kissed her again and smiled as they looked into each other's eyes. It was the last time Senta ever doubted how Jerrick felt.

Soon they were under way, lines cast off as the engine slowly brought them away from the dock, and the trawler crept through the marina. Senta looked out the starboard window of the pilothouse and watched the cars pass on the street that bordered the harbor. She wondered if anyone noticed the big, white yacht moving across the water. Then she remembered pulling the milk cart to the road years before and seeing cars driving by and wondering who they were. Jerrick switched on the Nav lights because it was still dark from the cloud cover even though it was nine o'clock in the morning. He then brought the engine RPM up and adjusted the radar. Senta turned from the window and walked over to Jerrick. She looked in his coffee cup and smiled at him lovingly, then went below to the galley to bring them more coffee.

Soon the city was behind them, and it was once again forest and stone cliffs along the water's edge. They watched deer on the bank, drinking from the river. They observed a great blue heron flying a foot off the water looking for his breakfast, a couple of egrets, and a kingfisher. "There are so many water birds," Senta said. "They're so pretty."

Jerrick reached down to a drawer and pulled out a green book entitled *The Audubon Society Field Guide to North American Birds* and handed it to Senta. "Look at the pictures," he said. "There must be 50 different types of ducks alone. Then there are all the hawks and the gulls and the wading birds. Thousands of different types of birds. It's fun to look at them with the binoculars and then try to find them in the book." Senta's eyes lit up as she looked at the colored plates of birds in the book. "The males look different than the females, and they also can look different at different times of the year," he explained. Every time Senta spotted a bird, she would get the binoculars and then try to identify it in the field guide. She was very pleased when she was able to do so, and Jerrick liked how much she enjoyed it.

Later in the morning, Jerrick said, "Come here, Senta. I want to show you something." Senta went and stood by the helm chair. Pointing out the window at the water and then at the digital display of their speed, he said, "You can see that we're moving because it says so and because we can see the shore passing by. But look at this. We're doing 9.6 knots. At this RPM, we should be doing 8.6 knots. How can we be going faster than what we should be going?"

Senta studied the number and, shrugging her shoulders, said, "I don't know."

"What if I told you that if we turned around and went the other way that we'd only be doing 7.6 knots. Now, what do you think?" he asked.

Senta thought about it and then said, "The water is moving. Are we going faster because the current is carrying us along?"

Jerrick smiled and said, "That's right. The river is flowing. Right now, right here, around one nautical mile per hour which is one knot. You can't see it. You can't tell by looking at it, but millions of gallons per hour are moving. Do you know why?"

Looking behind her, she said, "Because of all the water that's coming downstream from beyond Nashville."

"And all the other rivers that empty into this one, and all the streams and creeks and springs from millions of acres. Then this flows into the Ohio that flows into the Mississippi and on to the sea. And it never stops flowing."

"Music flows, too," she said. "You can't see it, but you can feel it."

Pointing up, Jerrick said, "The sky flows, too. Not many people notice it, but if you lie on your back up on the forward deck and watch the sky, it moves."

"So if you were flowing along on the boat, and listening to music flow, and watching the sky flow, everything would be flowing," she said.

He looked at her and smiled, pleased that she was understanding it. Then leaning toward her, he kissed her.

Once again she felt the electricity of the kiss and in a moment of illumination, she said, "Does love flow, too? Like the river, like the sky, like music?"

Jerrick nodded slowly, watching her as she understood it. "And it all flows from the same place. It's all the same thing," he said.

Senta's mind raced. She reflected on the music she knew and how it made her feel. About living under the sky moving over her and only now noticing. The big river flowing so close her entire life; yet she had not realized it. Then finally about him and the love she never had until now. She thought about how the flowing was all around her and within her. "Is it God?" she asked, looking at Jerrick. "Is it all flowing from Him?" He smiled and nodded.

Quietly, they shared the moment as the boat moved through the water. Jerrick put his arm around Senta and brought her close to him. She felt secure in the warmth of his body. Both were contemplating what had just been said. For Senta, it was almost overwhelming. How amazing that she had never seen it before! Just then the wind picked up and for the first time Senta saw whitecaps on the water and experienced a slight motion in the boat. And her mind made the connections. *The sky is flowing and the water is flowing; when they meet, we have waves,* she thought. *I feel the love of this man beside me. I can feel all of this. In fact, I'm surrounded by it. Thank You, God, for Your creation and making me part of it!*

A short while later, the first rain drops appeared on the windows. The reverse angle on the front windows kept most of the rain off so it wasn't necessary for Jerrick to turn on the wipers. Senta went to the galley a little after noon and made sandwiches for lunch. As she prepared the food, she wondered, *Does food flow, too? Is flow in everything?* When she looked at the beautiful roses in the vase, she remembered how red roses symbolize love. Smiling, she thanked God for roses. When Senta looked out the galley window she saw the gray skies and rain. *I'm so grateful that we're warm and dry here inside Arcadia,* she thought. *And I love this new sweater.* Senta thought about the people who had made her sweater, their lives and the love they had for their families. Her mind spinning, it came to her, *It's everywhere. It's all around me.*

After passing Dover and the Confederate fortifications that remained from the Civil War, they sailed a bit further and then found a creek that flowed into the Cumberland. Senta thought it was too small for *Arcadia* to fit in, but Jerrick slowly moved through the tight opening. A short distance later, she saw the creek open into a much wider anchorage. Senta watched as he skillfully brought the boat up into the wind and then operating the controls to the windlass, payed out the CQR anchor and one hundred feet of chain as the yacht reversed. Soon the anchor was set, and Jerrick hit the *off* button to the engine. The boat became silent with the engine stopped and the only sound the raindrops hitting the windows.

"It's beautiful, don't you think?" he asked her. "Not a house in sight. We've got the place all to ourselves. It's supposed to rain like this all afternoon and all night. It'll drop into the low 40's."

"Does *Arcadia* have heat, too, since it has air-conditioning?" Senta asked. "I'm guessing it does. I'm just cold natured, and I wondered if the boat would get cold tonight."

"It does," he said. "I'll turn on the heat if necessary, but I probably won't need to. There's a little trick. We can crack the door to the engine room, and heat will come out into the boat. It takes the engine a full 24 hours to completely cool down. They put out heat for a long time. There's that, and the reverse cycle heating system." He paused for a moment then added, "And there are other ways to keep warm." For a moment, Senta wondered what he meant. As her heart skipped a beat, she thought, *Could this be the day? If he wants me, I won't tell him no.*

After Jerrick had turned off the electronics and turned on the 360 degree anchor light outside, he said, "Let's go out on the aft deck for a second. We'll be under cover and not get wet." Senta followed him down the stairs and through the salon to the aft door and they stepped out on the covered aft deck. It was much colder outside, but the breeze was blocked by the boat since a boat at anchor will always point into the wind. The aft deck was dry. They stood for a moment, watching it rain as millions of raindrops tap-danced on the water surrounding the boat. Jerrick moved behind her and put his arms around her. "It's beautiful, isn't it?" he asked, softly.

"It is," she answered, thinking that the moment couldn't have been more perfect as she felt his strong arms surround her. She placed her hands over his. She couldn't help but notice his hands were close to her breasts and think about how it would feel for him to touch her. Listening to the rain, she closed her eyes and felt his hard body against her back. *I want to please him so badly.* Then he leaned down and kissed her ear, then kissed it again and again, moving down to her earlobe. Lightly biting her earlobe and then gently touching it with his tongue, he whispered, "I love you." *Oh, my God*, she thought, *The electricity .... I'm so warm even though it's cold. And that feeling inside, down there. I know I'm not supposed to think like this, but I can't help it. I want him so badly.*

He turned her around and gently kissed her on the lips. "Let's go in before you get too cold; we can get some food out for dinner." He bent over and pulled open a hatch. Letting go of her hands, he descended a ladder into the room below and then motioned her to follow. "This is the lazarette," he said. "It's just storage, the steering and the freezer. This is where I came yesterday to check the pressure in the steering hydraulics," he said, pointing to some machinery behind him. Senta looked around thinking, *There are so many different places on this boat, and I thought I'd seen it all.* "I wanted to show you so if I ask you to get something from here you'll know where the lazarette is," he said, opening cabinets which held spare parts and various food items. Senta took a deep breath, trying to calm herself and concentrate on his words. She still felt her knees weak from what he'd just done up on the aft deck. "No restaurants here as you can see so we'll be dining in tonight. I'm thinking two filets, asparagus, and baked potatoes," he said, opening a chest freezer full of food and found two filets and asparagus. "How does that sound?"

"That sounds wonderful," she said, still trying to get her bearings.

"OK, let's go back up and get inside," he said, closing the freezer and guiding her to the ladder.

Once inside the salon, he took the vase out of the sink and put it on the table. He put the frozen food in the sink to thaw. Senta sat on the white couch and looked at her roses and then at Jerrick as he opened a bottle of rosè and took two glasses out of the wine cabinet. Sitting down beside her, he poured the wine. Then turning on his iPad, he hit the Spotify icon, and brought up Senta's playlist. "I found your playlist, you know," he told her.

"You did?" she asked. "I had no idea people could see others' playlists."

"Yeah, you can see other people's playlists and listen to their songs if you like. See," he said, showing her the Senta playlist on his iPad. "But first, a toast to Senta Miller," he said, handing her a glass and raising his. "To Senta, who is perfect even if she doesn't know it." Senta teared up as she clicked her glass against his, blinking her eyes trying to stop the tears.

"Now, I have a question," he said, reaching over and gently touching her cheek where a tear had run down. "Today is Wednesday. We will be to Haven Harbor by Friday or Saturday at the latest. We have plenty of time. The weather doesn't look very good for tomorrow, so we may just stay here tomorrow, too, going all the way to Haven Harbor on Friday. Saturday is the Commodore's Ball. Have you thought any more about it? Would you like to go?" Jerrick took another sip of wine, and Senta did, too.

"Yes, but I want you to tell me about it. What to expect. What I'm supposed to do," she explained. "Honestly, I'm very intimidated by it. Something occurred to me last night. When I've fantasized about things like this, like going to a ball, I've never worried about anything going wrong. Now that it's real, that's all I think about."

"Well, do you remember when you, Abigail, and I ate lunch at the Farmers' Market?" he asked. Senta nodded. "It's really very much like that. There were lots of people in the food court, and there will be lots of people at the Commodore's Ball. You didn't talk to everyone at the food court, and you won't talk to most of the people at the ball. You'll get introduced to people, and you won't remember all their names. But you don't have to. Just like we talked with Abigail at the food court, you'll talk to the people at your table. Do you remember the first time we met? Do you remember the three other couples who bought cheese and bread?" he asked. Senta nodded while listening closely. "That's who will be at your table. So, you've already met them." Senta thought about the points he was making, finding them encouraging. "One thing that's different is dancing," he said. "No dancing at the food court. There is dancing at the ball, but, and I'm serious, you're a better dancer than most there. It's easy. It's just foxtrot."

"So there's no bachata?" she asked.

"No, I'm afraid not," he answered. "I'll show you how to foxtrot. And remember you don't have to dance every dance. You can sit some out if you don't care for the song or if you're tired or even if your shoes are hurting your feet." He watched her as she processed everything.

"Yes, I want to try," she said. "But I have to practice dancing."

Jerrick looked at her playlist and said, "Here we go. I didn't know you liked Frank Sinatra. "The Way You Look Tonight." This would be good to teach you how to foxtrot."

"I heard it at the Farmers' Market. I liked it, so I saved it on my Spotify list," she said.

"Ok, come here and let me show you," he said, touching the play button on the iPad. "Foxtrot is easy. It'll be easy for you. Remember, just like bachata, if you pay attention to my lead, it will be easier because you'll know what to do." Jerrick showed her the steps and how they fit to the music. Dancing together in the salon, Senta thought, *I am so happy. Every day is wonderful. I didn't know life could be so grand. He's right of course, this is much easier than bachata. I do like it, but I like bachata better.*

When the song ended, she said, "Jerrick, could we dance bachata?"

Jerrick smiled and looking at the iPad touched "Promise." The song started off slow as they came together. Not having as much room in the salon, they danced close and didn't do all the turns and spins that required more room. Senta thought, as she felt his body against hers, *I can't believe he loves me. I'm on this boat, anchored somewhere no one knows about, and I'm dancing with this handsome man.* Outside, the rain continued to fall, and the temperature dropped. When the song ended, Jerrick didn't release her but held her tightly against him. They looked into each other's eyes for a long time. Then he kissed her, gently at first but then harder.

The dam of desire finally broke, and he was unable to control himself any longer. He kissed her forcing his tongue between her lips. Senta exploded inside as his tongue penetrated her. Then he stopped for just a moment, and brushing the hair back from her face, said, "I love you. I love you like I didn't know I could love anyone." And then started kissing her forehead and cheeks and nose.

Senta was overwhelmed with emotion and desire, but as she had experienced before, she found herself unable to speak."

Taking a deep breath and slowing himself down, he said, "I want you. Now." Then slowly he started pulling her sweater off over her head.

Oh, my God in Heaven, Senta thought. Her mind raced. *It's going to happen. Is this what I want?* Her sweater was off, and he was unbuttoning her blouse. *But I don't want to stop him*, she thought. *I do want this.* She looked at him, breathing hard, his chest rising and falling under his shirt. Then she looked down at her unbuttoned blouse and saw her breasts rising and falling. *We love each other, so I can't do this wrong even if I do*, she thought. Then in an act of courage that surprised even her, Senta slowly unbuttoned his shirt and kissed his chest over and over while he lovingly looked down at her.

Taking her by the hand, he led her down the three stairs to the hallway and then down, past her cabin to the last door, the master cabin. He slowly took off her blouse and then unbuttoned and unzipped her jeans. When she only had on her bra and panties, he said, "You're beautiful." Then he unhooked her bra, and, moving his hands down her hips, slipped off her panties.

She stood as she had many times before in front of a mirror, but this time watching his face for his reaction. He looked at her then up to her eyes and smiled, and she thought, *He's pleased with me. He does think I'm beautiful.* Then he undid his jeans and removed them along with his boxers, in one motion. Senta had never seen a man naked before, and she stood looking at him. *He does want me*, she thought. *He definitely wants me. And I want him.*

Jerrick pulled back the comforter, the blanket and the sheet. He led her to the side of the bed and lay her down slowly, then crawled in beside her. He kissed her gently and asked, "Are you sure this is what you want, Senta?"

"I love you so much," she said, looking up at him, touching his face and running her fingers through his hair. "Yes, I want to make love to you. But I'm a little nervous," she said, looking into his eyes.

"I'm going to go slow and be gentle with you," he whispered. Then he kissed her and touched her slowly. After a bit, he could feel her relax as she kissed him back. He touched her again and a moan escaped her lips. "You are perfect," he said. Then he parted her legs, and he was on top of her. Bringing her knees up, he felt her tense again. "I love you and you are perfect," he repeated and kissed her again. She felt him press into her and felt herself break and she cried out softly as he entered her. He pushed in deeper then stopped for a second, kissing her again. Then he started moving and she could feel him inside of her, making love to her faster and faster until he climaxed. Outside the river flowed, the clouds moved across the sky and the wind made whitecaps on the water. Senta felt it all, all the flowing, all the love, and completely overwhelmed, she burst into tears of joy.

Jerrick lay on his back, holding Senta as she cried into his chest. He reached down and pulled the covers over them. Stroking her hair and kissing her head, he felt the softness of her naked body against his. Looking up at the twin hatches over the bed, he could see the rain falling. Exhausted from emotions and the lovemaking, they both drifted off into blissful sleep.

When Jerrick woke up an hour later, he found Senta watching him sleep as she lay beside him. "Hi there," he said, stretching his legs and feeling her body against his.

"Hi," she answered, smiling a hopeful smile. "Did you have a nice nap?"

"Yeah, I did," he said, smiling back at her. "How about you? How are you feeling?"

"I'm fine," she said. "I hurt a little."

"That's normal," he said. "I'm sorry. I tried to be gentle."

"You were wonderful," she said. "But how was it for you? Did I please you?"

"You were wonderful," he said, turning on his side and putting his arms around her. "Everything was just right."

Senta noticed the sparkle in his eyes as he told her the lovemaking was wonderful. "Liar!" she said, gently slapping his chest. She thought she had read his mind.

When Jerrick laughed, she started to laugh, too. "You know this changes everything, don't you?" he asked. Senta looked at him, wondering what he was going to say. "You have to sleep here from now on," he said. "You can keep your clothes in your cabin, and you can keep your bathroom, but you are sleeping here."

"What if I don't want to?" she asked, playfully.

"Oh, but you have to," he said, seriously, continuing the charade.

"Captain," Senta said. "I have a confession to make." Jerrick looked at her with a puzzled smile, curious as to what she might say. "Yesterday, while you were below, I went out on the foredeck and touched the windlass. I know I shouldn't have done it, so I'm confessing."

"That's serious. I told you not to touch it, and you've disobeyed me," he replied seriously.

"Does that mean you're going to punish me?" she asked, trying not to smile.

"It does," he said and for a moment looked at her seriously without cracking a smile. Then before she knew what had happened, he grabbed her and started tickling her. Senta squealed as he tickled her ribs and under her arms; then he grabbed her hands and pinned her arms over her head. "Now comes the real punishment," he said and starting slowly kissing her neck and then down to her breasts.

Feeling him again on her thigh, she said, "Jerrick, again already? Should we do that?"

"Yes, we should," he said, continuing to kiss her breasts. "And you were concerned you wouldn't turn me on."

Senta ran her fingers through his hair, watching him as he kissed her breasts. She let out a little cry as he touched her again, and soon she was moving her body, arching her back. *This feels even better than the first time,* she thought. *I didn't know I could feel like this. I feel like I'm going to explode.* "I love you sweetheart," she said as he spread her legs, and they made love again.

Afterward, they lay next to each other, listening to the rain. Senta got up and walked down the hall to her bathroom. She returned, wearing Jerrick's white shirt that he'd given her the first day. Climbing into bed and sitting next to him, she said,

"Jerrick, we have to slow down a bit. I'm sore. It hurts when I walk."

"I'm sorry," he said, reaching over touching her leg.

"You can't help it," she said. "I just don't think we should do it any more today." She curled up next to him and rested her head on his shoulder. At that moment, Senta realized that in bed they were the same height as she felt his muscular calves with her feet and looked him directly in the eyes instead of looking up at him. *He is so powerful*, she thought. *Does he realize that?*

Her thoughts returned to home. *Abigail and John and Rachel are probably eating dinner. John has milked the cows. Sugar is grazing in the pasture. Eric Yost is in prison.* She smiled to herself, content in the certainty she was safe from the former bishop. *And I'm here with Jerrick, making love all afternoon.* That brought a different kind of smile, bringing her back to the present. "Jerrick, are you hungry? Should I make dinner?" she asked.

"I am starved," he said. "And I wonder whose fault that is?" he said, reaching for her as she jumped away from him.

"No, no, no," she said. "No tickling. You'll end up getting aroused again, and I don't think I'd be able to do it again." Jerrick smiled.

"I'll get some clothes on and get the grill going on the aft deck," he said. "I'll grill the filets, and you can bake the potatoes and fix the asparagus. Just let me fire up the generator, so you can use the oven and electric range."

Senta watched him as he climbed out of bed, pulled on his jeans, and got a sweatshirt out of the hanging locker. She watched the muscles in his arms and his messed-up hair and thought, *I can't believe he's mine! He's mine.*

It was dark by the time dinner was ready. Jerrick lit two candles and placed them on the table in the salon. There was still rosé left from earlier. "Are you a little cool?" he asked, and she nodded. "I'll turn on the heat for a while just to warm it up a bit. You know by Saturday it's supposed to be hot again, and we'll be running the air-conditioning," he said, smiling. As they ate, he watched her and asked, "So, how was day four?"

"I can't even begin to describe how happy I am," she said. "Today could not have been more perfect." Senta took a sip of the wine. Her thoughts turned to Ruth. "I'm not sure why, but I'm thinking about my friend Ruth. She is so unhappy. It shouldn't be that way. I suspect her husband may hit her. You would never hurt me."

Jerrick reached across the table and lightly touched Senta's hand. "No, I could never," he said. "I don't understand why some men do that. To me, it should be just the opposite. You should protect, not hurt, the one you love."

"I have another confession," Senta said. "I didn't really touch the windlass. I just said that to see your reaction. So, if you're not paying me enough attention, I guess I just have to tell you I touched the windlass." Jerrick smiled at her, and they both laughed.

After dinner was cleaned up, they went to the bridge. Senta was a bit chilly, so Jerrick went down to the linen locker and brought up a blanket to wrap around her. As they sat looking out into the darkness, the clouds would sometimes clear from the full moon, and the anchorage would be bathed in soft moonlight. "Jerrick, you never told me what *Arcadia* means," she asked. "You were going to tell me once, but someone interrupted you."

"You can tell a lot about someone by what they name their boat," he said. "So you tell me if you think the name of this boat is appropriate. Arcadia was, and still is, the central part of Greece. Back in ancient times, it was considered a peaceful and tranquil place because it was away from the hustle and traffic of the busy, more heavily-populated port cities. Arcadia was agricultural and pastoral. It was a peaceful place."

"Of course, it's perfect," she replied. "Why do you think like that? How do you see the water like you do and the sky, when others don't? You are so different. It's like you're not from this time. It's like you are from a long time ago or from the future."

"There are some who understand or could if they'd stop and think," he said. "You can't simply talk about it because people won't understand. Seeing love in that way is so foreign to them," he explained. He watched her eyes as she embraced his words. The moonlight shown in through the windows. The clouds moved silently across the night sky, and the river flowed.

CHAPTER EIGHTEEN

At Anchor

Jerrick woke up twenty minutes before Senta. He enjoyed feeling the sheets against his skin and her warmth against his body. He listened for any mechanical sounds in the boat and heard nothing until the refrigerator compressor kicked on in the galley. He felt no motion, confirming that the front had passed and the wind had died down. He slowly got out of bed being careful to not wake her. Grabbing his robe, he made a mental note to buy her a robe so they weren't sharing the same one. Up in the galley, he made coffee and walked around the salon looking out at the anchorage. The rain had stopped, and while it was still overcast, there were a few patches of blue. He got his iPad and taking it up to the bridge opened the weather program. He looked at the radar for two hundred miles out. When he heard the coffeemaker beep, he went down to the galley just as Senta came up the stairs from their cabin. "Good morning," he said.

"Good morning, sweetheart," she replied, smiling.

"You're just in time for coffee," he said. "Let's drink it on the bridge." He poured coffee and carried the two mugs up the stairs as she followed. Senta was still wearing his white shirt. He wrapped her in a blanket and they sat on the bridge settee, looking out on the anchorage as they sipped the hot coffee. "Did you sleep OK?" he asked.

"Yes, I slept wonderfully," she answered. "But it was different. Different good. I love feeling you there next to me. But I've never slept with anyone before. Thankfully, it's a big bed because you take up a lot of room," she said, smiling at him. "Did you sleep OK with me?"

"It was fine," he said, "except for the snoring."

"I do not snore!" she said, reaching a hand out from under the blanket wrapped around her. She tried to playfully smack him as he pulled away, laughing.

"No, you don't snore," he said, trying not to laugh. "I'm just trying to get even for the windlass confession."

"Really, I don't snore, do I?' she asked concerned.

"No, you don't snore," he said, still trying not to laugh. "Really."

"You're terrible," she said, laughing. "You're probably being this way because you're hungry. Shall I make breakfast?"

"That would be great," he said. "I'll start the generator so we have power and hot water. I'll take a shower while you cook."

"Jerrick, I must tell you something," Senta said, looking down. "It's about the bed. I'm sorry, but yesterday... There's blood on the sheets. I just now saw it. I'll change the sheets, so don't make the bed. I know you always make your bed, but let me do it today."

"It's OK," he said, pulling her to him. Giving her a hug and a kiss on the top of her head, he added. "It's not your fault."

"Well, you're right, Captain," she said. "It's actually your fault." He smiled at her and thought for a second about making love to her again but decided it best that she recover a little longer.

Over a breakfast of bacon and eggs, orange juice and a little more coffee, the two discussed cruising plans for the day. "The weather is looking better today than what I expected," Jerrick said. "I think we'll go to Eddy Creek today. Then on Friday, we'll take her on home to Haven Harbor."

"Is Eddy Creek an anchorage like this, or is it a marina?" Senta asked.

"Both," he answered. "You can anchor out or stay at the marina. I think we'll tie up at the transient dock and go out for dinner tonight. There are Amish somewhere around Eddy Creek. I've seen a group of them rent a pontoon boat and take it out on the lake."

"Some of our community would go on the Blue Heron Cruise at Ashland City to see all the birds. I never went, but I wanted to. Now, I have my own personal cruise ship. I didn't realize what a different experience this would be! And then .... after what we did last night! When I look at myself in the mirror while brushing my hair, I'm not sure who I am. I feel like I'm the Amish Senta on a farm in Cheatham County, but then I feel like I'm Jerrick Douglas' girlfriend, Senta, on his yacht, cruising on the Cumberland. The clothes confuse me, too. When I'm wearing all the beautiful new clothes you've bought me and I see myself in the mirror, I'm not sure it's me," she said.

"Do you like the new Senta, or do you miss the old one?" he asked.

"Both," she answered, looking at him seriously. "But don't misunderstand me. This is where I want to be. I want to be with you. Though sometimes I think about putting my blue dress and apron and cap on, just to see if the old me is still there."

They cruised down river that Thursday, making 9.1 knots as they journeyed further from Cheatham Dam. As the river widened, the current slowed. Senta enjoyed passing the time by using the binoculars to spot birds. When she'd spot a new species, she would try to identify it with the field guide. Jerrick delighted in watching her experience the excitement of seeing things for the first time. Because they left the anchorage late, it wasn't until four o'clock that they arrived at Eddy Creek. When the boat was squared away, they walked up to the office to pay for the slip for the night and have dinner. The waitress watched the couple as she took their order. She couldn't help but notice how happy they were, hoping that someday she would find someone and be as fortunate.

That night after dinner as the two were settled in for the evening, Senta summoned the courage to bring up some things that were on her mind. "Jerrick," she said, "you know I tend to worry sometimes. Right now, I'm fretting about two things." Jerrick sat down by her in the salon and listened. "The first is about making love. I'm not sure, but I think I'm supposed to do something at the end, like you do. But I don't think I did. Would I know if I did? I'm afraid you won't tell me if I'm doing something wrong."

"And what is the second thing?" he asked.

"I'm apprehensive about Sunday, the day after the ball. You said you'd take me back to Cheatham County after our week. I don't want the week to be over. I'll have to go back to work, and then you'll be gone," she said, biting her lip hard and trying not to cry.

"Do you remember when you said it scares you sometimes to think about all the things that could have gone wrong when we met? What if you and Abigail hadn't gone to the Farmers' Market that Saturday? Or what if you'd sold out earlier and had not been at your table? Or what if I had been two minutes later and walked past you and never stopped?" he asked, watching her. Senta nodded, blinking back tears. "But those things didn't happen, did they? We were both there, and we did meet. Then the problems with your mother and the others not approving of me because I'm not Amish. Then Eric Yost. But what happened with all those problems? One way or the other, they all worked out. I can tell you the solution to both your problems, if you want to know."

"Yes, I want to know," she replied.

"Have faith, and try not to be afraid," he said, taking her hands in his. "Your first problem isn't really a problem. You've only made love twice. It takes time. Just relax, and don't worry about those things. I am sure what you're talking about will happen in good time. And, you will know it when it happens." She nodded and smiled. "The solution to your second problem is the same as the first. Have faith, and don't worry." Jerrick watched her as she considered his words. "Why are we here right now?"

"Because you asked me to come with you," she said.

"And why did I do that?" he asked.

"Because you love me?" she answered.

"And why will this river keep flowing, and the clouds keep flowing, and music keep flowing, and why will our lovemaking keep getting better and better?" he asked.

"Love," she answered. Jerrick nodded.

"So just enjoy the water and the sky. Enjoy the music. Enjoy me as I enjoy you. These are gifts and gifts are meant to be enjoyed." He stood and led her to the master cabin where they made love again, long and slow and patient. It came over her like the surf on a beach, suddenly sweeping her off her feet and enveloping her in ecstasy. Then a short time later it happened again, even stronger than the first. She cried out as she felt herself explode in a million pieces as he did the same.

They lay together afterward while Jerrick held her in his arms, both their bodies tingling. "Jerrick, oh my God," Senta said, her breathing still fast. "Twice. I didn't know it could happen twice. That was incredible. I'm so spent. I can hardly move. I love you." As she held him tightly, her breathing slowed. Then, he pulled the blanket over her, and they drifted off to sleep together.

CHAPTER NINETEEN

Haven Harbor

Friday came, sunny and calm. The temperature rose back into the 70's, and it felt like summer again. Jerrick filled the water tank on *Arcadia* and hosed off the boat. Inside, Senta was busy making pancakes. She could see him on the dock working as she made breakfast and thought, *There is no one else like him on this earth, and he's mine! I'm going to do as he advised and not worry about anything. He was certainly right last night. He's always right, and I trust him.* Senta set the table outside on the aft deck, and once everything was ready, she called him. He could see that she was more relaxed, and he complimented her profusely on the pancakes. She glowed with the praise, full of joy.

"It's so pretty today, let's run *Arcadia* from the flybridge," he said, and they began preparations for departure. While Jerrick was coiling the spring lines, he caught Senta watching him. They stood 20 feet apart on the starboard deck, just looking at each other. After casting off, they moved up to the flybridge. Jerrick guided the big trawler out of the transient slip, around the long covered dock and out into open water. The sky was a brilliant blue with big, fluffy cumulus clouds that appeared stationary but weren't. The water was flat with hardly a ripple, except for the occasional fish jumping.

Jerrick gave Senta a lesson in operating the boat, explaining all the controls. Then he let her drive. The Cumberland no longer looked like a river because it had widened to two miles. He assured her there was enough room and that it would be impossible for her to hit anything. Later, as they passed the town of Kuttawa, Jerrick put the ship on autopilot. If someone seated at the tiki bar in Kuttawa had been looking beyond the breakwater with a pair of binoculars, they would have seen them, Jerrick and Senta, dancing.

"We're almost there," Jerrick said, pointing to the white roofs of covered piers almost five miles ahead. "That's Haven Harbor. There's a restaurant there called Emily's. I'd like to take you there for dinner." Senta looked at where he was pointing and then picked up the binoculars for a better look. "If you see a blue roof that's taller than the other buildings, that's the Dominion Yacht Club. That's where the Commodore's Ball is tomorrow night." Senta didn't say a word as she viewed the harbor through the binoculars. She recalled her Google search of this place and the pictures she had seen on the internet as they approached their destination.

They brought *Arcadia* into her slip at Haven Harbor. It was the first time Senta docked on a pier with a roof, and it seemed odd. To her, it was reminiscent of entering the barn. Senta was surprised by the number of people walking up and down the pier. But it was Friday, after all, and there were lots of people arriving for the weekend. Some were pushing carts loaded with groceries; others were carrying duffle bags. It was also surprising that everyone knew Jerrick and was curious about his traveling companion. This would happen again and again that weekend.

With *Arcadia* secured to the dock and connected to shore power, Jerrick was inside the yacht switching over the electrical panel. Senta was standing on the dock waiting for him when she heard a familiar voice say, "Hey, what's happenin', Capt'n?" Senta turned to see Joe, the same Joe from the Farmers' Market, walking up to her. "Hey there, young lady," he said, looking at her like he was trying to place her. "Is Jerrick on board? Did you come in on *Arcadia*? You seem familiar, but I can't place you."

"Yes, I came with Jerrick. He's inside tending to the electric panel," she explained.

"I know you, but I can't remember from where," he said, scratching his head trying to figure it out. "Y'all just got back from Nashville, right?"

"Yes, and he brought me with him. He's invited me to the Commodore's Ball tomorrow night," she explained. "My name is Senta. You may remember me from the Farmers' Market in Nashville. I remember you. You and your wife and friends were there with Jerrick; you all bought cheese and bread."

"Son of a gun!" he exclaimed, looking at her still puzzled. "You and the other lady make cheese! I'm sorry, but aren't you Amish?" Before Senta could answer, Jerrick came out of the boat and onto the dock.

"Joe!" he said. "How are you?"

"A better question is, how are you?" Joe said, looking at Senta then back to Jerrick. "I've just been talking to Senta, you know, about the Farmers' Market and cheese." Then, looking down the pier to his boat, Joe saw his wife and shouted, "Ann, get down here! Jerrick wants you to meet someone!"

Ann came walking quickly down the dock to see what was going on. Jerrick grinned, knowing that this was just the first of many introductions he would be making. Senta stood nervously waiting for Joe's wife to make her way down the pier. "Joe, Ann," Jerrick said, as Ann arrived. "This is Senta. You may remember her from the Farmers' Market in Nashville. You bought cheese from her when we were there back in the spring." Ann welcomed her with a hug while Joe gave Jerrick a *come on and tell me about this* look.

"Senta and I have been dating this summer, and she's my date for the Commodore's Ball tomorrow night," Jerrick explained. "I believe we'll be sitting with you."

"Oh, good," said Ann. Putting an arm around Senta, Ann moved her off to the side and walked down the pier for some girl talk. "Do you have your dress? I'm wearing one I wore three years ago. I don't think anyone will remember. What does your dress look like?"

"Well, it's black. It's sleeveless with a square neckline.

It's full length with an empire waist," Senta responded. "Jerrick helped me pick it out in Nashville."

"That sounds beautiful," said Ann. "I had a dress like that years ago when we lived in Texas. It was black. No, it was blue. I really like the dress you're wearing now. It looks so cool. So nice when it's hot. You're so pretty."

"So, you've been dating the Amish girl from the Farmers' Market, and you didn't tell me?" asked Joe, grilling his friend. "She looks different in civilian clothes. Very nice. Very nice, indeed," he said, patting Jerrick on the back. Ann and Senta walked back to Jerrick and Joe.

"So, what are you guys doing for dinner tonight?" asked Joe.

"Joe," said Ann, slapping his arm. "They probably have plans."

"We're going to Emily's," Jerrick said, looking at Senta. "I can call and probably make it four if you'd like to join."

"Sounds great," said Joe. "We've got to get to know this pretty girl better."

"Joe!" scolded Ann. "Behave yourself."

Jerrick called the restaurant from his cell phone while the three talked, then came back with the news, "I got it changed to four at 6:30 this evening. We'll meet you there at Emily's because I want to take Senta around Haven Harbor and give her the grand tour.

"That'll take all of two minutes," teased Joe.

"Joe!" said Ann, slapping his arm.

"Actually, Joe, I want to take her on a walk out on the jetty after dinner, and I don't want you to be there," Jerrick grinned. "So we'll see you at Emily's at 6:30."

"See, Joe!" Ann exclaimed. Everyone laughed except Senta who wasn't sure yet how to take Jerrick's friend.

Back in the boat, Jerrick said to Senta, "Don't take Joe too seriously. He's always cutting up like that. He's a great guy. He'd do anything for you."

"I thought he was kidding around," said Senta. "But I wasn't sure."

"No, if I'd said I didn't want them to join us for dinner that would have been fine," Jerrick said. "They like you. I can tell." Jerrick went down in the engine room and checked everything out since he knew he wouldn't be running *Arcadia* for a while.

While he was there, Senta stuck her head in the door and asked, "What's a jetty, Jerrick?" He looked up from the oil dipstick in his hand and smiled.

"It's like a pier. Sometimes you'll hear dock, or pier, or jetty. It's over on the Kentucky Lake side. There's a gazebo on the end. It's a pretty place for a walk. It will be cooler by then so you might want to switch to jeans and a sweater."

"Will jeans be OK for this restaurant?" she asked seriously.

"Jeans will be just fine," he said as he continued checking the engines. Senta smiled and admired him from the doorway. "When I finish here, I'm going to get on the computer and pay some bills. Then, if you like, we can walk our pier. You'll meet more people whose names you won't remember." Just then, there was a knocking on the hull. "Someone's here. Probably to meet you. Go on up, and see who it is; I'll be right up," he said, wiping his hands on a paper towel.

Senta went up the stairs thinking, *Jerrick is right, and why wouldn't he be? He always is. Everyone wants to meet me, it seems.* She opened the aft door and went out on the aft deck to find another couple standing on the dock beside *Arcadia*.

"Permission to come aboard, Senta," came a booming voice. Senta didn't know what to say for a moment. Then she realized why these people knew her name; she'd met them before.

"Permission granted," said Jerrick, walking up behind Senta. The couple on the pier came through the starboard gate onto the aft deck.

"Word travels fast, doesn't it!" said Jerrick.

"Yes, it does!" said Dave, another neighbor on the pier. "Do you remember us, Senta? We were at the Farmers' Market, too." And it went on like that for the next several hours. People would come by the boat, or when Jerrick and Senta were walking around, people would stop them to talk. It seemed to Senta that everyone knew Jerrick.

Finally, when it seemed they had met everyone on Jerrick's

pier, he said to Senta, "Come on, let's go aboard and go down in the cabin and not answer if someone comes."

"Do you mean we're going to hide?" she asked.

"That's exactly what I mean," he said, looking down the pier as they boarded *Arcadia*. "We may have to go anchor out to get some peace!"

"I know. I can't remember everyone's names," she said, following close behind. "It's funny. I can remember their boats' names better than their last names."

"I'm going to turn on the air-conditioning. It's a little warm," Jerrick said as he touched the controls in the salon as they quickly went below. "We've got a few hours before dinner. Let's take a nap."

"Does that mean take a nap, or is that code for something else?" Senta asked, giggling.

"I meant take a nap, but, obviously, you're wanting to do something else," Jerrick replied with a wink.

"I do not," said Senta. "You're the one who always wants to do it. You're always after me. I'm still sore from what you've done to me."

As they got to the master cabin and Jerrick flopped down on the bed he said, "OK then, we'll just take a nap, a real nap."

Senta lay down and curled up next to Jerrick with her head on his shoulder. He reached an arm around her and kissed the top of her head. They lay snuggled together for a few minutes when Senta whispered, "I didn't actually do it, but I was thinking about touching the windlass."

"I knew it," he said, and turning over, started tickling her. She squealed and tried to put up a fight; instantly, they were both laughing. Then with her arms pinned above her head, he kissed her and soon they were making love again. Slow sensual love, then hard passionate love. Senta once again exploded in ecstacy, and Jerrick put his hand over her mouth and said, "Shhh. We have neighbors here. I don't want them to think I'm killing you!"

"I'm sorry," she said apologetically, catching her breath. "Was I being too loud? I'm so embarrassed. I couldn't help it."

"You're fine," he said, smiling at her. "Just try to be a

little quieter here in the marina in the middle of the afternoon." He started to move again slowly, watching her as he did. "Hold still, and don't move," he told her. Slowly, he moved into her, watching her as she watched him. Pulling back, he slowly made love to her. "Don't move," he said, moving his tongue down to her nipples, and reaching between her legs, he gently teased her with his finger.

"Oh, my God, Jerrick," she whispered, her breathing coming in hitches. "You're torturing me." Then, when she couldn't take anymore, he plunged into her, and they were .... enraptured.

They lay together afterward. Jerrick was on his back and Senta was on her side next to him, her head on his shoulder. "Jerrick, you're wonderful," she whispered, breathlessly. "You make love so nicely."

"And you were worried you wouldn't be able to do that. Remember?" he said.

"I know," she said. "I just had no idea it could be so good, so intense. You make me. I can't stop it. You knew I couldn't hold still for very long. It was torture but such sweet torture."

"I love you, Senta. It's very important that you know how much you are loved," Jerrick said. "It's important that you know how much I cherish you."

As Senta held him tightly, her mind was flooded with emotion. *How can any of this be happening? He brings me happiness that I didn't know could exist. I couldn't even begin to explain this to someone because there aren't words to describe it.* Then Jerrick touched her shoulder and noticing its coolness he pulled a blanket up to cover her. *He is always taking care of me,* she thought. *He always covers me if he thinks I'm getting cold .... He's so patient with me .... I'm never going to let him go away from me again .... Not that I could stop him .... I'll go with him ....I'll go with him anywhere .... I never want to be separated from him again .... He's so warm and strong .... And he loves me.*

The afternoon passed as the two drifted in and out of sleep, basking in the afterglow of lovemaking. From time to time they would turn, finding a new position and would drift off again intertwined. *There must be an infinite number of ways for us to sleep, our arms and legs wrapped around each other*, she thought. *And we could make love an infinite number of ways, sleeping in each other's arms. We are going to be together forever, loving each other forever.*

They got up an hour or so before they were to meet Joe and Ann. Senta fixed her hair while Jerrick got dressed. Then they walked up the pier to where Jerrick's car was parked and drove into the village. Jerrick gave her the tour explaining how there was water on three sides of Haven Harbor making it a peninsula. They drove out to where the parking was for the jetty, and he showed her where they would walk after dinner so she could see it in daylight. As she looked south past the lighthouse Jerrick explained why they couldn't see land. If the other shore was greater than fifteen miles away, the curvature of the earth puts the shore beyond the horizon. She was surprised at how much bigger the Tennessee River side was. He explained that 600 miles south was Mobile Bay and from there you could go anywhere in the world. They drove through the north side of the marina, and he showed her the yacht club where they would go Saturday night. He showed her the chandlery and boat works where there were several big boats out of the water for repairs. Parking back in town, they walked around the antique stores and dress shops. The couple walked back to the old grist mill and watched the water wheel turn. He always held her hand as they walked and gently guided her along the way. At the grist mill, she stood in front of the water wheel and he took her picture with his phone.

Upon arriving at Emily's restaurant, Senta immediately felt at ease. The charming country décor brought back pleasant memories of her life in Cheatham County. Joe and Ann were already seated and were eagerly waving to them from a back, corner table. Throughout the meal, Joe told stories on Jerrick, and then Jerrick told stories on Joe which kept everyone laughing.

When it was time for dessert, Jerrick insisted Senta order a piece of lemon merengue pie. *Why isn't anyone else ordering dessert?* she wondered. She couldn't believe her eyes when the waitress brought the pie to the table. The pie was topped with a merengue that made each slice a foot tall. Everyone laughed at her reaction, insisting she had to eat all of it.   "If I eat all of that, I won't be able to fit into my new dress for tomorrow night!" Senta protested, laughing along with them. She liked being teased by Jerrick's friends. When the waitress placed four forks on the table, Senta was relieved. For some reason, she thought about the time Mrs. King and Mrs. Belier asked her if she'd lost weight. Then she thought, *I can't eat like this all the time or I'll look like them! I want to look nice for Jerrick.*

After a delightful evening, they said goodbye to Joe and Ann who went home to their boat. Jerrick and Senta drove the short distance to the jetty which extended far out into the water. Stars in the clear, night sky shown down on the couple as they strolled down the jetty to the gazebo at the end. To the north, the lights of Kentucky Dam twinkled in a line almost two miles long. To the southeast, the beacon of the lighthouse swept across the water, guiding the way for travelers. Having reached the gazebo and looking west, they could see the lights of houses several miles away across the water. There was only darkness to the south as the water continued over the horizon. Senta turned to Jerrick, wrapped her arms around him and said, "Jerrick, please don't ever leave me. You are such a part of me now that to lose you would be losing part of me. I would die."

Jerrick stroked her hair as he held her. "Do you know the stars move, too? They flow like the water."

"Where did you come from?" she murmured. "I've never known anyone like you."

Then reaching in his pocket for his phone, he tapped the phone a few times, and music filled the night air. He lay the phone on one of the benches by the gazebo and held out his left hand to Senta. She smiled and placed her right hand in his. He brought her to him, and they began dancing under the stars. In one of the cottages on top of the white cliffs above the jetty, a woman said to her husband, "There's a couple dancing out on the end of the jetty. Can we do that? Tomorrow night, would you dance with me on the jetty?"

CHAPTER TWENTY

The Ball

It was a glorious Saturday morning. Having slept late, Jerrick and Senta enjoyed a leisurely breakfast on *Arcadia's* aft deck which had a wonderful view of the harbor. Sipping coffee, they watched boats come and go while talking and enjoying each other.

"This is one of my favorite things in the world," Jerrick said to Senta as he reached over and squeezed her hand.

"What is?" she asked, not sure what he meant.

"Just having a cup of coffee on the aft deck, savoring the tranquility," he said. "Another favorite being snowbound and drinking coffee by the fireplace with nothing better to do but watch the snow falling outside." Senta listened and decided it would be wonderful to be snowed in with him.

The conversation naturally changed to that evening's Commodore's Ball. Senta said, "I think I'm dancing better. I think every time we dance, it gets a little easier. I'm still not very good, but I love to dance with you."

"Let me show you something," Jerrick said, picking up his iPad and typing in some words. "You know about YouTube, right?" he asked, and Senta nodded. "OK, I'm going to show you two videos. Both are the same song, "Qué Bonito." I want you to watch them and tell me what you think. The first is Daniel and Desiree, who are incredible dancers."

Senta watched as the couple danced bachata to the song she liked so much. Their style and movements flowed into a stream of ever-changing steps and turns that left Senta marveling at how they were able to do it. They were spectacular.

When it ended, Jerrick asked, "What do you think?"

"They are incredible," she said. "I can't describe how good they are. She's beautiful!"

"They may be the best bachata dancers in the world," he said.

"I wish I could dance like that," said Senta. "I could never. I'm just not that coordinated or that pretty. She has a fantastic figure."

"OK, now I'm going to show you something very different," Jerrick explained. "This is *Policía Nacional del Perú*, "Qué Bonito." It's kind of surprising, but the police department in Lima, Peru has a band. They're going to do the same song, 'Qué Bonito.'"

The video started and Senta watched as a man in uniform conducted. "They're in uniform," she commented, and Jerrick nodded. Then the camera switched to a young police woman also in uniform who sang the song. Senta watched her and listened as she sang the song exquisitely. Her voice and the music and the words described how beautiful her lover was.

When it ended, Jerrick asked, "What do you think?"

"She's very pretty," Senta said. "She sings wonderfully!"

"But she's just a police woman in Lima, Peru," said Jerrick. "And she's wearing her police uniform."

"I know, but she's still lovely," said Senta.

"So, who is more beautiful?" asked Jerrick.

"Oh, that's a hard question," said Senta. "They both are. But if I have to choose, I think the girl from Peru."

"Did you notice how she moved when she sang?" asked Jerrick. "Very small, delicate movements." Senta nodded in agreement. "So what I'm saying is that both are very talented, and both are beautiful. The second girl isn't as dramatic, but is every bit as beautiful as Desiree, even wearing a police uniform. So, you don't have to be Desiree to be attractive or to dance well. It's possible to be beautiful in a quieter, softer way, like the girl from Peru. You are beautiful, Senta, discovering how to dance as you discover yourself. I find you enchanting right now, and I think you dance perfectly right now. Tonight, you will be radiant and dance splendidly."

Senta pondered Jerrick's words in the quiet moments that followed. *He thinks I'm beautiful because he loves me, but is it possible that I am? He makes me feel gorgeous when we make love. I never thought I was. He looks at me with so much love that I must be beautiful. Do I think he's handsome because I love him? No, he is handsome. It's love. Love makes us beautiful. Our love.* Senta watched Jerrick as they sat together, sharing the pure blissfulness of the morning. Then, looking out on the water of the harbor, she was reminded of the concept of love flowing through everything.

That afternoon, they danced on the aft deck. In part, it was because Senta wanted to practice more. But, it was also because they just wanted to dance. Afterward, Jerrick said, "I'm going to go check my white shirt to see if it needs ironing and see if my shoes are shined. You should go lay out your things."

"What do men wear to the ball?" asked Senta.

"A uniform. It's a formal yacht club uniform," he answered.

"Can I see it?" she asked. Jerrick went below and came back with a black uniform jacket and trousers. The double-breasted jacket was accented with black metal buttons, each depicting a fouled anchor. Each sleeve's cuff had four black, soutache braids. Just above those braids, the soutache formed three loops, each loop having a gold star within.

"It's elegant. I've never seen a suit or a uniform like this," she said. "I'm going to go lay out my clothes and start getting ready."

She went to her bathroom, showered and shampooed her hair. Once her hair was dried, she put it up in a French twist. She spent the next twenty minutes working to get it exactly perfect. Returning to her cabin to dress, she slipped into a black bra and matching panties. Carefully, Senta unzipped the dress and stepped into it. Once the dress was on, she was able to reach behind and zip it up herself. Next, she took her new shoes out of the box, admiring them for a moment before slipping them on. Finally dressed, Senta stood before the full-length mirror and thought, *I love my dress. It's just right for me. I think it looks like me. It's simple and elegant. I have never been this beautiful, never in my life.* Then she walked confidently out of her cabin, down the hall and up the steps to the salon where she found Jerrick reading. He stood up when he saw her. "You are so handsome in that uniform," she said. "Oh, my!"

"You are breathtaking," he said. "Absolutely stunning. Come here, and turn around. Let me look at you." Senta beamed from his praise, walked toward him, turned and then turned again. "Enchanting," he said. "Here, sit down," he said, motioning towards the couch. Jerrick already had a bottle of wine chilling and two glasses out on the table. "I thought we'd have a glass of wine before we leave for the yacht club." He poured and handed her a glass. "Really, you look fantastic," he said, as he raised his glass to her and they drank.

"I've never seen you in a suit," she said. "I'm used to seeing you in shorts and flip flops. Not that you look bad in shorts and flip flops. But I do like this," she said reaching over and touching the braid on the sleeve.

Jerrick sat back and studied Senta as he drank the wine and then said, "But there's something missing. I'm not sure what. You have the black clutch, don't you?"

"Yes, it's down in my cabin," she answered, concerned. "Should I get it now?"

"No, not until we leave," he answered, still looking at her like he was trying to decide what was missing.

"What's wrong?" Senta asked with worry in her voice. "Is it my dress? Or my hair? Do you not like it up like this?"

"No, it's not that," he said. "I just can't put my finger on it. Wait, I know what it is. I know what's missing."

Senta watched him with concern as he reached over beside the couch and retrieved a small, black box. "I think this will complete your outfit," he said, handing it to her.

"What is this?" she asked.

"You should open it and find out," he answered.

Slowly, Senta opened the velvet box to see the flash of

a diamond that at first confused her. Then she realized she was looking at an engagement ring. It was hers.

"Senta," Jerrick said. "Will you marry me?"

Tears streamed down her face. She held the ring box in her hands and trembled with emotion. Snapshots flashed before her mind's eye .... the farm, her parents, milking the cows and pulling the heavy cart to the road, the Farmers' Market on the day she met him, their date in Nashville, dancing with him, their trip together, making love. Overwrought with emotion, Senta was unable to respond. Jerrick moved closer and put his arm around her, waiting for her to regain control.

Jerrick took a handkerchief from his jacket pocket and gave it to Senta. Finally, wiping her eyes, she spoke, "Yes, Jerrick Douglas, yes, yes, yes, a million times, yes." Jerrick took the ring from the box and slipped it on the ring finger of her trembling hand. She started to say something but couldn't and threw her arms around his neck. He held her and stroked her hair. Finally, composing herself, she released him. "I love you," she said. "I can't believe this. I had no idea. When did you have time to buy this ring? There are no jewelry stores here, are there?"

"I bought the ring a long time ago," he answered. "Do you remember when we had lunch at the Farmers' Market?" Senta nodded. "After I left you there, I went to a jewelry store in Nashville and bought it."

"You've wanted to marry me all this time?" she asked, her eyes full of surprise.

"I actually thought about it the first time we met," he said.

"I did, too," she said, starting to cry again. "I loved you from the first moment I saw you. I couldn't even talk I was so smitten. I've thought about you every minute of every day since." Jerrick nodded and smiled. "And this ring," she said, looking at her hand. "It's beautiful. It sparkles so nicely. Jerrick, it's really big. You spent a lot of money on me again! What am I to do with you?" Jerrick smiled, and Senta laughed through her tears.

Walking into the Commodore's Ball on the arm of Jerrick

Douglas was a magical moment for Senta. She had been so proud to be his girlfriend, and now she was his fiancée. It was thrilling to be introduced that way! Senta felt very comfortable seated with the people from Jerrick's pier since she had met them previously.

"Why is there a flag in front of your plate?" she asked Jerrick, pointing to a small blue flag with an anchor and three stars.

"That's a past commodore's flag. It means I was a previous commodore. Do you remember the same flag that flies on the masthead of *Arcadia*? Three stars on the flag. Three stars on the sleeve," he said, pointing to the sleeve of his jacket.

"A good turnout for the Commodore's Ball," said Joe. "Except I understand the Commodore is pretty upset."

"What's wrong?" asked Jerrick.

"Did you notice there's no band? Apparently, the band that was booked got sick and had to cancel," said Joe. "Brown bottle flu, I imagine. It's OK. They found a DJ. Couldn't get another band on such short notice."

After a delicious dinner, the Commodore gave a short speech thanking everyone for a great season. Then he apologized for there not being a band. Finally, he proposed a toast to Jerrick and Senta on their engagement. Senta was overwhelmed as she thanked everyone, still not believing everything that had happened. She glanced at her hand from time to time to admire the ring. She had been worried about dancing, but she was rather relieved when the music started because everyone was drinking and dancing. The spotlight was off her.

Jerrick asked the DJ to play "The Way You Look Tonight". Dancing together was romantic even though the dance floor was crowded. Afterward, they sat down and visited with their neighbors from the pier, and then, a few songs later, Senta heard something familiar. "Bachata," Jerrick whispered in her ear. He stood, took her hand and led her onto the dance floor. No one else knew the song or how to dance to it. Jerrick had requested "Déjà Vu" at the same time he'd requested the Frank Sinatra song. At first, Senta was nervous being the only couple on the dance floor. Jerrick could tell and whispered in her ear, "Close your eyes." She did, and she was back at the Farmers' Market dancing with him the first time. Except this time, she knew what to do and danced in perfect unison with him, responding to every turn and spin. She opened her eyes, and all she saw was her future husband. As they danced, she was aware of his arms around her and his body pressing against her. She felt the music flow and knew that below them the water was flowing as were the stars above.

As the song ended, Senta felt in perfect harmony with Jerrick. Then the applause interrupted the moment, bringing her back to reality. As Jerrick led her back to their table, she recalled that the day she'd won the cobbler contest had been the best day of her life. Then, her best day had become the day she'd met Jerrick at the Farmers' Market. Now, today was the best day. And she wondered, *Is it possible to have an infinite number of best days?*

They left the Commodore's Ball around eleven o'clock, taking at least thirty minutes to get out to the Range Rover because everyone wanted to offer congratulations and wish them well. Everyone, it seemed, wanted to meet Senta and compliment her on her dress and her dancing. She'd never received so much attention in her life! As they drove back to their pier on the other side of the harbor, Jerrick asked, "Did you have a good time, Senta? You did great. You are beautiful. I love that dress."

Senta's eyes were shining as she reached for his hand and said, "My heart is overflowing. Yes, I had a wonderful time. But every day is wonderful with you. Is it possible for life to be this wonderful?"

Jerrick glanced over to her and said, "Yes, it is possible."

Back at their pier, they walked down the gangway. The air was getting cooler, and the night was still. They walked together hand in hand down the pier, illuminated by the small dock lights. "Let's open the portholes in the master cabin," he said as they walked between the boats on either side. "I love how the air feels in the fall. I'll throw an extra blanket on the bed so we stay warm." They boarded *Arcadia* and went below to the master cabin. Jerrick helped her out of her dress before he took off his uniform. Having opened two portholes, they crawled into bed together and were soon fast asleep.

CHAPTER TWENTY-ONE

The Blue Gate

Senta woke and for a moment thought she was back in her bed in her house on the farm. But the feeling of him next to her quickly brought her back to reality. She watched Jerrick sleeping next to her. Then she brought her left hand out from under the covers to see if her ring was there or if it had been a dream. She looked at the ring, touching it with her finger to confirm that it was real. *It wasn't a dream*, she thought. *I'm here, and Jerrick is with me on this boat. He proposed to me yesterday. We're engaged.* Jerrick, still asleep, turned on his side toward her. *Oh my*, she thought, *I still can't believe it! This amazing man loves me.*

She slipped out of bed quietly so as not to wake him, and grabbing his robe, she wrapped it around her and tiptoed out of the cabin. Up in the galley, she pushed the button and the coffee started brewing. She walked into the salon and found the ring box still on the table from the previous evening. She picked it up and admired it briefly before putting it in the robe pocket. Peeking out the aft door, she looked at the quiet harbor and then up at the sky. How much more attuned to the weather she had become in just one week!

When the coffeemaker *beeped*, she walked back to the galley only to meet Jerrick coming up the stairs, wearing a pair of half zipped-up jeans and rubbing his eyes. She ran the rest of the way to him and, hugging him, said, "Good morning, my love! Good morning!"

"Good morning to you," he said, groggily.

"I'll pour some coffee," she said. "Sit down. Let me get a blanket to wrap you up in. It got a little cool last night with the windows... portholes open. I stole your robe again. I'm sorry. I'd give it to you, but I'm naked."

"You know I was going to buy you a robe today when we went back to Nashville, but I kind of like you naked. Maybe I won't," he said, teasing her. Senta brought them two mugs of coffee and sat down next to him.

"I love you, Mr. Douglas," she said, holding the coffee between her hands enjoying the warmth.

"And I love you, Miss Miller," he answered, watching as he memorized every nuance of her face. "Do you remember what today is?"

"Yes," Senta answered, with a worried tone in her voice. "I know. But... I don't know how to say it, but please don't take me back and leave me there. I can't bear to be without you."

Jerrick smiled as he took a drink of coffee, "Do you not remember what happened yesterday?" he asked, gently touching her ring finger.

"Yes," she answered.

"That means I'm never going to leave you," he said, "because I never want to be separated from you again either."

"Where you go, I will go, and where you stay, I will stay," she said, looking at him intently.

"Today, we'll drive back to Cheatham County. We'll check on your house and then go see Abigail and John."

"And Rachel," said Senta, smiling.

"You'll need to talk to Mr. Campbell," Jerrick said. "And I don't want to be engaged for a year. I want to marry you soon, like in the next week or two. Whenever we can make the arrangements. Do you know where you'd like to be married?"

"Oh, Jerrick," she said, moving closer to him and touching his arm. "I want to be married soon, too. I think I would like to be married at my house. I know my parents are gone, but it would seem like they were there with me. And I have an idea for Mr. Campbell, but I need to talk to Abigail first."

"I have an idea for our honeymoon," Jerrick said, watching Senta's reaction.

"A honeymoon!" exclaimed Senta. "Jerrick, you absolutely spoil me every second of every day. I don't have to have a honeymoon. Every day with you is a honeymoon."

"You deserve a honeymoon," he said. "Do you want to hear my idea?" Senta nodded, taking another sip of coffee.

"It's fall, October," he said. "We would get married, then come back to the boat. We'd head south on the Tennessee River. Then 200 miles south of here, we'd get on the TennTom and take that down to Mobile Bay. We'd follow the Intercoastal Waterway, then cut across the Gulf to Ft. Meyers. We'd cross Florida on the Okeechobee and come out on the Atlantic at St. Lucy." Senta listened with her mouth open. "Then we'd cross to the Bahamas and island hop to the Abacos, then the Exumas. I don't know where we'd end up. We'd just cruise until, I don't know, February sometime, then work our way back. We'd be back here sometime in the spring."

"Jerrick," she said, full of emotion. "That sounds like the best honeymoon anyone could ever imagine. I know it sounds very expensive, but I'm trying to learn to leave that to you. I love you, and I will go with you anywhere you want to go."

"I love you," he said, "I want to show you the rivers and the oceans, the islands and the mountains .... All the things you've dreamed of. That's where I want to take you."

They ate breakfast, talking about the future. Then Senta showered while Jerrick checked everything out on the boat. Standing on her tiptoes, she looked out the porthole in the shower. Seeing the boat in the slip next to them, she wondered how it would be to look out and see an island covered in palm trees.

They drove on Interstate 24 to Tennessee and then took the Ashland City exit. Soon, they were driving down the road toward Senta's house. With his left hand on the wheel, Jerrick reached over with his right and took her hand. He sensed some tension as they got closer to their destination. Senta said, "I don't know why I feel so apprehensive. I've only been gone a week, but I feel like I've been gone for a long time." When they pulled up in the driveway of the house, Senta inhaled quickly and brought her hands up to her mouth in disbelief.

"What's wrong?" Jerrick asked, watching her reaction to something he didn't see.

Without a word, Senta got out of the SUV and slowly walked up the sidewalk to the gate. Jerrick followed, not understanding what was happening. With tears streaming down her cheeks, Senta reached out and touched the blue gate. "What's wrong, Senta?" he asked.

"Nothing's wrong," she said, crying and smiling. "It's my gate. It's blue."

"It was white before," Jerrick said, puzzled as to the change in color as well as the tears.

"Yes, it was," she sobbed. "But now it's blue. Abigail must have painted it," she said, touching the gate.

"Does that mean something?" he asked. "Why would Abigail paint your gate blue, and why are you crying?"

"A blue gate means that it's the home of a girl of marriageable age," she explained through the tears. "It means that I can court and can get married." Then, Senta put her arms around him and cried against his chest, "It means that I'm going to marry you." They stood in front of the white farmhouse with the blue gate and held each other while Senta cried. All the years and all the memories came back to her. Playing in the yard as a girl, the tornado with her mother in the cellar, drinking coffee with Sally in the kitchen. Then the day her father had the stroke, the day Yost came with the imposter, the day her mother passed away. Looking up at Jerrick, she said, "Let's go inside. You've never been in my house before, only outside."

They walked to the kitchen door, and Senta unlocked it and led him into the kitchen. "It looks just the same," she said, "but it seems smaller somehow." She showed him the parlor where she explained, "This is where Yost and all the others came with the actor we believed to be the Attorney General. I sat here and my mother sat there," she said, remembering that day for a moment. Then she led Jerrick up the stairs and down the hall to her bedroom. Standing in the middle of the simple room, she asked him, "Jerrick, you may think this is a strange request, but would you mind if I changed back into Amish clothes to go see Abigail and John and Rachel? I know I have violated the rules of the order, and they will probably officially remove me. But, for today, because Abigail has never seen me wearing clothes like this, could I just change back to my Amish clothes?"

Jerrick nodded and kissed her on the forehead, then turned and walked down the hall, "I'll wait for you downstairs."

Senta stood looking at herself in the mirror, wearing her white blouse, jeans and sandals. Then, slowly, she unbuttoned her blouse and slipped off her jeans and paused to think about all the years this had been her bedroom. She opened her closet door and took out a blue dress, a white apron, and a white cap. She took down her hair, then brushed it and redid it into a bun. Next, she put on her dress and apron, and then her white cap. Lastly, she found her black shoes in the closet and put those on, tying the laces. Senta walked down the stairs and into the parlor where Jerrick was waiting. She stopped, stood completely still and remembered that this was how she looked when they first met. He read her mind and he, too, recalled that moment.

"So, is your name really Senta?" he asked. She nodded. "Well, Senta, I'm going to come back and see you again. And I won't wait seven years." She ran to him, and they held each other in a long embrace.

They walked out to the driveway together. He opened the door for her and helped her into the Range Rover. She thought about how he had done the same thing in the same place on their first date. "Are you ready to go see your friends?" he asked.

"Yes, and I'll try not to cry. This is all just very emotional for me," she said. They drove the quarter mile down the road and pulled into the drive. Having parked the SUV in front of the Lapps' house, Jerrick walked around and helped Senta out.

Inside the house, Abigail heard the sound of tires on gravel and looked out the parlor window. "John, it's Senta! She's back!" Abigail cried out, but remembered John was in the barn. She hurried to the front door and then ran down the sidewalk to her friend. The two ran to each other and then into each other's arms. Jerrick slowly walked up the sidewalk to give the women a few moments alone. Then Jerrick caught sight of John coming around the house.

"I heard tires," said John with a big smile.

"She's back, John!" cried Abigail, now holding her friend at arm's length and brushing some fallen hair away from Senta's eyes. "We have missed you so much. How are you?" she asked.

"I am fine," Senta assured her friend. "We were just at the house. I saw the blue gate."

"I hope that's alright?" said Abigail. "I just thought you should have one, all things considered, so John and I found the can of blue paint your father had bought years ago. We painted it."

"I love it!" said Senta. "I'm never going to repaint it white. I'm going to leave it blue. Always!"

"Mr. Douglas, it is good to see you again," said Abigail, in a more formal tone. "Please, let's all go in the parlor."

"Abigail," said Jerrick, with a grin. "What am I going to have to do to get you to call me by my first name?"

"Yes," said Senta as they all walked into the house. "You do need to work on that, Abigail. You can't be calling him Mr. Douglas forever," Senta said, holding up her left hand so Abigail could see her engagement ring.

"Oh, my God in heaven!" exclaimed Abigail. "You're engaged? You two are to be married?" Senta nodded, and then the two women hugged again as the two men looked on, smiling. "John, you and ......Jerrick, sit down and Senta and I will go get some lemonade for us," she said, pulling Senta out of the parlor and down the hallway to the kitchen.

"Oh, Senta, I can't believe it!" cried Abigail when they reached the kitchen. "Did everything go alright? We've been worried sick. Has he been good to you? Oh, what am I saying? You are positively glowing. Look at that ring. That's a sizable diamond, Senta. I don't know anything about diamonds, but I think that's big."

"Abigail, everything was magical. This week has been like a dream. He is always very kind to me. He's very patient and doesn't get mad at me even when he could. I love him so much. I can't live without him, but I knew that from the first time I saw him. He thinks I'm pretty, Abigail, and tells me all the time."

"Of course you're pretty, Senta," said Abigail. "He may be English, but he's not blind!"

"I know, you say so, but I've never thought I was," confessed Senta. "I was afraid that he might not find me appealing, you know," Senta said whispering. "That I might not arouse him."

"Senta? Did you?" gasped Abigail.

"Yes," said Senta, biting her lower lip and watching her friend's reaction. "We did. I needn't have worried about him not finding me desirable." Abigail stood stock-still with her hands on her face, listening to her friend. "I'm a little sore. Did that happen to you, Abigail?"

"You poor thing," cried Abigail. "But he's good to you?" she said, looking at her friend.

"Yes, yes, Abigail. He's very good to me. And he's very gentle with me. He's wonderful. I just didn't know what to expect. I was so worried because Ruth always said she didn't like being married and that her husband made her do terrible things. But Jerrick is wonderful."

Abigail held Senta's hands and listened intently as her friend shared her excitement.

"But Abigail, I had no idea how wonderful this could be!" Senta paused and looked around the corner of the kitchen back toward the parlor to be sure no one was hearing. "Abigail, the first two times we made love, it was wonderful, but I didn't .... you know." Abigail watched her friend, trying to suppress a smile. "But Jerrick told me to relax, so I did. Then the third time, oh my goodness! I love him so much. On Saturday night, he proposed and gave me this ring."

"Senta," said Abigail. "We're going to have to sit down with some coffee and talk about this. Sometime when the men aren't around. Yes, I understand what you mean. You apparently learn much faster than I did," she said, laughing. "But that's a conversation for another time. Let's get the lemonade."

The four sat in the parlor, talking. Senta related the events of the past week and their voyage down the Cumberland River. "Sleeping on the boat is incredible," said Senta. "Most of the time, you can't feel it moving. It's just so peaceful."

Then Abigail told Senta about what had transpired while she'd been away. "We have your deed, Senta," said Abigail, handing her an envelope. "A Tennessee State Policeman dropped it off Friday and asked us to give it to you. Your farm is back in your name." Senta opened the envelope and looked at the deed and then handed it to Jerrick to read.

"It's finally over," sighed Senta.

"Yes, Bishop Yost pled guilty to all the charges," said John. "He's in jail in Ashland City and will be transported to prison tomorrow morning. We've had an election, and Mr. King is the new bishop."

"Senta, we don't know what will happen," said Abigail. "We expected something might have been said about you, but Bishop King has said nothing. I think people know that you went with Jerrick. We've not said anything, but people did see you leave with Jerrick and the Attorney General. So far, there's been nothing said about removing you from the order."

"They probably will," said Senta, sadly. "I've broken the vows, and I'm going to break them again when we marry," she said, reaching over and taking Jerrick's hand.

"Abigail, I have another situation to discuss," Senta continued. "I have so enjoyed my job with Mr. Campbell, but it is time for me to resign. My place now is with Jerrick. I expect Mr. Campbell may be upset, but if I had a solution, maybe he would take it better. Abigail, do you think you might want to take over my position with Mr. Campbell?"

"Oh, Senta!" Abigail exclaimed. "I guess great minds think the same. I must confess that I had thought of that, too. Yes, I could try it. It has worked out well for you, and I think it could be the same for me."

"When I go and talk to Mr. Campbell, may I tell him you'd like to take over for me?" asked Senta. "Gosh, the computer is even here already."

"Yes," said Abigail, looking at John. He nodded in affirmation. The four talked until Rachel woke up and required attention. Then Senta held the baby and played with her until it was time for Abigail to nurse her.

Abigail and John insisted that Jerrick and Senta have lunch with them. During the meal, the conversation turned to making plans for the wedding. It would be held the following Saturday at Senta's house in the front yard by the blue gate. Abigail said she would take care of food and flowers. Senta said that she would like everyone in the Amish community to be invited and John volunteered to spread the word. By the time lunch was over, the plans were mostly complete. After lunch, Abigail packed some leftovers for them to take home while John took Jerrick to the barn and showed him the dairy operation. When they returned from the barn, Jerrick and Senta said their goodbyes until Saturday.

They drove the quarter mile back to Senta's house to spend the night before going to see Mr. Campbell Monday morning. Upon entering the house, Senta once again felt a flood of memories. Then turning to Jerrick, she said, "I want to take you to the creek and show you where I like to sit and listen to music." The remainder of the day was spent walking around the farm and sitting by the creek. Senta got out her phone while they were by the creek and put on her playlist. They danced there in the woods next to the creek.

When the sun started to set, it was time to return to the house. As they came in the kitchen door, Senta turned on the light and said, "I don't think we can sleep in my room. You're much too big to fit in my bed, much less both of us. The bed in my office bedroom is bigger. It's not as big as our bed in the boat, but for just one night it should work." They climbed the stairs together, and as they walked in Senta's bedroom office, Jerrick turned her to him and kissed her. As they kissed and she felt his arms around her and his body against her, she couldn't believe that he was there and that it was real. Stopping for a second, she said, "Jerrick, I'll be right back." She hurried down the hallway to her room and picked up the pillow from her bed, the pillow she had hugged for so many nights. She paused for a few moments, remembering every detail. Then she lay the pillow down on her bed and ran back to the other bedroom and Jerrick.

They woke up early the next morning, wanting to arrive at

the accounting office just as it opened. "I'll take you to breakfast after you've talked to Mr. Campbell," Jerrick said.

"I feel guilty quitting my job like this," said Senta as they drove to Ashland City. "He has been so good to me, and I've really enjoyed working there."

"I think he will understand, and I like your idea about Abigail taking over for you," said Jerrick. "You should invite everyone from your office to the wedding."

When they arrived at the accounting office, both Sally and Suzanne immediately noticed Senta. "Everybody, look who's here!" screamed Sally as she jumped up and ran to Senta. "And this must be Jerrick?" she asked before Senta had a chance to make introductions. "Good job, Senta!" Sally exclaimed, raising her eyebrows as she gave Jerrick the once over. "I'm so sorry I hung up on you when you called," Sally apologized to Jerrick. "I thought …. I hope you understand. I'm sorry." Jerrick accepted her apology, remembering when he'd called in an attempt to find Senta. Suzanne hugged Senta, and everyone in the office gathered around.

"Senta," said Suzanne. "We've all been wondering how you were, where you were and what was happening."

Senta smiled and held up her left hand. There was silence for a split second as all the ladies focused on the ring, then the office erupted into squeals. Senta, who had always disliked being the center of attention, found herself being exactly that. Happy tears began to flow down her cheeks. When things quieted down, Mr. Campbell came out of his office. "What's all the ruckus out here?" he asked.

"Senta's back, and she engaged!" exclaimed Sally. Everyone talked at once as Mr. Campbell got the whole story in bits and pieces.

"Senta, I assume you'll be wanting to take more vacation since you're getting married," said Mr. Campbell.

Everyone hushed and listened as Senta said, "Actually, Mr. Campbell, I will need to resign as I will be with Jerrick and won't be able to work for you anymore. I'm so sorry. I really appreciate the work you've given me over the years, and I've really enjoyed it."   She watched him as he listened to what she was saying and then looked at Jerrick. "But, Mr. Campbell, may I suggest a replacement for me unless you already know of someone. May I suggest Abigail Lapp? Sally and Suzanne already know her. She's John Lapp's wife. My computer, your computer is already at her house. She's Amish, so Mr. and Mrs. Stoll will approve of her. She's very smart, and I am certain she will do a good job."

Mr. Campbell's frown turned to a smile as he said, "Sally and Suzanne had already suggested her, anticipating that you might be leaving us. Yes, I think we will give her a try."

"Thank you, Mr. Campbell," said Senta. "I've already asked if she'd like to try it, and she is agreeable. I'd hoped you'd like the idea, so I left my company cell phone with her." Jerrick and Senta then invited everyone to the wedding the following Saturday. They left the office with everyone standing outside, waving goodbye to them. "I didn't know how much they cared about me," remarked Senta as they drove away.

"Senta, lots of people care about you," said Jerrick. "Me, most of all." Senta looked over at him and smiled.

"Jerrick?" she asked. "Is it alright if I get married in my Amish dress? I know that English girls all want very fancy, white wedding dresses, but we don't do that. If it wouldn't disappoint you, I'd like to get married in my Amish dress."

Jerrick looked over at her, and smiling, said, "I want you to wear whatever makes you happy. Your Amish dress is just fine with me. All I care about is your happiness. I just want to be with you, live with you, and love you."

Senta smiled at him as they drove down the road, his left hand on the wheel as she held his other hand between both of hers.

CHAPTER TWENTY-TWO

Autumn

The following Saturday was a resplendent, sunny day in October. The leaves were changing, and the colors of the trees were stunning. Jerrick and Senta got up early and drove to Cheatham County where they met John and Abigail at Senta's house. When they arrived, Abigail was out front, decorating the fence and gate with flowers. John was walking up the drive, leading Sugar who even had her mane braided. "Everything is taken care of, Senta," said Abigail. "You should just relax and enjoy your day."

Jerrick walked back to the barn with John while Abigail led Senta into the kitchen to show her the food preparations. Senta was surprised to find Mrs. King and Mrs. Belier there working. "Senta," said Mrs. King, giving her a hug. "Mr. King won't be here today because, you know, he's our new bishop, but he told me I could come. He wanted to, but the circumstances being what they are, he can't. But we wish you the greatest happiness. Mrs. Belier also hugged Senta and wished her well. Then, Senta went back outside with Abigail, still amazed that the two ladies were working so hard on her behalf.

When the guests started arriving, it was in a combination of motor vehicles and buggies. There were six cars full of people from the accounting office, along with their spouses. Mr. Campbell led the convoy in his Cadillac with Jason Schneider bringing up the rear in his JS Computer Services van. Sally had been kind enough to recruit her pastor from the First Baptist Church in Ashland City to officiate since the new bishop would not be able to perform the ceremony. Senta couldn't believe her eyes when Luisa Fernanda and Carlos got out of their pick-up truck. Then, Amish buggies started arriving. For whatever reason, as Mrs. King had alluded, Bishop King had chosen to ignore the situation, and Senta had not been shunned. A surprising number of her neighbors from the Amish community came for the wedding. Several cars arrived with friends of Jerrick's, friends who were eager to meet Senta. Four cars brought friends from *Arcadia's* pier back at Haven Harbor. Finally, the familiar black Suburban with two state police cruisers pulled into the driveway, transporting the Attorney General.

After so many years of being alone and at times of feeling forgotten, Senta looked around at everyone gathered in support and celebration of her and Jerrick. Her heart was full, and she was overwhelmed with emotion. Shortly before the service was to start, one last buggy arrived. Ruth stepped out by herself, tied up her horse, and hurried to find a seat.

It was certainly a non-traditional Amish wedding since the groom wasn't Amish, and the pastor was Baptist. Jason took care of the music and chose two songs from Senta's Spotify playlist. "I Don't Want To Miss A Thing" for the processional and "Baby I'm Yours" for the recessional. Abigail served as the maid of honor, drafting Sally, Suzanne, and Ruth to be bride's maids. Jerrick recruited Joe to be his best man, and John Lapp, Carlos, and the Attorney General to be groomsmen. Mr. Campbell was chosen to walk Senta down the aisle and give her away.

As she waited in the house, watching out the window for Abigail to signal her to come out, Senta prayed. She thanked God for that moment, for that day, and for her life which was full of more love and promise than she could comprehend. She looked out the window and saw the man who would, in a few minutes, be her husband and was overwhelmed with emotion as to how they had been brought together. She looked at the guests and thought about how much she loved all of them. She saw Sugar tethered to the big tree directly behind the pastor and thought of her parents. She knew they were watching that day from heaven. Then, looking up, she watched the clouds flow across the sky and thought of the stream behind the barn and the big river a few miles away that flowed to the sea, and finally of the love flowing through her to Jerrick and beyond. *You who dwell in the gardens with friends, let me hear your voice.*

Seeing Abigail's signal through the window, Mr. Campbell opened the door and guided Senta out onto the porch. She placed her hand around his arm as he walked her down the sidewalk and through the blue gate in front of the house. *How beautiful your sandaled feet, O prince's daughter.* As she walked down the aisle formed by the chairs on the lawn, she saw the glorious leaves of autumn as they fell from the trees above and thought they were prettier than any rose pedals.

Holding the bouquet Abigail had made and trying her best not to cry as her eyes met with friends, Senta made her way toward Jerrick. Hearing the processional, Senta remembered the first time she'd heard the song when Jerrick had sent it to her in the letter. She thought it was perfect because she didn't want to miss a second with Jerrick and swore to herself to always be by his side. *Place me like a seal over your heart, like a seal on your arm.* With each step closer to him, she started crying, overcome with the pure joy of his love for her. Everyone said afterward that it was one of the best weddings they had ever attended. Senta made it a point to visit all her guests, and finally spoke to Ruth who was sitting with Mrs. Belier.

"I wish you love and happiness," said Ruth.

"Thank you, Ruth," responded Senta.

"You're very happy. I can tell," said Ruth, smiling.

"I am," said Senta. The two friends shared a hug, and Senta promised to come visit when she could.

There was plenty of food and drink. Everyone stayed a long time, but as it got later, the guests started to leave. Jerrick and Senta thanked each and every friend. When the sun started to set and finally Jerrick and Senta had a moment to talk, he asked her, "Are you happy, Senta?"

"It's not possible in any dictionary or any language to find words to describe how happy I am," she answered.

"It's almost time to start our honeymoon," he said.

"Yes," she said, smiling up at him. "We were going to drive back to the boat tonight, but could we stay here instead? I know the bed is too small for you, but to be in my house and to have you here with me is so important for me. This is where I waited for you for so long."

"Of course," he said. "I'd like that."

Senta and Jerrick talked with Abigail and John about keeping an eye on the farm for the next four months while they were away on their honeymoon cruise. As the last guests left, Senta stood in the front yard by the blue gate, petting her horse. When everyone was gone, and Sugar was back in her stall in the barn, Senta led her husband upstairs to the bedroom where they made love and fell asleep in each other's arms.

CHAPTER TWENTY-THREE

The Farm

One Year Later

The white Range Rover took the Ashland City exit on Interstate 24 and headed south. It was a beautiful, sunny Saturday in October, and the trees were at their peak of color. "How are you feeling?" he asked as he glanced over at her.

"I'm fine, truly," she said. "But I will admit, I'll be glad when she arrives. I remember when Abigail was pregnant and how hard it was for her at the end. But I've been blessed with such an easy pregnancy. I didn't even have morning sickness."

"You've done great," Jerrick said, taking her hand. "You've not had any problems to speak of, but I know it's still hard."

"As soon as our baby is born and I'm able, I want to start dancing again," Senta said. "I want to dance with you every day."

"We haven't danced in over a month," Jerrick teased. "You've probably forgotten how." Senta smiled and lightly slapped his hand.

"I can't wait to see how it's going at the farm," she said. "What a wonderful idea Abigail had!"

"Yes, and I think there are lots of possibilities for expansion," Jerrick said.

"Thank you so much for helping us," Senta said. "You know so much about all this because of your coffee business."

"Senta, you don't have to thank me," he said. "I love helping you and Abigail."

"We shouldn't even say it like that. It's *us.* You, me, Abigail and John. We're partners," she said, and Jerrick smiled and nodded.

Arriving at Senta's farm, Jerrick said, "It looks a little different than it used to." The driveway was wider and a larger parking area had been built next to the barn. There were several dozen cars parked there, and the sign in front by the road read *Blue Gate Farmers' Market.*

Abigail greeted them as they walked into the barn that had been converted into a Farmers' Market. The stalls where dairy cows had been were now spaces for vendors. There were bread and other baked goods, jellies, and preserves. There was also furniture from Stoll Woodworking. It was too late in the year for most vegetables, but there was a stall with cauliflower and broccoli. Four Amish ladies helped customers and checked them out. "Come and see our new label," said Abigail, leading Senta to the refrigerated cheese case. Abigail picked up a package of cheese and handed it to her. Senta saw the new label that read *Blue Gate Cheese,* complete with a picture of a blue gate.

"Abigail," said Senta. "It's perfect!"

"I like it, Abigail," Jerrick agreed.

"Business is good," said Abigail. "I'm just so busy. I may have to do what you did and turn my job with Mr. Campbell over to someone else. I have that someone in mind," Abigail said as she discretely pointed to one of the women helping in the Farmers' Market. The three of them walked back outside. Abigail pointed toward the parking area and said, "Well, will you look there! It's Ethan Ward, the Attorney General. I'm amazed at how many people from Nashville will drive all the way here to come to the Blue Gate Farmers' Market."

"I'll go talk to Ethan," said Jerrick, "and leave you girls to visit."

Abigail watched Senta as her eyes followed Jerrick. "You two were made for each other," Abigail said to her friend.

"I know most people wouldn't believe me, but every day is wonderful," she said. "The more I know him, the more I love him. I thank God every day for him."

Then, just as some customers were going into the barn, one of the Amish ladies came out and said, "Hi, Senta! Abigail, can you come here a minute? We need your help with a cheese question."

Abigail said, "I'll be right back." She left Senta standing by the door as she ran back in to handle the question. Senta looked around, watching customers arriving and leaving. She looked at her house, remembering her life there before Jerrick. Senta smiled as she watched him talking to Ethan in the parking lot. Then she turned and walked back behind the barn to look for Sugar. As she came around the corner, she found a young woman standing by the fence petting her horse.

"Hello," said Senta to the young woman as she turned around.

"Hi," the woman replied, smiling and continuing to stroke the horse's neck. Senta walked up to the fence and rubbed Sugar's nose.

"Did you know that this is Sugar, Senta's horse?" the young woman asked Senta.

Surprised and puzzled, Senta replied, "Well, yes, I did know that, but how in the world do you know that?"

"Well, this is her house," the girl replied. "She lived here all her life until she got married. That's why the gate is blue. It's some Amish tradition, I think."

Senta hugged her horse and the young woman watched her, noticing the horse's affection for Senta. "I'll be back, Sugar," Senta said and together the two women walked slowly back around the barn. Then Senta asked, "I am so curious. How do you know all this? How do you know about Senta, and her horse, and the blue gate?"

"My friend Kayla. She's inside buying some cheese. She was the first one to tell me about it. Then, I had a patient tell me the story, too. My name is Alexis," the young woman said, extending her hand to shake Senta's. "Someone in Nashville told her about this place and the story of Senta, so we drove out to see. I live in Nashville. I'm a dental hygienist for a dentist in Brentwood. Patients tell me all sorts of things. How did you find out about Senta?" she asked.

Senta stood in front of the barn, smiling at her new friend, marveling at how the world works. "Well, Alexis, I *am* Senta," she answered. "This is my house, and Sugar is my horse."

Alexis looked at Senta with surprise that changed to disbelief, "You're Senta? Kayla won't believe this! But, I thought you were Amish."

"Well, I was," Senta answered. "I am still, sort of. But my husband isn't. So, most of the time I'm not."

"And you're expecting?" asked Alexis, glancing down at Senta.

"Yes, next month," answered Senta.

"And, can I ask?" inquired Alexis. "Was there some bad guy who tried to steal your farm? Kayla was telling me the story. She saw it on TV."

"I can't believe you know this, but yes, that is true," Senta replied. "That's my husband over there. Do you see those two men?" she asked, pointing them out for Alexis. "The one on the right is my husband, Jerrick. The other man is Ethan Ward, the Attorney General. He's the one that prosecuted the man who stole my farm."

"Wow, he looks very young to be the Attorney General," said Alexis. "I can't believe I met you, the real Senta. May I call you Senta?"

"Yes, please call me Senta," she replied. "And I will call you Alexis. Alexis, by the way, are you married?" Senta asked.

"No, I'm not," Alexis replied, wondering why Senta had asked.

"You're not Presbyterian are you?" Senta asked.

"No, I was raised Southern Baptist," she replied, puzzled by the question. "But my friend, Kayla, is Presbyterian, and she's always inviting me to go to church with her."

Senta smiled, looked up at the sky and watched the white clouds flowing across the blue. Then, she turned to Alexis and said, "Come with me, Alexis. I want to introduce you to my husband and Mr. Ward. If Mr. Ward asks you if you're Presbyterian, I don't want you to lie, but you might say you're considering switching denominations."

Alexis gave Senta a puzzled look, then smiled as they walked toward Jerrick and Ethan. Then she said, "Senta, this will sound odd, but I feel like I know you. It's impossible, but you're so familiar to me. It's like I've known you before."

"Who knows," said Senta, smiling. "Maybe it's déjà vu."

The End

ABOUT THE AUTHOR

This is LL Fox's first novel. Learn more about LL Fox's inspiration at his website: www.llfoxbooks.com.

Made in the USA
Las Vegas, NV
09 December 2020